WICKED FOLK

JAMIE McFARLANE

Cover Artwork: Fiona Jayde Media

ISBN: 1-943792-13-5
ISBN-13: 978-1-943792-13-9

CONTENTS

ACKNOWLEDGMENTS

To Diane Greenwood Muir for excellence in editing and fine word-smithery. My wife, Janet, for carefully and kindly pointing out my poor grammatical habits. I cannot imagine working through these projects without you both.

To my beta readers: Carol Greenwood, Linda Baker, Kelli Whyte, and Nancy Higgins Quist for wonderful and thoughtful suggestions. It is a joy to work with this intelligent and considerate group of people.

SUMMONED

Faa Farmstead, just outside Eppy Faire, five years ago

Lace Faa stared out at the waning crescent moon through the wavy glass of the old farmhouse window, wishing for even the slightest breeze. The day's heat refused to dissipate from the humid, summer air which clung to her as she tried unsuccessfully to fall asleep. As if on command, a slight puff of wind rustled the sheer curtains of her second floor window, carrying with it the faint sound of chanting. She strained her ears, curiosity piqued, wondering who might be working her family's hidden craft so late at night. Her gaze shifted to the barn across the gravel driveway. A flickering glow between weathered siding exposed the presence of lit candles and a ritual in progress.

She dropped her legs over the side of the bed and placed her feet in just the right spot to keep the weathered floor from creaking. At the age of sixteen, Lace wasn't fully initiated in the subtle magics of her kin, but moving silently had been drilled into her from an early age. She walked carefully, rolling from heel to toe along the unseen joists that supported the floor, avoiding loose boards as she slipped from bedroom to hallway. The hem of her white cotton nightgown thumped quietly, caressing the wooden stair treads as she descended to the kitchen.

For a moment, she paused at the screen door and considered its habit of screeching when opened. Wetting forefinger and thumb in her mouth, she rubbed them on the old, rusted top hinge. Tall and slender, Lace slipped through the door, opening it only a crack. Relief from the heat held in the old house was welcome as she picked her way gingerly across the gravel. Her eyes focused on the flickering light leaking from the ancient barn.

Lace negotiated the piles of junk that had found their final resting place next to the building and carefully placed both hands on the rough siding, leaning forward to look through one of the many cracks in its façade. Her eye came to rest on the edge of a white circle, drawn on the dirt floor only feet from her position. With her limited view, she glimpsed two black candles burning brightly at the tips of what she suspected was a pentagram, although without full view of the circle, she couldn't know for certain.

"Phezore Gesteriph Feoro, I summon you." The bold voice, her uncle Willum Gordon's, resumed chanting in the ancient language Lace believed was only known by her extended family. Her heart thudded in her chest, recognizing the simple ritual - if only from her reading.

"Oh, Willum," she whispered involuntarily before bringing her hand to her mouth.

"Who's there?" Willum asked loudly from within the barn.

Lace stepped back, startled, catching her heel on a piece of long forgotten machinery. She spun, trying to save herself, but in the poor light, her knee came in contact with a stack of precariously balanced wooden crates. She lunged, diving away from the collapsing junk, all pretense of stealth abandoned. The tall door of the barn slid open as she twisted, trying to free her legs.

"Madge?" Willum asked, the low angle of wavering candles eerily illuminating him from behind.

Lace hastily scrawled a rune in the air with her finger, turning away from Willum's position so he wouldn't see the faint sparkling trail as she did. As an initiate of her clan's magic, she'd mastered the one spell that had come easily to her – shadow walk.

Willum stepped from the barn, closing the door behind him. Lace used the noise to her advantage and gained her feet, moving slowly from her original position. Willum turned and stared directly at her, standing stock still – a hunter trying to locate its quarry. Lace froze. She knew him to be cruel when cornered and he would not take kindly to her spying on his ritual. A weak practitioner by family standards, he'd often taken out his frustrations on her. With the provocation of an interrupted ritual, Lace well understood the danger she'd placed herself in.

2

Willum took a few steps forward, cutting the distance between them in half. Lace breathed slowly, trying to calm her heart, the lack of oxygen demanding deeper breaths. Swiping the air between them, Willum moved toward her. Slowly, she stepped aside, anticipating his movements. Sweat beaded on her forehead as his fingers came within inches of her face.

"That better not be you, Lace," Willum growled and turned back toward the barn.

Lace watched as he turned and disappeared, closing the door behind him. For several minutes, she refused to move and only did so when her uncle's chanting resumed. Even with the danger of Willum's anger, Lace's curiosity drove her to creep around the side of the barn, losing her shadow step as she exited the small radius the spell allowed.

A snort from the first stall greeted her as she approached the proud, aging Belgium draft horse, Lester; his head bobbing up and down in greeting. She quickly moved between the bars of the tubular steel fence and melted into the beast's neck, wrapping an arm across its massive chest. She projected calm to her lifelong friend and he happily accepted, brushing the underside of his head against her back. After a few moments of greeting, Lace freed herself and picked her way through the stall to the inside of the barn, not completely avoiding Lester's mess.

Her hand searched for and found a makeshift ladder of two-by-fours strapped across interior studs. She climbed into the hayloft and crawled forward over the warm, spring hay bales she'd helped put up only a few weeks before. Shrouded in darkness, Lace peered down at the scene below.

Willum sat hunched on his knees, arms open in supplication to the pentagram-etched circle. The flames of the black candles lifted higher and higher as his voice rose, the name *Phezore Gesteriph Feoro* etching itself into Lace's mind as he continued. She had no reference for the named being, but she also knew that there were only a few types of beings that could be summoned - all of them demonic. The very knowledge of its name, a danger to her.

Without warning, a flash of light burst through the barn and the candles extinguished. Darkness filled the room and the horses whinnied in their stalls as a fell wind rushed from the ritual circle. A shimmer caught Lace's eye. The pentagram-inscribed circle glowed, faintly at first, but grew in intensity. She found she couldn't tear her eyes from the circle as a thick green claw erupted from the dirt floor. The claw was followed by a muscular arm and then another, both frantically scratching and pawing the earth. With a puff of acrid smoke, a grotesque, man-shaped demon pulled itself from the ground and stood on the dirt floor within the circle.

The demon slowly turned, taking in the barn and appeared to ignore her uncle Willum's supplicated form. Subtly at first, its visage shifted to that of a human. The short knobby horns along the center of its cranium and running down its back changed to hair. Pallid green skin shifted to a dark olive.

"Who are you and why have you summoned me, foolish human?" it finally asked, its voice a velvety, deep baritone.

"Lord Iurabon. It is I, Willum of Eppy, who seeks your counsel," Willum replied, not daring to look up from his kneeling position on the floor.

"And you, Faa whelp? Why does an Eppy princess hide in the shadows?" A voice whispered in Lace's ear. "Release me from this circle and I will train you to rule this world at my side."

"What makes you think I would help a sniveling, pathetic grub such as yourself?" the demon asked in full voice, having made a complete transformation to human. Shirtless and gleaming in the light of the spell circle, a more beautiful man Lace had never seen.

"Lord Iurabon, it is true, I am unworthy," Willum replied, still looking at the floor.

"Come down here and tip but one candle over," the demon whispered to Lace. "I will reward you beyond your greatest dreams."

"Stop using my name, you idiot!" the demon spat. "If you must address me you may call me Lord Gester. Now tell me what you wish from me or send me back from whence I came."

"Lord Gester, my apologies," Willum replied. "I desire to learn the arts of necromancy."

"You're losing your opportunity. You should move quickly," Gester whispered in Lace's ear.

"I must admit, you humans never cease to surprise me," Gester replied aloud. "Did you lose your first love to the grave? Don't answer that, I care not. What is that it you have to offer? "

"A Faa princess of Clan Eppy," Willum replied. "Young and tender."

"Willum, no," Lace said, horrified, forgetting she lay hidden. She'd always considered it a joke that she was the last in a line of gypsy queens, but there had always been those who took the matter seriously.

Willum straightened and stared up to the loft. In his confusion, Willum's knee dragged across the spell circle's fragile line. While the summoned could not affect the circle no matter what it tried, the summoner could.

"What are you … "

"Willum, the circle," Lace pointed.

Willum froze, regaining his senses at the last moment. He looked down at the circle. His knee had obscured all but the final eighth of an inch. The demon laid his head back and cackled maniacally.

"Pathetic!" Gester roared. "Somehow you discover my name, yet on your first summoning, you release me. You are weaker than I could have imagined. I will so enjoy devouring you."

"But … it's still intact," Willum whined, looking up at the demon.

Lace bolted from her position, her eyes having caught what Willum had not - the fact that his right hand had also brushed through the chalk as he'd pushed himself around to find her. She lost no time descending the two-by-four ladder next to Lester's stall. The massive draft-horse pranced wildly, kicking at the interior wooden walls. Without the threat of the demon, Lace would never have considered entering such a small space with the terrified two-thousand-pound animal. She also knew the beast was not to be calmed, so she waited until he turned. Moving quickly, Lace dropped the stall chain and raced down the forty-foot run-out that led to a larger turnout area for the horses.

"I'll be coming for you," the demon's voice whispered in her ear.

A scream from the front of the barn echoed back through the aisles of the stalls. It was a scream of agony and regret and lasted longer than she imagined someone might have breath for. The sound was too much for Lester, who shot into the run-out and thundered toward Lace, Willum's scream having removed any question as to which direction was the safest.

As Lester careened toward her, Lace sprang onto the mid bar of the tubular steel fence. The horse reared and spun back toward the barn, bumping the fence and nearly pinning Lace's legs. At the last moment she flung herself onto its back, a crazed move, borne out of necessity. Frantically, she grabbed at his thick mane for purchase.

A fresh scream cut through night, causing Lester to spin again as he reached the stall. Lace scrabbled forward, pulling on his thick mane and bringing her face up next to his ear. She spurred him onward, urging him with her feet as well as her voice. The giant animal had no chance of clearing the five-foot tall fence but Lace knew no fence could physically restrain him.

A loud popping sound was all she heard as Lester's broad chest struck the gate, flinging it to the side. Freed from the confines of the run-out, Lester charged down the hill as Lace clung to his back. A fell wind blew at her back and she dared a glance, but saw nothing, instead feeling the evil presence closing on them. If it was to be a race, she'd chosen poorly. A draft horse's speed was only sixty percent of a light horse's, but there was nothing to be done about it now. Accepting her fate, she laid her head down and caressed the beast as it jumped the small stream and thundered up the other side of the hill and along a familiar path.

Twenty minutes later, Lace finally gained enough control to slow her friend. No longer sensing the demon's pursuit and with concern for Lester's well-being, she brought him to a walk. A bond of sweat had joined the two together. She continued to cool him down for several minutes, not allowing him to fully stop.

She looked longingly down the trail behind them as she turned Lester around and slid from his back. Her once clean white night gown was covered in grime and sweat. She slapped the animal's thick hind quarters and sent him back along the trail. He would find his way home, but she knew she could never return. It was a decision that had been a long time coming. There was nothing for her on the Faa Farmstead. Her mother, the so-called Queen of the Gypsies, was a pathetic drunk, having done nothing but squander the small fortune passed down by Lace's grandmother.

Lace was only a few miles from Bakersville, where her friend Billie lived. Together, they'd dreamed of running away to a big city like Charlotte. While it was only a pipe dream for Billie, Lace knew she could count on her friend to help and remain quiet about her plans.

Lace arrived at the trailer park before dawn where Billie and her younger brother, Jack, lived with their mother.

"Billie, wake up," Lace whispered near the narrow louvered glass panels open on the side of the trailer. "Billie!"

It took a few tries, but finally Billie replied.

"Lace? What's going on? Is it time for school?" her friend asked groggily.

"No. I'm in trouble. I need help. Is your mom home?"

"What time is it?"

"I don't know. Look at your clock," Lace whispered back.

"Shit, Lace. It's five-fifteen in the morning! Mom's still at work," Billie replied. "Come around front. I'll let you in."

Lace crept around to the stoop of the wide trailer, unhappy to be forced into the bright pool of light beneath the mercury vapor lamp.

"What the hell, Lace?" Billie asked, looking at Lace's dirty nightgown and bleeding feet. She pulled Lace in and hugged her.

"It's bad, Billie," Lace said. "I have to leave."

"In your nightgown?"

"I need clothes," she said.

"You need a shower."

"I don't have time. They'll be coming for me."

"Who? Your mom? Like she'll be awake before noon." Billie scoffed. "If you don't want to be noticed, you'll clean up."

"A quick shower," Lace agreed, getting a whiff of something bad.

Billie pushed her toward the bathroom. "I'll get you some clothes and we can talk about it."

Fifteen minutes later, Lace exited, dressed in the loose black dress Billie set out for her.

"Sorry I didn't have any underwear your size. Besides, that's icky," Billie explained as Lace brushed out her long, black hair.

Lace smiled. She would miss her best friend. "I'm going to catch the six-thirty to Charlotte," Lace explained.

"You're really going?" Billie asked.

"Something bad happened," Lace said. "If anyone comes looking for me, you have to say you never saw me. Don't believe 'em if they say I did it."

"You're scaring me, Lace, and you can't take that train. We've never actually tried to make the jump," Billie said.

"I'm not expecting you to come with me," Lace said. "Your mom needs you, but I have to go."

"Here." Billie held out her hand with a small wad of cash. "It's all I have; I wish it was more."

Lace accepted the money and hugged her friend goodbye. "I'll look for you someday, Billie."

"I'm sure I'll still be here. I love you, Lace ..."

Lace brushed tears from her eyes as she walked down the gravel street of Bakersville toward the train tracks. Billie had graciously given up her black combat boots. They were too big, but much more comfortable than walking in bare feet. The freight train passed through every morning at six-thirty, but didn't actually stop. Bakersville sat at the base of granite bluffs by Cane Creek. A huge bend in the line brought the tracks alongside the bluffs and over to the bridge, slowing all trains to nearly walking speed.

It turned out that jumping onto a moving freight car was easier than she'd expected. Lace simply ran along-side until she matched its pace, then grabbed a hand rail and swung her body onto the narrow ladder attached to the car. The unlocked door was heavy and hard to open, but relented so she could slip inside. Perched atop a large carton, she lay back and fell into an exhausted sleep.

The sound of rain pinging on the metal roof woke Lace. Sliding open the freight car's door, she caught her first sight of the bright lights of Charlotte as rain splashed in her face.

BLESSING

Leotown, Current Day

"You understand we can't warranty this grass seed," the man from Green Solutions Hydro Seeding stated for about the fiftieth time. His balloon-wheeled tank truck was pulled up next to the nearly completed greenhouse on the north lawn of my new home, Tenebrius Manerium. "Those trees will never allow enough sun to germinate a lawn."

"Don't you have a special shade-mix?" the red-headed Andy Brandlemeir asked. He climbed down from the ladder leaning against the greenhouse and crossed his arms. What Andy gave up in "book-smarts," as he called it, he more than made up for in loyalty and I'd become one of his wards.

The seeder grimaced, not wanting to get into it with Andy. "Yeah, that's what we have loaded, but I'm just saying, there won't be a warranty."

"It's okay, Andy," I said and turned back to the concerned man. "As I explained to your boss, the soil back here is particularly fertile. A warranty isn't necessary."

"Is that a …?" I followed the man's gaze to the top of the mansion. My older sister, Maggie, padded along the mansion's stone rampart three stories in the air, still in her new favorite form – a black panther. Noticing our attention, she quickly disappeared from view.

"Cat?" I filled in for him. "The light back here plays tricks on your eyes." I pushed my words with a suggestion.

"Looked bigger," the man said, but turned away. "I guess we'll get to it, then. Sign here." He held a metal clipboard out to me and I signed off.

"I've seen that cat up there before," Andy said after the man was out of earshot. "Ain't no house cat, either."

I sighed. Andy was the husband of Kelli, one of the two remaining members of Whyte Wood coven. Somehow, he'd retained his belief that magic wasn't real and I had to credit him for sticking to his guns in the face of overwhelming contrary evidence.

"I ain't gonna say nothing," he said. "I figure people got a right to their secrets."

"How much work before the greenhouse is ready?" I asked, mostly interested in changing the subject. I had to raise my voice above the pump motor on the hydro-seeder as the workman dragged a large hose over the freshly graded dirt. The previously overgrown, heavily-treed landscape had been denuded by the over-zealous Left-Hand Coven in an attempt to destroy my family and take control of Tenebrius Manerium.

"Last of the glass panels is coming this afternoon. I'm just checking to make sure we're ready."

I was excited at his progress. The interior of the greenhouse was now outfitted with long, cypress shelves along the exterior walls and a wide work table down the center. As a wizard, I was willing to skimp on just about anything but my greenhouse. I had delayed several other projects in order to complete this beautiful building.

The toot of a car horn caught my attention and I turned to look up the cobblestone path that meandered around to the front of the house. Unsurprisingly, it was Willow Katty in her restored 1950s vintage work truck. She carried a load of seedlings we'd been setting aside at her nursery over the winter.

Willow was one of three sisters who owned and operated the local witch's haunt and restaurant, Chatty Katty's. I was happy to see she'd brought her daughter, Cypress (or Cy), along. Willow was a curvy woman in her late forties and had difficulty suppressing her often overt sexual overtures. Thank goodness, with her eighteen-year-old daughter back from college, she tended to be less forward. It wasn't that I found Willow unattractive. She was all that and more, but I was a one-woman man.

"Uncle Felix!" Cypress bounded out of the truck before it fully rolled to a stop and ran over to give me a hug. It was a running joke between Cy and her two cousins, Dandelion (Dande) and Solstice (Sol), that they referred to me as Uncle Felix. I was barely ten years their senior, but they enjoyed needling me about my elderly status all the same.

"Welcome back, Cy," I said, enjoying the attention. "When did you get in?"

"We came back last night," she said. "I can't believe we're through our freshman year."

"Are you ready to do some planting?" I asked, walking to the back of the sage-green truck. Cypress grabbed my hand.

"Mom is so excited about your greenhouse," she said. "And Aunt Belle sent sandwiches. Is Clarita here?" Clarita was, of course, my six-year-old niece.

I chuckled. "Yes. Gabriella dropped her off and last I saw; she was playing with Maggie."

"I see her. I'll be back!" Cypress dropped my hand and sprinted toward the doors of the glassed-in atrium at the back of the house that served as an informal dining room.

"Good help is hard to find." Willow laughed as I lowered the tailgate of the truck and helped her roll back the protective blanket covering the tiny plants.

"She's a sweet one," I replied. "You all are. I would have happily come over and helped load this up. You didn't have to do it by yourself."

"The girls are all back," Willow said. "We had it loaded in minutes. Besides, I wanted to see your progress." She waved to Andy, who was walking purposefully away. Although his wife was a witch - a fact he never acknowledged - Andy had no interest in being around other witches. He nodded tersely but kept his head pointed forward.

"Queer little man," Willow said. "Isn't that Kelli Brandlemeir's husband?"

"I think you make him nervous," I said.

"I have that effect on most men," she said huskily with a

waggle of her eyebrows.

I nodded in acknowledgment. "You definitely make me nervous."

"You are such a tease, Felix Slade." She pulled a tray of tiny green plants from the truck. "How long will *they* be here?" She was referring to the men spraying green slurry onto the bare dirt. Willow had made it clear she didn't think it necessary to hire the truck. I'd argued that planting three acres of grass seed by hand was more work than I was interested in.

"This is their last trip," I said. "He's concerned the grass won't grow back here because of the shade."

Willow harrumphed as she set her load on the cypress counter. "We'll see about that," she said. "A blessing ceremony is in order."

I shook my head mournfully. What she had in mind was exactly what Tenebrius Manerium needed, but I also knew it would entail plenty of personal discomfort. Wordlessly, I walked back to the truck to pick up another flat, this one filled with white jasmine plants.

"I'd love to have you over, but it's such short notice," I said.

"You're just worried about Mom and her sisters taking off their clothes," Cy said from the other side of the truck. I hadn't seen her approach and she had my six-year-old niece, Clarita, firmly planted on her hip.

"There is nothing more beautiful than the human form in its natural setting," Willow said. "We will restore your land's fertility and rejoice."

"Not to mention get drunk off our asses," Cy said.

"Cypress. Not in front of Clarita," Willow scolded with a mischievous smile on her face.

"Can we invite Gabriella?" Technically, Tenebrius Manerium was smack dab in the middle of Veiled Circle Coven's territory. And Gabriella, my – I wasn't really sure what we were – was of a different, albeit friendly coven.

"Already taken care of," Willow said.

"So this plan is already in motion?" I asked with a sigh. Why did I even bother to think I was in control of things?

"Mari was hoping you'd pick up a few bottles of that Moscato she likes," Willow answered, referring to her sister and Dande's mother.

"Anything else I should get?" I asked. I really couldn't complain. Having a coven of witches weave a fertility blessing into my land was a rare opportunity and I was fortunate to have such good friends. If I had a complaint, it was that I hadn't been consulted about it. A weak argument, to be sure.

"I have a list," Willow said and pulled a piece of paper from her lacy bra. A whiff of her sultry perfume hit me as I accepted it, no doubt she'd doused it liberally.

"You play dirty."

"If you only knew," she said, causing my heart to race. There was something about the older woman that … well, I didn't want to dwell on that thought too much. I pushed the list into my pocket.

"Just how are you and Gabriella doing?" Willow asked, her concern genuine.

"Okay, I think," I said. The truth was that I was crazy about Gabriella Valverde. I thought we'd crossed whatever boundary constituted a relationship, but we'd recently regressed into some sort of more-than-friends-but-less-than-lovers-land. I didn't like the ambiguity.

"The two of you need to work this out. She is very much in love you with, Felix, but whatever has come between you could cause a schism." Willow turned from the truck and started back to the greenhouse, having said her piece.

An innocent laugh caught my attention and I turned to see Clarita skipping across the cobblestone drive toward me. She was the one woman in my life with whom I found no ambiguity. I scooped her into my arms, spinning as we laughed, and followed Willow and Cypress back to the greenhouse.

"Tomorrow morning we'll start transplanting these into larger containers," I said to Clarita, setting her on the counter.

"There aren't enough," Clarita observed, and she was right. Even though Willow had brought an entire pickup load, the greenhouse had room for ten times as many plants, if not more.

"That's the fun of it," I said. "We'll split these, add more and soon we'll fill this entire greenhouse."

"Mr. Slade?" The hydro seeder knocked on the open door, looking at the four of us as we worked with the plants.

"Yup," I answered.

"We're done here," he said. "You'll need to stay off the seeds for the next four to six weeks as they germinate. Like I said before, we can't guarantee the planting due to the excessive tree canopy. Since you'll have a lot of bare spots, I'd recommend a second application. Would you like to make that appointment now?"

"I don't think that'll be necessary," I said. "Do you know your way out?"

"We get pretty busy come summer, but it's your decision," he said and turned away.

"Hey, Felix?" Andy's voice caught my attention. "Is it possible to move this pickup truck? The rest of the glass has arrived."

"That's our cue," Willow said. "We'll see you tonight, sweetie." She plucked at Clarita's cheek affectionately. "Don't forget the Moscato. Mari hasn't talked about anything else for a few days."

I frowned at her. " You've known for a few days?"

Willow winked while sidling up to me. "I even picked out a new sheer camisole. I think you'll like it."

"Mom," Cypress complained. "Stop. It's embarrassing."

"I'm afraid this talk of fertility blessings has me all worked up." Willow fanned her face with her hand. "You know how I get."

"I do," Cypress replied, hooking her arm through her mother's to guide her back to the truck.

I took Clarita into my arms and followed the pickup out along the cobblestones. Movement in the shrubs next to the house caught my eye and Clarita wiggled so I'd place her on the ground. Maggie, my sister who preferred to stay in panther form, slipped around the corner and nuzzled against Clarita, leading her off.

"You're causing rumors," I said loudly to Maggie's retreating form, earning me a chuff.

The throaty sound of a big motor caught my attention. Coming down the long drive was Amak in her Jeep complete with oversized tires, stream snorkel, and blaring music.

"I didn't know you were coming out this morning," I said, as my six-and-a-half-foot tall best friend and Senwe Troll princess swung easily from her rig. We'd actually started out as enemies, worked our way around to lovers and finally settled on being friends. I know what you're thinking - she's a troll. Don't judge me. She's gorgeous in her own right and I'm not the sort to let skin color and tusks get in the way of true love. In the end, it was Amak who turned me down on the relationship front, unable to make a commitment due to her station in the Senwe tribe.

"We're going to attack your garage today," she said. "I can't believe you've never opened it."

"I have," I said defensively. "I park the truck in the end bay."

"Which doesn't even have a door on it," she said. "Are you afraid of something?"

"It's not like that," I protested.

"So you are," she said. "Spill it, Slade. Something's got you going about the garage. "

I sighed. "Today's as good a day as any."

The five-stall garage sat on the east side of the circular courtyard, perpendicular to the house and attached to the breezeway. Both the garage and breezeway were in poor repair and I knew when we started working on one, it would require work on the other. I'd been using excuses like limited funds and winter weather, but now Amak was calling me out.

I approached the first stall and pulled at the door. Initially, it was stuck. I felt somewhat let down when we finally opened the door and found nothing more than a pile of old crates. It might be interesting to go through them, but not today.

We moved on to the second and pulled it open. This time the task was easier, having figured out how best to work with the old doors. Sitting inside was a canvas cover that when pulled back, exposed a dusty, but gorgeous, old Indian motorcycle.

"That's something," Amak said. "Ten years old, I'd guess. Want me to get my cuz to come pick it up? She's got a tow-truck with a flatbed."

I shrugged. "Sure. Can't just let it sit here."

"This is great," Amak said. "Just think of the fun we could have on it."

I smiled. She was right. It did look fun. I slowly moved to the next garage. I knew what we were going to find and wasn't ready for the rollercoaster of feelings it would cause.

"What is it, Slade? You bury a body in here when you were a kid?"

"No," I said. "Let's keep going."

"Suit yourself," she said.

I pulled at the third door. Even with a tarp covering it, I knew exactly what I was looking at.

"What is this?" Amak asked excitedly, pulling at the tarp and exposing my dad's medium blue and white 1972 Classic Chevy Suburban. It was strange that I couldn't remember what he looked like, but I knew every detail of his Suburban. "Slade. You've been holding out on me. Tell me again why you didn't want to find this?"

"It's my dad's," I said. "The only thing I remember about him is riding in this truck."

"It's in pristine condition," she continued excitedly. "Those seats are leather and I think it's got the 454 big-block in there."

I walked along the passenger's side and peered in. It had been cleaned out before being stored. Nothing but a thin film of dust could be seen, although I recall the truck always being clean. I pulled the door open and slid into the front seat. The interior smelled familiar, threatening to dislodge a memory. I struggled to chase it down, to no avail.

"Hey, you okay in there, Slade?" Amak asked opening the driver's side door. "You look like you've seen a ghost."

"It's familiar," I said.

My mother had cast a spell on me for my own protection, causing me to forget most of my childhood. It hadn't worked perfectly, because twenty years later, I'd shown up in town and inadvertently laid claim to the family fortune, including Tenebrius

Manerium. Unfortunately, much of my memory was still lost, either due to too many years having passed or because of what she'd done to me. If you believed my sister, Maggie, Mom had abandoned us for the good of the family. She'd fled for some reason Maggie either didn't know or wouldn't share.

"Pretty nifty," Amak said. "Tell me we're going to get this fixed too?"

"Think your cousin has a discount for multiple projects?"

***

Later that night, I lay back on the warm blankets spread on the wide granite steps leading down to the fire pit. The buzz of too much alcohol kept me well relaxed. The Katty sisters, their daughters, Gabriella, Kelli and a couple of other witches whose names I couldn't recall, danced beautifully in the cold, spring air. Clarita had finally given up and lying next to me, snuggled in amongst the thick comforters.

In my current state, the general nakedness of the older women didn't bother me as much as it did when I was sober. I appreciated that the younger women, like Gabriella, kept things at a P.G. rating, only stripping down to leotards.

Willow explained to me on numerous occasions that to be sexually stimulated by a fertility dance, or really any of the blessings performed by modern witches, was natural. In fact, she'd argued that it was very much the point. Nature was the very force they celebrated and reproduction was at the heart of everything natural.

I tacitly agreed, as there wasn't much I could say. To deny that I was attracted to just about every naked female form I'd witnessed would have been a lie. Certainly, there were degrees of attraction - as well as taboos. I found the easiest way to avoid being confronted by these issues was by simply getting drunk enough that I no longer cared. If and when that plan broke down, I sought out Gabriella, whose beauty was at a whole different level from those around her. Petite and graceful, she danced in a way that brought tears to my eyes. Her connection to everything and everyone around her allowed her to mingle selflessly with her sisters.

Feeling my attention, she would often dance over to me and draw me in, coaxing me from my safe position. Our dance together was ephemeral, leaving me wanting more as she joined back with her sisters. It was nights like this when I found myself jealous of the bond the sisterhood of witches shared. I questioned what any of them saw in me. Why did they allow me to witness and participate, if only somewhat, in their rituals?

***

The next morning, I awoke. The fire had died and the crowd thinned to a small number, many of whom were stirring, just as I had, with dawn's break.

Gabriella pulled me back into the nest we shared with Clarita and Maggie, in panther form. I'd let cold air in under the covers, a sin that could only be rectified by closer contact. I tossed a leg over Gabriella and pulled her up against my chest where she snuggled for warmth, making it impossible for me to consider leaving, though urgent duty called.

I smiled at Belle, Sol's mother, as she gathered her blankets and quietly pulled on her shoes. She greeted me by returning my smile, then gestured down the hill. The sun's low rays breaking through the trees gave me just enough light to behold a transformation unlike anything I'd expected. Instead of the gray-green dried slurry of fertilizer and grass seed, there lay a thick field of blue flowers and grass. In the middle of this field lay the three young Kattys; Sol, Cypress and Dande, curled around each other as they slept.

NAKED TRUTH

"Gia, do we have any more of those rosemary soaps?" Judy Babcock called out from where she sat on the floor of her small shop, reloading shelves that had been picked clean by a steady stream of tourists.

"Sweetie, I'm going to need you up front," Georgia Baker, or Gia, Judy's coven sister and friend of fifteen years, called back to her.

Judy stood and brushed dust from the back of her jeans. Gia, a heavyset black woman, stood behind the counter looking skeptically at a rail-thin young woman in her early twenties, who wore a ratty grey sweatshirt and short black skirt.

"Oh," Judy said, drawing the girl's attention away from Gia. "I'm sorry, we're closed just now. We'll open tomorrow morning around ten."

"That's what I tried to tell her," Gia said. "I don't even know how she got in. I know I locked that door."

Judy glanced at the closed front door. The sign had been turned around and dead bolt thrown.

"I just need a job," the woman said. "Please, I need your help."

"We aren't looking for any help," Gia answered, crossing arms defiantly beneath her heavy bosom.

"I know how to do things." The young woman looked pleadingly at Judy. "I tell fortunes for the Dark Folk. People will pay for that."

"I'm sorry, dear one, that is not the nature of our shop," Judy said. "But perhaps there is something else. Are you hungry?"

"I just need your help!" The girl growled unnaturally, her eyes bulging as she did.

"Gia, run!" Judy exclaimed.

"You cannot leave." The girl's voice lowered as she spoke and her body shook. The skin of her face drew taut and then split down the middle as a hideous, horned skull ripped through. The transformation continued as both women stood rooted in place, seemingly frozen. "I just needed your help."

Transformation complete, the demon shed the last visage of the girl and brought its clawed hand up to strike …

"Felix!" Maggie shouted. "Felix, wake up!"

I tried to free myself, but found my arms were pinned by my unnaturally thin and completely naked sister, Maggie, who was sitting on my chest.

"Get off!" Unkindly, I threw her to the side as I scrabbled away, still having trouble distinguishing what was real and what wasn't. I'd been watching the scene from my foster mother, Judy Babcock's eyes, as if I were her. The clarity of the vision had been so real I could still smell the scent of lavender and rosemary.

"Pull it together, Felix," Maggie said. "You were screaming. What's got you all freaked out?"

"Put some clothes on already," I said, exhaling a troubled breath. "That was the third dream I've had about a girl who's in trouble. This time she was in Judy's shop in Crabtree."

Maggie tried to calm me. "There's no reason to believe Judy is in trouble if she wasn't in your first two dreams."

"I have to call her. I can't take that risk," I said.

"Tell me what you saw." Maggie, unabashed by nudity, sat on her heels facing me.

"The same girl is in all the dreams. Each dream is about her and a monster. The first two times the monster attacked her. This time, it came out of her and attacked Judy," I said.

"You're skipping details," Maggie said. "Dreams are all about small details. Start over and don't skip anything. Memories of dreams are fleeting."

I let out a sigh. With the lights on, I could see that I was in my own bed and wasn't about to be attacked by a grey, horned monster. I walked her through the details I could recall.

"Three times you've dreamed of this girl and a monster," Maggie said. "In two, she's running from it, in the other it possessed and killed her. This most recent dream references Dark Folk and Judy. Have you heard of Dark Folk before? It's not a term I recognize."

I shook my head. "Never heard of it. What makes you think that thing is a demon?"

"Just your description," she said. "Only major demons have the ability to possess. Dreams are figurative, not literal. You shouldn't get hung up on specific details, but look at the whole."

"That's confusing. You first said details are important. Now they're not?" I asked.

"Some are. Some aren't. Mostly, you don't know until some guy's chasing you with a chainsaw," she said.

"Too many horror movies?" I quipped.

"I'm not the one screaming his head off in the middle of the night. And what's that saying? Third time's a charm?"

She was right. In my life, important things announced themselves in threes. The fact I'd had three roughly similar dreams put it outside of coincidence for me.

"There's a section of books on demons in the lab," I said and got up. "Any chance you'll put some clothing on?"

"Don't be such a prude," she said. "I thought you were in trouble and I shifted very quickly. It's not like I carry clothing. Why? You getting turned on by your sister?"

"Oh, shit. You didn't just say that," I said.

"Happens with animals all the time," Maggie said, calling over her shoulder as she padded from my room. "Only taboo with humans. I wouldn't hold it against you, but I'd appreciate it if you'd keep it to yourself."

I tossed a pillow at her as hard as I could. I knew she was just messing with me.

"Meet me in the lab?" I asked.

"Getting some burritos," she called from the hallway. "I'll see you there."

"Seriously. Put some clothes on," I yelled after her.

***

Early the next morning, Clarita ran in to the atrium dining room and climbed onto my lap, waking me. The atrium was my favorite room in the house. It extended out the back of the house, next to the kitchen. It seemed like part of the back yard with trees visible through the glass roof and three walls of tall sliding glass.

"Hey, monkey," I said groggily, setting the book I'd fallen asleep reading onto the stack next to me.

"A little cool in here, don't you think?" Gabriella asked as she slid cold hands under my t-shirt and onto my chest. The delicate scent of lavender and pine had arrived just before she had.

"Yup, sorry. I had another dream, got up to read, and must have fallen asleep."

It was a chilly fifty degrees and I'd opened the glass door panels in the corner where I sat. As an earth wizard, I wasn't generally bothered by minor temperature variations, but I knew it was cooler than Clarita would appreciate. I stood, pulled an umbrella shaped propane heater from the open veranda, closed the doors, and lit the wick.

"The same girl?" Gabriella asked as Clarita gave me a wordless hug, popped off my lap and ran off, no doubt in search of her built-in baby sitter, Aunt Maggie.

"This time she turned into a demon and attacked Judy," I said and flopped back into the wide wicker chair that had no business in the dining area. I'd dragged it in from the veranda in the middle the night so I could recline better.

"Have you called Judy? Is she okay?" she asked, sitting on my lap and taking a drink of my orange juice. She was apparently on her way to work as she was wearing a blood-red linen suit, complete with matching spiked heels.

"No. I checked her website. Her coven was out in the woods last night and she won't be up until after noon," I said.

"How do you know it's a demon?" she asked, looking at the stack of old leather-bound books lying on the table.

"Something Maggie said." I grabbed a book from the top of the pile and opened it to where I'd inserted a napkin. An old charcoal sketch was preserved by a yellowed, transparent film taped to the page. It depicted a demon within a spell circle. The demon had several small horns protruding from its hairless skull. Its torso was naked from the waist up, boasting a thick musculature with arms ending in clawed fingers. "I'd say he'd stand out in a crowd."

"He was in your dream?" Gabriella asked.

"Could have been that guy's twin," I said pointing at the picture.

Just then, my phone rang.

"It's Judy," I said, looking at the screen.

"I thought you hadn't called her yet."

"I haven't," I said and answered the phone. "Good morning, Queen of the Forest." It was one of the many nicknames I had for Judy.

"Good morning, Lord Toadstool," Judy replied.

"You're up early. I thought I saw on your site that you and the girls had a romp planned last night."

"We did. I don't suppose you happened to have noticed what type of *romp* that was?" she asked. I always appreciated that she didn't mind my playful references to her coven's rituals. If anything, she seemed to enjoy the banter.

"Oh geez, sorry, I didn't. I just looked for a time when I could call you," I said. "Let me guess; it had something to do with getting in touch with family. I hope I didn't keep you awake."

"*Familia Unom*," Judy replied. "Dolly has been fighting with her daughter, Petaluma, and asked the coven for help."

"How late were you up?" I asked. The *Familia Unom* ritual helped family members become more empathetic toward each other for a short period of time. Judy and I had a very close relationship, considering we didn't have blood bonds, and she must have felt my stress.

"One thirty sound familiar?" Judy asked.

"Sorry. I've been having a repetitive dream," I said. "You and Gia showed up last night and were attacked in it."

"We probably pushed ourselves into your dream with the ritual," she said. "I don't think there's anything to be concerned about."

"What do you know about Dark Folk?" I asked.

"Why would you bring them up?" Judy asked, her voice suddenly serious.

"The girl I've been dreaming about mentioned them," I said. "Why? Who are they?"

"Dark Folk refers to a community of Scottish gypsies here on Sugar Mountain. They live in a community called Eppy Faire, just outside of Asheville," Judy said. "Felix, a man was found murdered at Eppy Faire two weeks ago. Some people are saying witchcraft was involved."

"Why would they think that?" I asked. It was an old wound. Anytime something unexplained happened, people pointed fingers at good witches like Judy because she didn't hide her craft in the shadows.

"Rumor is the man had been dead for days when they found him, but people said they'd seen him walking around the Faire earlier that day," she said.

"Necromancy?" I asked. "That was in my dreams."

"Necromancy would explain it," she said.

"I'm coming down," I said.

"Don't be silly. This has nothing to do with me," she said.

"Then it will be a fun visit," I said.

"I can live with that," she agreed. "I'll tell the girls. They'll be so excited. Have you thought about what you're going to say to Thea? She says you haven't talked to her since you left."

"No," I replied weakly. Thea was one of Judy's coven sisters and we'd been a thing up until the point I'd injured her and two other witches in my attempt to join their circle. If that hadn't been bad enough, a week later I'd put Thea in the hospital after we'd taken things too far on a camping trip on the Appalachian Trail. That had happened almost two years ago.

"Just be honest, Felix," she said. "Thea's a strong woman and she's been going through some changes lately. It would be good for you guys to talk."

We conversed for another twenty minutes and I finally hung

up, feeling like we'd managed to reconnect.

Gabriella looked at me expectantly. "What'd she say?"

I explained most of the conversation, leaving out the part about Thea.

"You're going to North Carolina?" Gabriella asked.

"I'm hoping you'll go too," I said.

"What about Clarita? What about my job?" she asked.

"Would Kelli Brandlemeir take care of Clarita for a few days?" I asked.

She nodded. "That's a possibility. What if I flew down next weekend and stayed for a few days?"

Mentally, I breathed a sigh of relief. It would give me time to clear the air with Thea without a larger audience. "I was thinking about heading out tonight. Do you think Kelli would watch Clarita in the meanwhile? I don't want to take her down there if that thing is really on the loose."

"Kelli's been bugging me to have Clarita spend time with Nelson. If I offered to pay her, she'd appreciate it. I know they've been having trouble making ends meet."

"I've been trying to toss Andy as much work as I can," I said.

"Kelli says that's been a real blessing," Gabriella said. "I'll be a little late tonight, around seven. Is that a problem?"

Something in the way she said it put me on guard. The tone of the conversation had changed and I wasn't sure where we were headed. I picked up her hand and looked her in the eyes. "Nope, but I'd wait for you even if it was."

"Felix, I feel like I need to tell you something."

I closed my eyes, then opened them to look at her. "Sounds ominous."

"I had lunch with Dean yesterday," she said. "I don't want to lie to you, and it didn't mean anything. We're friends."

"Don't kid a kidder," I said as evenly as I could manage.

"Nothing happened, Felix," she said.

I knew what she was saying was true, but it was part of who I was to know just a little more. I couldn't read minds, but I certainly received vibes, especially from my close friends.

"I'm not accusing you, Gabriella," I said. "You're a decent, honest woman. The thing is, I also know you're moving away from me. I've felt it since that night we took down Liise Straightrod and her Order of the Left-Hand."

"Felix, I don't want to lose you." Tears streamed down her perfect cheeks, ruining her carefully applied, albeit unnecessary, makeup.

"Shhh, don't cry," I said, dabbing at her face with a napkin, trying not to further ruin her makeup. "I'm yours for as long as you'll have me."

"You're so distant. Every time we start to get close, you pull away," she said. "I can't keep going like this."

"Just want to be friends, then?" Maggie walked into the room holding an overflowing plate of eggs, bacon, and toast. "Never heard that one before."

"Maggie!" I scolded, turning toward her. "This is a private conversation."

"Geez, fine." She turned and walked back to the kitchen through the swinging door.

Gabriella slid off my lap and straightened her dress, the mood broken. "I should go."

"Wait," I said, standing with her. "One chance?"

"For what, Felix? Maybe we *should* just be friends," Gabriella said.

"Is it because I won't have sex with you?" I asked.

She momentarily pursed her lips. "No ... Sort of ... not really ..."

"*For fuck's sake! You put it to a troll.*" Maggie's voice floated through the door.

"Maggie!" Both Gabriella and I said in unison.

"She's not - not right, you know," Gabriella said softly. "You were intimate with Amak, but you refuse to be with me. What am I supposed to think?"

I pushed my arms out toward her and bared my wrists. It was the ultimate gesture of surrender for our kind. By allowing Gabriella access to my blood, I wouldn't be able to lie to her. I'd wanted to spare her the details that explained my predicament, but I knew to let her leave my home today without resolution would end our relationship.

"I can't," Gabriella said. "You have reasons for your privacy."

"Do it for me."

I closed my eyes as her cool fingers found the soft spots on my wrists, just behind the carpel tunnel.

"You don't have to do this," she said.

"The trouble started when I asked to join Judy's circle. It was a simple ritual; I don't even remember for what. I swear, it was to run the bugs out of Judy's shop or something like that." I appreciated that Gabriella giggled with me, recognizing that I was both telling the truth and that sometimes witches often did practical things that seemed fairly pedestrian.

"For a while, things were working," I continued. "I could feel the other women in the circle and power flowed between us like giant ocean waves."

"That's a lot of power." Gabriella responded to my emotional recollection of the circle's energy.

"Yes. I didn't understand that it was me, that I was causing a feedback loop or a giant power dump or something. Fortunately, Gia realized something was wrong and broke the circle just as it crested. The thing is, we all thought it was caused by a storm. Two of the girls had to be taken to the hospital.

"That's horrible," Gabriella said. "Were they okay?"

The memory of that experience caused me to wobble, my knees going weak. "I broke two of Iris's ribs and Dolly sprained an ankle. How do you live with that? Two of the sweetest ladies you'd ever meet and I threw them across a room like rag dolls."

"You didn't know, Felix. It wasn't your fault."

"It was my fault. No, I get it," I said interrupting her defense. "I didn't mean to do it and that'd be pretty sick if I did. But I had no business joining a witch's circle. If Gia hadn't stopped it, I can't fathom what might have happened.

"That's not everything, is it?" Gabriella said what she could feel was coming next.

"Her name is Thea." I brought an image of my previous girlfriend to mind. I smiled as I remembered her flipping her long, blond hair around as we chased through the woods. We'd been on a spell components gathering sortie. It was my happiest memory with her. Gabriella smiled as she shared in the moment.

"I met Thea while she was in school and introduced her to Judy. Even though Thea brought some baggage with her, Judy welcomed her all the same. I guess Thea and I had a lot in common. The real trouble came a couple of weeks later. To be honest, I've always thought Thea might have been drawn to me because of that ritual - moth to flame, that sort of thing. The bottom line is she got burned ... big time. We were still trying to decide what our relationship was and we were drunk, sitting in the back of my pickup, staring up at the stars. Thea just started taking her clothing off. You gotta know, I was all in. Talk about your beauties ..." I said and then immediately wished I could take it back.

"Go on." Gabriella wasn't impressed, but wasn't about to hang me while I was baring my soul.

"One thing led to another," I said. I winced at the imagery I was sending Gabriella's way - a leggy blonde Thea straddling me, head thrown back in the moonlight. "I'm so sorry, Gabriella."

"Go on," she replied, her voice breathy.

"I'd never been with a witch," I said. "Not for lack of offers. As you know, some of the girls are pretty liberated in their thinking. I'd always thought it best not mix my romantic life with Judy's coven sisters. I felt it would be weird."

"But not with Thea, apparently," Gabriella said. This time the disapproval in her voice was clear.

"No. You're right," I said. "Thea ... well, it just seemed like we'd be good together."

"So what happened?"

"As things intensified ..." I pulled the memory of Thea back to mind. "We'd switched positions and I remember looking down at her, out of my mind with pleasure. I felt her reach out for me, trying to join."

"As in a witch's circle?" Gabriella asked.

"Yes. Only I didn't know how dangerous it was and I'm not sure I could have stopped myself if I had. In my excitement, I nearly killed her. One moment, we were joined as one, the next she was lying unconscious beneath me, blood running out of her eyes and nose. If I hadn't opened my eyes, I would have finished the job."

I pulled my arms away. I had nothing left to share but shame and I couldn't bear to look at this woman who I so desperately didn't want to lose. Hot tears rolled down my face and I sat back into my chair.

Cool fingers brushed my cheeks and Gabriella's silky black hair fell across my face just before her lips met my own.

"That's a heavy burden to carry alone," she whispered, cradling my head in her hands.

"I couldn't tell you," I said. "It's ... "

"Seriously! That *has* to be the first rule. Don't talk about screwing old girlfriends!" Maggie said, walking back into the room and flopping into a chair. She was wearing one of my t-shirts which hung baggily on her thin frame. "And talking about killing them has to be *way* up on that list too. So this was your big plan, brother? You're more hopeless than I thought."

Having bared my soul, I had no capacity for moral indignation. Even more, Maggie was right.

"I've changed my mind," Gabriella said. "I'm coming with you to North Carolina."

"What about work?" I asked, confused by the sudden shift of energy.

She smiled at me and then Maggie. "I'm loaded with vacation time and I've always wanted to meet Judy and Gia."

"What's going on?" I asked.

"Felix, I can't read you, not without sharing the blood bond. Just like I can't read Maggie. That's unusual for me," she said. "I've taken your hesitance as non-interest, but that's not at all what I just felt. You've been protecting me by denying yourself something we both very much want."

"Sex. Shit, can't anyone just use the word?" Maggie asked.

Gabriella looked at Maggie and her smile broke into a grin. "She kind of grows on you, doesn't she?"

ROAD TRIP

"Witches," Maggie lamented, breaking the silence after Gabriella left.

"You're not much help," I said.

"Just keeping it real," she replied. "We're headed to Judy's?"

"How long were you eavesdropping?"

"You remember when Gabriella arrived?"

"Yes."

"Since about then," Maggie said. "Bad habit from when I was a crow. Do you hear that?" She cocked her head toward the kitchen.

"What?" I had phenomenal hearing, but only picked up the sound of wind through the trees. I'd recently come to realize that Maggie's senses were even sharper than my own. We hadn't talked about it much, but I suspected it had something to do with the way magic had been passed to her from our parents. I'd never seen her cast a spell or stir an enchantment, but she easily transformed into whatever creature she had in mind with virtually no thought, although it used a considerable amount of energy.

"Beefy motorcycle rolling down our lane," she replied.

I strained my ears and finally picked up the low thwupping of an approaching bike.

"Probably Amak." I grabbed dishes from the table as I walked out of the dining room.

"I didn't think she had a bike," Maggie said, following me into the kitchen.

"She doesn't. I found that one in the garage last week," I said. "Only eight years old. Know anything about that?"

"It was Geoff's, not that he'll be needing it anymore," she said darkly.

Geoff was our older brother of whom I had no memory. More

significantly, he was Clarita's father, and Maggie described him as a relatively weak wizard. To the extent that his death in the silver spell circle inside Tenebrius's laboratory was a measure of strength, I suppose she was right.

I pushed through the swinging door into the mud room and out onto the breezeway that joined the house to the garage. With her heel, Amak kicked the stand, resting the bike on the brick-paved circular parking as she shut off the engine. The bike was an Indian Chief and sported the willow green and ivory cream two-tone paint, complete with light brown leather side bags. I'd never be mistaken for a gangster with this bike, but it fit my personality.

Amak swung her long leg over the back, clearing the short passenger back rest as she did. As was common for Amak, she wore shorts and a loose shirt which I suspected bordered on pornographic when she rode.

"That has a nice sound," I said, as Maggie and I approached.

"My cuz Caradu had to send the bike out to a friend; she doesn't do motorcycles. They got you all fixed up, though," Amak said, pulling off a minimal helmet. "The Burb took a bit more, but it's ready too. If you hop on, we could go pick it up."

"Ama'." Clarita came rolling around the corner of the house, apparently done watching cartoons for the morning. Amak scooped the small girl into her arms.

"Any chance you're up for a road trip?" I asked.

"Further than the shop?" she asked.

"North Carolina," I said.

"What's in North Carolina?"

"Crabtree Valley. It's where Judy lives," I said. "Know anything about demons?"

"That sounds ominous. You think there's a demon running around?"

"I'm not sure. I've been having dreams," I said.

"Tell her about the stiff," Maggie said. "You know, the one who was walking around dead."

Amak lifted an eyebrow.

"Judy saw a news report about a dead guy seen walking

around town. It has people pointing their fingers at the local witches," I explained. "They found him in the same place I've been dreaming about."

"And you're not buying coincidence." Amak already knew the answer.

"If there's any chance Judy's in trouble ..."

"Wish I could come with you, but I'm in the middle of installing a new security system out at the mansion. I shouldn't leave town," Amak said.

"It would be great to have you along, but I understand," I said. "I'd love to take the Indian." I stepped toward the motorcycle that, at a minimum, had received new tires.

Amak followed my gaze. "Eleven hundred miles is a long trip on a motorcycle, especially if you haven't been riding."

"Don't think you're leaving me behind, and I'm not flying all the way down there as a crow again," Maggie said. I turned just in time to see her cross arms in front and pull the t-shirt she'd been wearing over her head.

"What in the hell, Maggie?" I asked, turning away, her pale, naked form now burned permanently into my mind.

"Baroof." The woof of a dog caught my attention and I looked back to where she'd been standing. In her place, I found a flop-eared, bright-eyed, golden-rust colored dog.

"You've got to be kidding me," I said. "A Vizsla?"

Maggie, in the form of an athletic looking red hound, trotted past me and proceeded to squat on the recently mulched path leading from the parking area to the breezeway.

"Damn it, Maggie, couldn't you at least take it a little further out?"

She looked over her shoulder petulantly and gave one good thrust of her back leg, flinging a stream of mulch nowhere close to the pile she'd just dropped. Leaning her head back, she howled defiantly and trotted over to where Clarita had extricated herself from Amak. The small girl wrapped her arms around the dog's neck and planted a kiss on its red nose. With a scream of delight, Clarita ran off across the pavers toward the heavily forested back yard with Maggie loping along happily behind her.

"Looks like Maggie's traveling light," Amak said. "When are you leaving?"

"After Gabriella gets off work? I figured we could make it as far as Big Spring in the Ozarks," I said. "You should ride the Indian while we're gone. It'd be a shame to leave it in the garage."

***

I woke to the sound of Maggie's low growl. I checked my phone and groaned. It was four in the morning and we'd only arrived at Big Spring campground a couple of hours before. We'd done nothing more complicated than set up the tent and gang our sleeping bags together. It was the first time I'd trusted myself to sleep in the same bed with Gabriella. We were locked together, with her back to me and my arm holding her close. My hand cupped her breast and her small arms were wrapped around my forearm. It was innocent enough while we were both sleeping, but now that I was awake, she had my full attention.

"You feel good," she whispered, eyes still closed. She pushed against the bag with her feet and slid back into me, making contact with things that needed to be avoided.

"You play dirty," I said.

"Best role reversal … ever," she said, gently rocking her hips and causing my eyes to cross. For a moment I considered taking her up on her invitation.

What appeared to be the palm of someone's hand touched the outside of the tent and slid across the fabric. The tent shook violently as the intruder stumbled against a support line. Maggie barked menacingly, struggled to rise from the jumble of blankets and clumsily stepped over us, her big paws sliding on the uneven tangle of cloth and bodies.

"That looked like someone's hand," Gabriella whispered, pulling a pair of jeans into the sleeping bag.

Moonlight streamed in through the front screen as I hastily unzipped it. The smell of rot assaulted my nose as I wriggled out the door behind Maggie.

"I need you to stay here. Maggie and I are going to see what's going on," I said.

Gabriella laid her hand on my own. "Don't go."

"Maggie smells something," I said. "We'll be right back."

"Be careful," she said. "We don't know these woods."

Outside the tent, I waited for my eyes to adjust to the light of the waning moon. The sound of the nearby Current River was loud in the otherwise quiet early morning. I breathed deeply and again picked up on the malodor, the smell of rotted flesh and death.

Impatient, Maggie took off into the woods in the direction of the river. A yip of pain twenty yards into the trees drew my attention.

"Maggie," I whispered harshly and sprinted toward her cry.

"*Augendae*," I incanted. It was a new zero-component spell I'd been working on. Without the energies of spell components and my blood to activate it, the sensory enhancement spell wasn't particularly strong. What it did do, however, was help me pick out the shapes of ankle twisting limbs and rocks as I wove through the dense undergrowth.

Without hearing Maggie's throaty growl, I would have run right over the top of a dark haired woman Maggie was facing down.

"Maggie, stop," I said. I wasn't sure what the woman was doing in the woods so late or why she'd been messing with our tent, but nighttime definitely made people less settled. "Are you okay?" I asked, reaching out.

The woman turned toward me and a fresh wave of putrescence assaulted my sensitized nose. Maggie barked loudly and rushed the two of us. The world slowed as my brain processed the face in front of my own. Cloudy irises and drooping cheeks startled me and I tried to pull away. The woman's fingers clawed at my bare chest, finally finding purchase on my outstretched arm. Her grip was vicelike and boney, digging into my skin. A blackened, viscous liquid dripped from her open mouth.

Maggie barreled into the two of us, clamping down on the woman's forearm. Protesting with a low moan, the woman was thrown to the side as Maggie pushed off her torso. I stumbled back, free from the woman's death grip.

"*Scutum.*" I ignited my pinky ring's protection spell. The glowing shape of a round buckler shield appeared in front of me. I'd never been able to see the shield before and wondered if it was due to the *Augendae* spell.

"Leave," the zombified woman mumbled after she'd regained her footing. "Leave."

"Definitely not my type, sweet cheeks. I'm having enough trouble with my girlfriend as it is," I quipped, looking around for a limb or something to use as a weapon as I retreated onto the sandy bank. I could go more offensive, but it would be a last resort. I'd read somewhere that zombies and the undead in general weren't in favor of fresh, running water. What I didn't know was whether this was a good application of that knowledge.

"Leeeave ...." She scratched at the shield, her fingertips nothing more than bone claws. The contact made no sound, but she was unable to reach through. I backed further onto the sandbar that ran alongside the river. My hope was to lead this thing away from Gabriella as quickly as possible. My ring had started to tap into my own energy reserves. It was a neat trick - the ability to channel extra energy to recharge my rings in real-time. The problem was, the shield spell was extremely expensive and I might need that energy for other purposes.

While I considered all of this, Gabriella emerged from the tree line, branch in hand. In a single, fluid motion, she tagged the woman just behind the ear. The sound of crunching was not nearly as bothersome as the sickly squishing of interior matter.

"What is that?" she asked, breathing hard from exertion.

"*Lucem,*" I said, causing my silver ring to emit a bright light which I directed onto the corpse. What we hadn't been able to see previously was the condition of the woman. It was clear, even to a casual observer, that this woman was well past her expiration date.

"What's this?" Gabriella asked, crouching next to the woman's head. I thought she was going to ask about the rather large indention she'd caused, but she gingerly pulled back the woman's shirt, revealing the top of a scar in the shape of an upside down goat's head.

"Satanists?" I asked, moving closer to illuminate the scar that looked like it had been burned into the flesh, possibly after her death.

"Not Satanists. It's upside down," Gabriella said. "We should check her for identification."

I steeled myself for the task and quickly searched through her pockets, coming up with nothing. I pulled out my phone and took a picture of the scar on her back. It was grisly, but I wanted to be able to refer to it in the future.

"Is this the girl from your dreams?" Gabriella asked.

"Too old and her face isn't right," I said. "I'll grab a shovel. We can at least give her a decent resting place."

"We need to call the sheriff," Gabriella said. "This woman had family."

I groaned. Gabriella was right, but I didn't want to get mixed up with the police.

"That's fine, but the story is we just found her like this," I said, pulling out my phone.

Two hours later the sun was just starting to rise and the sheriff finally showed up. He was an older man with a substantial paunch and a generous greying mustache. He was accompanied by a middle-aged woman dressed in khaki slacks and a lab jacket.

"Were you the group that called in the DB?" His hand rested casually on a holstered pistol.

"Yup, that was me." We'd packed everything but the coffee pot and camp chairs by now and I was anxious to get back on the road, even though I was tired from interrupted sleep.

"I'm Sheriff Burford and this here's the coroner, Dr. Grant," he said.

"Thanks for coming out, Sheriff." I offered my hand. For a moment he considered me and then reciprocated. "I moved her a little, trying to find some identification."

"Why don't you show me the body, son," he said patronizingly as he pulled at his belt, not making any progress against his overhanging gut.

"All-righty, pops." I'd always hated being called son. "She's right over here. My dog found her this morning." I led them down to the bank of the river.

The coroner walked over to the body and knelt next to it, pulling on latex gloves.

"How do you know this girl?" the sheriff asked.

"Mostly from her perfume," I said.

He raised his eyebrows. "You getting cute with me?"

"Yeah, bad habit," I said, not meaning it. "You're making an assumption that's annoying. We don't know her. We're just passing through, trying to do our civic duty."

"You just happened to run across a dead girl?" he said.

"If my dog hadn't found her, we'd never have known she was there," I said. "Didn't seem right, just letting her lie there, not telling anyone."

He nodded and looked back to the coroner. "What do you have, Helen?" he asked.

"This body's been moved," she said, looking at the body that lay face down in the weeds.

"Preliminary cause?"

"No. We'll have to get her back to the morgue," she said. "The body's in bad shape."

He turned back to me. "You mind if I take a look in the truck?"

Gabriella stepped between us. "What are you looking for?"

"Maybe another DB. Just trying to validate your story, little lady," The sheriff looked over his sunglasses at her, tapping them downward with a chubby finger.

Gabriella's eyebrows shot up at the last remark and she leaned forward, not at all intimidated. "You want to search our vehicle because we had the misfortune to camp next to a dead woman?"

"It's called law enforcement. If I don't find anything, you'll be on your way. You can either let me search the truck or I'll call a judge and get a warrant," he said. "Regardless, I'm getting a look in there."

"What's up?" I asked, turning to Gabriella. I got that she didn't like the guy, but looking through the Suburban to rule us out seemed reasonable.

"He's asking to do a search without cause. Anything he finds and deems suspicious, he's able to use. A warrant requires cause, which he doesn't have. I'm advising you not to let him search," she said.

"You're the district attorney," I said, shading the truth. She'd once been an assistant district attorney and was now working as a corporate lawyer.

"I don't give a god-damn if you're his fairy godmother. Big town law isn't going to work down here," Sheriff Burford said, resting his hands on his belt. "You don't want to be messing with me on this. I'll impound that truck and we'll take it apart piece by piece."

"Hope you're ready for a lawsuit in that case. Law is law, sheriff. Just because you say something doesn't make it right," Gabriella said.

"Sheriff?" The coroner called from where the dead woman lay. "You're going to want to see this."

"Stay put and shut up." Burford snapped and stalked over to where his coroner was looking at her phone.

"I like it when you're all momma-bear," I said. "I'm not sure we should antagonize him, though."

"My shirt has blood on it," Gabriella said so quietly I could barely hear her. My heart sank. If he found her shirt with the girl's blood on it, we'd be in trouble. I held my finger to my lips and strained to listen to the sheriff's conversation.

"... body is one of ours." I caught the coroner saying.

"Say that again?" Burford wasn't trying at all to be quiet.

"She's from our morgue," the coroner said. "Exposure case, came in three days ago."

"That's impossible," he said.

"Just verified her prints."

"These dumb-asses are up to something. I can feel it," he replied.

"I examined her body myself," she said. "Those are my stitches."

I strained to see what she was pointing at, but the tall grass and distance didn't allow for it.

"Shit," he said and walked back to us.

"I'm going to need to get some information," he sighed. "Let's start with names, addresses, and phone numbers."

About forty minutes later a dark blue van arrived and two men in coveralls emblazoned with Carter County on their backs packed up the corpse and carried it away.

"Looks like you've no outstanding warrants and your stories check out about being in Leotown yesterday. I'm inclined to let you go for now," the sheriff said, dragging his eyes up from the ground, disappointment written on his face.

"No good deed," I said.

"What's that?" The set of his mouth showed his annoyance.

"No good deed goes unpunished is the whole quote," I said.

"Word of advice," he said. "Lose the attitude."

It was good advice, not that I was likely to follow it.

"At least we got to see the river," I said as the sheriff walked off. "You know it's completely spring fed? That's why it's so clear."

"I just need a minute to change, these jeans have blood on them," She pulled a pair of dark red, leather pants from one of her three bags and slipped her jeans off right where we stood. I just watched, mouth agape, as she wriggled into the tight pants.

"Shit, I think my heart just stopped," I said, when she snapped the final button in place.

She looked up at me and grinned. "See anything you like?"

"Wonder what Sheriff Bumble-Butt would have said if you'd been wearing those when he arrived?" I asked.

"Pretty sure all that man saw was brown skin."

I took a deep breath, shaking my head to clear it. "If he'd seen all the brown skin I just saw, he might have changed his tune. Although part of me hoped he'd get his search warrant so you could take him apart in court."

Gabriella flashed a smile as she pulled on and laced up shiny, black leather boots. Straightening, she subconsciously ran a hand over her bottom, smoothing the leather. From my perspective, her well-rounded posterior was one of her best assets, although I knew she felt it was oversized.

The serenity of the morning had long since been disrupted and the roar of the Suburban's throaty engine was discordant with the beautiful wooded setting. Not caring to make it worse, I idled down the gravel path to the entrance of the park. With tires on the asphalt, I depressed the accelerator and roared out onto the narrow highway. The events of the morning dissipated as the wind buffeted through the open windows. Maggie barked happily, her head stuck out the window behind me; cheeks flapping in the wind.

NIGHTSHADE AND OLD LACE

The small town of Crabtree Valley hadn't changed in the two years since I'd left. A proud old courthouse stood at the center of the town square which was surrounded and faced by well-maintained red-brick two and three story buildings. While Crabtree wasn't a tourist town per se, nearby Asheville was. When people drove through or explored the area, a fair number of visitors landed here each year. As a result, tourism had become a primary business and Crabtree Valley boasted higher than average per capita coffee shops, restaurants, and gift shops.

Judy's shop, Nightshade and Old Lace, was on Jefferson street, half a block from the square. It sat just around the corner, in the same building as Mugsies, a twenties-themed coffee shop. I pointed to Judy's awning and slid into an open parking spot right in front.

Maggie jumped from the open window of the Suburban and joined Gabriella and me as I pushed open the old wooden door. I smiled at the sound of jingling bells, recalling a moment not so long ago when a similar sound had brought my attention to Gabriella entering a bakery. Maggie pushed past, nearly taking out my knees.

"Well, hello there, girl." It was Gia's voice, who I soon found, bent over, petting Maggie along the back. "I'm afraid we don't allow animals in the shop. It's a city ordinance," she said without looking up.

"How about service animals?" I asked.

"Oh dear!" Gia exclaimed, using the counter to help her stand up straight. The heavyset woman worked her way around Maggie and pulled me in for a bone crushing hug. I wrapped my arms around her and breathed in her lilac scented perfume. She'd always smelled like home to me, having been one of the few, steady, positive influences in my life. For a moment, I soaked up the joy she exuded.

"Gia, who is it?" Judy called from the back room. I suspected she'd been in the basement if she hadn't heard us come in.

"Felix! And he brought friends," Gia called back.

A moment later, Judy emerged from the curtained doorway which separated the shop from a small office and storage room. "Gabriella?" she asked, as her eyes moved from me to Gabriella.

"Judy, Gia, I'd like to introduce you to Lady Gabriella Valverde of Whyte Wood," I said formally. I didn't know much about witch protocol, but I did know that getting things on the table was important. "Gabriella, Mistress Judy Babcock and Georgia Baker of Nightshade and Old Lace."

Demurely, Gabriella made a slight curtsey, bowing her head, an action I'd never seen her perform.

"I am sorry to hear of the passing of Mistress Barrios, Lady Valverde." Judy bowed her head respectfully, closing her eyes as she did.

"Blessings to you and the earth beneath your feet," Gabriella replied.

I cut my eyes to Gia who looked on with a huge smile. "Am I the only one who feels they're in a movie and someone forgot to give them a script? What are you guys on about?" I asked.

"It is lovely to be greeted in the traditions of our mothers," Judy said. "May the fresh breath of spring forever embrace you."

A slight motion at the curtained doorway that led back to the non-public area of the shop caught my attention. When I looked up, my heart skipped a beat and my palms started sweating. In the doorway stood the woman I'd seen in my dreams. Older, thinner and dressed in a black dress that hung loosely on her frame, she stared intently at me, arms crossed, her fingers and ears laden with ornate, silver jewelry.

I quickly stepped around Judy and Gia, placing myself between them and her. "What do you want?" I demanded.

She looked curiously at me, raising a pierced eyebrow that boasted a low profile gem, but otherwise didn't move. Lace was just as beautiful as I remembered in my vision.

"Felix?" Judy asked.

"Stay back, Judy," I said. "She's dangerous."

This caused both of Lace's eyebrows to lift in surprise.

"Felix, stop. You're being rude. Lace works here," Judy replied.

"For how long?"

"I don't know what's gotten into you. Lace, I apologize for my son's behavior." Judy stepped around and turned to face me, her back to the woman she called Lace.

"It is of no concern," Lace replied. "I am not unaccustomed to being judged on my appearance."

"It's not your appearance that concerns me," I said. "You bring trouble."

"That's quite enough," Judy said. "Felix. Outside." Judy nodded to the door, her face pinched. When I didn't immediately turn, she pushed my shoulder.

"Don't bother," Lace replied. "My shift is over anyway."

"Wait," Judy said. "We can't leave things like this."

"No, it's cool," Lace shrugged and slipped behind the curtain.

"I'll talk to you later," Judy said to me and hustled after the woman.

***

"Your dragon's breath isn't happy," I observed, walking through Judy's front garden patch. She hadn't said much at the shop and when it was time to close, we'd followed her and Gia home.

"It can be fickle," Judy replied. "Do you want to tell me what happened back there with Lace?"

"She's trouble," I said.

Judy tipped her head forward just slightly and gave me the "no-kidding" look she reserved for such moments. "As are you all."

"She's the girl from my dream, Judy. I saw her kill Gia," I said.

"A sweet young child like that would not have such an easy

45

time facing off with me." Gia's lilac perfume arrived at the same moment her hand came to rest on my waist. I'd always enjoyed how freely Gia shared her affection. She preferred to be in physical contact with people as she talked. I wrapped a free arm around the portly woman.

"You cannot trust the narrative of your dreams, Felix," Judy said. "What you saw was a portent. There is danger around this girl, but she is not necessarily the cause of it. I've seen this much myself."

"But I saw her ..."

"Stop. I invited her and the girls for a picnic tonight. Have you been developing your wizard's sight?" she asked.

I smiled. I was proud of the progress I'd made and was ready to fall into a familiar pattern of bragging to Judy and Gia. I'd also grown and wrestled with my need for approval.

"Then look at her aura before you accuse her," she said. "You need to be careful about who knows of your capabilities, Felix. Not all witches are to be trusted. We're as susceptible to lust for power as any people."

"This particular witch has 'different capabilities' she'd like to explore with him," Gabriella offered as she pulled up a long strand of Creeping Jenny.

Gia giggled. "I believe that's a different type of lust. And a nice looking, trustworthy male practitioner is never for want of companionship."

"I expect you to be nice to Lace if she comes tonight," Judy said. "She might bring trouble, but I won't abandon a sister who needs help and neither should you."

I sighed. "I might have overreacted, but you didn't see what happened. She turned into a demon."

"Look at her aura and then we'll talk," Judy said. "I have. She's bruised, but there is much good in her."

I saw auras much differently than Judy and Gabriella. They seemed to discern a person's history, their emotions and general bearing. For me, I saw a person's or object's power signature. The more powerful, the brighter the aura. Dark colors tended toward destructive capability, where lighter colors were restorative in nature. I had difficulty with intent, however, something Judy and Gabriella seemed to more easily understand. I'd learned from Willow Katty, however, that gauging intent wasn't an ability all witches shared. The first time we'd met, she had taken one look at my aura and been ready for a fight.

"I'll give her a chance," I said. "But I'm not happy about it. So tell me what's going on with your fickle dragon's breath?"

"Gia moved it last week and we're having a devil of a time. We're trying to get more light to it. The poor thing was already unhappy and the move might have been too much."

As with many witches, Judy's yard was given to useful plants and beautiful flowers. Having lived with her, I knew the really interesting stuff was in the back, hidden from casual observers.

"Do you want to fill this entire square?" I asked, looking at the recently tilled earth surrounding the anemic looking plant.

"Your lavender is beautiful," Gabriella observed hesitantly, still not past the I'm-just-a-visitor stage of her visit.

"Thank you, dear. Gia makes such beautiful candles with it," Judy acknowledged. "Yes, Felix, the entire patch."

I pulled off my boots and socks, laying them to the side. Digging my toes in, I was immediately able to feel the stored energy in the fertile soil. Having worked with Willow in Chatty Katty's greenhouse and gardens, I'd honed my ability to sense different signatures which reflected the auras of people who had worked the soil. Gia had definitely poured herself into this small plant. Her velvety, pale purple aura coursed through the dragon's breath and nearby soil. The problem, however, was the presence of larval cutworms, over-fat from dining on a plant that should have died days ago, but was being sustained by Gia's attention.

"You have cutworms, Gia," I said. "They're quite pleased with your snacks."

"I'll have their hides," she spat.

"Give me a minute," I said. "I don't think it's fatal."

I closed my eyes, sank to my knees and reached out for the mountain beneath me. It was something I'd been working on at

Chatty Katty's. The witches nurtured plants with their hands and with blessings. Willow had pushed me to work less with my hands, to try reaching out more with my spirit. I wasn't sure if all wizards had this ability or if the talent was unique to me, but I felt I was tapping into the very soul of the Earth. Whatever the connection, it allowed me to access and benefit from Tenebrius Manerium's deep store of energy when I'd needed it desperately. According to Willow, it was a talent I shared with my missing mother.

Everything on this mountain was familiar; like a long lost friend. I hadn't known how to reach out to the earth's essence two years ago, but I recognized its presence and welcomed it like an old friend.

"Sweetie, what are you doing?" Gia gently grasped my hand with her own.

"Don't join," I whispered. "Just feel it."

I allowed the energies to pass over us, the first flows reflecting mostly Judy and Gia, although I also recognized my own latent energy from when I'd lived here. Reaching deeper, I discovered the energy I'd been searching for - the very mountain itself, faint, but not stagnant. The mountain was alive, albeit slumbering peacefully.

I pulled what appeared as a small gossamer thread toward Judy's property and a trickle of the mountain's wild energy snaked toward us. With a wave of my free hand, I gently nudged what felt like a thimbleful into the dragon's breath but ended up with more. It was too much for the plant, so I shunted it off into garden around us. A crackling sound broke my concentration and I opened my eyes to see the plant thickening. I pushed the energy across the small plot and shoots erupted from the red earth, growing into stems and leaves, sprouting until there was a thick mat in front of us.

"Felix?" Judy asked, standing with her hands on Gia's shoulders. "When did you learn this?"

"I've been helping a witch in Leotown with her garden. I guess it was something I developed over time," I said.

"I felt it," Gia said, hoarsely. "I felt the mountain whispering to us. It was beautiful."

"Look at the trees," Judy said, drawing our attention to a pair of dwarf apple trees that arched over the shallow streambed we'd worked so hard to re-route when we'd moved into the dilapidated log cabin so many years ago. The branches were weeping toward the ground, heavy with ripened fruit. "Those were barely the size of acorns this morning."

"Sorry, boss," I said. "I guess I was showing off."

Our conversation was cut short by the sound of a vehicle approaching, going well over the recommended forty-five miles an hour for gravel roads. A black convertible sports car careened into the small lane and skidded to a halt behind the Suburban.

"Oh, lordy," Gia said and worked to get off her knees. I stood and helped her. "I'll be inside, working on dinner if you need me."

"Who's that?" I asked.

"Dinner guests are starting to arrive," Judy said uncomfortably, confusing me with her demeanor. I should have seen the trouble coming, but I didn't.

"That's great," I said, excitedly.

A flash of blonde hair caught my attention and while I recognized her, I was shocked at the transformation. Thea had changed. Two years ago, she'd been an attractive, leggy blonde; playful, but having no real sense of herself and not willing to let herself be pushed into a stereotype. The woman who approached now was confident and had fully embraced the model's body she'd been given. She was dressed in a short purple leather skirt, and a medium blue blouse with a deep plunging neckline.

"That's Thea?" Gabriella asked, brushing off her jeans and straightening her hair.

"I guess it is," I said.

"I meant to say something," Judy said, revealing the source of her discomfort.

"Peaches!" Thea threw open the garden gate, causing it to fall off one of its hinges. "I knew you'd come back for me. What? Are you just going to stand there? No hug for the girl you put in the hospital and left behind?"

I blew out a hot breath filled with adrenaline. She had me. I'd never made things right and she definitely hadn't forgotten.

"Hi, Thea," I said weakly and approached, not sure what I was in for. She opened her arms. I'd forgotten how tall she was and her heels put her right at my height. Her smile was friendly and I returned her embrace, her heavy breasts pushing into my chest.

"You smell of magic, Felix," she whispered as her hand dropped to my rear to cup my butt. "We have unfinished business."

I tried to pull back, but as I did she slid her hands up and grabbed the back of my head, pulling me in for a rough kiss.

She'd gone too far and I pushed away from her.

Laughing loudly, she pointed at me. "You should see your face right now. Fuck. You can't, but it's priceless."

"Thea," Judy said disapprovingly. "Don't you think that's enough?"

"What?" Thea asked, turning serious suddenly. "Was it *enough* he left me to die? *Enough* he left town and abandoned me? Is that the *enough* you're talking about?"

"I waited by your bed for weeks," I said.

Thea smiled, losing whatever pretense of anger she held. "I'm just kidding. I knew it was going to be awkward. I was just seeing how far I could push it. Who's this?" she asked, looking at Gabriella.

"This is my friend, Gabriella," I said. A momentary look of pain from Gabriella prompted me to amend. "My girlfriend. Gabriella, this is Thea."

"His *old* girlfriend," Thea added, holding her hand out as if to shake. I noticed that she held it out limply. "And aren't you just the cutest little thing? Felix does seem to like a little variety, right, sweetie? Trading a lot of treble for a ... hmm ... a little bass?"

I wasn't sure what she was saying but Gabriella seemed to be clear on it and took offense. "Nice to meet you," Gabriella answered coldly, not bothering to pick up Thea's hand.

"Don't be like that," Thea said. "I'm just kidding. I think you fill out those jeans beautifully. Do you have them custom fit? "

Judy stepped forward. "Thea, if you can't behave, I'll ask you to leave."

We were saved by an old passenger van pulling up. "Felix!" An olive skinned woman waved as she stepped from the driver's seat, sliding the door behind her open. I took advantage of the interruption and grabbed Gabriella's hand, pulling her around Thea.

"Oh gawd, it's the mom-squad," Thea complained. "Maybe I will get going. Let's do lunch, eh, skinny? Bring your friend with you. I'll play nice. Judy has my number since you seemed to have forgotten it."

She followed us out to the drive where five kids, all girls, were pouring out of the van. It had been two years, but I recognized them each, although I was shocked at how much they'd grown in what seemed like such a short period of time.

Luana Burgio, only a few years older than myself, turned after handing parcels to her kids. "Hugs!" she said and flashed a bright smile at Gabriella as she pulled me in. Luana was a ball-of-fire, single mother of three. "Introduce me to this extraordinary woman you've clearly brought home to show off."

"One more, one more," Dolly Applebaum, a chubby, gregarious woman danced around the front of the vehicle, arms outstretched. I let go of Luana, who immediately moved on to Gabriella, and hugged Dolly.

"Sisters, I'd like to introduce you to Lady Gabriella Valverde of Whyte Wood," I said formally, then turned. "Gabriella, Dolly and Luana, two of the finest witches you'll meet this side of the Mississippi."

The women all nodded and smiled at each other. It felt good to have my friends and family finally meet each other.

"Can these really be yours?" I asked, looking at the girls "They're so big."

Thea, who'd become entangled in the small flood of girls pouring from the van, extracted herself and jumped into her convertible. "Let me know if you decide to make it a real party," she called, waving as she roared down the lane.

A tall girl I knew to be Dolly's, chose that moment to come around the back of the van, directly in line with the gravel being sprayed from Thea's vehicle. It might not have been intentional on Thea's part, but it certainly was dangerous.

I turned and whispered, "*Scutum*," projecting a shield just behind the tallest of Dolly's girls, Petaluma. She looked at me quizzically, obviously recognizing that I'd incanted a spell in her direction, but not able to see its end result. Gravel ricocheted harmlessly away and I released the spell.

Dolly tsked, once the noise had sufficiently abated. "Poor dear, but she's really had a rough run of things."

"Dolly!" Luana said, looking at me horrified.

"Oh." Dolly clasped her hand over her mouth. "I'm so sorry, Felix. I didn't mean ..."

"It's true," I said.

BAD INFLUENCE

"What else can you tell us about the dead guy at Eppy Faire?" I asked the narrow-framed Iris Besset. She was the sixth and final member of Judy's coven and had arrived midway through dinner. After dinner, we'd adjourned to the back deck and were watching the girls play with Maggie in the back yard among the more exotic plants. Having grown up with witches for mothers, they were well accustomed to which plants to avoid.

"There's not a lot to tell," Iris said, "beyond the fact that his body showed signs of significant post mortem chafing of the skin on his hands and feet. Of course we're not releasing that information to the public and he's not with us anymore. The FBI picked him up shortly after he arrived."

"They probably don't want you to talk about your walking dead any more than they want us talking about werewolves in Leotown," I said and winced. I hadn't meant to bring it up.

"What's this about werewolves and the FBI?" Luana asked.

"I didn't know if you wanted me to spread that around." Judy looked at me apologetically. "I sensed it was something of a secret."

"I'm sorry," I said. "I shouldn't have said anything."

"Why were you attacked by werewolves?" Dolly asked. "And why are you sorry?"

"He's protecting my feelings," Gabriella said. "The lycan were hired by one of my coven sisters. She turned to the left-hand and had the werewolves kill our mistress."

"Why would she do that?" Dolly asked, her voice pitching higher with every word.

"Seduced by power," Gabriella answered. "It was horrible. The lycan kidnapped an uninitiated child and killed her mother who was also one of my coven sisters."

"What did you do? How could you stand against werewolves and left-hand witches?" Dolly asked, sitting forward on her chair.

Gabriella looked at me for help. She'd already said more than she wanted to.

"Alone, we couldn't have," I said. "But the fact is, we weren't alone. The Katty Sisters of the Veiled Circle stood with us. A troll princess, Amak, and her cousin, Rose, helped, as well as a newly born lycan who had previously been a policeman. It was hard, but we figured it out."

"What happened to the coven sister who turned to the left-hand?" Dolly asked, unable to contain herself.

"Killed by the left-hand mistress."

"You poor dear."

"My god-daughter was the real victim," Gabriella said. "She had to watch her mother be killed by lycan."

"What do you know about Dark Folk?" I asked, looking to change the subject.

Just then, a new voice from next to the kitchen's sliding glass door interrupted the conversation. "Sorry I'm late." Lace announced.

Judy stood, grabbed a beer from the cooler and held it out to her. "Nonsense. I'm glad you made it out so you could meet everyone."

I stood. Now was the right time to rectify things. Lace accepted the beer from Judy and looked in my direction. The lines in her young face were hard and it took no imagination to realize she'd seen more than her share of trouble.

"I was out of line, earlier," I said. "I'm sorry."

A flicker of surprise flitted through her eyes and then was gone. "I'm used to being judged."

Gabriella sidled up next to me and held out her hand. "How long have you been seeking?"

"Seeking?" Lace asked. "Look, I don't know what kind of goofy crap you're into, but count me out."

"She was separated from her mother," Judy said. "There were no sisters to guide her."

"Don't talk about me like I'm not here," Lace replied. "Seriously, if this turns weird, I'm outta here - job or no. My mom was a drunk and a freak. I'm nothing like her."

"But you've seen things. Felt things," Judy continued.

"Whispers in the dark, lies on your friend's lips," Gabriella continued. "You are not alone, Lace. We are few and we are your sisters."

"I knew this job was too good to be true," Lace replied. "You're just a bunch of nutty old ladies." She turned and ran back into the house.

I wasn't sure why they were pushing her so hard. I jumped from the deck and ran around to the front just in time to see her slam the door of a broken-down, foreign two-door vehicle. The engine grudgingly turned over as she tried to start it.

"Go! You piece of shit." She cursed as her foot thumped the floor boards while she pumped the accelerator. The engine caught and she jammed the vehicle into gear.

"Lace," I yelled into her open passenger side window. "I saw the demon too. You have to stop running. We can help you."

"Fuck!" she exclaimed and accelerated, throwing rocks from the front tires in her attempt to turn around.

I reached forward and twisted my hand, pinching and pulling back. There was no guarantee my manipulation would grab the ignition key, but the engine shut off and her brake lights illuminated. When I caught up to her she was bent over in her seat, rummaging on the floor for her keys.

"Fuck, fuck, fuck," she repeated. Worriedly she glanced through the passenger side window at me. "Leave me alone!"

"The demon is a ghrelin," I said. "I saw what it did to Willum."

She stopped fumbling for the keys and looked over at me. "You couldn't have." The comment was not intended for me as much as it was something she couldn't keep in.

"But you know I'm telling the truth," I said.

"I don't understand."

"Sure you do," I said, leaning in the open window. "You just don't want to admit it to yourself."

"Admit what?" she asked, sitting up, considering me.

"You're a witch," Judy appeared suddenly at the driver's side window. I startled and banged my head on the doorframe. Judy went on. "Magic runs through your blood and you feel the bond of sisterhood. Do not be afraid."

"Shit, Judy," I said as I rubbed my head.

"Good to see I still have a few surprises for you, dear boy," she replied.

Lace puffed air from her mouth and gave a quick shake of her head. "Let's say I believe you. This isn't going to get weird or anything."

I smiled sardonically and shook my head. "I'd like to weigh in on this."

"No, dear," Judy replied, ignoring me. "There is nothing weird about coming to understand yourself. Sometimes we have to let go of our fears and misunderstandings to do so."

"So far, I've only seen parlor tricks." Lace abruptly turned defiant. "Prove to me that your magic is real."

"You need no such proof," Judy said. "You've seen the magic and it is part of you."

"*Altum Visu.*" I inspected the girl in front of me. Her aura was a gorgeous shade of turquoise; bright greens streaks swirling around blue eddies. Her untapped power was significant, glowing brighter than Judy's leaf green behind her.

"What? Your eyes ..." she said.

"*Finis,*" I said. "Witches have trouble demonstrating magic on command."

"Displays of power aren't necessary; Lace already knows the truth. Would you like to come back and finish your beer?" Judy asked.

Lace sagged, and finally nodded agreement. "Is everyone here a witch?" Lace asked as we walked through the side yard.

"Yes," Judy answered. "Except for Felix."

Gabriella covertly caught my eye as we arrived back in the yard and I gave her a quick smile. Dolly and Luana's girls had given up any pretense of noninterest and tracked our progress.

"Why were you asking about Dark Folk?" Lace asked, accepting her beer from Irene.

"I've had visions, Lace," I said. "You were in them. You mentioned Dark Folk."

"It used to be a derogatory term, but people accepted it," she said. "My mother was one of them and was … important."

"Eppy Clan?" I asked, recalling the name from my vision.

"That's right," Lace answered, searching my face for more information.

I already knew from my vision that her mother was Queen of the Dark Folk and Lace was a Princess in line for the title. What I didn't know, and wasn't willing to push, was what it meant to be royalty and why she needed to hide it. That said, I could understand not spilling everything you knew to strangers.

"Rumor is the Dark Folk practice black magic," Dolly said.

"I don't know about that," Lace replied. A lie even I recognized.

Judy shook her head. "Dark Folk are known to sell curses and hexes. That's not exactly black magic, but it's still wrong. The rumors are mostly hogwash. Although, we've had more than a few people come to us looking for a cure from something they believed came from gypsies."

"The dead man isn't hogwash," Iris said quietly.

Gia waggled her eyebrows. "Nor was that fungal infection on poor Mrs. Williamson's backside."

"Does this look familiar?" I pulled out my phone and flipped to the picture of the scar on the woman who'd attacked us back at Big Spring. I handed it to Iris.

"Identical to the scar on our DB," Iris said after looking at it closely. "Where'd you get this?"

"This lovely paid us a visit at our campground. She kept telling us to leave," I said. "I'm not even sure how she knew we were there. It's not like we told anyone."

Lace pulled the phone closer so she could see. "This woman is dead."

I lifted an eyebrow. "She was when she came into our camp site. What I can't figure out is how she found us."

"Simplest answers are almost always the right ones," Luana offered. "Something located you and sent her after you."

"She came from the morgue," I said. "That would have been a heck of a walk for a zombie in the middle of the night."

"First, she wasn't a zombie, but an undead. Undead under the control of a necromancer aren't going to walk around in the daylight. Daylight breaks the spell and the corpse is ruined." Petaluma, Dolly's thirteen-year-old daughter had surreptitiously placed herself near the porch while we talked. She had appeared to be engrossed in a book and I might have been more careful with the conversation if I'd thought she was listening.

"Luma, you're supposed to be playing," Dolly reprimanded lightly.

"Petaluma is correct," Iris said. "We're seeing the craft of a necromancer and a darn powerful one."

"Can I see the picture?" Petaluma asked. "Mom, don't treat me like a kid. I'm old enough."

Dolly looked apologetic. "Luma, why can't you just go play with the girls?"

"Because I grew out of playing with lightening bugs when I was ten," she said. "I know these things aren't zombies because of the scars you're talking about. I'll bet you don't know that those scars show up after the body is taken over. Can I see the picture?"

"Luma, stop," Dolly said.

"It's an upside down goat's head," Iris answered. "It was on both bodies. How do you know they were applied after death?"

"That's easy," Petaluma answered. "Necromancers have no power over the living. The scars are part of their ritual. How far away is Missouri?"

"I just don't know where she gets all these ideas," Dolly complained.

"Books, Mom," Petaluma replied.

That got everyone's attention. Books that had true magic references were highly protected resources and not the sort of thing handed to children.

"Luma, where have you found books that talk about

necromancy?" Judy kept her voice level so as not to let on how concerned she was, but I recognized that tone.

"In the library, where else?" the girl responded.

I quietly breathed a sigh of relief. A young witch's developing powers combined with the right manuscripts could and had spelled trouble. And yes, the double entendre was intended.

Gabriella pointed to the glossy covered book Petaluma held at her side. "Is that one of them?"

Petaluma looked at the book in her hand guiltily and then stared at the ground. She was a frail girl, with long, straight black hair that she allowed to fall in front of her face. From my position, it seemed clear there was something off about the book she held.

"Petaluma Morticia Applebaum, you will answer the question and hand me that book," Dolly ordered, straightening in her chair and leaning over her considerable bulk.

Petaluma hesitantly handed the book to her mother who pulled the dust sleeve from it, revealing a leather bound sheaf of yellowing papers. Instinctively, Dolly opened the book.

"Dolly, stop!" I said, sensing power building around her. I jumped to my feet and grabbed Luma in a running tackle, pushing her to the ground. Dolly, frozen by fear, shrieked as the book ignited in her hands and too late, she let it go. In slow motion, the flaming book fell and exploded in her lap. I turned away and curled protectively over the frail girl as Dolly was propelled violently into the deck's wooden railing.

I quickly checked Luma who was beneath me. "Are you hurt?" I asked over the sounds of chaos building around us. She struggled to free herself from my arms and scrabbled to her feet.

"Mom!"

The scene behind me was madness. While Dolly had taken the brunt of the explosion, Luana was also down. Judy and Gabriella had both jumped into action and were assessing the damage. The explosion had brought the flock of small girls swarming around the porch, screaming for their mothers. There was nothing I could do for the fallen that Gabriella and Judy wouldn't, so I surveyed the scene. Iris, always the calm and sensible one, already had her phone out and was talking with a 911 operator.

When my eyes found Gia, she was still seated in her wicker chair, her hand resting on her neck; shell-shocked. Lace knelt beside her and held her own hand on top of Gia's. Blood flowed freely over both their hands. My eyes lit on a piece of chair shrapnel sticking out from between their fingers. Gia's eyes looked into my own imploringly. Understanding passed between us - she was in trouble and knew it.

"Don't move," I said and approached. She nodded, keeping her soft brown eyes locked on my own. I pulled my t-shirt off and folded it over, ignoring the scorched holes that hadn't been there when I'd put it on. Lace accepted the shirt and gently placed the makeshift compress against Gia's neck, next to the protruding steel wire. "We'll keep pressure on it. You have a piece of steel wire in your neck. I don't think we should remove it. Iris has already called 911. It sounds like they're sending flight-for-life."

Gia nodded her head slightly in understanding.

I felt Iris's presence as she approached. "That's right, Gia. If we've nicked anything important, removing the object might open it up more. Be brave, sister." It was an unnecessary statement.

The Georgia I knew was deeper than most people gave her credit for. Some might dismiss the overweight, ebony-skinned, middle-aged woman, but it would be their mistake. We all knew her to be quick-witted, loving, intelligent, and loyal to a fault.

"Are you hurt anywhere else?" I asked.

Subtly, she shook her head no, her pain too great to allow for speech. I ran my free hand down her side, unconcerned about impropriety. If she had been struck somewhere else, it was important I locate it immediately. I nodded and smiled at her once I was convinced she had no further injuries.

"Felix, Judy needs you," Iris said, her eyes conveying a sense of urgency.

I'd just settled to my knees, uninterested in leaving Gia's side.

"I'll stay with Georgia," the dignified woman assured me quietly.

"I'll be right back," I said to Gia.

"What's going on with Georgia?" Judy asked as I approached. She sat with Dolly's head in her lap at the edge of the deck. They'd cleared room for the unconscious woman and someone had fetched towels. Judy had put the girls to work, holding compresses against Dolly's legs and stomach. Luana had fared better and sat against the railing with Gabriella tending to her.

"There's a projectile in Gia's neck," I said. "She's losing blood, but still conscious, though I don't know for how long."

"You need to deal with that book," Judy said.

I followed her eyes over to a smoldering pile in front of a hedge of holly. I looked around the once-tranquil deck and shook my head at the bedlam caused by the bespelled book and understood her point. We'd reached a state of equilibrium and Judy wanted no further mishaps.

In a witch's house, components for spells, even those that are common household items, are often found in unusually large quantities. Such was the case with salt, vinegar, and honey in Judy's home. Opening the cupboard on the porch which doubled as a pantry, I grabbed a dark blue bag of granulated salt and made my way over to the book. Luana's oldest, a ten-year-old I used to call Bug, caught up with me and grabbed my hand as I walked.

"How's your mom, Estelle?" I asked, not sure how much the girl remembered me. I'd spent plenty of time in the past babysitting her and her younger sister Roxanne, but she hadn't paid much attention to me since I'd arrived.

"Mom says she's okay and you can still call me Bug," she said. "I'm grown up, but it's okay. Just don't call me Stella. You didn't hug me when I got here." Like her mom, she was olive skinned and had unusually light green eyes.

I stopped and smiled. "I'm sorry, Bug. You're right, that was rude of me. Do you forgive me?"

She opened her arms and gave me a big hug. I guess she remembered me just fine and I hated that I'd ignored her.

"Yes. You're forgiven," she said.

"We have to be careful with this book. We can't touch it," I said. "Someone enchanted it with something bad."

"I know. It's why Mom said we're not supposed to play with her special books. But she never said they could blow up."

"I've never seen it happen before," I explained. "Mostly, we're worried about your magic combining with a spell that will hurt you or someone else."

"My magic hasn't come in," she said matter-of-factly. "Mom says she was a late bloomer too and I shouldn't worry."

"Not everyone's magic is the same. Your magic might be here already, but maybe you don't know how to find it." It was something we'd seen before. Magic affected people differently. Witches turned out to have the most common magic of all, which was why their numbers were greater than other magical types. "I know one thing though and it's that you're special, no matter what."

Bug bounced along beside me. "Mom says that too, but I think she's worried I won't be a witch like her and grandma."

I didn't have much I could say about that, so I turned to the book that now lay in its own blackened circle. The plumbago ground cover had burned back where it came into contact with the fiery missile. As we closed in on it, the smoking book burst into flame again. "First thing to do is cut the enchantment off from the world around it," I said. "I believe it's drawing power from the witches nearby."

"And wizards," she corrected.

"Right you are," I agreed. "Do you feel anything?"

She closed her eyes, concentrating. I had no idea where the book was gaining energy, but it was a reasonable guess. She shook her head no.

"You might when I close it off." I poured a thick ring of salt around the book.

"What are you doing with the salt?" she asked.

"I'm making a spell circle. It's wizard magic," I said. "Once I form it, nothing physical or magical can enter or exit."

"It's also necromancer magic," Petaluma said. She'd very quietly approached us from behind.

I acknowledged her presence with a nod. "You're right, Luma.

62

The circle will cut it off from necromancer magic."

In and of itself, necromancy wasn't evil. It was pretty disgusting and dealt with a side of the grave I had no interest in. That said, I'd only heard of evil necros, but hadn't known any firsthand. The thing was, if that's where Luma's magic abilities were, it would be devastating if she were ostracized because of small thinkers.

"I don't know why the book hurt Mom," she said in her normal, quiet voice.

"*Sphaera*," I incanted. A translucent bubble popped into existence over the flaming book. As it did, I kept an eye on both Petaluma and Estelle. Both girls rocked forward slightly as they were cut off from the book's draw and then Petaluma's face screwed up in pain and she yelped as if she'd been bitten.

I reached out for her in concern. "Luma, are you okay?"

"I feel so empty," she replied, sounding spacey.

I dropped the bag of salt and caught her as she passed out. It was the second time in twenty minutes I'd found myself holding the frail child and the third time I'd rescued her that day. They say third time's a charm, but for me it was a warning. Something was telling me that the girl would need my continued protection.

The sound of an approaching helicopter caught my attention as I stood and carried Petaluma back to the deck. Judy's home was deep in the heavy forest of Sugar Mountain and the nearest place where a helicopter could set down was in the field behind her neighbor's house. I laid Petaluma onto the couch.

"What's going on with Luma?" Judy asked.

"I think she might have been connected to that book," I said. "She's breathing. Bug, stay with her, hold her hand. I need to show the paramedics how to get here."

Estelle did as I asked and I ran around the side-yard, hopped into the Suburban, drove up Judy's lane, and then back down the neighbor's. It had been a long time since the Jenkins' had horses, although their property was still enclosed by fence. I pulled to a stop in front of the steel gate and waved my hand at the cheap lock that hung on a chain. The chain swung free as I flicked my fingers. I carefully nudged the gate open with my bumper and drove into their pasture which was giving way to the encroaching forest.

The white and red helicopter swung around in an arc, not sure where to land. I jumped from the truck and held my hand in the air, careful to aim well away from the trajectory of the aircraft. "*Adoleret.*" My ruby ring blazed momentarily and three smoky fire balls blooped into the air. I waved my arms and the craft turned in my direction and descended, throwing grass and dirt everywhere. I hastily pulled our luggage and tents from the truck to make room for passengers. Removing the seats was more work, but I was able to remove it just as a man wearing a blue jumpsuit approached.

"Where do we need to go?"

"Next house over. I can drive, but it's through there." I pointed at the thick hedge of trees separating Judy from her neighbor.

"Give us a minute to load equipment." He turned back to the helicopter where two more people had emerged in similar suits.

I drove the truck closer to the helicopter, staying clear of the rotors. Once I stopped, the three quickly placed backboards and portable equipment in the back. Wordlessly, they climbed in, shutting the doors as they did. Adrenaline was flowing, but I did my best not to speed through the bumpy field.

"Jackson Baskin." The man in the seat next to me announced once we were moving. "We've been on the phone with Iris Besset?"

"Yes. She has some medical training," I said.

"Right. Two people hurt?" he asked as I pulled through the gate and sped down the lane.

"Three," I said. "Four if you count the girl who passed out. I believe Iris is helping prioritize. There is an unconscious woman who was very near an explosion. The second has a piece of shrapnel in her neck and is bleeding. The third is conscious, but has several wounds."

"Copy that. Tanya, you triage the neck wound. Prich and I will see to the others."

Entering the back yard, I chose the least damaging path I could manage. My eyes cut over to the book and discovered I'd kept sufficient contact with my spell circle. The shimmering sphere still protectively surrounded the book. If my passengers saw the magical sphere they didn't mention it.

Gabriella met us at the back of the truck and escorted us to Dolly where Jackson and Prich got to work immediately, checking vitals and calling back to the hospital.

"You're doing really well, Ms.?" Tanya started, as we approached Georgia.

"Gia," I filled in for her.

"Gia. I'm Tanya and I need to get a look at your neck," she said. "You're doing really well and I'm not seeing enough blood to make me think you hit anything important. You up for a helicopter ride today?"

Gia's eyes grew wide as she shook her head slightly side to side.

"Don't be like that, sweetie," Tanya said. "I ride in them every day. They're loud but they'll get us there quickly. Do you have any allergies?"

Gia again shook her head.

"We're just going to take your vitals really quick," Tanya said, wrapping a blood pressure cuff on Gia's wrist. For a witch, it was a particularly sensitive spot, but Tanya had no idea and inflated the cuff.

"Do you think you can walk? It's going to be a bumpy ride back to the chopper. That's why it's not a good idea to ride all the way back down the mountain," she continued in calm, professional tones. There was no way Gia was getting out of the ride, although I wasn't sure she understood that yet. "The doc is worried about damage we can't see with the equipment we brought along. We can bring a board over if you need."

Gia harrumphed and then closed her eyes at the pain she'd caused herself.

"Sounds like you're up for a walk then," Tanya said as she and Iris helped Gia from the chair.

By the time we settled Gia into the Suburban, Prich was climbing into the back, pulling on the backboard where Dolly lay unconscious. It had taken most of the women to help Jackson and Prich carry their friend to the truck and they carefully slid her in.

"We'll get our equipment and get going," Jackson directed.

"What of Luana?" I asked.

"You'll need to bring her down; we don't have room for another passenger."

EVIL IS AS EVIL DOES

The neighbor, Rob Jenkins, looked quizzically at me as I labored to lift the middle seat into the Suburban.

"Everyone okay?" he asked, standing in his bathrobe and slippers, a cigarette hanging limply between his lips and what I suspected was scotch in a highball glass.

"Not sure," I said. "Sorry about all this."

"At least everyone has their clothing on. Just make sure to lock the gate on the way out and try not to rut up the grass any more than you have," He turned and walked back toward his house.

I shook my head as I loaded into the truck and hurried back to Judy's property. As I pulled into the drive, Iris was carefully loading Luana into the front seat of the mini-van. Estelle, Luana's eldest, had taken charge of the younger girls and already had them buckled in.

"I'm going to follow Iris to the hospital," Judy said, pulling keys from her purse as she approached the Suburban.

"We'll be right behind you. Did Lace leave and where's Petaluma?" I asked not seeing her in the van.

"Mildew and troll spit," Judy said, looking around sharply. "Luma woke just after you left for the helicopter and I think Lace decided she'd had enough for one evening."

"Will Lace be okay?" I asked.

"We're a lot to take in – even without an accident like this," Judy replied. "I guess we'll know if she shows up to work tomorrow."

"I suppose that's right. You go ahead. Gabriella and I will bring Petaluma," I said. "You can't leave Iris to look after all those girls."

"You're right," Judy agreed. "Just so you know, Petaluma is at an awkward age."

I opened the door of the Suburban and jumped out. "What

woman isn't?" I asked.

"Funny." She opened the door to her car and slid in.

I walked back along the tracks my Suburban had left in the mat of ground cover that flanked Judy's home. I winced at the crushed foliage, but there'd been no other choice. I took a short cut through the white painted arbor which was covered with vines that were just now waking up after their winter slumber. I recalled helping Judy place the arbor in the fence line several years back and planting the wisteria vines at the base.

"Have you seen Petaluma?" I asked, finding Gabriella straightening up the mess on the deck.

"I thought she left with the rest of them," Gabriella replied. "She's not back here."

"She wasn't out front," I said. "Luma," I called, cupping my hand next to my mouth. Gabriella joined me in calling out for her as we separated, walking out into the grassy part of the yard, just short of Judy's well-tended gardens. The sun was setting and I started to become concerned.

"What's back there?" Gabriella swept her arm at the thick trees just past Judy's herb gardens.

"Several hundred square miles of national forest," I said. "It's what drew Judy to this spot."

"We should check the house," I said, turning back.

"Felix, look." Gabriella pointed at the burned spot, the line of salt interrupted by what looked like the toe of a shoe.

"She's taken it." I said, heading back toward the house. Through the sliding patio door, we entered the simple home and hustled toward the hallway that led to the three bedrooms. "Check the basement."

I swung the door open on my old room. My bed was still there, but the room was otherwise filled with supplies destined for Judy's shop in town; a corner table held candle making tools. The room smelled of pungent herbs and flower extracts. Not finding Petaluma, I quickly closed the door, my sensitive nose unhappy with the myriad of scents. The door to the next room was open and I stepped in. Light blue colors and everything neatly tucked in its place. Once again, the most prominent feature was the smell, although this time lilac gave away the room's primary occupant as Gia.

Finally, I searched Judy's room. Unlike Gia, her room was less organized. Piles of various things littered every horizontal surface. It wasn't as messy as it was cluttered. Regardless, Petaluma wasn't to be found. By the time I made it back into the hallway, Gabriella was back up from the basement, winded. The look on her face told me what I already knew.

"I'm going next door to see if Mr. Jenkins has seen her," I said.

"Should we call the sheriff?" Gabriella asked.

"I'm calling Judy," I said, not wanting to make that decision on my own.

"I'll check the neighbor." Gabriella pulled open the front door. "Uh. Felix," she said, not stepping through the door.

I looked up from my phone and saw flashing lights atop a brown law enforcement vehicle pulling down the drive. A barrel-chested, middle-aged man stepped from the vehicle, placed a dark-brown, wide brimmed hat on his head and straightened his utility belt. I hung up the phone and stuffed it in my pocket.

"This could be trouble," I said and stepped past Gabriella. About halfway down the sagging wooden steps I recognized the man.

"Deputy Merritt," I said, holding my hand out.

Merritt and I were about the same height, but he easily outweighed me by fifty pounds. Recognition flickered through his eyes and he accepted my hand into his own. The man's burly forearms bespoke considerable strength, but his handshake was just firm with no attempt to cause damage.

"Is Judy home?" he asked. "I received a call from emergency services."

I felt Gabriella's hand on my waist as she stepped to my side. Merritt nodded his head in acknowledgement and touched the brim of his hat. "Ma'am."

"Judy is on her way to the hospital with a friend. There was an accident; flight-for-life was called."

"Flight-for-life is normally under the purview of my office," he said.

"Iris Besset called it in," I said.

"Understood, and you are?"

"Felix Slade and this is Gabriella Valverde. You might remember me from Nightshade and Old Lace," I said. "I used to work there and you'd stop in once in a while."

"Ah, right," he said. "You lived with Judy up until a couple of years back. I wondered if that was you. Would you mind if I saw some identification? Same for you, ma'am."

"There's a girl missing," I said. "A thirteen-year-old daughter of the woman taken in the helicopter." I handed him my driver's license.

"Define missing," he replied.

"We're not sure. We can't locate her, but it got pretty chaotic around here after the explosion," I said.

"Are you sure she wasn't in a vehicle headed to Asheville? Or maybe on the helicopter?"

"We don't think so," I said. "That's why we're looking for her."

"Let's take a look," he said nodding at the house.

"Would you mind if I ran over to the neighbor's house to ask if he saw Petaluma?" Gabriella asked.

"That would be fine, Ms. Valverde," he agreed.

I pulled out my phone as I led Deputy Merritt through the house and out to the back porch.

"Hello?" Judy answered the phone immediately.

"We haven't found Petaluma yet and Deputy Merritt just showed up. Says he got a call from emergency services," I said. "Are you sure she's not in the van?"

"That's Sheriff Merritt and Luma is *not* in the van," Judy replied. "I'm turning around."

"Understood. Be careful," I said.

"What happened here?" Sheriff Merritt asked, looking at the remaining chaos. "You said there was an explosion."

"One of the kids was handing something to Dolly and it exploded," I said. "Maybe a fire cracker?"

The sheriff's aura was straightforward and like other lawmen and women I'd met, he had a natural ability to recognize outright lies. I hoped his abilities didn't extend to truth shading.

"Same child who's missing?" he asked.

I nodded. "It is. But I didn't get the sense she meant any harm."

"Work with me here. The way I see it is we have three possibilities; abduction, runaway, or she's simply lost in the confusion," he said. "Obviously, we hope it's the latter."

Just then, Gabriella returned, her face flushed. "Mr. Jenkins has not seen her," she said. "You could have warned me about his proclivities."

I raised my eyebrows. I wasn't familiar with any of Rob Jenkins' proclivities. "Like what?"

"He came to the door naked," she said.

This caught the sheriff's attention and he snapped his head in the direction of Jenkin's property. "He exposed himself to you?"

"Yes. Quite proud of himself, too," she said.

"Give me a minute," he said and pulled the radio from his belt. "Pol, I'm going to need a couple more units up here at the Babcock place. We have a possible missing child."

A woman's voice answered. "Will do, Aaron. Jason and Drew are on duty. Do you want me to send them both?"

"Roger that, Polly. Have Jason bring the four-wheelers," he answered and clipped the radio back on his belt.

"What's going on, Sheriff?" If my adjustment to his honorific caught his attention, he didn't show it.

"It's dusk right now and in forty minutes it'll be too dark to effectively search this mountain. What I need from you is a good description of the missing child."

I described Petaluma and looked around nervously. We were losing time getting organized and the mention of abduction worried me. There'd been enough weird stuff happening that I couldn't rule the idea out.

"Sheriff, I know these woods," I said. "Let me get going and see if I can find her."

"In a minute," he said. "I'll need your cell phone numbers. The service up here is good and that'll be a good way for us to communicate. Right now, my office is calling in volunteers who help with these types of things. If you think you have an idea of where she went, I'd like to follow up on that."

"It's not that," I said. "It's just that I know the trails."

"Be practical for a moment. You don't have water and you don't have a flashlight. Both things you're going to need," he said.

Maggie trotted into the back yard, tongue hanging from her mouth. "Maggie, where have you been?" I asked, knowing she wouldn't be able to answer.

"That your dog?" he asked.

"Sure is," I said, scratching her shoulders affectionately.

"Not sure a bird-dog is going to be much help," he mused.

"Here are our phone numbers," Gabriella said, handing Merritt a piece of paper. "We have hiking gear in the truck out front and the dog is familiar with Luma. Can't hurt to start looking."

"Right," he said. He didn't appear to be a man who appreciated letting a situation get beyond his control and he was struggling to assimilate the information bombarding him. "I'll have my deputy call these numbers in a few minutes so you have a contact number."

Maggie nuzzled my hand, her maw wet from being dunked in a water bowl. She was definitely ready to get going.

"Let's go girl." I patted my leg, making a show for the sheriff who would not likely understand if I just talked to Maggie normally. "Hunt 'em up." I tapped the couch where I'd laid Petaluma after she'd passed out.

Maggie baroofed and spun in a circle, making a big show of getting excited, finally smelling at the location where I was gesturing.

"What's the plan?" Gabriella asked once we were out of ear shot of the sheriff.

"There's a main trail back about half a mile. It goes east-west. I'm hoping Maggie will get a hit off it," I said.

"What about that Seer's Glass or the compass you made last year when you were tracking Shaggy," Gabriella asked. "Can't you make one of those?"

"I have no idea if Judy has the components available," I said. "And I'd need Petaluma's blood to make the compass." I pulled my day pack from the back of the truck and checked the water bottles. Flicking on a flashlight, I led us over to the forest.

"*Augendae*." I cast the sensory enhancement spell on myself, which would work better than a flashlight for me.

"Baroof, Baroof," Maggie barked excitedly. I wasn't sure if she was on scent or just impatient to get going."

"What's up, girl? Timmy fell in the well?" I couldn't help myself and smiled as Maggie growled menacingly.

Gabriella swatted my arm with her flashlight. Apparently, I wasn't supposed to make jokes while running through the dark creepy forest. "You're such a dumb-ass," she said.

"We'll find you, Maggie. Go!" I urged.

Maggie barked a final time and vaulted into the forest, her narrow body easily slicing through the undergrowth. As a bird-dog, she was particularly adept at traveling quietly and quickly.

"What now?" Gabriella asked.

"Turn off your flashlight."

Gabriella complied and we stood at the edge of the darkened forest, the last rays of the sun's light an orange glow filtering through the deciduous canopy.

"What are you doing?" she asked quietly.

"Shhh." I closed my eyes and picked up her hand. The spirit of this forest was familiar to me and I quieted, allowing myself to become attuned. It wasn't like the forest would tell me where Petaluma was. I'd never been on a speaking basis with nature, but I felt the forest welcome me all the same. A natural habitat is a living, breathing organism; all beings within it are interconnected. I'd have enjoyed drawing a spell circle and meditating for an hour or two, but I didn't have the time. I had learned as much as I could in a short period.

"This way," I said, opening my eyes and leading Gabriella in the direction of a heavier path.

"You found her?" Gabriella asked.

I chuckled, loving her wide-eyed faith in my wizardly powers. I would have loved to say yes, but lying to a witch was a fool's errand. "No. I needed to say hello to an old friend."

"You're so full of crap," Gabriella said. "And I can't see without my flashlight."

"*Augendae*." I waved my hands across her eyes.

"Oh." She sounded startled. "That's amazing. The colors are beautiful. It's almost like daylight."

I shook my head. Somehow, every spell I cast on Gabriella worked better for her than me. The surrounding terrain, for me, was considerably more muted than she was describing. To me, the forest appeared to be in a perpetual state of late dusk.

The trail we were on was only used by Judy and her coven when they entered the forest and even then it was one of several. If Petaluma wanted to disappear into the woods of her own volition, I had a couple of places in mind to check. I reasoned that she wouldn't go directly to any of the coven's ritual sites. As a young man, I'd visited the forest during more blessings, rituals, and celebrations than I could remember and had discovered my own share of unique hiding places.

A distant sound of breaking branches and Maggie's excited baying caught our attention. "Sounds like she's on to something. This way," I said.

"But she's over there," Gabriella pointed toward what I knew to be a deep ravine.

"Trust me," I said as we ran as fast as we could safely manage.

Jumping across a narrow stream, I turned back to offer my hand to Gabriella. She'd worn light tennis shoes to dinner and was having trouble with the slippery mud. Having crossed, we continued on through the wild undergrowth, using Maggie's baying as a beacon. My confidence grew as we closed in on a position I was more than familiar with.

"There." I pointed at a quad of giant oaks that had grown together. The massive trees competed for position next to and surrounding a thick slab of granite. From beneath the slab, a steady stream of water exited into a marshy area, eventually turning into the stream we'd crossed below. A careful observer - which I was certain Petaluma was - would have tracked the running stream back to the lichen covered rock which had been overgrown by the proud guardian oaks. When I'd been younger, I'd been able to slip between the trunks by climbing only a few feet. Over the years, the trunks and my own growth had forced me to climb higher, but I'd always been able to find access. The reward had been a private retreat with a crystal clear pool.

Maggie quieted as we approached; human understanding overriding the beast. When Maggie transformed, she shared a duality with her beast form. She was capable of overriding the animal's behaviors, but more often than not, she simply enjoying the form's natural, instinctual abilities.

"There's a hollow inside the trees," I said. "The spring bubbles up inside and flows under the rock. We have to climb up to find a way in between the trunks. There's room - just enough for a small girl."

"Luma, I'm coming in," I raised my voice to the tree, seeking out familiar footholds.

I'd lost a certain flexibility since the last time I'd entered this private sanctuary and it took me several tries to boost myself over the first branch and into the cleft which would give me the purchase I required. In the wan light, I peered down, my eyes coming to rest on the thin teen. Her knees were pulled tight against her chest and she refused to acknowledge my presence.

"Is she there?" Gabriella called up to me as I turned back.

"Yes," I said. "Call Merritt."

I turned back and carefully lowered myself down next to Luma. She shivered as my arm brushed against her own. I pulled off the shirt I'd grabbed from the truck and wrapped it around her. My eyes caught a glimpse of the book held tightly against her chest.

"I can't go back," she said through gritted teeth.

I pulled a fist-sized chunk of granite from the cold pool of water beneath us. "*Adoleret.*" I focused the stored energy from my ring into the rock until it was almost too warm for an ordinary person to hold and set the rock next to her.

"I won't let anyone take your book until you're ready," I said.

"Why did it hurt my mother?" Petaluma asked. "It's never done that before."

"It's a spell," I said, telling her something she already knew. "It was worried you were giving it up."

"Spells don't worry," she said. "Don't treat me like a child. I know you're going to try to take it again."

"How long have you known?" I asked.

"Known what?"

"Don't treat *me* like an idiot," I replied. "How long have you known you have power over dead things?"

"I'm not left-hand," she replied without conviction.

"Is that what you think? That you're bad because of your magic?"

"I tried to kill my mother. I think it's pretty clear what I am," she said. "You don't know the things I've done."

I wrapped an arm around her and pulled her close to me. "Luma, only you decide what path you walk. Having necromancer magic doesn't make you evil." Initially she resisted, but then loosened her grip around her knees.

She placed the book beneath her thighs and buried her face into my chest, crying softly. "I can't stop myself."

"When a practitioner's magic comes in, it can be overwhelming," I said. "Did you know I burned down the gymnasium of my high school?"

She placed her hand on my chest and pushed back, looking me in the face. "You did not." Her words didn't match what her face seemed to understand.

"It's how Judy found me," I said. "I was a mess."

"Thea says you're dark, but you hide it."

I wasn't expecting the slap and it set me back. For a moment, I just looked at the small girl, not sure how to respond. "I guess I don't see it as black and white. I've done things I'm not proud of, I know that."

"You hurt her," Petaluma continued. "She says it was really

bad, but she's glad it happened."

"It was an accident," I said. "Just like your book hurting your mom. Why would Thea be glad it happened?"

"Not sure," Petaluma replied.

"*Altum Visu.*" I waved my hand across my eyes and opened them slowly.

"What are you doing," she whispered. "Your eyes are glowing."

"Wizardy stuff," I said. The book she was holding had a deep purple glow with bright streaks of yellow along its leather cover. A translucent slimy brown and green algae-like film covered the book and rode up along Petaluma's arm, encircling her throat. A small amount of energy appeared to flow from the girl, most likely feeding the parasitic spell.

"If I promise no one is taking that book from you, can we get out of here? I think your mom would like to see you when she wakes up," I said.

"She's afraid of me."

I considered her words. If I were talking to a normal kid, I'd deny what she was saying, but I was talking to a witch whose magic had come in. I'd risk alienating her if I lied. "Is Judy?"

"No. But Mom's been trying to hide me from Judy. I think she's ashamed."

"She's afraid of how other people will treat you when they learn of your magic," I said. "Believe me, if Judy can deal with me, she'll know how to help you too."

"I'm not giving her my book."

"Of course not," I said. "It's too valuable. Where did you find it?"

"At the faire last fall," she said.

"Faire?"

"Eppy. The gypsy faire. They have a store with old books. I couldn't believe I found it," she said.

"Yeah. Me either."

PLEA

"It doesn't get busy until afternoon," Lace said. "And by busy, I mean we might get a handful of real customers. Mostly, people come to talk. I have some work to do in the back, if you guys can deal with the front." She had been curious about how the girls were doing, but not as freaked out as I might have been in her position.

Gabriella and I had offered to help at Judy's shop while she sat with Dolly and Gia in the hospital. Dolly's recovery would take a while, given the concussion and second degree burns on her stomach and thighs. Gia, on the other hand, had been fortunate. Her neck wound, while initially concerning, was healing quite well although she was likely to have a considerable scar.

"Do you have any of those soaps in the back?" Gabriella called from behind the second aisle. "They smell like rosemary." I quirked my head at the familiar phrase and swiveled toward the front of the shop.

Perfectly timed with my dream, the front door opened, causing the brass bell to ding cheerfully. I quickly stepped from behind the counter, positioning myself between the newcomer and Gabriella. If we were going to step in the crap, I was facing it head on.

To my surprise, not to mention considerable confusion, the woman who entered was FBI Agent Dana Anderson. Anderson was medium height with auburn hair, porcelain white skin and today, she wore a tailored gray suit with a white blouse. Her attire was quite different from the last time we'd met when she had been wearing a dark blue jumpsuit. I might have mistaken her for a mild-mannered business woman if I hadn't seen her arrest a werewolf and a couple of rogue witches without breaking a sweat.

"Agent Anderson?" I asked.

She gave me what I can only describe as a look. "Mr. Slade. Why am I not surprised to see you here?"

"I think that's a good question," Gabriella said, standing. "Why *aren't* you surprised?"

"Have we met?" Anderson asked, turning toward Gabriella.

"Not directly." Gabriella joined me at the counter.

"And you are?" Anderson asked. I wasn't sure why Gabriella was playing coy, so I watched her intently.

"Gabriella Valverde," she replied, holding out her hand. "Tell me your name again?"

"Special Agent Dana Anderson," she replied, accepting Gabriella's hand. "You are Whyte Wood then?" It took her a moment to recall the information.

"You should know better than to lie to a witch," Gabriella said coolly. "Could you have picked a cheesier alias?"

Anderson hitched an eyebrow and looked at me. I gave her a shrug. I wasn't sure what Gabriella's issue was, but I sure wasn't about to question her in front of Anderson.

"You caught that, did you?" Anderson asked.

"I was suspicious when Felix told me about you and Mulper back in Leotown," Gabriella said.

"For the record, it's the first time I've been outed," Anderson admitted. "Most of the people I run into don't watch much TV."

"Why the alias?" I asked.

"Consider the type of people we're likely to run into," Anderson replied.

"Criminals?" I asked.

"Yes, and given names are targets for all sorts of spells and curses. I'm not about to give them that power," she replied.

"Social visit then?" I quipped.

"No. Mr. Slade, I'd like to ask you about a corpse I examined two nights ago in Missouri," she said. "The local sheriff thinks you're involved, but didn't have anything concrete. Want to tell me what that's all about?"

"Not much to tell," I said. "We found a woman next to the river."

"She had a wound on the side of her neck and a rather large dog bite on her arm. Strangely, both of those wounds were received post mortem," Anderson replied. "I understand you were traveling with a dog. Perhaps I should get a warrant for an impression of its teeth, so I could match it up with the wound pattern." Maggie had come out from the back of the shop and looked up at Anderson inquisitively.

"Coroner told me the woman had been dead for a few days," I said as innocently as I could manage.

"No judge would give you a warrant for dog mouth prints on a corpse. There's no crime," Gabriella said, annoyed.

Anderson sighed. "I feel like we're getting off to a bad start. But first, is anyone else in the store?"

"Aside from Maggie here, we're alone," I said, hoping Lace wouldn't join us. "What's going on?"

She crossed to the front door, flipped the sign from open to closed, and twisted the lock. "Level with me," she said. "I know you didn't hurt that woman in Missouri. Not, at least, while she was alive. However, the marks on her body bear a strong resemblance to those on an agent who was killed in much the same manner only a few miles from here."

"As in special agent?" I asked.

"Yes. An undercover."

"Why was he undercover?" Gabriella asked.

"Do you recognize this man?" She held out a picture of an early thirties-something man dressed in khakis and a polo shirt.

I looked at it and handed the picture to Gabriella. "Never seen him before. Is that him?" I asked.

She ignored my question. "What's your relationship to the woman in Missouri?"

"Similar taste in camping spots?"

"Funny." She didn't seem to be amused.

"We lost Agent Pileggi a few weeks ago," Anderson continued. "He was undercover, investigating a string of unsolved murders."

"How many people?" Gabriella asked, handing the picture back.

"Could be as many as thirty," she said. "Maybe more."

"Why are you talking to us?" I asked. "Are we suspects?"

"You haven't told me about the woman in Missouri," she said, redirecting the conversation.

"You shouldn't say anything, Felix," Gabriella said.

"He's not mirandized," Anderson said.

"Still ..."

"The dead woman drew us down to the river and then attacked us," I said. "It's not a big mystery and I have no idea how she could have even known we were there."

"In her state, she didn't know anything." Anderson confirmed something I suspected. "She was being driven by someone or something from another location."

"You think that someone is from here?" I asked, my mind immediately going to Petaluma and dismissing the idea just as quickly.

"Frankly, it's baffling," she agreed. "How many people knew you were coming here and when did you tell them?"

"No one knew we'd be spending the night at Big Spring," I said.

"Except Amak," Gabriella said.

"Fine. Except Amak - and she's a good friend."

"Is Amak a witch?"

"Troll," I said, biting off the word princess as I thought better of sharing that information with someone I had no reason to trust. "You met her last year. She and her cousin dropped off those two lycan they hunted down."

"Doesn't exactly fit the profile," Anderson answered. "If I recall, those trolls are Senwe Tribe. Senwe have witch doctors, but don't do necromancy."

"You didn't answer my question," Gabriella said. "Why aren't you surprised to see Felix?" That's my tenacious girl.

"I've been looking for him," she replied plainly. "Coffee at Mugsies this morning was a pretty good clue."

Gabriella stiffened. "Snooping through Felix's credit card purchases is an invasion of privacy."

"We need your help," Anderson's face, normally impassive,

showed the strain behind her words. "I need your help." Her voice softened as she said the last.

"How long have these murders been going on?" Gabriella asked.

"Six years, but the death toll has accelerated."

I took a breath. This was going to get worse. "Tell us what you know."

"Felix. We shouldn't get involved," Gabriella said. "It's horrible, but we don't need to be part of this."

"We already are," I said. "Go ahead, Dana."

"Do you recognize this woman?" Anderson pulled another picture from her suit coat. As she did, she exposed the badge and revolver at her waist.

It was a picture of a much younger Lace Faa. "Uh. I sort of recognizer her ... but no, I don't really know her. Who is she?"

"The woman's name is Lace Faa," she answered, lifting a skeptical eyebrow. "Originally one of the missing. We think she was at ground-zero."

"Ground-zero? Sounds like you're describing a bomb," I said.

"What do you mean by 'originally'?" Gabriella asked.

"Law enforcement ran across her in Charlotte a few months back," she said. "Her boyfriend was murdered. Local LEOs ran her prints through IAFIS and she popped because of an unrelated incident when she was a juvie."

"Where is she now?" I asked.

"She wasn't held and by the time we realized she was important, she was in the wind," Anderson said.

"Do you think she's part of it?"

Anderson paused, considering her words. "Do we think she's murdered more than a couple dozen people? No. But whatever's going on, she knows something."

"That's the help you needed?"

"Finding Faa would be helpful, but no. I need something else." She swallowed hard. "It's my partner, Mulper. He's gone missing."

"Describe missing. Was he undercover too?"

"Not officially," she said. "Technically he's on vacation and the

FBI isn't prepared to do anything for another week at a minimum. But I know him."

"Simple as that? Just find him?" I asked. "It sounds like looking for him would be dangerous. Seems like we should just go back to Leotown."

"That would be the smart move," Anderson agreed. "I might mention; I have access to information about your mother."

Maggie stood, issuing a low growl as she did.

"It's okay, Maggie." I dropped my hand and smoothed the hackles on her back. "What kind of information?"

"I don't actually have it," she said. "I've just heard a few references and can put you in touch with someone who knows more. Fact is, I'm not authorized to give you that information unless you're helping with the investigation."

Maggie barked and I had to step between her and Anderson.

"Is there an issue with your dog?" Anderson asked, backing away. To her credit she didn't reach for the gun at her waist.

"I'm not sure what's bothering her; she's generally friendly," I said.

"What do you make of the walking dead?" Gabriella asked, helpfully changing the subject. "How do you explain that?"

"Necromancy?" Anderson said, although it sounded like a question. I was surprised to hear her use the word so blatantly. I guess I was expecting more along the lines of denial, which she must have read in my face. "You don't need to look so surprised. You already figured it out. The thing with necromancers is they are often cult based and impossible to pick out in a crowd. They appear normal to the people around them, but they're anything but."

"Dark Folk," I said, mostly to myself.

"Some of them, yes," Anderson agreed. "We think the ring leader is one Willum Gordon; a man who should be avoided at all costs. He runs the community called Eppy Faire."

"Necromancers don't need to kill," I said. "Sure, they deal with dead things, but there's no reason to draw that kind of attention."

"Yes and no," Anderson answered. "We've dealt with plenty of necromancers and they're not all bad. There are even a couple employed by the FBI. Even with the bad ones, it's never this bad, though. Necromancers gain both power and satisfaction from working with the dead. The bad ones cross the line, pushing people into dangerous situations, but they rarely resort to murder. These killings are entirely different. In this case, someone or something seems to relish in these acts. Necromancers generally take little joy or interest in the act of dying. It is the dead they're interested in."

"What about Gordon?" I asked.

"He's a real mystery. As far as we can tell, he arrived five years ago, taking over leadership of the community. Two months after Lace Faa's missing person's report was filed, her mother was murdered and Willum moved to Eppy Faire. Six months after that, we started finding bodies," she said. "It wasn't until recently and with great sacrifice that we put this together, ironically, with the help of a necromancer who is able to see the last few moments of life under certain circumstances."

"That's powerful," I said.

"Yes, although not always helpful," she said. "Often times, a person is so focused on what they're losing in their last moments that they have no thoughts of the person doing the murder."

"We're going out to Eppy Faire tonight and we'll see what we can find. No promises, though," I said.

"Anything you could do to help," Anderson said and turned to go, leaving a picture of Mulper on the counter.

As soon as Anderson was gone, I went to the back room. Lace had already taken off, not that I could blame her.

***

"You're not supposed to bring food into a hospital," Estelle scolded me, looking into the plastic bag I'd set on the rolling tray next to Gia's bed. Someone had arranged for Gia and Dolly to share a room in the small hospital.

"Nosey little bug, aren't you?" I tweaked her ear affectionately.

"What if I said it's Gia and Dolly's favorite and will make them feel better?"

Estelle turned and walked over to the door, carefully closing it after scanning the hallway. I chuckled at her cloak and dagger routine.

"Actually, we're going to get going," Luana said, standing. "I've a passel of girls who will be hungry soon. Estelle, give Felix your hug and say goodbye to Gia and Dolly." Luana wore bandages on her face and arms from the explosion and her hair had been cut shorter due to singe. Word was, however, she would not have any residual scars.

"But he just got here ..." Estelle complained.

"If you give your hugs to Gia and Dolly, I'll walk out with you," I said.

"You better." She wore a fierce look on her face, clearly not wanting to be trifled with.

"Estelle ... " Luana chided gently.

"I'll walk with you, too," Judy said. "Come on, girls."

Gabriella opened her mouth to speak and Gia interrupted her. "Gabriella, would you be a dear and locate a fried wonton for an old woman? They're no good once they get cold." Gabriella smiled kindly and nodded. Apparently, Judy wanted to talk to me alone – such was the subtlety of communication with witches.

"Dolly is still sick." Estelle informed me once we were in the hallway and walking toward the parking lot. "Mom says she'll be better, but we'll have to take good care of her. She doesn't know why the bad book acted like that, but she says Luma gets to keep it for now. I don't know why that is. Do you know?"

It occurred to me that we were down a girl and I wondered where Luma had gotten off to.

"Where *is* Luma?" I asked.

"She's with Thea. They're buddies," Estelle said.

"You're getting pretty old. Have you started learning the blessings?" I asked, changing the subject.

"I know all of them and Mom says next year I can join in the Spring Equinox. She doesn't want me doing too many things, but

Luma is already in the circle." I chuckled at the girl's exuberance.

"We'll have to get pizza before Gabriella and I head back home," I said as we arrived at Luana's van. "You get to pick the movie."

"When are you leaving? And ... I like Gabriella. She's so pretty. You have to bring her to movie night, too," Estelle chattered on, only stopping to take quick breaths.

I waved at the van full of girls as they pulled away, leaving Judy and me in the parking lot.

"That is a lot of energy," I said.

Judy gave a warm smile as she watched the van leave the parking lot. "They are the future of Nightshade."

"How is Dolly's husband holding up?" I asked. "I haven't seen him."

"Herb left Dolly last year," Judy said. "He said he felt they'd grown apart, although I think something happened between him and Luma and he got scared."

"How long has she been experimenting with necromancy?" I asked, reading confirmation in her face.

"Little over a year," she answered. "Dolly is upset about it all. I'm glad you were here yesterday. Did you work things out with Thea?"

"We talked, but it was awkward," I said. "She's changed. She was rude to Gabriella."

"You've changed," Judy replied. "Thea has always been rude and she sees Gabriella as competition."

"For me?"

"Thea still talks about you," she answered. "But that's not why I wanted to get you alone. What is Petaluma still doing with that book? Dolly's not going to like it."

"You were there," I said. "You saw what separation from the book did to her. She and the book are intertwined."

"Are you sure?"

"I am," I said. "The book has a parasitic spell which latched onto her. It would hurt her to remove it without first destroying that spell."

"I don't know how to do that," Judy said. "Where could she have possibly found this book? It hasn't been handed down, as Dolly doesn't come from a long line of witches. Her mother was the first and she was just a kitchen witch."

I grinned at the term 'Kitchen Witch.' It was one of Judy's least favorite terms. It referred to a time when magically inclined women hid their actions by practicing in kitchens, often with no support network to help them discover their craft.

"I have a couple of books that I think might have some information on parasitic spells," I said.

"You need to be careful with your family's library, Felix. Look what's happening with Luma," she said.

"Someone planted that book, Judy," I said. "It was placed specifically where Luma would find it. There's no way she found it at a book store, even one run by Dark Folk."

"Is that what she told you? That she found the book at Eppy Faire?" Judy asked.

"It is," I said. "You can't stand between Luma and necromancy. If that's her magic, she'll learn it with or without you. It's no different than when you found me."

"Except Petaluma has parents. One of whom is a practicing witch," she said.

"The FBI is involved at Eppy," I said. "They're trying to keep a lid on a series of murders. That man Iris examined, he was an FBI undercover."

"How do you know this?"

"I had an unofficial visitor at the shop this morning," I said. "There's a missing agent they want me to look for."

"You'll do no such thing," she said. "You need to get in your truck and go back to Leotown." She glowered at me, standing with arms akimbo.

"FBI says they know there's a link to necromancy," I said. "Don't you see? Petaluma might be mixed up in this."

"How does the FBI know about things like necromancy?"

"I don't think all of the FBI does, but there's a group that looks into things like this. Apparently, they even have a few witches in their employ," I said.

"I heard rumors," she said, leading me back into the hospital.

"The agent who came to the shop today was looking for me," I said. "She thinks Lace is involved in the murders. Lace overheard and disappeared."

"Poor girl," Judy said. "Whatever she's involved in, it's not her doing. This much I believe. The FBI isn't to be trusted, Felix. They are not above dealing with threats quite harshly. For every generation of witches, there has been an opposing group of self-appointed bigots who find power through fear. Salem is not so long ago. We must always remember to keep our confidences."

I nodded solemnly. It was a well-worn conversation. Judy had no trust for authority figures where it related to practitioners. Once, as a know-it-all teen, I'd pointed out that Salem was three hundred years ago. She'd forced me to read a history of the events and then shown me how her own family tree had been severely pruned throughout history. It was a brutal, bloody past and I wasn't about to get into it with her.

"All the more reason for me to check into it. If there's a tie to Luma I need to be there," I said. "Gabriella and I are headed to Eppy Faire tonight. I want to get a look at the book store where she found that manuscript."

"I won't stop you, but you need to be careful, Felix," she said. "And for the record, Gabriella seems like quite a catch. Try not to mess it up."

"Seriously?" I asked, scandalized, as we pushed back into the hospital room, the smell of Chinese food seeping into the hallway. Gabriella had placed herself next to the head of Gia's bed and was eating noodles with chopsticks.

"You didn't tell me about your niece," Gia said, looking at Gabriella's phone.

Judy's hand caught my arm and she spun me toward her. "A niece? You found your family?"

"Clarita is my older brother, Geoff's, daughter. The court awarded custody to Gabriella when no other living relatives were found," I said.

"You're a relative," Dolly pitched. She'd been uncharacteristically quiet for most of our visit due to the heavy pain medication she was under.

"Custody was granted before we knew of Felix's familial line. Clarita is a powerful, early emerging witch," Gabriella said. "For her safety and guidance, I've accepted her into my coven."

"How powerful?" Judy asked.

"Not here," I said. "Not where there are phones."

Gia's eyebrows shot up and she started coughing, which caused her to grab her neck and groan. "Only hurts when I laugh, sneeze or cough," she sputtered. "Just a little tea would help."

Gabriella handed an insulated cup to her. "We have a wonderful arrangement. She visits Felix and Mag …" She stopped short and then continued. "She visits Felix every day while I'm at work and plays with Maggie."

If any of the women caught her bobble - and I was sure both Gia and Judy had - they just smiled politely. The older witches were comfortable with shaded truth and recognized it for what it was.

"When are they letting you out?" I asked Gia.

"They said tomorrow morning, but you know hospitals. One thing will turn into another and it'll end up being late afternoon," she answered. "I'll be quite happy to be disconnected from all this." She lifted her arm to show off the IV.

"We'll take good care of you," Judy said.

"I think Gabriella and I are going to take off," I said. "We thought we'd check out Eppy Faire."

"It's pretty at night," Dolly offered. "The carousels and big-top are all so cheerful."

EPPY FAIRE

"What did you talk with Judy about?" Gabriella asked once we were on the road.

"She wanted to know about Petaluma and why she still had the book," I said.

"Did you tell her about the parasitic spell?"

"Yes. I also told her we had to leave it alone until we could figure out how to safely remove it. The aura of the spell is familiar, but I don't recall from what. It's not like any witch magic I've run into."

"Describe it."

"Oily. Slimy. Revolting," I said. "The book itself was different. It's not your standard witch fare, but not that far off either. It was darker, but not as repugnant as the thing wrapped around it."

"And that thing is touching Luma?" Gabriella asked.

"It's even siphoning a small amount of energy from her," I said. "The spell is bad stuff, but we could harm Luma if we just cut her off again."

We drove in silence, finally turning at an old road sign which hadn't seen maintenance in years. The crumbling asphalt road wound up a mountain holler with thick trees that crowded the road, darkening the already dusk-dimmed route. I pulled on the headlights as we drove deeper into the dark side of the mountain, the sun having long since dropped behind the tall ridge.

"There it is." Gabriella pointed at a glow of lights off to our right. I turned onto a gravel road, where a better maintained sign simply read 'Eppy Faire.'

Cresting a hill, we got a good look into the forested valley below. Lights dotted the hillside where homes were nestled. A flattened area, separated from the trees, was lit up like a Christmas tree. My eyes traced the tracks of a small wooden roller coaster. Through the open window we could hear the thrilled cries of excited passengers. A man with an orange-tipped flashlight waved us down and pointed at a parking area already brimming with vehicles.

"Put your sun visor down," Gabriella instructed once I'd stopped.

"What?"

"Didn't you read the sign? They'll put a bumper sticker on your car if you don't," she said.

I dropped the visor and met her behind the truck. "What do you want to do first?" I asked. "I bet they have a fun-house. You know, where people try to scare you and they have mirrors that make you look grotesque."

"I've never seen a movie where people went into a fun-house and didn't get attacked," she said.

"That's why I love you," I said. "You get me."

Gabriella stopped walking and turned to me. "Did you mean to say that?"

"Say what?" I asked, still sporting a goofy grin.

"You said you love me," she said.

"Has there ever been any doubt?" I asked. "You're the woman of my dreams."

"I'm not the only woman of your dreams," she said.

"I know I'm sarcastic sometimes," I said. "But yeah, you're it for me."

"What about Amak and Thea?" she asked.

"Even when I was with Amak, in the back of my mind, I knew it was you," I said. "Amak even told me that was true."

"She did?"

"Apparently, we smell different when we're in love," I said. "She pointed that out several times. I think that whole Senwe Princess business was a lie. She knew it was you I wanted and stepped out of the way."

"I like the way you see her," Gabriella said. "I grew up with a mistrust of trolls. Witches aren't immune to petty hatred and if there was ever a group that it was okay to demean, it was trolls. I see how that's wrong. Would you really have gone the distance with her?"

"Nothing like talking about old girlfriends," I said, handing a couple of twenties to a teen manning the gate to the amusement park section of the faire.

"Would you?" She pressed after we'd walked through the turnstile.

"No idea. She shut it down pretty quickly after realizing my interest," I said. "I won't insult you by telling you I had no interest. She's a remarkable woman, but I'm a one-woman kind of guy and she wasn't available. After that, she just became a friend and I stopped thinking about her in that way."

"You can turn it off? Just like that?" Gabriella asked.

We'd been having this conversation in one form or another during the entire trip. It was the first time she'd been quite so blunt, however. "Is that what this is about? You're afraid I'll just decide to abandon you?"

"You abandoned *me*," a familiar voice announced over our shoulders. Of all the people in the county I didn't expect or want to see, Thea was top of that list. Gabriella and I turned to meet her. "Have you had sex with her yet? I'm telling you, he's a love 'em-and-leave 'em kind of guy."

"Thea," I said. "That's not fair."

"Oh. You haven't, then," she said with a fake pout. "That's awkward … again."

"What do you want, Thea?" Gabriella asked. "Besides making Felix feel bad."

"Oh, I'm just messing around," she said. "I guess Felix here never told you about my lack of manners. I promise I'm done now. I just had a lot of pent-up anger and you're getting the sharp end of that stick."

"Doesn't sound like you're done," Gabriella pushed back.

Thea gave Gabriella a surprised look. "Kitty has some claws." She turned to me. "I approve, Slade. She's a keeper."

"What are you doing here, Thea?" I asked.

"Me? Oh, I guess Judy didn't tell you," she said. "I work here. I just broke up a fight over by the target range. Drunk townies and all. Tell you what, dinner is on me tonight." She pulled a couple of tickets from her pocket and handed them to me. "Ask for Jayce. She'll get you set up."

"You don't have to do that," I said, trying not to take the tickets.

"No. I've been rude. The least you can do is let me buy dinner," she said. "Maybe I'll see you over there."

"That'd be great," I said. It was the bad thing about being around witches. They both knew I didn't mean it.

"This is me … burying the hatchet," Thea said, miming throwing an axe to the ground before walking off.

"She's not in a good place," Gabriella said after Thea was out of earshot.

"Tilt-o-whirl?" I asked not wanting to focus on the negative.

"Seriously?" Gabriella laughed nervously.

"We can't come here without trying a few rides," I said.

"Fine, but I'm not getting on that roller-coaster."

"We'll see." I grabbed her hand and dragged her through the crowd.

An hour later, my eyes were spinning - an after-effect of too many rides. It had been a number of years since I'd last enjoyed a carnival and I didn't have the endurance for it any more.

"Should we find the fortune teller? Maybe we'll get lucky," I said.

"What about the book-store?"

"Let's find a map," I said.

As it turned out, maps weren't particularly available, but the people of the fair were more than happy to point us in the right direction. Not surprisingly, there were two fortune tellers on the campus. Madame Celise was the closest, located right in the center of the bustling village just outside the gated carnival rides. The businesses along the street were all named and numbered on signs that swung from antique street lamps. The column of brightly colored rectangular wooden signs was separated by small chains that squeaked as we passed. The Madame's entrance was part of a two story row-house. We walked between flanking wind chimes to a large glass door which stood open. Inside, a picture window looked out onto the busy street behind us.

"Come in, travelers," a smoky alto voice intoned from within the building. I looked at Gabriella and she returned an excited smile, clearly looking forward to the performance. Gypsy fortune tellers were well known for their show. I was on the fence as to whether that meant they really had an ability to see the future or were just good con artists. Believing that a person could constantly tell fortunes, day in and day out, was a bit of a stretch for me. It also seemed that magic might not want to expose the secrets of everyone quite so routinely. Those issues aside, I wasn't ready to put Madame Celise in either category just yet.

"Travelers," Gabriella tittered quietly, picking up on the woman's quick observation.

"Madame Celise?"

Lit only by candle light, a woman's face peered at us over a glowing glass ball.

"Please come in." She gestured to the chairs opposite her.

"Your top is beautiful," Gabriella said, admiring the woman's fluffy white blouse that had gold and blue embroidered stitching throughout.

"Greetings, Lady," she said. "You honor Celise with your presence." Gabriella quirked an eyebrow and suppressed the giggle forming in her throat. She was like a kid in a candy store. "Is it love that brings you to my table this eve?"

Gabriella squeezed my hand harder, which I thought wasn't possible. "Madame, tell me of our relationship. Will it last?" she asked.

"Allow me to hold your hands, dear ones," she said. "I will ask the spirits."

We laid our hands on the table and Madame Celise picked them up into her own.

"I tell you this for your safety," she said. "Do not release my hands while in the presence of the spirits. It is only through our contact that I'm able to provide protection. Do I have your solemn word?"

We both agreed and just as we did, she snapped her eyes closed. Perfectly timed, four candles on the fireplace mantle behind her snuffed out. As a wizard and a skeptic, I desperately wanted to inspect the wall for modifications. I had to admit though, it was a neat trick.

"Spirits, I call you for a most important question," she started, huskily. "Please answer our call. The Lady ... " She popped open an eye and looked at Gabriella questioningly.

"Gabriella," Gabriella filled in.

"The Lady Gabriella has asked if her love for ... "

When the second eye popped open I answered immediately.

"Felix and his love for her will stand the test of time ... "

At that point she started swinging her head around dramatically and pulling on our hands as she swayed back and forth - either humming or moaning, I wasn't completely sure. She repeated her question a second time and as she did, a light mist filled the room from floor level. Again, a neat trick.

On the third chant, as her voice lowered, her eyes popped open. This time her eyes were featureless, her pupils no longer visible.

"Be careful, my children, for the spirits are with us." She continued pulling us as she swayed in more or less a circular pattern, her long braided hair moving wildly from side to side.

From nowhere, a ghostly shape appeared, floating on the mists that had settled above the table. It was indistinct and moving in a lazy circle.

"Tell us now, spirit!" she commanded and resumed her moaning. A low vibration emanated from the floor and all at once, just as she seemed to be reaching the end of her crescendo, everything stopped. There was no moaning or thrashing and the vibration was gone, even the little glowing slug that I was pretty sure was being projected from somewhere behind the curtains next to the window disappeared.

"I have your answer, dear children," the woman, who couldn't be more than forty years old, said after slowly opening her restored eyes. The mists dissipated into small ducts low on the wall.

"Tell us, Madame Celise. What did the spirit share with you?" Gabriella asked with no lack of drama.

She slid a card across the table at us which showed her rates; ten dollars for a basic reading, twenty for a personalized reading and ten dollars for each person beyond the first. Tips were appreciated. I reached into my pocket and pulled out two twenties, figuring it should cover us.

"I cannot be sullied by such mundane exchanges, but alas rents must be paid," she said. "Please leave your offering in the bowl." She nodded her head to a glass bowl that sat next to the table and I placed the bills in.

She continued. "There is uncertainty in your future, my children. While there is no lack of true love, I see great conflicts ahead. It is only by staying true to each other that you will overcome these conflicts and realize the future together that you seek. Such is what the spirits have said and so it is true."

Gabriella giggled and grabbed my hand. Who knew she'd enjoy visiting with a psychic so much. "Thank you, Madame Celise. Were the spirits able to share the nature of these conflicts?"

"No, my dear, but you will know them for what they are when you face them. The spirits were quite adamant about this. I'm afraid your faithfulness might be a matter of life and death." Once again she spoke dramatically, much more than the situation called for.

"A second question, Madame Celise?" I asked.

"If it is within my power," she replied.

I pulled two more bills from my pocket and placed them in her glass bowl. "Have you seen this man?" I handed her a picture of Agent Mulper.

The woman held the picture between her hands and closed her eyes, opening them a moment later. "I have not, but danger surrounds him. You should proceed carefully."

"Thank you, Madam Celise," I said. She returned the picture and gave a half-hearted smile.

"That was weird," Gabriella said as we left.

"Weird, how?"

"She lied when she said she'd never seen him," Gabriella said. "She wasn't lying about the danger, however."

"You're better than a lie detector," I said. "Best not show that skill to Special Agent Anderson."

"Doesn't work on everyone," she said. "I'm surprised she was that direct. Witches are used to not being able to lie to each other and it is practice to prepare vague answers," she said.

"How do you think she knew your title?" I asked.

"It is a safe guess to call someone 'Lady.' Our reactions reinforced her responses," she said. "She really was delightful, wasn't she?"

Not far from Madame Celise's, we found the quaint old book store. Where Celise's storefront had been bright and colorful, the bookstore was earthy. It was grounded with a worn wooden floor and tall shelves of books proudly displayed a huge inventory. Small reading nooks were sprinkled throughout, with comfortable benches and thick, albeit worn, pillows. I could see what Dolly liked about the bookstore as it catered to a wide variety of subjects.

Gabriella guided me to a coffee bar she'd spied and we sat on a couple of stools while the barista brewed a latte for us to share.

"Point us to the occult section?" I asked, after Gabriella purchased the coffee.

He pointed. "Modern is G-10, historical is an aisle over. There's also a young-adult section at the end of G."

"Young adult?" I asked of Gabriella as we walked back in the direction he'd pointed.

"Kids have questions too," she said.

I'd never seen witchcraft or wizardry as a religion. That's not to say I didn't recognize the religious implications of things like necromancy or even demonic possession. But basic wizardry seemed a lot more like tapping into a power within the earth that was part of nature, not a statement about a creator. I also knew better than to argue this position with most people, as it made them think I was nuts or worse - a heretic.

"Block me for a minute." I stepped around her into the aisle. There was a quick way to look for magical books and a slow way. The recent development of my eyes glowing when I cast my wizard's sight was hard to mask, but I'd be able to pick up on magical books very quickly. "*Altum Visu*." I waved my hand in front of my eyes and felt the familiar burning sensation that accompanied the planar view.

"May I help you?" A man's voice asked from behind us.

I turned away as Gabriella moved to intercept. "We're just browsing, but I would be interested in any texts you have on Hinduism."

"This is occult. Hinduism is two aisles over," he answered. "Here, I'll show you."

I worked my way down the aisle, scanning through the books. I could see residual energy on the books and a small amount on the shelves. The energy was transfer, common for mundane objects that had come into contact with people who were magical. I worked my way around the corner and into the young adult section.

"Whoa." A boy looked up from his seated position. When I'd scouted the aisles I hadn't considered a kid sitting on the floor. "Your eyes are on fire."

I held my finger up to my lips. "Don't tell anyone, it's a secret." His aura was bright blue with streaks of magenta and sparkles of yellow flashing around his hands and eyes. I imagined he had latent magical talents and wondered if he had a mentor or if he would ever even discover his capabilities.

The book he held was another thing. The same greasy mud green covering as was on Petaluma's crawled all over it and was surging onto the boy's hands.

"What do you have there?" I whispered, feeling creepy that I was keeping my voice down while talking to a child in a book aisle.

"Just a book."

"Tobin? What are you doing back here?" A woman's voice asked.

I plucked a book from the shelf and turned my back to the approaching woman.

"Look at this book I found," he said.

"*Finis*," I whispered, dropping my wizard's sight.

"Great, bring it along. We need to get going," she said.

I turned and placed my book back on the shelf. Tobin looked at me, no doubt confused that my eyes were no longer glowing.

"His eyes. They're not on fire anymore," Tobin said, pointing back at me. I looked to the woman and then back down to the boy. I hated throwing him under the bus, but wasn't about to have this conversation. I also wasn't about to let him leave with the book. I shrugged apologetically at the woman.

"I'm sorry, he has quite an imagination," she explained. From the sound of her voice, it hadn't been the first time she'd had to make excuses for him. I wanted to explain to her that it wasn't going to get better, but it wasn't up to me to out her son's emerging magic.

"Kids who read are a blessing," I said. "No apology necessary."

I flicked my finger, using my capability to manipulate small objects and forced the book out of his hands and to the floor. Before he could bend to pick it up, I cast a quick spell – "*Scutum*." I raised a shield over the book which harmlessly deflected his attempts to pick it up.

"Tobin, stop messing around," the boy's mom scolded.

"I'm not!" He looked at me accusatorily. "I can't pick it up."

"I don't have time for this, Tobin," she said and grabbed his hand, dragging him down the aisle. He looked back at me and I mouthed 'sorry' back at him. He wasn't impressed and stuck out his tongue, which caused me to chuckle.

"Is that one of them?" Gabriella asked, nodding at the book on the floor.

"Yes," I said. "It was trying to slime that boy."

"He couldn't have been older than ten," she said. "What would someone want with him?"

"He's a latent," I said. "Not overly powerful, but he certainly has something."

I looked at the title of the book, not yet willing to pick it up. It read – 'Spirit's Guide – A Warlock's Intro.'

"What are you going to do with it? We can't leave it here, but it could be dangerous," she said.

"Only one way to find out," I said. "Stand back."

"Felix, don't," Gabriella backpedaled.

I reached for the book and it felt as if my hand had come in contact with gelatin, not quite firm but not quite solid either. The feeling dissipated quickly as I turned the book over in my hand and inspected the colorful dust jacket. It was then I realized I was just looking at a stupid kid's book, way beneath my dignity to be reading. I couldn't imagine why a person would find it interesting. The feelings mixed with embarrassment for even considering a child's book. What would people think of me for choosing such a book as a grown man? I hastily set the book back onto the shelf, not caring if I'd found the correct location. I couldn't be associated with it any further – what if someone had seen me holding it?

"We should leave," I said.

"What about the book? We can't leave it for another child to find," she said.

I looked at her, blinking my eyes. She made sense, but the feeling of embarrassment persisted. "I've been spelled," I said, realizing the truth of it. Turning toward the back wall, I cast my wizard's sight and looked down at my hands. The slimy green ichor that covered the book was slowly creeping up my arm. I tried to pull it off with my other hand and succeeded only in transferring an equal part.

I looked over to the book and realized every book on the entire six-foot section of the second shelf was dripping with the malevolent spell.

"What's wrong?" Gabriella asked.

"We need to leave," I said. "It's on me."

"What about the book?"

"It's not just this one, it's the entire section. It's too dangerous," I said.

"We can't leave it for other kids."

"We'll have to," I said. "Gabriella, it still has me."

Impulsively, she grabbed the book from the shelf. Immediately the spell started interacting with her hands.

"Damn it," I said. "That was stupid. I don't know how to remove that curse."

"Oh, toadstools and slime," she reacted, obviously not listening to me. "It's making me nauseous."

"*Finis*." I cancelled my wizard's sight and grabbed her arm, dragging her up to the checkout.

"Is this everything?" The clerk asked. I noticed he was wearing gloves.

"Why the gloves?"

"Books are a way of life for us. This way we don't allow the oils of our hands to spoil your treasures," he said, accepting my credit card.

"Convenient," I said.

He looked at me perplexed, but smiled and ran my card. "Are you going to join us for the book fair?" He pointed to a sign advertising a morning event in a couple of days.

"Yeah, I don't think so," I said and led Gabriella out of the store. "Where's that diner?" I pulled the tickets from my pocket and looked at the address. We were close and I turned quickly into an alley.

"Wait." Gabriella pulled on my arm, she staggered to the building next to us, leaned over and threw up.

I gently pulled the book from her hand and held her hair away from her face as her back spasmed in dry heaves. After a few minutes, she stood back up, steadying herself on the brick wall.

"Better?" I asked.

"The book. It wanted me to drop it," she said. "I thought I could resist, but I couldn't."

"Come with me," I said, wrapping my arm around her slender waist.

"We don't serve alcohol." The waiter sniped as we walked into the diner.

"Way to work for your tips, junior," I sniped right back. "We're not drinking; she's motion sick."

"Find a table. I'll be back in a few." He glowered at me and then bustled away.

The diner was relatively empty with only a few of the tables occupied. I led Gabriella over to a booth by the window, but changed my mind, grabbing the salt shaker and turning toward the back of the restaurant. Helping Gabriella back to the bathroom, I managed to snag three more shakers.

Once inside the women's bathroom, I made a beeline for the handicapped stall. If I'd had any previous illusions about women's bathrooms being cleaner than men's, they were at that moment dispelled. The problem was we didn't have time to be shopping around for a more suitable environment. Whatever the magic was, it was still having a profound effect on Gabriella.

Hardly able to bear the thought of my next actions, I pulled heaping wads of toilet paper from the industrial roll and wiped out the toilet's bowl as best I could and flushed it. Next, I pulled a similar wad of paper from the roll and jammed it into the hole, plugging the toilet.

Gabriella slumped to the floor, not quite unconscious, but woozy. With eyes fluttering and her head was rolling back and forth against the wall, her legs slid under the stall door. "Hold on Gabriella," I said. "I've got you." I pulled her back to a seated position after tossing the salt shakers into the bowl, without opening them up.

"What's going on in there?" A woman's voice asked, knocking on the door.

"My friend is sick," I said. "Go away."

"Perverts. I'm telling management," she said.

I ignored her and plunged my hands into the bowl, loosening the lids of the shakers and allowing them to dump out into the water.

"I'm sorry, babe," I said as I stood over her and lifted her by her armpits, guiding her hands into the toilet's bowl. With my knee holding her in place, I picked up the book and prepared to drop it into the makeshift porcelain cauldron.

I wasn't prepared for what happened next. An inhuman voice emitted from the book, starting as a whine and transitioning into an eerie howl. The book bucked in my hands and in my distraction, I released Gabriella who slumped to the floor, her jaw ricocheting off the bowl's rim. "Shit! Get in there, you little bastard."

A loud rapping on the door behind me could only mean someone in authority had been alerted to the 'problem' in the bathroom. "What's going on in there?" While I didn't much care, I did recognize the voice of the snotty waiter who already thought we were drunks.

I struggled with the kid's book-turned-bull and finally wrestled it into the water.

"I'm coming in," he said, rattling the lock on the door. I heard the deadbolt slide open, so I released the book with one hand for a moment and flicked it closed, jamming the heel of my boot into the door. I gave up all pretense of dignity and lay down on the book, forcing it into the bowl. Upon contact with the water, a final, desperate scream emanated from within the toilet and then all was quiet.

"I'm so sorry," I said as I gently pulled Gabriella from the floor, her eyes fluttering open as I did. I managed to lift her to the seat just as the door was pulled open.

"Security is on the way," the pissy waiter informed us.

"Get out, you pervert," Gabriella choked.

The waiter grabbed my shoulder, intent on rescuing the damsel. It was more than I could take - given the stress I'd been dealing with. I stood, grabbed his wrist, and twisted it as I turned into him and pushed him from the stall.

"She's talking to you," I said, releasing him as I pushed the door closed behind me. "Or do you not understand a woman's need for privacy?"

He sputtered, unable to form a complete sentence, finally throwing up his hands in anger and stalking out.

"How are you doing in there?" I asked, opening the door.

"Better ..."

"Put your hands on your head, jackass," a voice commanded from behind me.

DAMASCUS

The weapon the man held was a stun-gun. Its gray body and bright yellow lightning bolt where a barrel should protrude were dead giveaways.

"Hold on there, tiger." I said, raising my hands. "Nothing to get excited about."

"Step away from the stall," he ordered, lowering his weapon.

"Felix? What's going on?" Gabriella asked weakly.

"That idiot called security on us," I said.

"Move it!" The security guard demanded.

"Take it easy, buddy, unless you're going to shoot an unarmed man for helping his sick girlfriend."

"Step away from the stall," he continued, although less sure of himself.

I stepped toward him and he backed out of the bathroom allowing a second man in uniform to enter the room. This one held handcuffs.

"I'm just going to restrain you for our safety," the older man said in a conciliatory tone. "We got a report of an assault and have to follow through on it. If everything checks out, we'll have you on your way."

Firm hands grabbed my wrists and one by one my arms were twisted behind my back. I'd been cuffed a few times in my life and knew that it was painful if I resisted.

"Ma'am? Are you okay in there?" The second guard asked.

"Are you going to arrest me for needing to use the toilet?" Gabriella asked, her voice stronger.

"No, but we're going to ask you to come down to the station," he said. "We'll get this cleared up."

"Give me a minute," she said. "I'll be out in a second."

"We'll be right outside this door," he said, pushing me so I was forced to walk through the hallway and into the back of the restaurant's main dining room. The waiter caught my eye as he emerged from the swinging door, palming a large tray of food. His smug grin was interrupted when he tripped on seemingly nothing and the tray toppled back into him as he tried to steady it.

"Karma's a bitch," I said.

"That's enough." The guard pushed me forward, perp-walked me through the dining room, and steered me out the front door to his waiting golf-cart. The small vehicle was adorned with official looking stickers and a flashing light. He removed the cuff from one hand and locked me into a rear facing seat.

A few minutes later, Gabriella emerged followed by the first security guard. The fact that he walked several feet ahead, cheeks reddened, suggested that Gabriella had given him a piece of her mind on the way out.

"You'll need to ride up front," the man who'd cuffed me informed her as she sat next to me.

"As I explained to your friend, you're currently in violation of the law. You're restraining a person without cause," she said haughtily.

"I apologize for the inconvenience, but in that you were creating a public disturbance, we're well within our jurisdiction to remove you from the premises," he said. "I take it you're a lawyer?"

She gave him a short, unfriendly smile. "Good call."

"It's a short ride to the station where we can work this out," he said. The vehicle's electric motor caught and we started forward.

"Book?" I asked quietly.

"Trash in the bathroom. Best I could manage," she said.

"How are you feeling?" I'd like to have cast the planar view, but I couldn't due to the attention we were receiving from people on the street.

"Much better. How'd you know to do that?" she asked.

"Some old wives' tales are based in reality," I said. "That and I had a salt-water aquarium once and it kept blowing out my rings."

"I feel violated," she said. "That thing was trying to get in me."

"And here I thought I was going to get busted for giving you a swirly," I said, still worried about how pale she looked.

She chuckled as I wiped wet bangs from her eyes with my free hand. I was pleased, however, when my touch didn't sense any residual magic from the book. I couldn't imagine how the children who'd picked up those books must feel. Worse yet, I suspected they felt as Petaluma did – attached.

The cart pulled to a stop in front of a wooden building that was fashioned after a wild-west sheriff's station, complete with wooden porch and golden star on the front window. I flicked off the cuffs and handed them to the guard.

Recovering from their surprise, the two officers guided us up the stairs and into a more modern room than I'd expected, given the façade. A woman behind the counter looked up as we entered.

"She's in the interview room." The woman said without introduction.

"This way." A push in the small of my back wasn't unexpected and I walked through the opening in the counter that separated staff from visitors.

The hallway we entered wasn't long and with urging from behind, I entered a nondescript room with a stainless steel table. On the other side of the room, Thea paced back and forth.

"Shit, Felix. What are you doing?" she asked as I was pushed into one of the two chairs. "And Gabby, you don't mind if I call you that, do you? Is that toilet water all over your pretty blouse? Good thing you're wearing a matching bra, wouldn't want … right … not much to cover."

"Really?" I asked, annoyed by Thea's ability to insult Gabriella every time she opened her mouth.

Thea gestured to the guards. "Leave us,"

"Are you sure? He could be a handful." The younger of the two said.

"Felix isn't going to be a problem, are you dear?" she said in a falsely sweet voice.

"Why are you holding us?" Gabriella asked.

"Why are you asking about FBI agents?" Thea asked, ignoring

Gabriella.

"What are you into, Thea?" I asked. "This isn't like you."

"You've always been naïve," she replied. "I'll ask again. How do you know about David Mulper?"

"I must have heard about him in the news," I said. "Madam Celise was just so much fun that I thought maybe she had the inside scoop."

"Celise is the real deal," Thea replied. "Did you figure that out? Drove me nuts for the longest time. It's funny, she had added all those smoke and lights so people could choose to believe she was a fake. And for the record, nobody knows about the agent you were asking about."

"We're leaving," Gabriella said, standing.

"Tell me before you go what you were doing in the book store?" she asked, flipping on a TV monitor hanging from the wall.

"What do you think?" I asked. "Looking for books."

She produced a remote control and un-paused a frozen picture of me in the bookstore rounding the shelf, eyes ablaze, confronting the small boy, Tobin. She allowed the scene to play out.

"Nice trick with the shield. You've really dialed that spell in," she said. "You know how few moms actually allow their kids into the occult aisle? And then you go and screw it up."

"I bought your book," I said. "How long have you been part of this?"

"Part of what? The mystical world? You know me, Felix. I'm not a joiner," she said.

"From where I'm sitting you are," I said. "Did you have anything to do with Luma getting her book?"

"That fat cow she calls a mother couldn't see the brilliant child for what she was," Thea spat. "She had more raw talent at nine years than her mother has to this day. That bitch was ruining her - all daffodils and roses. Damn it! The girl's a necro and a fucking amazing one. Did you know it was Luma who sent that thrall to warn you off?"

"In Missouri?" I asked.

"Yup," she said. "Never seen the like before. She reached out nearly a thousand miles, plucked a host from the morgue and walked her out to your campsite - all from her bedroom. Did it talk to you?"

"That was Luma?"

"Fucking right it was," she said.

"How'd she know we were coming here?" I asked.

"Let's just say her loyalties are currently confused. And she might have overheard some things," Thea said. "It's no problem, she's a long play."

"If you hurt her, so help me," I said.

"What? You'll leave me battered and in the hospital?" she asked. "Sorry, lover. Been there, done that."

I sighed. She really knew how to punch buttons.

"You've been watching Felix?" Gabriella asked. "Why is that?"

"An old friend of his mother's would like to have a word with him. Let's take a little walk." Thea crossed to the door and knocked. When it opened, she spoke to the guard. "You'll accompany us to the temple."

"Cuffs?" It was the younger, surlier of the two guards who asked.

"Still doing that thing with locks?" Thea asked. When I didn't answer, she continued. "Cuffs won't be necessary."

"This is kidnapping," Gabriella said. "You're holding us against our will."

"Just figuring that out are you?" Thea asked. "Don't worry, you won't want to miss this. Apparently, Willum wanted me to make you understand that he's an old friend of Atronia's."

"My mother," I filled in for Gabriella's benefit. I found it interesting that now two different people were using her name as a lure.

The security office sat at the edge of Eppy Faire, blocked off by semi-permanent barricades to discourage pedestrian traffic into the actual town where the gypsies lived. With one guard in front and one behind, we were led out of the building, past the barricades and up a cobblestone street.

"Who ... who ..." An owl called from a nearby tree as we passed.

"That reminds me; is that crazy crow still following you around?" Thea asked as we turned toward a white clapboard church structure.

The sound of huge wings pushing against the air startled us into looking up. What appeared to be a great horned owl crossed in front of us and sailed upward, landing conspicuously on the church roof.

"I still see her from time to time," I said. "What's your end-goal here, Thea?"

"Be patient," she said. "No sense having to repeat all your questions for Willum."

"How long have you been acolyting for him?" Gabriella asked.

"Acolyte. That's shit," she said. "We're partners. Been that way since we hooked up in college."

I raised my eyebrows at the time reference. I'd met Thea about the time she'd washed out of school. It had been me who introduced her to Judy. "Wait. You were with Willum when we ...? "

We'd arrived at a side door to what had been referred to as 'the temple.' It seemed to have the basic architecture of most churches I'd seen, but lacked any symbols of Christianity or even Judaism. If a demon was involved, that made sense. The Star of David and the cross of Christ were both powerful symbols. I understood from my reading that demons and sub-demons couldn't reside on soil sanctified by the God of David.

"And immediately there fell from his eyes as if it had been scales." A man I recognized from my dreams to be Willum had opened the door and smiled welcomingly. He was dressed simply in a black linen robe with a light-brown braided belt pulled into a knot at his waist.

"Is this the road to Damascus?" Gabriella asked, annoyed.

"Ah, how delicious! A believer," Willum replied. "Please come in. And yes, the passage is appropriate for when a man learns of his true calling. But by all means, Althea, answer Mr. Slade's question."

He led us into the sanctuary of the old building. The pews still remained, but in place of the altar sat a chair that would better be described as a throne.

"To answer your question, Willum and I were friends before you and I met, Felix," Thea answered.

"What really happened the last night you were together?" Gabriella asked. "I refuse to believe Felix hurt you."

"We don't have time for this," Thea answered and for the first time her cheeks were flush.

"Why not?" Willum asked. "Do you not believe that the truth shall set you free?"

"I thought we agreed; we weren't going to talk about this," Thea said.

"Embarrassment is not becoming of you," Willum said. "Where is my devil-may-care warrior? Is it possible you've developed feelings for the wizard?"

"You're such an ass," she retorted.

Willum threw back his head and laughed loudly. "I prefer goat." He snorted at his not-so-hidden reference. "I'm surprised you never figured it out. For a wizard, you're easily manipulated by guilt. Did you never once wonder what was within you that would cause such damage without your intent?"

He watched me, waiting for me to reply.

"Oh, hell's gates," he said. "Thea spelled you, you big dolt. She was trying to take from you and you fought back."

"There was no fight," I said, then turned to Thea. "What could you take from me?"

"I blame your mother," he said. "She really did you up with that memory spell. I thought it'd work to our benefit, but your subconscious fought back. And what the hell do you *think* we'd try to steal? Your good looks?"

"My magic," I answered feebly.

His eyes widened in disbelief. "I rarely find it appropriate to use curse words, but could you *be* more dense? Of course, your grace-damned magic."

"Maybe it's because you suck at cursing," I said.

"Respect!" The younger guard demanded, landing a blow with his night stick against my back, causing me to fall forward.

"*Adoloret!*" I pointed my hand at the guard behind me, but nothing happened.

"Mr. Barnes, there is no need for violence," Willum said calmly. "The wizard and the Lady are our guests. Perhaps you should remove yourself so as not to be a further distraction."

"Yes, Master," he replied.

"What do you want from us, Willum?" I asked as Gabriella helped me stand back up.

"Tell me why you've been consorting with the FBI. They are such a pain."

Before I could answer, he continued. "Don't deny it. I suppose they're upset at the loss of their agents. Couldn't be helped. As for what I want with you, it is the same thing I want with the Applebaum child, although I'd hoped to grow that one a tad more. Can't be helped, though. Must make hay while the sun shines. I'm sure Althea would quite enjoy a chance to rectify past failures."

"To *take* my magic?" I asked. It hadn't been lost on me that he'd referred to the loss of multiple agents.

"Precisely. But I believe you'll give it to me quite willingly," he said.

"You're nutters."

He turned his hand over, forming a claw, pointed skyward, and incanted something. The evil of the spell gathering around him was palpable even without my wizard's sight. When he turned his claw toward Gabriella, she shrieked in agony, her back arching as she rose from the ground.

"*Scutum,*" I attempted to cast a shield spell and failed. My rings weren't just exhausted; they'd been dispelled in the toilet-water saline bath. A flicker of the spell attempted to ignite and I forced my thoughts down into the ground, only to be met with a layer of putrescent energy that had been woven beneath the dark church.

"Oh, you are a sumptuous one. Beautiful," he cackled over Gabriella's screams of agony. "I'd forgotten how I enjoy the taste of the light witches. And a believer to boot."

"Stop!" I yelled.

"I don't know if I can," he said. "She's so lovely."

"Stop! Whatever you want. I'll do it," I said.

"Drat," he said after a few more seconds, lowering his arm and allowing Gabriella to fall back to the ground. I rushed to her and pulled her into my lap, cursing myself for bringing us into this beast's den.

"Take them to the cell." Thea fired off the order to the remaining guard. "I'll assemble the church."

"Not tonight, the moon is still gibbous. Three nights hence will be fine, you can arrange to have them taken to the Cathedral in the morning," Willum said.

"Is your soul dead?" I asked, looking at Thea, the depth of her betrayal finally sinking in.

"Lock them in the tower then and take his rings," Thea said, ignoring my chastisement. "Make sure to set the bar; our wizard can manipulate simple locks."

The remaining guard thumped me painfully on the shoulder. "Let's go."

I helped Gabriella to her feet. I wasn't about to ask how she felt as tears streamed down her face. I wanted to lash out, but my offensive capabilities had been literally flushed down the toilet.

"Arrange to bring the Applebaum girl at the same time," Willum said before we were out of earshot.

The cell was in the church's tower, up two flights of stairs. Each step was agonizing for Gabriella, so I resorted to carrying her. While she was light weight, it was an arduous task. The cell was an eight by eight room with a high barred window that had a view of the night sky. A cot with a thin mattress; the only furniture in the room.

"Jewelry in the bowl," the guard demanded. "We'll know if you're holding back. I'd hate to have to use the stun-gun on you, but I will. If you behave, I'll bring water later on. "

Classic carrot and stick. I pulled my rings and bracelet off. I hated letting them go, not because they had any magical value left in them, but because of the sentimental value I held for them. That said, I wasn't about to get Gabriella hurt again.

"And the girl," he said.

"What? Her jewelry is useless," I said.

"Is that the conversation you want to have?" he asked, placing a hand on the handle of his stun-gun.

"Didn't anyone ever tell you not to cross a wizard?" I asked.

"Dark Folk have been looking after ourselves for centuries. We don't fear the likes of you," he said. "Now do what I said or I'll taze you, just as sure as I'm standing here."

"No. I'll get it," I said and picked up Gabriella's hand. On her right hand she wore her grandmother's wedding ring. It was simple, a rhodium-plated band lacking even a diamond, but it had immense sentimental value. On her left, she wore a couple of rings I wasn't familiar with. I pulled off the rings while palming the wedding band. I made a show of dropping all but the wedding ring into the bowl and handed it back.

"Place the bowl outside the door." I did as I was required, after which he placed a plastic bottle of water on the floor. "Take the water and back off. I'd go easy on the water though. It's the last you'll get until tomorrow."

I watched as the door swung closed. The sound of something heavy scraping against the thick wooden door confirmed their commitment to locking us in. Gabriella stirred and tried unsuccessfully to lift herself from the mattress. I went to her and helped her up, sitting next to her. She lay heavily against me as I placed her grandmother's ring back on her finger and pulled her in tightly.

"Do you suppose this is what Madam Celise saw in her glass ball?" I wondered idly, smoothing her hair with my fingers. I watched in surprise when all at once her hair turned a silvery gray as she nodded off into unconsciousness.

I'LL HUFF AND I'LL PUFF

I sat for about an hour, mostly in shock, I suppose. I'd never felt as useless as I did at that moment. Without my charged jewelry, I had few spells that would work against the guards. I couldn't imagine how I'd combat Willum, especially if he were able to lift me with the same strength he'd used on Gabriella. As far as I could tell, he hadn't even struggled.

I cast my wizard's sight and was surprised to see that the stone cell was mundane and completely devoid of what I assumed was Willum or the ghrelin's energy. It made sense. While demons were extraordinarily powerful beings, a ghrelin wasn't at the top of that food chain. A ghrelin would have to build energy over time and conserve its use if it was going to maintain a matrix like the one I'd found beneath the church.

It was sometime around midnight when Gabriella stirred. She'd been sleeping fitfully and I finally heard her inhale deeply right before she sat bolt-upright, looking around wildly.

"Silici Scintillam Excudit." A small ball of flame ignited, hovering above the palm of my hand. A moment later, the ghostly outline of a lantern formed around it. The outline was something I'd been experimenting with and I might have taken more pleasure from it appearing if we weren't in such a grim situation.

"Where are we?" Gabriella asked.

"Locked in a tower by an evil witch," I said.

She looked at my face to see if I was seriously cracking wise. "Smartass," she said. "My body aches all over."

I used my free hand to pass her the water bottle. "Drink something."

She opened the bottle and took a generous swig, wincing as she swallowed. "What are we going to do?" she asked.

"I've been thinking about that," I said. "Can you walk?"

"Walk? Yes," she said and then dropped her head into her hands. "It was horrible, Felix. I felt like my soul was being torn apart. Every fiber of my body was on fire. It was agony and all I could think about was how I had failed you and Clarita. It felt like nothing in the world would be right again."

A dark shape fluttered across the window, interrupting the bright moonlight that shone in.

"I'm sorry," I said. "I wish I'd never brought us to North Carolina."

"And what of Petaluma and Tobin?" she asked.

"How could you have heard that? He was … You know …"

"Torturing me," she filled in. "His words were as clear as if I were sitting next to him at mass. His intent was even more clear. He plans to torture and kill those kids and more, Felix. His church. *This* church is a death cult. He plans to murder everyone."

"How can you know that?" I asked.

"I felt him in my head, Felix. We shared space and time together," she said. "He wanted me to know what he has planned. I've seen what he's done to other people, not just in this life, but in other times and places. He's growing more powerful with every kill."

"What is Lace Faa to him?"

Gabriella shook her head and looked at the floor. "I don't know. He didn't care to share that with me."

"You're not alone, Gabriella. People care about you. I care about you."

"When he was attacking me, I felt nothing but despair. I was paralyzed by it," she said.

The moon beams were once again broken by something flying across the window and I extinguished the flaming ball we were using for light.

"What was that?"

"Hope," I said as a familiar raven landed carefully on the windowsill and wriggled through the bars. I held my arm up for a landing pad as Maggie glided over to us.

"I thought you were an owl," Gabriella said.

"Cawwk," Maggie replied, annoyed. She couldn't answer complex questions in her current form.

"Can you find the Suburban and bring it back up here?" I asked. "I think I can get us out, but it's going to make a lot of noise."

Maggie nodded her head up and down.

"Aren't you worried about Willum?" Gabriella asked.

"If we fail, Maggie will have to get help," I said, lifting her back up to the window sill.

"What are you going to do?" Gabriella asked.

"Make a mess," I said.

Gabriella nodded and looked at me expectantly.

"I need to move the cot over so I can see when Maggie is coming up the hill. She might draw a crowd, since there are a few fences between here and there," I said.

"Can she even drive? Hasn't she been a crow most of her adult life?"

***

"Shit. We're on," I said, standing on the cot and peering out the window. Fortunately, the tower had good line-of-sight to the village below.

Our concerns regarding her driving skills hadn't been entirely unfounded as soon I saw headlights bumping up and the scream of an engine working too hard in too low of a gear for its speed.

I sat down on the floor and closed my eyes. "Hold the mattress over us and watch for falling objects."

"What are you doing? And don't say making a mess."

"You know when I said an evil witch locked us in the tower and you thought Rapunzel? Think more like three little pigs," I said.

I reached out to the stones around me. Being an earth wizard, I had a special bond with natural building materials and nothing was more natural than a stone tower. Even the mortar was just a blend of sand, cement and lime. It seemed an obvious mistake, but then not even Gabriella knew where the source of my magic emanated from. It was a lesson I would remember forever. Had I told Thea about my bond with the earth, she would not have made the mistake of putting us up here. No wonder wizards worked hard to keep their secrets.

Unbinding the mortar was a simple matter, although at first, it seemed to do nothing beyond cause the building to shake and plaster dust to fall from the ceiling. The tower had been well constructed and the stones lined up nicely, one on top of the other.

"I hear someone outside," Gabriella whispered, harshly.

I pushed at the stones beneath the wall that separated us from our guard. Contrary to scientific belief, systems aren't always as easily transitioned from order to chaos as the fourth law of thermodynamics might suggest. That said, the notion of a tipping point was something I could easily embrace. I concentrated on the wall until I'd managed to wiggle free a key block from beneath us. The trick was to collapse only the parts of the building that would allow our escape, while keeping the roof from falling in on top of us.

"What's going on in there?" I heard through the door. Until that point, I hadn't realized someone was standing guard and I suspected he'd been sleeping.

"Who are you, what are you doing here?" He asked, obviously surprised. "How'd you get in here? What ... No ..." The rest of his speech a wet gurgling. Someone or something had gotten to him and it was to our advantage.

The wall I'd been working on sagged and then crumbled onto the stairs below, taking our cell door and most of the wall it had been attached to with it. We found ourselves staring at the guard, who lay against the outer wall, one hand still on his stun-gun, the other grasping at his throat which had been viciously torn open. We were still far from free, so I forced my eyes away and continued to push at the base of the wall. After what seemed like ages, I managed to free an exterior block, and then another from the level below. Soon the outside wall began to crumble and the floor beneath the dead guard gave way. He tumbled down, landing on a pile of stone below.

"Now," I said. "We go now!"

I stood, grabbed Gabriella's hand, and pulled her up. The two of us carefully picked our way through the shifting cascade of ruined stone blocks and over the fallen guard. We weren't very far off the ground when we reached open air and saw the Suburban. The problem was that my naked sister, Maggie, was exiting the driver's side, hands up, in front of the guard, Barnes.

"On the ground," he ordered, pulling handcuffs from a pouch on the back of his belt.

"Ground this!" Gabriella exclaimed as she stepped forward and fired off the guard's stun-gun I hadn't seen her pick up. The familiar click-click-click of capacitors discharging was followed by Barnes going stiff as a board and falling to the ground.

"About time," Maggie said, running back to the Suburban and diving into the driver's seat.

"Get in back," I shouted, as I piled in behind her and Gabriella yanked open the passenger door.

"Go! Go!" Gabriella shouted unnecessarily, as I threw the truck into gear and stepped on the gas, swinging the tail around.

If I'd been thinking, it might have been quicker to find a way out on this residential side of Eppy Faire. No doubt, the village had an entrance for residents. In my mind, however, all I knew was the exact route we'd come in and I was in no mood for improvisation.

"Over there," Maggie squawked in my ear, pointing at a section of chain link fence she'd already run through. I swung the vehicle to the side and gunned it.

"Is anyone following us?" I asked.

Gabriella turned around and looked. "I don't know. I can't see anyone."

We bumped violently over cement parking strips and back into the Faire's mostly empty parking lot. There was a booth ahead, but for those exiting, there were no obstructions. I didn't breathe easy until we finally made it out onto the main highway.

"How did you destroy the tower?" Gabriella asked.

"Let's say I don't like tight places and keep it at that," I said.

"Guys, I need something to eat," Maggie complained. I hadn't looked at her since we'd started our pell-mell race from Eppy Faire. In the rearview mirror, her skin was tightly stretched and every bone in her face and shoulders was prominently visible. "I think I changed too quickly. And what the hell happened to your hair?"

"Trail mix in the camping bag," Gabriella said, ignoring the question as she climbed over the seats.

"Sports drink in the cooler," I said, thinking about the problem of delivering quick calories. I found a lane to pull the truck into where we'd have some cover in the trees. I jumped out and opened the back door, horrified by Maggie's quivering, emaciated form. "She's going into shock. Stay with us, Maggie."

"Just need food," she mumbled.

Gabriella handed me a bottle of red electrolyte-rich water and I lifted it to Maggie's mouth. She drank greedily and then coughed a portion of it back out as she was unable to negotiate both her breathing and drinking.

"Blanket." Gabriella handed me a light quilt she'd brought along. I was shocked at how easy it was to lift my tiny sister from the seat and wrap the blanket around her.

"Did we get away?" Maggie asked, eyes rolling around in her head.

"You saved us, Maggie, but now you need to stay with us," I said.

Gabriella handed me a bag of trail mix. "Why did she change from the owl?"

"I don't know," I said, unsure if she'd be able to eat the trail mix in her current state. "Do we have anything softer?"

"Owls are pretty," Maggie mumbled as she ripped the trail mix from my hand and sloppily pushed it into her mouth.

"Tamale? It's been thawed, but it's mostly frozen," Gabriella said, handing a corn-leaf wrap to me.

"*Adoloret.*" I pushed a small amount of heat into the tamale and held it out to Maggie. This time she opened wide the second it came into contact with her tongue.

A few moments later her eyes blinked open. "Get off," she said, struggling to free an arm. Once free, she pulled the sports drink from my hand and drank deeply. After finishing half the bottle, she laid her head back.

"I'll ride with her," Gabriella said, slumping into the chair and resting her hand over Maggie's arm. The evident pain in her face and the silvery hair were a grim reminder of the night's events. A surge of guilt caused my stomach to roll. Gabriella and Maggie had both faced death tonight because of my lack of caution. It was a lesson I would not soon allow myself to forget.

We finally pulled up to Judy's cabin after two in the morning. Her car was in the driveway and her bedroom light was lit. Gabriella and Maggie slept, leaning into each other for support. I'd turned the heat up and was glad to step from the vehicle into the cool night. The fetid smell of rotting flesh caught my attention and I quickly locked the Suburban's doors. Once again, I had few offensive options, but if Judy was in trouble I would not hold back. I raced to the house and pulled at the locked door and knocked furiously.

"Judy!"

I jumped from the porch and ran to the backyard, not caring what plants were trampled. Following the stench, I headed away from the house, slipping on the bank of the stream bed in my haste. Falling forward, I caught a glimpse of a lantern at the edge of the forest, just inside the tree line. A moving figure interrupted the lantern's glow. I scrabbled over the bank and raced toward the lamp's light.

"Felix, there you are." Judy looked up from her labor. The smell of death hung heavy in the cool, damp air.

"What happened?" I asked, surveying the scene. Two corpses lay next to an unfinished, shallow pit. Both showed considerable decay.

She stepped from the shallow grave and handed me the shovel. "Beyond the obvious?"

"Maybe you could cover the obvious, too," I said.

She smiled. "All right, I had a couple of unwelcome visitors and had to dust off my wand. Now I'm burying them so they can rest."

"Wand?"

"I haven't always been the matronly flower child you've known and loved," she said. "There was a time when I felt a witch needed some bite to be respected."

'Matronly' and 'flower child' were far from descriptions I'd have used to describe Judy, but it wasn't the time. I jammed the shovel into the ground. "Gabriella and Maggie are in the truck. We ran into trouble."

"What kind of trouble?"

"The kind that might follow us home," I said.

"I have a place that's safe for tonight," she said. "How did Maggie find you? Last I saw, she was sunning herself on the back porch. Did she run all the way out to Eppy?"

"Something like that," I said.

"Trouble does seem to find you," she said. "Cover these poor fellows up, we'll have to do a better job of it later."

"Petaluma is in danger," I said. "We need to find her." I grabbed the first corpse by its ankles and dragged it into Judy's pit. Judy had done quite a number on her visitors and I winced as body parts were left behind or dragged along unceremoniously - not all that well attached.

"I just talked to Thea an hour ago. Luma is fine."

"What did Thea want?"

"Said she was looking for you. Wanted me to tell you that she had a nice time this evening and you should come out for another visit."

"What about Luma?"

"She's staying with Thea for a few days while Dolly is in the hospital."

"Thea's not who you think she is," I said. "She's part of this." I gestured at the pit which now held the majority of the two corpses.

Judy studied my face before replying. "I'm such an idiot," she

122

said with a sigh.

"I'm going after her, but not tonight," I said. "We need to gather some things before we head out."

The shallow grave was anything but perfect and it wouldn't fool anyone for very long if they happened by. I was curious about Judy's decision not to call the sheriff, but that was a discussion we could have later.

"Do you have your phone?" I asked, having left mine back at Eppy Faire.

She fished into her jeans pocket and handed me a newer smartphone. I dialed the number I'd been given for Agent Anderson.

"This is Dana," the woman answered after the fourth ring, her voice heavy with sleep.

"Hey. This is Felix," I said. "There are two corpses in my foster mother's back yard."

"Foster mother? As in Judy Babcock?" Anderson asked.

"Yes. They shouldn't be too hard to find."

"Describe the corpses," she said, coming fully awake.

"Mottled flesh, bones sticking out, really bad breath," I said.

"Shit. Is everyone okay?" I was surprised to hear the generally formal-speaking Anderson cuss.

"Willum has taken Petaluma Applebaum," I said. "Althea Sanders is helping him. They were planning something big for tomorrow night, but I might have messed up those plans."

"Messed them up, how?"

"By escaping," I said. "Long story, but Willum definitely knows you're on to him and it sounds like he's looking for a big finale."

"You need to stay away from that man," Anderson said. "He's dangerous."

"Right. Dangerous," I agreed. "Look. We're not going to be here when you arrive. It isn't safe."

"I'll deal with it," she said. "Don't forget my warning, Felix."

"Thank you, Dana." I hung up and handed the phone back to Judy. "The FBI will deal with the bodies and they'll be discreet."

"That doesn't sound like any FBI I'm familiar with," Judy said.

***

The sky was just starting to lighten when I finished packing the last of the items we'd take up to Judy's safe location.

"What's going on?" Gabriella asked sleepily as I started the Suburban and backed around.

"We're relocating," I said. "How are you feeling?"

"Better," she said. I'd checked on her and Maggie several times while we'd packed Judy's car and the Suburban with supplies. Both women seemed to be resting comfortably.

"It's a short drive," I said. "Just rest, we'll be there soon."

I marveled at just how well Judy's sedan handled the degrading road conditions. We'd transitioned from the main highway to a gravel road and then to a dirt two-track. The suspension of the Suburban was made for the rough travel, but Judy negotiated it all with considerable finesse, only bottoming out a few times.

"Missed one." Maggie stirred for the first time since we'd fed her tamales.

"One what?" I asked.

"Hole in the road." She grinned, pleased that I'd fallen for her question. "You should go back; it might feel left out."

"I guess you're feeling better."

"Did you know Gabriella's hair turned silver?" Maggie asked.

"Geez, Maggie. Yes, but she might not like someone pushing it in her face."

"Small price to pay for being attacked by a demon." Gabriella pushed herself up in the seat and drew the blanket up around her shoulders.

"I gotta pee," Maggie said.

"We're almost there," I said, although I had no real idea if that were true.

Maggie picked up the bag of trail mix and shoveled it into her mouth. "Do you have any more of those tamales?"

Gabriella reached over the seat and opened the cooler. "What's all this stuff back here?"

"We had visitors at Judy's last night," I said. "We're going to make it harder for them to find us."

Gabriella looked around. "This is beautiful country,"

Judy pulled into a small clearing and I stopped next to her. She'd already stepped out and was stretching in the dappled rays of the morning sun. I took a deep breath and smelled nothing but clean mountain air, damp with the morning dew.

"What happened to Gabriella's hair and why is a naked woman climbing out of your truck?" Judy asked.

"Why is she naked? Or why is she in my truck?" I asked.

"Pick one."

"That's my sister, Sevena. She's naked because it makes me uncomfortable," I said.

"She looks so familiar, what am I missing?"

"That's Maggie," I said.

"Maggie. As in the vizsla?"

"Maggie. As in the raven, the panther, the owl and ..."

"Not an owl, but it's so nice to finally meet you in person, Mistress." Maggie gave a half curtsey as she took Judy's hand.

BEFORE THE STORM

"Just whose place is this?" I asked, eyeing the stuffed antelope head mounted on the wall. It was the sort of thing Judy despised.

"Aaron Merritt," she answered.

"Sheriff?" I asked.

"Don't make more out of it than there is," she said. "He's a friend."

"Good for you," I said and then scowled at her. "Like you have to hide that from me."

"I wasn't hiding anything. It just didn't come up," she said. "You didn't say what happened to Gabriella."

"It was bad," I said. "But the whole story will have to wait. Do you know where that jewelry I asked you to bring along got to?"

"I'm exhausted, Felix. You have to be too," she said. "Let's deal with it in a couple of hours."

"I was attacked by a demon," Gabriella filled in. "And Judy's right, you need to rest, Felix. Magic shouldn't be undertaken when you're exhausted.

"We're vulnerable," I said. "And Luma is depending on us."

Gabriella patted my arm, reminding me to take it easy. "In your current condition, you'll be of no help to anyone. I'm also worried for Luma, but I know you cannot hope to face a demon as you are now."

"Two enchantments," I negotiated. "Then I'll rest."

Judy sighed, but acquiesced, pulling a tissue bundle from the deep pocket of an apron she'd donned before we'd left the house.

"I'd hoped these would remain keepsakes, memories of a time forgotten," Judy said, unwrapping the tissue as Gabriella joined us next to the fire pit. I'd lined up my primary spell book, nettles, rose thorns and poison oak, along with a narrow strip of leather, a small piece of pure silver foil and block of paraffin.

"That's beautiful," Gabriella observed. Resting atop the tissue was a silver oak leaf attached to a leather cord. The detailing on the leaf was very intricate.

"I thought perhaps you could wear this around your neck," Judy said. "It belonged to a friend of mine and was used in circumstances not so different from what we faced today. He would be pleased that you would take it up in the service of good."

"What was his name?" I asked.

"Lane."

I wanted to tell her it was too much. I sensed how important the jewelry was to her and I would hate to have anything happen to it. I also knew she had already thought her offer through and it would be futile to argue. I accepted the silver leaf. It was heavier in my hand than I'd expected.

"This also came from Lane," Judy said, digging into her pocket. She pulled out a smooth, pencil-sized stick and handed it to me. I accepted the narrow instrument and inspected the silver clasp which dangled from one end. "That clips onto the leather cord. He always hated the idea of a wand, so he wore it around his neck. The clasp pulls free with a little pressure."

I held the wand and Judy moved my fingers so the butt end rested against my palm and the pointy end barely protruded past the end of my index finger.

"You never told me about Lane," I said.

Judy smiled wistfully. "It was well before you came into my life. Perhaps, once we're through this ..." Her words trailed off. "I don't know how those will work for you. Witches don't imbue their instruments with enchantments; we just use the objects as foci."

"They'll work," I said, confidently. "It's just ... they have great sentimental value to you."

"And have been sitting in a box, forgotten," she said. "Lane would want them used, especially this way. I can feel him smiling."

I nodded. I wouldn't push her on the subject any further. I

removed the leather cord, preparing the items. Even as I mourned the loss of my old jewelry, I felt a sense of excitement about something new.

From a tote I'd dragged up from the truck, I set aside the tubers, herbs, plants and other items required to enchant both the fire and shield spells. I'd have to make do with an aluminum pot for a cauldron, but the vessel had only a small impact on the final outcome.

For most enchantments, the ingredients weren't a precise recipe. Variation between practitioners was common. Indeed, the spell book I used was one of my own making. I'd done a lot of experimenting with a variety of recipes, each with slight tweaks. Even today, the mix would be slightly different from the last time, as I was using rose thorns instead of raspberries. It would reshape the enchantment slightly. I'd also decided to use the rose thorns to extract the essential drops of my blood.

"Oh goodie." Maggie walked out with a jumbled plate of food in one hand and a peanut butter sandwich in the other. "I love watching him do enchantments." Gabriella backed off, joining Maggie, sitting gingerly on the porch next to her. She wouldn't admit it out loud, but she was still hurting.

"Wait!" Maggie interrupted as I dropped the paraffin into the pot. I looked up at her, wondering what new revelation she might have. "When Willum was diatribing, didn't he say you guys could have sex now?"

Gabriella giggled, but I couldn't let my mind even consider what she was saying. "Maggie! Stop," I said. "I need to concentrate." The idea lit like a fire in my mind. Could she be right? Was the danger I posed to witches merely a misconception crafted by Thea?

Judy looked at me quizzically, but remained silent, working her way back to the porch to sit on Maggie's other side. Three women I loved, all in a row. Great.

I ignored their whispering and continued adding ingredients one at a time until all I had left was the leaf and a single rose thorn. While stirring the mixture with a rose stem, I gripped the still-attached thorn. The puncture was not a pleasant sensation. While I didn't enjoy drawing blood by knife-point or with a sharp blade, at least those methods drew blood quickly. On the other hand, the thorn was dull by comparison and required more effort than I appreciated. Finally, after what seemed like forever, I felt the familiar trickle of blood on the palm of my hand. I chanted *'veni foras scutum'* over and over. Once the first drop of blood hit the material in the pot, I twisted the thorn from the stem and dropped it in. A moment later, the mixture clarified, turning from a concoction of disparate items into a single, clear viscous fluid resembling anti-bacterial hand cleaner. With nothing more to be done, I dropped the silver leaf jewelry into the mixture. The action wasn't without a bit of drama as a poof of smoke billowed from the pot and expanded up into the air, dissipating as it did.

I reached into the pot and pulled the leaf out, holding it up for all to see.

"Did it work?" Judy asked.

"It doesn't have a charge yet, but the enchantment has taken." I'd been confident when I started. The shield was one of my bread-and-butter spells and my familiarity almost guaranteed success.

"Prove it," Maggie said, tossing a grape in my direction.

I easily dodged the grape. "I said it doesn't have a charge."

"Meh, you don't need a charge," she teased, leaning over and picking up a golf-ball sized rock and throwing it. I dodged, again.

"Maggie, stop!" I said, getting annoyed as I eyed her picking up an even larger rock. "Do not throw that." I warned as she glared defiantly at me, bringing her arm back.

"Maggie." Gabriella tried de-escalating.

Maggie let go of the rock, big enough to do significant damage. I reached for the energy of the mountain beneath my feet. For whatever reason, I failed to make contact.

"*Scutum*," I said, using my own energy as Clarita had shown me. For a moment, a blood red shield appeared in front of me and the rock bounced off harmlessly, breaking in two as it struck the ground. If I wasn't mistaken, the shield had actually damaged the rock.

"See? Stop your whining," Maggie said, apparently justified.

I wasn't about to explain to her that I'd used my internal reserves. I had yet to learn how to quickly connect with the energy in the environment around me, only successfully tapping the power source when under extreme duress or when I was completely relaxed and could take my time.

"Yeah, great," I said. "Now let me finish this."

Next, I turned my attention to the fire spell. Judy had a rare ingredient I was excited to try. She hated the fact that she still had it, having stopped trading in the more exotic crafting ingredients a few years back. Just because she'd stopped trading, however, didn't mean she'd been able to bring herself to throw things away. The tiny dark lump didn't look like much but if the inscription on the small re-sealable plastic bag was to be believed, I would be adding a salamander's heart to my enchantment.

After several minutes of mixing and incanting, I finally threw the precious wooden wand into the flaming mixture of coals and about a dozen other ingredients. I then carefully extracted the wand from the pot.

"Feel like playing catch now?" I looked at Maggie. "*Adoloret*," I chucked a goldfish sized ball of flame at her, giving it a little zip to make things interesting.

"Damn it!" She rolled out of the way. The flaming ember singed the side of the cabin upon contact and I hustled over to make sure it didn't do any further damage.

"Can you rest now?" Gabriella asked.

"One more," Judy said and reached around her neck and removed a simple crystal hanging from a golden chain.

"Judy, I can't," I protested.

"I can't think of anyone I'd rather give this to," she said. "Pass it to a loved one when the time comes. For me, that time is today."

"You're getting downright sentimental," I said, hugging her.

She swatted my butt playfully. "Don't push it."

"It's beautiful, Judy," Gabriella said. "Lane?"

Judy gave her a warm smile. "My mother gave it to me when I

joined her circle."

I took a deep breath, not wanting either of them to see me choking up. Then I smiled. Like I could hide emotion from either of them.

"What are you enchanting that with?" Maggie called from the porch, still shoveling food from her plate.

"Light," I said. "Like my big silver ring."

"Oh, I liked that ring," she said and then caught herself. "But crap, that crystal should be even better than a ring."

I repeated much the same process as I had for the silver oak leaf and the fingerling wand, only this time, applying the components for the *Lucem* enchantment. Maggie was right. The crystal seemed to take to the enchantment very well and when I was done, it glowed slightly.

"Now we rest," I said.

"Good," Gabriella said as I followed her into the cabin where she climbed up onto a high bunk bed that held a full-sized mattress. She'd already laid out a couple of our quilts as well as our pillows.

"Do you really think they won't send zombies up here after us? It's not like they had trouble finding us in Missouri," she said, lying next to me in the upper bunk. We'd set an old-fashioned wind-up alarm to wake us later in the afternoon, although Maggie had promised she wasn't going to sleep.

The sheriff's cabin was well set up for sleeping and food preparation, but little else. There was no indoor plumbing and the facilities consisted of a privy several yards down the hill. It was, however, beautifully perched near the top of the mountain and looked out over a deep, forested valley.

"It'd be quite a walk for a zombie. We're sixty miles from the nearest hospital or morgue," I said.

She was quiet for a few minutes and then whispered. "What if my hair never turns black again?"

"I think it's sexy," I said.

"You would." She wrapped her hands around my own and laid her face next to them, kissing my hand. "Where do you think Lace went? I hope she's safe."

"Me too," I said and drifted off to sleep.

I'm not a big fan of daytime naps. When Gabriella nudged me awake, I had no concept of what was happening or where we were. Slowly, reality came rushing back and the weight of our situation settled back upon me.

"Coffee?" Judy handed me an old mug.

"I've been trying to come up with some way to locate Petaluma," I said.

"What if we're overthinking this?" Gabriella asked. "Judy, do you have a signal on your phone?"

"Sure, they upgraded the tower just last year," she said. "Better signal than the house."

"Perfect." Gabriella pushed away from the table and ran out the door. A moment later, she arrived with her tablet computer.

"What are you doing?" I asked.

"Give me a minute," she said, taking Judy's phone. "Crap, can you unlock it?"

Judy unlocked the phone and handed it back.

"I'm putting your phone in hotspot mode." I had no earthly idea what she was talking about. Gesturing furiously for a minute, she finally announced, "Bingo! We're online."

"And?" Judy asked.

"Just wait." Gabriella navigated to a website for something called the find-my-phone application. "Voila," she said triumphantly as a map filled the screen, showing Eppy Faire. A red dot sat prominently in the center.

"Why is it red?" Judy asked.

"I didn't have much battery left last night. It must have run out," she said. "It's showing I was at the sheriff's office when it ran out."

"More like the back yard of the sheriff office's," I said observing that the dot appeared to be at least forty yards behind where the sheriff's office was located.

"I don't think the GPS is that accurate. What about your phone?" Gabriella asked.

"Do flip-phones do that?" I asked.

She looked crestfallen. "No."

"What about Luma?" I asked. "What if she has a phone?"

"You have to know the password," she said.

"Like a witch can keep a secret from her mother," I said.

"She hid that book," Gabriella replied.

After a prolonged conversation with Dolly, Judy finally extricated herself from the phone conversation. "The FBI came by the hospital today. They were already on Petaluma's trail. Unfortunately, she left her phone at the house. Thea has fallen completely off the radar and the Feds issued an amber alert for Luma."

"Damn," Gabriella said. "Now what?"

"Let me try something," I said, pulling the tablet over. I punched in an email address I hadn't used in a number of years and tried a familiar password.

"What are you doing?" Gabriella asked.

A map took over the screen. It zoomed in to a section of the national forest that had a common boundary with Judy's home as well as Eppy Faire. A dot was moving along one of the roads, just exiting the forest a few miles up from the Faire.

"Who is that?" Gabriella pushed.

"That's Thea," I said. "She hasn't changed her password."

"You remember it from two years ago?"

"It's my birthday," I said.

"That's awesome," Maggie said. "She's so fricking twisted."

"I don't suppose you'd stay behind?" I asked Gabriella. She didn't answer beyond a tip of her head and pursed lips.

Judy handed Gabriella a smoothed stick with a single green jewel inlaid at the thickest end. "I have something for you,"

"A wand? Judy, I can't take your wand," she said.

"It's not mine," she said. "It was my mother's."

Gabriella took a deep breath. "That's too much."

"Nonsense. Maybe if it were my grandmother's," Judy said.

Gabriella looked suspiciously at Judy. "Is it your grandmother's?"

Judy chuckled. "Caught red-handed, but you'll still take it. I heard about that spell your coven cast allowing you to pin Felix down on the couch. Use that same incantation with the wand. It won't have the force of your coven, but it will help you focus the spell. You'll need to concentrate your energy as much as possible if you are going to win against the undead they've been throwing at us."

"The spell we used on Felix seemed awfully dark to me," she said. "I didn't know it then, but my mistress was flirting with black magic."

"A decision you will have to make. Personally, I've shied from conflict whenever possible. If pushed to it, however, you wouldn't catch me chasing demons and undead without a wand," Judy replied and then chuckled. "Of course, you wouldn't find me chasing demons either way."

Gabriella smiled and waved the wand around experimentally. "And yet, you didn't seem to have trouble with those undead at your home."

"There was a time ..." Judy stopped. "The thing to remember is that they are no longer people. Their spirits have long departed and they are nothing more than puppets, doing the bidding of someone who would hurt you and your family. Also, go for their legs. Their controller will lose interest if they have to crawl after you."

"I don't know," Gabriella said. "I don't know if I can make that spell work under pressure."

"You didn't have any problem in my apartment," I said.

"That was different. I had my coven behind me and I was doing the bidding of my mistress. Plus, I knew I wasn't going to hurt you," she said.

Judy picked up Gabriella's hand. "Come with me. We can take a few practice swings." It was something I loved about Judy; she was quick to empathize with other's needs.

While I'd have enjoyed watching Gabriella practice with Judy, I needed to get organized if we were going into the forest where we'd seen Thea's cell phone. Willum's ceremonies would take a fairly large space, possibly hidden some distance from the road Thea had been traveling. Once we turned down that road, we truly wouldn't be able to see the forest for the trees. I was thinking we'd benefit from an eye or two in the sky.

"Is it safe for you to shift again?" I asked Maggie, who'd finally donned one of my t-shirts.

Maggie waggled her eyebrows. "Tired of looking at me already?"

"Apparently, I'm the only one with issues about you being naked all the time," I said. It was true that neither Judy nor Gabriella seemed even the least bit perturbed by her nudity. I'd have expected it from Judy, who felt the human form in its natural state was beautiful, but I'd have thought Gabriella would have been at least somewhat disconcerted.

"I've been shifting a lot," she said. "I should be able to safely transition after all the calories I've taken in over the last ten hours, but I'll want to stay in that form for a few days. Why, what do you have in mind?"

I pushed the tablet over to her, having zoomed the map into a ten square mile area of the forest. "There's no way Gabriella and I can cover this much ground, especially on foot. I'll bet anything there are people coming and going to this cathedral. It can't be that hard to find from the air."

"Nobody pays attention to a raven," she said. "Just so you know. I like old meat - the rottener the better - and don't be refrigerating it."

"That's disgusting."

"It's softer and tastes better," she said, pulling off her t-shirt and walking over to the refrigerator. From the freezer, she pulled out an ancient looking packet of mystery meat and stuck it in the microwave. "When this is done, throw it on the roof."

I sighed and followed Maggie out the front door, recognizing that I was becoming inured to her naked state. The sound of popping, like that of bubble wrap, caught my attention and a rock the size of my fist jumped up in front of Judy and Gabriella. Gabriella swung her wand and a puff of dust erupted to the right of the rock.

"I'm never going to get this," Gabriella complained.

"That was very close and your aim will improve over time," Judy said. "Besides, those zombies are larger than rocks and they move slowly. Don't underestimate their strength, though. Do not let them get ahold of you under any circumstance."

"Bonsai!" Maggie exclaimed, gaining everyone's attention. She sprinted toward the side of the mountain and jumped from a rock outcropping. I bit my lip as she plunged over the side. If she didn't shift and catch the wind, she'd fall forty feet into the wooded terrain below.

"Shit." I followed after her once she'd fallen below my sight line, still in human form.

"Felix?" Gabriella called after me, sensing my concern.

Just when I reached the edge of the mountain, my eyes caught sight of the large black raven I'd grown up with, soaring down into the valley, gaining speed as she cruised mere feet above the tops of the trees. A gust of wind and a wide turn lifted her hundreds of feet in just a few seconds. I marveled at her grace as she circled overhead, crowing loudly.

A LIGHT IN THE DARK

"Take mine," Judy said, handing me her phone. "I'll buy a temporary when I get to town."

I reached for my wallet, but she held up her hand to stop me.

"What will you do?" I asked.

"I need to tell Aaron what's going on," she said, meaning the sheriff. "He was willing to let us use his cabin, but he's going to want to know I'm okay."

"Will you tell him everything?" Gabriella asked.

"No, but I have experience modifying reality with a more palatable version of the truth."

"Does he know who you are? Who the girls are?" Gabriella asked.

Judy gave us a wan smile. "At some level he does. He doesn't push it too hard, though."

I hugged her. "Stay safe and call me if Lace or Petaluma show up."

She turned back as she walked toward her car. "I will."

As Judy put her hand on the car's door, her phone rang. I recognized the number as belonging to Agent Anderson. "Any word on Petaluma?" I asked, picking up.

"We had a lead out at Eppy, but it turned out to be a dead-end," she said. "Were you involved in the collapse of their church?"

"They've a secret location where they're performing their rituals," I said, ignoring her question. "Can you track them electronically?"

"If there were tracks to find," she said. "This group is smart."

"We have a lead," I said. "We're going to check it out."

"Bring me along," she said.

"That's not a good idea and besides, it's not like we know

whether it'll pan out," I said.

"My partner is missing, Slade. Other than ransacking every house in Eppy Faire, I have nothing else," she said, pleading in her voice. "My office is about to pull me back."

"They can't do that," I said. "What about Mulper?"

"They still believe he's on vacation."

"If you want a lead, check the security guards at Eppy. They kidnapped us last night and held us against our will," I said. "One of them was called Barnes."

"You need to fill out a complaint if we're going to hold him," she said. "But I could pick him up for questioning."

"He's dangerous. Take backup," I said.

"I will," she said and hung up.

"What about Maggie?" Gabriella asked as I put the Suburban in reverse and slowly backed onto the dirt track leading down the mountain.

"She'll find us," I said.

"She really did a number on the front of the truck," Gabriella observed. I'd been trying to ignore the bashed-in grill, dented hood, numerous scratches to the paint, and missing side mirror.

"She hasn't done much driving and there was that chain-link fence she had to take down," I said.

The entrance to the part of the forest we'd be searching was well-marked and we stopped to look at a permanent map mounted between pine logs and covered with plexiglass. A steel map holder stood empty and its accompanying donation box had been jimmied open at least once.

I pointed to the map as Gabriella joined me. "Judy's cabin is about ten miles over that ridge, just off this map. Eppy Faire is five miles over that way."

"Why did it take us so long to get there?"

"It wouldn't have if we were crows," I said. "The mountain roads wind all over the place up here."

"Cawwk," Maggie cried as she landed on top of the map-stand.

"This is the road Thea was on," I said, looking at Maggie. "It only goes another hundred yards north. Did you see anything like a church?" Maggie shook her head negatively to my disappointment. She should have seen a structure if they'd buried a church back in these hills. "Let's grab our hiking gear. There's a dirt road we can follow, hopefully Maggie will get a lead on something."

I pulled out a water bottle and stuffed Judy's phone into the lightweight day pack I used for hiking. We walked quietly down the deteriorating asphalt and stopped at a rusty chain hanging between two heavy posts. A sign that read 'No Admittance – Forest Service' hung precariously in the center.

"That's a new lock," Gabriella observed.

I agreed. "Curious."

We walked around the post and started down the easy grade. "There's been traffic on this road this spring."

"How can you tell?" Gabriella asked.

"Look at the plant growth on the shoulder, then look at the track. No reason for the weeds to be clear along the track unless people are driving on it," I said.

We continued for thirty minutes, which I estimated to be a mile in. As we trekked downhill, I thought I heard the trickle of a stream, probably within thirty yards, through the overgrown trees to our right.

"Someone's coming," Gabriella warned. I strained my ears and heard the low rumble of a vehicle.

"Over here." I jumped from the road and slid down into a ditch. We scrabbled up the other side and into the trees. Moments later a rusty old station wagon lumbered up the road, the people inside not bothering to look around as they drove past.

"They're from Eppy," Gabriella said.

"How do you know?"

"I recognized the woman sitting in the back from the security station." she said.

"Good eyes."

We waited a few minutes to make sure they weren't being followed by another vehicle and then climbed back onto the road.

"Look at that," I said, pointing to an opening in the trees where a number of cars had flattened the grass. A single pickup truck remained. Carefully, we crept up to it and Gabriella placed her hands on the hood.

"What are you doing?" I whispered.

"Do you really not watch TV? If the engine is warm it's been driven recently," she said.

"Is it?"

"No."

Maggie landed on a branch next to the impromptu parking area. "I think Maggie sees something," I said, walking over to where she'd landed. When I got there, I saw what her sharp eyes had easily picked out. A well-traveled dirt path disappeared around the tree where she sat.

"Thanks," I said as we passed beneath her.

The trail couldn't have been easier to follow. The people who'd recently used it had made no effort to cover their tracks. All manner of trash, bits of clothing and objects I had no interest in inspecting littered the edges.

"Do you smell that?" It was the third time I'd smelled that type of decay. It wasn't unusual to smell plant or animal decay in a natural setting, but this stench was in a whole different category.

Gabriella wrinkled her nose and pulled the wand from her waist pouch. "Yes."

The sound of water increased and we soon found ourselves crossing a stream, the muddy banks sporting numerous shoe and bare footprints.

"This can't be good." I pointed at one of the better defined footprints with a red-brown stain at its center.

It was about seven in the evening and I'd miscalculated the sunset, not factoring in that we were on the eastern slope of a mountain and traveling downward. For us, the sun was already behind the mountain and the hollow where we walked continued to get darker.

"Up there," Gabriella said as we came around a bend. She pointed at the side of the hill we'd started to climb after crossing the stream. The path we'd been on led to the mouth of a cave.

Wooden stairs had been built into the hill, making the final climb considerably easier than it would have been otherwise. "Tell me we're not going in there." We both looked into the gloom of the cave, the unmistakable stench of death in the air.

I gave a frustrated sigh and shook my head. "Yeah, I wish."

I incanted my ghostly lantern, pleased to feel the energy transfer smoothly from the crystal hanging around my neck. The color of the light had shifted slightly, which I suspected was due to the shift in the enchantment's ingredients. The fire within was a translucent yellow ball with bright red flames coursing over its surface. I smiled at the small comfort I took from it.

The entrance to the cave widened into a large room. It wasn't until we'd crossed the floor to where it narrowed into a hallway that I caught the fetid breeze that blew up from within. Where previously I'd had a few whiffs of decay, this was significantly more intense. I gagged, my ordinarily keen senses amplifying the effects.

"Damn. I don't know if I can do this." I stopped and waited for the bile in my stomach to settle.

"What if Luma is down there?" Gabriella asked. "We don't have a choice."

I nodded, closing my eyes. She was right, of course. I set my jaw and strode forward. The tunnel continued to narrow and we were forced to crawl on our knees a couple of times when the ceiling became too low to allow us to continue walking. Perhaps more disconcerting was the appearance of two and three-foot diameter holes that led to other branches of the tunnel. I wasn't particularly susceptible to claustrophobia, but between the low ceiling, the off-shoot tunnels and the horrible smell, my brain had pretty much decided we were in the worst possible place. Finally, we reached the end of the low ceiling and were able to stand up in a larger chamber.

"Felix ..." Gabriella's voice rose as she said my name. I recognized panic in her voice as she shined a bright beam of light from a pencil sized LED flashlight at her feet. A blackened hand had ensnared her ankle and was compressing her pant leg. I swung the ghost lantern closer, fully illuminating the remains of a woman who'd been dead for months, if not years.

Gabriella's eyes grew wild and I quickly placed my hand over her mouth, dropping the lantern, just as she started to scream in abject horror. Wildly, she kicked her foot and the undead woman lurched forward. With the lantern no longer in my control, the light extinguished. In her panic, Gabriella dropped the small but powerful LED. The sound of flesh tearing loose and a loud crack preceded the flight of the woman's forearm as it arced through the beam of the lost flashlight.

"It's not moving," I said with my face close to hers. There was enough light for me to see the terror in her eyes. "I'm taking my hand off your mouth. Okay?"

She nodded and I slowly removed my hand. "Is it off?" she whispered, not willing to look.

"*Silici Scintillam Excudit.*" I reignited the lantern. "See if you can hold this." I handed the lantern to her and slowly let go. She smiled the smile of a person grasping for sanity in a world gone crazy. Even so, the lantern remained lit for her. I reached for her fallen flashlight and as the beam played along the floor of the cavern, it fell across a line of corpses.

"Do you hear that?" I asked, quietly, turning off the flashlight.

"What?" Gabriella whispered.

"Listen," I said walking forward. The light of the ghost lantern didn't reach far and as long as we didn't get too close to the cavern's wall, the dead weren't overly illuminated. "Something's tapping."

We continued forward, not moving overly fast. As we turned another bend, the tapping sound grew louder and we turned our attention to water dripping from the end of a tall stalagmite and running down, disappearing into the ground. I turned on the flashlight and ran the beam into a parallel cavern, separated from our side by a jagged wall of both rising stalagmites and drooping stalactites. Further back in the room, a green-hued pool was ringed by calcium deposits as if someone had sprinkled the edge with salt. The undisturbed water perfectly reflected the spectacular scene above.

"There's something else," Gabriella whispered, pointing at her ears and then down the main corridor where we'd been walking. I strained my ears and heard a faint clanking of steel on steel.

"They'll see us approach," I whispered back. "There's no way to hide the light."

"Use that spell you cast in the forest to enhance our senses," she said.

"It won't work. It enhances existing light. We're too deep; there's not enough residual light," I explained. "Let me try something. And this is going to suck." I doused the ghost lantern and cast the enhancement spell she'd asked for, first on me then on her.

She gasped, grabbing my arm as the spell enhanced our ability to smell the stench of decaying flesh within the cavern. I clenched my teeth and fought a new wave of revulsion. The idea seemed more horrible upon implementation than I could have imagined. I suspected the magic, having little light, texture or sound to work with, had boosted the only thing we were actively using – our sense of smell. That or the stink of dead people kept in enclosed spaces follows an exponential curve.

I placed my hand over the end of the LED and turned it back on, then carefully uncovered a tiny portion of the lens, allowing a small amount of light to leak out. The cave glowed and the shadows lightened. I could just make out the smooth path that led down.

"Can you see well enough?" I asked. Gabriella nodded and we pushed forward.

At some point, I lost count of the dead we passed. Anderson's estimate of thirty wasn't close by half, although most of them were so decayed, I had to wonder if they'd been pulled from graveyards.

The periodic clanking grew louder as we continued on, soon rounding a final bend and ending at the edge of a steep ramp that led downward. The glow of an electric lantern forty yards ahead was the first thing I recognized and I shut off the LED, allowing our eyes to adjust. We'd entered a large room, within which rows of old church pews had been set out more or less in an even pattern. At the front, where the lamp burned, a solitary figure hung, chained, in what could best be described as a very narrow, iron banded bird cage. Next to the cage was a stone altar, dark liquid dripping from its large flat top. The smell of blood hung thick in the air.

"This must be the cathedral," I whispered.

"I hear weeping," Gabriella said. I closed my eyes and concentrated. For some reason Gabriella's hearing had responded extremely well to the enhancement, much better than my own. I finally picked up on the sound of muted sobbing.

"Someone's alive in that cage," Gabriella said, surging forward.

I caught her arm. "Careful. Let me go first." I made my way down the ramp and through the center of the ordered rows of pews, my eyes scanning back and forth for signs of danger. Just as in the hallway, more corpses lined the walls, only these appeared to be newer kills. A glimpse of a familiar face caused me to do a double-take. I scanned back until I located it. In the middle of the group sat a very dead Agent Mulper.

"Shit," I said, pointing him out to Gabriella.

"Is someone there?" A woman's voice asked from the cage.

"Lace?" Gabriella replied. "It's Gabriella and Felix. Are you hurt?"

"Get out of here," Lace said. "The whole place is spelled. They'll be coming; you need to run."

"We're not leaving you," Gabriella said.

"You have to. They'll be here any minute."

"*Lucem*." I pulled the brightly lit crystal from beneath my shirt. My eyes stung at the bright wash of light. I pulled off my day pack and unlocked Judy's phone. I wasn't surprised to discover I had no reception, but that wasn't my current end game.

"Here." I handed the phone to Gabriella. "Take pictures. They'll never believe us. I'll see to Lace."

Gabriella accepted the phone and I ran over to Lace's cell. A chain held the cage off the ground. I found the pulley mechanism by the cave wall and released the latch, quickly lowering her.

"No key," she said, looking at the heavy lock. "You can't break it off. It's too thick."

"Don't know a lot of wizards, do you?" I asked, twisting my fingers. The lock didn't budge, so I cast my wizard's sight – and laughed. The locks at Tenebrius Manerium had been a challenge, these were uninteresting at best. I twisted, lifted the locking mechanism and pulled the body sharply downward. The lock fell off easily and the door swung open. Lace collapsed through the door with a groan. The cage, short and narrow, had been designed to torture by not allowing a person enough room to sit or stand straight.

"I don't know any wizards," she answered.

"Any *other* wizards," I corrected. "And neither do I - unless you count my sister and even I'm not sure what she is."

As I talked, I scanned the room. It was coated in the green slimy aura I'd come to associate with Willum and the ghrelin.

"I'm good," Gabriella said, pushing the phone back into the pack. "Anderson isn't going to like that we found Mulper dead."

I helped Lace to her feet. "I think she already knows. We'll need to get word to her right away, though."

"All you need to do is get this phone within sight of a cell tower. I sent her a text with pictures and the location."

"Lace, did you see a little girl?" I asked.

"You mean the one with the book at Judy's barbeque?"

Lace stumbled forward as I tried to help her up the path.

"That's her," I said. "She's been abducted too."

"I'm not sure you've got that right," Lace said. "She and a blonde witch were the ones who snagged me. The girl didn't help, but she wasn't tied up either."

"Damn it," I said. "She's a good kid."

"Take it from someone who knows. Sometimes when you're in with the wrong crowd, you do the wrong things," she said. "The girl was definitely involved."

"Damn it," I repeated.

A wave of power surged through the cavern and for a moment,

nothing changed.

"Luuucy," I heard Thea's faint voice calling from above. "Luuucy. You have some 'splaining to do." She'd adopted a very poor Cuban accent.

The corpses near us started to move, very slowly at first, as they gathered their arms to their sides and started to rock forward, synchronized.

"If they brought necros, we can't get past all of them. We're trapped," Lace said, resigned.

"We're not staying here," I said.

Gabriella had already pulled her wand from her pocket and lashed out with it. A wave of power struck the closest corpse. The effect was immediate and the body was flung into the cavern wall. Unfortunately, it didn't break apart and gathered itself slowly for another push forward. Spurred by adrenaline, Gabriella swung her wand to the side and struck a second. This time the shambling cadaver fell to the side. It hadn't been permanently stopped either.

"I have an idea," I said, reaching up and dousing the crystal hanging around my neck.

"Are you crazy?" Gabriella whispered harshly.

"If we can't see them, they can't see us," I said. I quickly cast my planar view. All around us, the animated dead appeared as pale wisps. Small contrails of energy streaked up the ramp, coalescing into a single cord that wrapped around the bend above and out of sight.

I turned my attention to Lace, who was unable to walk, stumbling as she attempted to move. "Help me with Lace," I said. "I need to keep a hand free."

"I can't see anything," Gabriella's bright form stood out like a beacon in the darkness. I stepped closer to her and she jumped as Lace's foot made contact.

"It's us," I said. "Grab on." The nearest wispy figures were closing in on our position, but since I'd doused the lights, they'd dropped their arms to their sides. "They can't see us."

Thea's voice came down from above, baiting us. "That won't help when we get down there."

With Gabriella behind, I threaded us through the animated corpses. I was grateful not all of them had been lit up although the sheer number seeking us was still considerable.

"Why isn't Thea here yet?" Gabriella whispered.

I stumbled on a rock and was driven to my knee. The sound of my breath being pushed out was enough to redirect a pair in our direction.

"I'd guess they're waiting for reinforcements," I whispered back, once again gaining my feet. "If we could just get outside, they won't be able to follow."

We finally reached the top of the steep ramp and our pursuers appeared to have given up on finding us and were instead shambling along a parallel path to our own. It made sense, there was a choke point ahead where we'd have to crawl out. If the undead could beat us there, we'd be trapped.

For a few minutes, the entire journey took on a surreal sensation as we walked forward in lockstep, with our unseeing enemy both in front of us and behind. As we reached the point I was looking for, I angled to the edge of the cave and toward the stalactite room, shuffling unanimated skeletons from my path. Fortunately, Lace was able to crawl, where she hadn't been able to walk. The going was slower, but we'd separated ourselves from the herd.

When I finally felt the edge of the pool, I understood right where we were. It seemed like we'd taken forever to get this far. In that there was little magical energy in this portion of the cave, my wizard's sight was useless. I pulled out Gabriella's flashlight, once again blocking a majority of the light. We'd gotten turned around trying to navigate through the sediment formations, so I maneuvered us over to where the stalagmites were the densest and our light was less likely to be visible from the main passageway.

"Come out, come out, wherever you are," Thea cackled, sounding very close.

I stopped our forward movement and popped my head up, looking over a natural swale and came face to face with a glowing skeleton. Whoever was controlling this one had to have seen or heard me. Boney arms flopped against the top of the wall and swung at me. My heart hammered in my chest as I fell back, dropping the damn flashlight again. Gabriella scrambled to cover the light, but the damage had been done.

"Darling, you don't need to hide," Thea said, overly sweet. "Come out of the shadows and join us."

Three strong-beamed flashlights illuminated the cavern where we huddled.

I dismissed my wizard's sight. "Pull back your minions and we will."

"Did you not think we'd be monitoring our home?" Thea taunted as we inelegantly crawled through a break in the mineral deposits.

"Where's Petaluma?" I asked just before my eyes fell on the thirteen-year-old standing beside Thea. They were dressed identically, both wearing black leather pants and matching blouses. Luma's face showed conflict and Thea must have sensed it, because she turned and picked up Luma's hand.

"Right here, darling. She's been hoping you'd join us," she said.

"Please, Uncle Felix. It's who I am," Petaluma said quietly, her face looking at the floor.

"You don't have to do this, Luma," I said. "Necromancy is misunderstood, but you don't have to do bad things with it."

Thea chuckled. "Bad things? A moral argument from Felix Slade? I thought I'd never see the day. How can it be bad if it feels so good?" I recognized the words as my own, from when Thea and I had been dating. As a younger man, I'd rationalized breaking my own rule of not being involved with Judy's coven sisters with that same reasoning.

"That's not the same," I said, helping Lace stand. She seemed a little more stable on her feet, but I knew we'd never be able to make a run for it. Plus, we had at least ten feet of crawling between us and the next section of cave.

A man and woman I didn't recognize stood just behind Thea and Luma. Their manipulation of the minions was obvious as they moved their own bodies, if only slightly, bringing the small army in to surround us.

"Would you believe she's the most powerful necro in the group?" Thea asked, stroking Luma's hair. "She controls dozens, where most of these idiots can only handle two or three."

"Luma, you need to let us go. They'll kill us," I said, looking at the girl I'd babysat so many times.

"We'll do no such thing," Thea argued, looking directly into Petaluma's eyes. "Willum just needs them not to be messing it up for us. Don't listen to him."

Two more people arrived, sliding beneath the low wall that led to the entrance and immediately added to the army around us.

Petaluma closed her eyes and raised her arms out to her sides, palms up. "Mother would never allow me to reach my potential," she said. "I tried talking to her, but she won't even say the word necromancer. There's no place for me."

The power gathering around her was enormous and we all watched in horror as every remaining corpse rose to its feet. "Why?" Luma continued. "Why is this so wrong?" The clatter of feet on the ground was almost deafening in the enclosed space as perhaps a hundred corpses in varying degrees of decay stepped forward, moving at varying speeds depending on how far back they were.

My mind raced. We couldn't be captured again. Willum, under the ghrelin's control wouldn't make the mistake of leaving us alive a second time.

"Stop, Luma. Can't you see that when people discover what you're doing they'll have to stop you?" Gabriella pled. "There is a channel for your energy, but this isn't it."

"Thea says you're a bad witch. That you stole Uncle Felix from her," she said. A cadre of corpses moved toward Gabriella. I moved around to place myself between her and them.

"That's not right, Luma," I said. "Thea is with Willum. She never loved me."

"Don't listen to him, dear," Thea soothed. "The witch is certainly bad; we should remove her."

"NO!" I said. In a moment of perfect clarity the idea that I'd been missing struck me as if a bolt of lightning.

"*Lucem!*" I pulled the chain from around my neck and held the crystal in front of me, pushing it into the face of the nearest rotted face. Involuntarily, it turned from the glow, holding a skeletal hand up as an ineffective shield.

"Uncle Felix!" Petaluma shrieked. "You're hurting me."

I put as much command into my voice as I had. "Luma, pull them back."

"I can't," she whimpered. "He'll be angry."

The corpses surged forward and as they did, I pushed more of my energy into the crystal.

Luma screamed frantically as bodies dropped to the ground. "Stop! You're murdering them!"

I pressed forward, Lace and Gabriella close on my heels. "You must pull them back, Luma. I won't allow you to hurt my friends."

"No," Thea commanded. "Willum will punish us if they escape. Stop him." She gestured over her shoulder to the other necromancers.

As I swung the crystal in a wide arc, six of the approaching enemy fell, as did two necromancers. I reached down and pulled at the energy of the earth below. As with Judy's home, there was little to be found, but still it sustained my efforts and the crystal brightened. The radius of the crystal's light turned into a lethal wrecking ball of destruction.

Thea stepped in front of us and tried to physically block our path. Between helping Lace and channeling energy to the crystal, I was running at a hundred percent and almost missed her approach.

Gabriella stepped forward to block the woman. "Back off."

"Shut up," Thea countered, bringing her hands up to push Gabriella, who was considerably smaller, out of her way.

What happened next caught me completely by surprise, as Gabriella simply punched Thea straight in the nose. I didn't see it coming because I had no idea my girlfriend had such skills. Thea's hands popped up defensively to her face just in time for Gabriella to swing a second time, this time coming around on her eye. Thea fell to the floor, stumbling as she backpedaled.

"You'll pay," Luma said. The remaining corpses rushed us and I turned, focusing as much energy as I could draw from the ground beneath us. It felt as though I was trying to drink through a coffee straw. The energy was there, but constrained. I pulled at it and my eyes burned from the intensity of the light. As I closed my eyes, whatever was blocking me let go. My fingers felt as though they'd burst into flames and I released the crystal's chain.

"Felix! Stop!" Gabriella's cool hands closed over my face and I realized I'd fallen to my knees. When I finally opened my eyes, we were the only ones still upright in the chamber. The fallen lanterns brought in by the Dark Folk eerily illuminated mounds of rotted corpses.

"Luma?" I let go of Lace and ran to the fallen girl. Her eyes were closed, but her chest moved slowly as she pulled in breath.

"Felix, more will be coming," Lace warned.

"Go!" I said. "Get out." I placed my fingers on Thea's neck, feeling for a pulse, which I found.

I turned back to Luma and scooped her up, following after Lace and Gabriella who were starting to pick their way under the low hanging shelf. Coming out on the other side, we struggled back to our feet. As a group, we stumbled and ran to the entrance, the dim sky of dusk still brighter by orders of magnitude than the cave.

Shouts of excitement and the crack of a small caliber rifle spurred us down the steep embankment as we ignored the wooden stairs. Luma groaned as her head struck the hard-packed dirt beneath us. Gabriella whipped her wand around and caught the only figure we were able to see directly, his gun swinging wide.

"You there, stop!" he demanded, lowering his rifle at us once again.

"*Adoleret*," I pointed my finger at him, hurling a ball of flame into his chest. He screamed and dropped the rifle, running off into the trees.

As a group, we stumbled forward, making it into the thick forest. My plan was to get to the stream bed and wait out the hunters in the dark. If we had to make our stand, that's just what we'd do. The crashing of men through the undergrowth around us grew louder. They shouted excitedly to each other, having caught sight of us.

"We'll never make it," Gabriella said.

"Stop moving," Lace said simply.

"We can't," I said, misunderstanding her request as more fatalism.

The sounds of more men closing in around us caught my attention. It would be only moments before they discovered our position.

Lace clawed my shoulder, grabbing just enough material to spin me around. "Trust me," she implored.

I stopped.

She murmured what sounded like a prayer, her unkempt dark hair falling around her pale face. As she spoke, one of our pursuers came into view, looking around wildly.

"I don't see anyone," he yelled. "Try further downstream."

Two more men joined him, looking around. "They were just here," one argued, panting from exertion.

Gabriella lifted her wand and flicked it in the direction we'd been heading. The leaves of a bush shook as her spell impacted it.

"There!" The three men, all armed with rifles, ran forward through the undergrowth.

Ding. The phone in my backpack announced a text message receipt.

All three of us looked at the backs of the retreating men, paranoid the phone's sound would call them back. When it didn't, Gabriella slowly pulled at the zipper of my pack and fished out Judy's phone.

"Anderson got the pictures," she whispered. "She wants permission to track our phone's location."

"Permission?"

"I think she figured out my day job," Gabriella said. "She says

152

to hold on; the cavalry's coming."

"You need to be quiet," Lace warned. "My spell doesn't cover sound.".

DARKNESS EXPOSED

The bright beam of a high-powered flashlight lanced through the heavily treed forest, pausing momentarily as it illuminated the four of us still hunkered down next to the hillside leading to the cathedral's cave. Something about our position gave the invisible form behind the light pause, but so far it hadn't been enough to warrant more than a quick second look. Just as before, this searcher moved on, crashing into the forest to continue his frantic search.

I held the unconscious Petaluma in a seated position in front of me, hugging her protectively with my arms. I wanted to teleport the girl back a few years, to the happy moments I remembered with her as a preteen, playing in this very forest. Just how that sweet girl ended up in a cave full of monsters under her control, while she attacked me and mine, was something I couldn't bear to consider.

We'd been hiding for what felt like hours, but it was more like forty minutes when Petaluma stirred.

"Shh," I encouraged, as Lace's concerned eyes bored into us. She'd been against bringing Petaluma along given her less than positive experience with the girl so far.

"Uncle Felix?" Petaluma asked, groggily. "Where are we?"

"In the forest, hiding from the Dark Folk," I said.

She sagged back into my arms. "He'll kill us all."

"No, sweet child, he won't. The FBI is on their way."

"He's too strong," she said.

"Just rest," I said.

"Felix," Gabriella whispered. "Look."

At the mouth of the cave, Thea emerged, outlined by a light from behind. Apparently, she'd recovered and with her at least one of the necromancers with whom we'd tangled. She stumbled

154

forward and worked her way down the stairs.

"Lady Althea." A man approached from the path that led back to the parking area. "What are your orders?"

"Where is the Applebaum child?"

"Jorie saw her come out of the cave with the princess and the prisoners from last night." I recognized the voice as belonging to the first security guard who'd imprisoned Gabriella and me. "He fired a shot to get them back into the cave, but they ran."

"Kill them all," she said. "No survivors."

"Even the girl?" he asked, surprised.

"Especially the girl," Thea said coldly. "She's weak and knows too much."

I half expected Petaluma to gasp or become angry. Instead, she silently turned into my chest and wrapped her arms around me.

"Willum wants you back at the church immediately," he said.

Thea didn't reply other than to push past him.

"I don't know how much longer I can hold this," Lace said after a few more minutes. "I've never masked so many for so long."

"Have you ever joined with another sister?" Gabriella asked, reaching for Lace's hand.

Lace took Gabriella's hand, looking at her skeptically.

"Do you feel that?" Gabriella whispered. "The warmth in the palm of your hand. Please let me in. Allow my spirit to join with your own."

"I'm afraid," Lace said.

"I won't hurt you," Gabriella reassured.

Lace nodded, the tension in her face draining.

"Share your pain with me," Gabriella said soothingly. "You needn't carry this burden alone. Tonight we stand together, sister."

"I see you," Lace whispered.

"And I see you," Gabriella replied.

A small shuddering breath reminded me that I held a small witch who also needed support. With a free hand I wiped the quiet tears that had fallen on her cheeks. She'd no doubt heard Thea's death sentence. "All is not lost," I comforted, to which she had no response.

"Do you hear that?" I asked after perhaps another fifteen minutes had passed.

"What?" Gabriella asked, sounding like she was only about half there.

"Dogs," I said.

A moment later, a man in full tactical gear with FBI emblazoned on his chest, burst into view, wielding a large flashlight and being pulled along by a German Shepherd. The dog drew up short, five yards from our position and whined, pawing at the air.

"Drop the spell," I whispered. The dog barked frantically at my voice, but didn't advance.

"What is it, girl?" the man asked, shining his flashlight across our position just as Lace released her spell. I felt fortunate the agent didn't have a weapon drawn, as he startled and nearly dropped the leash. The dog, having discovered a target, lunged forward. "Freeze," he yelled, swinging the light back onto us. "Raise your hands. FBI."

"We're unarmed and injured," I said, raising my hands. "Agent Anderson is looking for us."

"Hold there," he said over the barking dog. "And don't move."

"Tactical, I've got a group of four saying they're the vics," he said. After a moment he replied to an unheard voice. "Two women, one child and one man." He paused, obviously listening to orders. "He's late twenties, straight dark hair."

"What are your names?" he called over, still not advancing.

Before I could answer, however, two men with rifles rose, and wearing night vision goggles silently entered the small clearing.

"Felix Slade, Gabriella Valverde, Lace Faa and Petaluma Applebaum," I said.

We waited while he relayed the information. "They're clear," he finally announced. "Henderson, take 'em back to the command post."

"The cave," I said, pointing up the hill. "There are several people still in there."

"Bobby. Secure that cave," the first agent said.

156

The agent who had been identified as Henderson slung his assault rifle over his shoulder and flipped the lens of his night vision goggles up. "Can you walk?"

"Yes." I helped Petaluma to her feet and then looped an arm under Lace's shoulder.

"Keep your lights pointed low and on the path. We don't need to blind the other agents," he said, pointing to the path. The sound of a shout and weapon-fire sent us all to our knees on the other side of the muddy stream bank. The shots had been fired at least a hundred yards away, but I knew better than to believe a bullet couldn't find us.

"We're clear," Henderson announced a couple of minutes later.

The large clearing where a few hours before, only a single truck had been parked had completely transformed. A white-tented command center stood next to a black, armored vehicle. Huge halogen lights shone out in all directions, illuminating a myriad of emergency vehicles, many with their light bars still flashing.

Henderson led us through the chaos and over to the back of one of three ambulances that sat up on the dirt track leading out.

"Anderson wants to see you after you're checked out," Henderson said as a man wearing an EMT uniform approached Lace, helping her to sit on the wide back bumper of his vehicle.

"I'm fine," I said, before Henderson could leave. "Gabriella, will you stay with Lace and Petaluma while I talk to Anderson?"

She nodded. "I've got it, Felix."

Henderson escorted me back to the command post, stopping to knock at the open door of the armored vehicle. "Anderson?"

"Felix. Good." Dana Anderson looked out the door. "Thank you, Agent."

Radio chatter behind her announced the capture of another person in the woods. I scanned the makeshift brig which was nothing more than ropes around a group of folding chairs. Of course there were several heavily armed agents standing by to enforce the detainment area. A dozen men and women, wearing the clothing I associated with inhabitants of Eppy Faire, sat handcuffed, looking very unhappy. While disappointed, it was no surprise Thea wasn't yet among the detainees.

"You didn't find Thea Sanders?" I asked.

"No," she said. "Was that Petaluma Applebaum with you?"

"She's a victim." I hoped Anderson wasn't able to see through my lack of confidence in that statement.

She didn't respond to my assertion, but moved on. "What's in the cave, Felix?"

"It's bad, Dana," I said. "Are you sure you want to be here for this?" An image of her dead partner replayed in my mind's eye.

Agent Anderson nodded at me, a weary look in her eyes. "I want to catch this bastard."

"There were seven or eight people in the cave when we escaped," I said. "Althea Sanders was one of them, I don't know any other names. We saw Althea and a couple more escape, probably headed back to Eppy."

"We'll get her; there's a warrant out on her. Was Willum Gordon involved?

"I'm sure he was calling the shots, but he wasn't down there," I said.

"Follows his pattern," she said. "Do you feel up to going in the cave?"

"Have you cleared it yet?" I asked.

"They're going in now," she said. The sounds of tactical chatter spilled from the back of the heavy vehicle and she moved me over to one of the tables beneath the white tent top. "I'd like to introduce you to one of our non-traditional profilers, Jardeep Farha."

A middle-aged man, early fifties, with dark, tanned skin rose. He looked to be middle-eastern and when he spoke, his accent sounded Arabian. "Pleased to meet you, Felix Slade," he said, extending his hand. "Jardeep Farha."

A tingle of energy passed between us as we shook and I searched his face, seeing something familiar in his eyes. I couldn't quite identify it, but I felt as though I recognized him. The slightest smile passed like a phantom across his face and was just as quickly gone, leaving me to wonder if I'd seen it at all.

"What's going on, Felix?" Gabriella asked across a state trooper who limited her access to where Anderson and I were talking.

"I'm going to lead Anderson down to the Cathedral," I said.

Her eyes reflected her concern. "Are you sure?"

"It'll be okay," I said. "Stay with Lace and Petaluma, they need you."

"Be careful."

"Let's move," Anderson said grimly, motioning for Farha to follow.

Just as the clearing had been transformed, so too had the entrance to the cave. Floodlights on temporary poles lit up the night, a pale wash on the face of the mountain. Two prisoners were cuffed and being held at gunpoint on their knees. A third was brought out; struggling to keep his feet and blinking wildly. Not far away, technicians worked beneath the same lights, unspooling long electric lines and assembling a ventilation tube.

"You're clear to go in, ma'am, but there are a lot of nooks and crannies down there, I'd be careful," an agent advised as we reached the top of the wooden stairs.

Anderson pulled her service pistol from a holster at her belt and nodded in response. The three of us entered the cave and were immediately struck with the all too familiar smell. Anderson stopped and pulled a white breathing mask over her nose and mouth, offering one to me.

"We'll have lights on in ten minutes," a technician in a white jump suit announced at our backs.

She snapped out an order. "Don't come in until I give the go ahead."

"Yes, ma'am," the technician replied.

Agent Anderson turned her head toward me. "How far down is Mulper?"

"Twenty yards on the other side of that low hanging ceiling," I said, my hot breath blowing back into my nose behind the mask. I wasn't sure why we were wearing the masks, as they didn't appear to do anything for the smell and I noticed that Jardeep had opted not to wear one.

To Anderson's credit, she had skipped the business suit and instead wore tight jeans, not hesitating to mimic me as I slid down to my back side and worked my way beneath. Glow sticks every few feet made the trek easier and we soon exited on the other side.

"My god," Anderson uttered. Her flashlight acted a pointer in the dim glow of the electric camp lanterns left behind by the tactical team. A near-perfect circle of corpses surrounded a bare spot of earth where we'd made our stand.

Jardeep's flashlight beam caught on the golden chain of the crystal pendant I'd dropped. "What is this?" he asked, carefully picking his way through the litter of bones and bending to inspect it. With tweezers, he picked it up for an easier look.

"That's mine," I said. "I must have dropped it."

"Care to explain how it's in the center of all of this?" Dana Anderson asked.

"You wouldn't like the explanation," I said.

"Perhaps we can save that discussion," Jardeep said, his voice smooth and authoritative as he slid the necklace into a plastic bag, careful not to touch it.

Anderson frowned and chastised him. "You should not be disturbing evidence."

"An artifact such as this shouldn't find its way into the hands of the uninitiated," he said, holding up the bag so he could more closely inspect it. "Tell me, Mr. Slade. What is special about this necklace?"

Up to that point, I hadn't determined if I liked or disliked Jardeep. Something in the way he asked made me uncomfortable, as if he already knew the answer but was testing me.

"It has sentimental value," I said. "I'd like it back."

He raised an eyebrow. "You enchanted this?"

I held out my hand. "It is mine."

"It's evidence," he replied, dropping it into his pocket.

"What's down there?" Anderson asked, shining her light down the slope.

"The Cathedral." I followed the trail of glow sticks, not interested in revealing I'd generated a pulse of light powerful

160

enough to knock out the entire room full of animated.

"Wait," Jardeep pushed. "What happened here?"

"Zombies tried to kill me and my family," I said. "Beyond that, I'm not ready to have that conversation."

"That's obstruction," he replied.

"Knock it off, Farha," Anderson said. "We're here for Gordon. Felix, would you care to speculate what the Dark Folk might have been doing in the Cathedral?"

The three of us rounded the corner and I, once again, took in the church-like setting.

"Dark mass," Jardeep answered. "Willum positioned himself as a deity with the Dark Folk. This room has been westernized and made to resemble a church, but that altar is unmistakable. The members were sacrificing to him. Who was in here?" He'd arrived at the steel cage, door open and chain slack. "It was recently occupied."

"David." Anderson's voice was low and filled with pain. I was about to correct her; it hadn't been Mulper in the cage. But when I turned, I realized that she'd walked off and found her partner, lying crumpled against the wall. I mentally kicked myself for not having warned her, although I knew Gabriella had sent pictures.

"I'm not sure," I said, dodging Jardeep's question. "We came to find Petaluma."

He gave me an appraising stare and I held his gaze. Something along the lines of a compulsion pushed at my tongue, but I resisted. Jardeep certainly had power, but I wasn't about to give away information that might endanger Lace or Petaluma. He broke eye contact and grinned, nodding his head slightly in acknowledgement of the exchange.

"Agent Anderson, I believe the room is clear enough that we might allow the forensics team entry," Jardeep said.

"Send them down," she said quietly, kneeling next to her partner. "I want David's body taken out first."

"You can trust me, Felix," Jardeep said as we walked up the ramp, out of the cathedral.

"It's not that I don't trust you. It's that I don't know you, Agent

Farha," I said.

"I am not an agent," he said. "I'm a civilian contractor. A specialist. Problem solver, as it were."

"Specializing in what?"

"Well, this," he said, spreading his arms to indicate the scene in front of us.

I raised my eyebrows. "Dead bodies? Caves? Mass murder?"

"I'd be willing to bet most of these people led ordinary lives and died ordinary deaths," he said. "This is far from the place for us to discuss such matters. What say we get out of here, go somewhere less … awful?"

I agreed. "If I never come back to this cave, it will be too soon."

"When forensics is done, no one will be coming back in this cave," he said.

"They'll bury the bodies in here?" I asked.

"No. The FBI is setting up a field morgue," he said. "They'll gather the biological material they need, document it and match it to records of the dead and missing. Most families won't be notified and the bodies will end up in unmarked graves in a special cemetery the government controls. The only record of who they once were will be stored as GPS coordinates and tissue samples in a big vault."

"Why won't families be notified?" I grunted as we crawled on hands and knees back under the shelf, the smell of fresh air welcome.

"Nobody knows they're missing," he said. "Felix, necromancers usually work with the already dead. The act of murder is just as abhorrent to them as it is to us. Those corpses were liberated from their graves long after family members have put them to rest."

"Not all of them," I said, gulping the clean forest air as we reached the mouth of the cave.

"Agent Anderson requests that you begin your work," Jardeep said to a technician. "There is an agent's body below and she would like it extracted first."

"String it up," the technician said to her team. "I want fresh air and lights in thirty minutes. Bolten, tell the morgue we need a bag and special handling for an agent."

"Do you have a vehicle?" Jardeep asked. "I came with Anderson."

"It's near the main entrance," I said. "I won't leave without my friends."

"I'll see what I can do."

We walked in relative silence, passing workers carrying heavy supplies, all going the other way.

"How long will they be here?" I asked, idle curiosity getting the better of me.

"With that many bodies, I'd guess ten days minimum," he said.

"Felix!" Gabriella pushed her way through the crowded clearing and embraced me. I held her tightly, soaking in the warmth she exuded.

"Where are Lace and Petaluma?" I asked.

"We're just over here," she said. "I think the agents are scared of us."

"They're under orders," Jardeep said.

"I tried calling Judy to let her know we'd found Petaluma, but I can't get a signal," Gabriella said. We found Lace and Petaluma sitting in folding chairs, each holding a bottle of water.

"Uncle Felix." Petaluma ran up to me and grabbed on desperately.

"Cell phones won't work," Jardeep explained. "We're jamming signals in the valley."

PROMISE IS A PROMISE

"We should adjourn to a location more conducive to private conversation," Jardeep said, glancing warily at the growing horde of law enforcement.

"Lace and Petaluma are in no condition to walk out," I said. "And my truck is over a mile away."

"I'll find an agent to stay with them," Jardeep said.

Lace caught my eye, brushing bangs from in front of her face. Her eyes pled with me not to leave her behind, but she didn't give voice to the request.

"I can walk, Uncle Felix, please don't leave me here." Petaluma wasn't willing to leave anything to chance – or unsaid.

Gabriella looked askance at both of us. "I'm not talking to anyone without a shower."

"Well, Mr. Problem Solver," I said. "There you have it."

"Fine," he sighed, pushing away from the tree he'd leaned against and stalking off.

"I don't trust him," Lace whispered.

"Neither do I," I answered. "But if he can get us out of here, it would be worth something."

A moment later Jardeep appeared, driving a four-person ATV. "Get in. Hurry," he said.

The five of us piled in. Gabriella took the seat next to Jardeep, allowing me to keep Petaluma on my lap. As soon as we were in, he started the machine forward, bouncing over the rough terrain.

"Let me guess, the vehicle has been repurposed," Gabriella said.

"Some problems are more difficult than others." He gunned the accelerator and the narrow vehicle climbed the side of the ditch.

At the end of the dirt track, where a chain had once denied entry, we found a state trooper's cruiser and a saw-horse barricade. A tall trooper flagged us down, stepping around the fender and into the glare of the cruiser's headlights.

"Identification?" he asked.

He handed his ID to the trooper. "Jardeep Farha. I'm taking this group to the station for questioning."

"I'll need to call it in," he answered, returning Jardeep's wallet.

"No need for that," Jardeep said. "I have authorization."

The trooper squinted and then smiled affably. "Right. That's all I need then. Carry on."

"These aren't the droids you're looking for?" Gabriella challenged when he drove off.

"Something like that," he agreed, pulling up to my parked Suburban. "What happened to this?" He'd parked so the ATV's headlights were illuminating the deep scratches in the Suburban's paint.

"My sister had a run-in with a fence," I said.

"Cawwk." Maggie's cry was high up in an overhead tree. I smiled as a generous dollop of poo hit my windshield.

"We'll get in the back," Gabriella offered, opening the side door and releasing the middle seat so it slid forward. Petaluma dutifully climbed into the back of my Burb and smiled for the first time that night when Gabriella climbed in after her.

I started the truck and drove out onto the paved road, turning toward Crabtree Valley. I didn't know what felt weirder, surviving a zombie apocalypse or simply driving away afterwards as if everything were normal.

Twenty minutes later Jardeep's phone rang. "Farha," he answered. The conversation he had was relatively one-sided, but I was able to get the gist. Dana Anderson was pissed he'd facilitated our removal from the scene and wanted us to come back. Jardeep, while contrite, wasn't interested in returning and believed we'd have a more interesting conversation away from the ears of curious agents who weren't allowed a full narrative of the events.

"Problems?" I asked once he'd hung up.

"Nothing unexpected," he replied.

"Don't forget showers," Gabriella called from the back seat.

"Crabtree Valley Inn," he said. "We have a bank of rooms and it's within walking distance of an all-night diner."

"Know it well," I said. "I'll need to call Judy to pick up Petaluma."

"I don't think that's smart," Jardeep said. "We have it on good authority she was part of this."

"If she was, it was because she was a victim of Thea Sanders," I said.

"She's a minor, Farha," Gabriella said. "You can't question her without her guardian present and I'll be advising them to say nothing."

He wasn't having it. "What happens when she does this again?"

"She didn't do this," I said. "Someone used a very confused and frightened girl and you'll get no cooperation from me if you go after her."

"*If* we have your cooperation, we should be able to keep the girl out of it. For now," he replied, not quite hiding his smugness.

I slowed the truck and pulled over to the side of the road. "Mr. Farha, you need to remove yourself from my vehicle."

"You don't want to do this. Let's just keep going," he said, once again using a persuasive magic. This time the push was significant and I almost did exactly what he requested.

"You're leveraging a twelve-year-old girl," I said, gritting my teeth and rebuffing his attack. "We'll take our chances."

For a moment the two of us sat there, locked in a battle of wills as he mounted heavier and heavier assaults. For the first time since I'd met Gabriella, I found myself pushed to the point of no return; where the darkness I'd once used to burn down my school's gymnasium threatened to overtake me. It was something I feared.

"You're right, of course," he said finally, as if we were having a minor disagreement. "There is no reason for threats. We want the same things – to have a mass murderer behind bars and the good folks of Eppy Faire and Crabtree Valley once again safe from harm."

"Felix?" Lace asked worriedly. "Your eyes."

I tilted down the rearview mirror. My eyes looked almost totally black, like my pupils had filled in the entirety of my eyes. They also glowed faintly in the dark of the vehicle. I sighed, closing my eyelids and concentrated on putting away my anger, calming myself. When I reopened them, my normal blue-gray gaze had returned.

"Your mother does not like to be pushed, either," Jardeep said.

"What do you know of my mother?"

"Anderson said you might be interested in Atronia Baltazoss," he said. "I say we get cleaned up and have some breakfast. I hear the diner's waffles are to die for." I had to hand it to him, he certainly enjoyed pushing buttons.

I fished in my backpack for Judy's phone and dialed her new number.

"What are you doing?" Jardeep asked.

I ignored him.

"Felix?" Judy answered the phone on the first ring.

"We have Petaluma and Lace, both," I said. "I need to get Petaluma somewhere safe. Can you help?"

"Of course," Judy said. "Where are you."

"We're just rolling into town. Headed to the Crabtree Valley Inn," I said.

"Divert to the United Methodist parsonage, just down from the shop on Jefferson," she said.

"Parsonage? The priest's house?" I asked.

"Not a priest," she said. "But otherwise, yes."

I hung up and pulled back onto the highway. A few minutes later, I slowed as we approached the stately old church and stopped in front of the old white two-story residence. The parsonage was nestled cozily into a corner formed by the church's main building and a much newer addition.

"What's going on?" Jardeep asked.

Before I could answer, the whoop whoop of a police siren sounded as Sheriff Merritt's vehicle slid in behind us.

"Sheriff is a friend of Judy's," I said.

"You can't get him involved. This is need-to-know only," he

replied.

I shrugged a shoulder." Sheriff Merritt only knows that Judy is eccentric and a little girl needs help. Stay cool and you've got nothing to worry about," I said.

Petaluma climbed over Lace, pushed the door open, and ran for Judy, grabbing on as if the older woman were her only lifeline. Judy raised her eyebrows on my approach.

"Why here?" Jardeep asked.

"I have no idea," I said, although I had an inkling.

"What happened to her?" Judy asked, looking at a limping Lace being helped out of the vehicle by Gabriella.

"Not sure. Nothing good, though."

"Were you a part of all that hubbub out at Julian's Peak?" Merritt asked.

"Yes. When I figured out Thea Sanders had kidnapped Petaluma, I decided to check out some places I thought she might go," I said. "I dated her back when I lived here. I guess we got lucky. Not sure what all is going on, but Mr. Farha escorted us out of there pretty quickly." I felt uncomfortable lying to the sheriff, especially under the scrutiny of four witches who understood my deception.

"They've locked that mountain down tight. Staties won't let local law back in there. Must be something big," he said.

"Do you mind if I have a quick word with Judy?" I asked.

He nodded and walked over to talk with Jardeep.

"What's really going on, Felix," Judy asked.

"We found Lace in an underground cathedral," I said. "She was in a cage, ready to be sacrificed, probably later tonight. Thea and a handful of necromancers showed up and made trouble."

Judy looked from me to Petaluma, standing next to her in the pale moonlight. "What aren't you telling me?" she asked.

"Petaluma was convinced that Willum Gordon was going to hurt her if she didn't help."

"You were helping them?"

"Willum said he'd hurt my family if I didn't help him," Petaluma said and even I could pick up on the shading of the truth.

"And?" Judy pushed.

"And I liked it," Petaluma said, with a hint of defiance. "Willum said I was powerful, that I should be a queen. He wanted to help me."

"You can't trust him," Judy said.

"Aye, Willum was bad enough before," Lace said, with a slight Scottish accent I hadn't previously picked up on. "But the demon crossed his circle nigh-unto five years ago. I witnessed it and have been running ever since."

"That was the night you escaped the barn on a draft horse," I said.

Lace looked at me questioningly. "How could yeh know this?"

"Took a train into Charlotte? I know because I saw it in a vision a few weeks back. Judy, if Willum Gordon is possessed and comes for Petaluma ... Wait. Is this consecrated ground?"

"This is Aaron's church and Pastor Clyde and his wife, Leona, are Aaron's friends," she said.

"I didn't think ... you know ... witches and the church," I said hesitantly.

"We're about to find out," she said glancing over my shoulder to the house. When I turned, a woman about my age stood on the front porch, obviously pregnant. Her husband had already advanced down the sidewalk and was approaching Merritt and Jardeep.

"Not to play devil's advocate, but are you sure the pastor can help?" Gabriella whispered.

The whole concept of churches and blessings was a conversation we'd had a number of times and was frankly, something I felt needed more investigation. While the faithful had no specific magic, many had very recognizable auras and their places of worship lit up like Christmas trees with residual energy. On the other hand, there were many churches that bore little residual energy from their parishioners and Gabriella was wise to ask. A demon would have no trouble entering a church such as that.

"I've always left demons to the clergy," Judy smiled. "There is little a demon can do to the faithful. And a more adorable couple you'll never meet. Would you believe she keeps mini goats in her back yard?"

"Aye, this is all well and good, but you need to be certain. Willum Gordon will not leave behind one as powerful as your beautiful child," Lace said.

"*Altum Visu*," I incanted, running my hands across my eyes. My worry for Petaluma drained away as I inspected the wavy-haired preacher whose entire body glowed a pale yellow. Daring a glance onto the porch, I saw that his wife's aura was much the same, although with streaks of orange. A thick swirl of color around her abdomen announced the presence of a new member of their family. Strong chords of the same yellow-white energy crisscrossed the property and into the church. I should have known Judy wouldn't take a chance.

"*Finis*."

"Satisfied?" Judy asked.

"It's beautiful."

"Pastor Clyde, you know Judy Babcock. Her stepson, Felix, and … well maybe you could finish the introductions." The sheriff looked to Judy who continued seamlessly.

My initial hesitation in shaking the man's hand gave way to surprise that it was simply a warm, friendly shake.

"Please. Call me John," he said. "Aaron says you've a problem you need our help with?" The man's smile was friendly, albeit confused.

"Would you mind if we speak in private?" Judy asked.

"I get it," Merritt said. "I'll be in the car."

"Thank you, Aaron," she said, running a hand down his arm. "Felix, I believe I've got it from here. Please be careful." She reached up and kissed me on the cheek.

"We will," I said, hugging her and then Petaluma.

"Before I forget," Judy said, pulling two phones from her purse. "They're just prepaids, but at least you'll have something until you can replace yours."

I handed back her smartphone and gratefully accepted the new devices.

"Felix, I'm not sure what you're mixed up in, but there's a lot of weight in town. The kind of weight that can swallow people's lives. Be careful, son," Sheriff Merritt said. For some reason, I didn't mind it when he called me son.

"Now can we talk?" Jardeep asked as we loaded back into the Suburban.

"Showers first," Gabriella reminded him.

"Great," he replied sarcastically as we headed toward the hotel.

"Grab my blue bag?" Gabriella asked as we stopped in front of the hotel. She positioned herself under Lace's arm and helped the girl limp across the slate entryway and through the automated doors.

"Anderson isn't going to like that you allowed the Applebaum girl to leave," Jardeep said after he talked to the night manager.

I accepted two room keys from him. He wasn't going to let up and I wasn't going to get into it with him. "We'll cross that bridge when we get to it."

"Meet me in the lobby in forty-five minutes," he said. "And don't pull a disappearing act. Believe me, there's nothing Anderson won't do at this point to get to the bottom of these murders."

The rooms he'd given us were nothing fancy; two queen beds in each room, a TV and a bathroom, but at least they adjoined.

I helped Gabriella prop Lace up on the bed, stacking pillows behind her so she could relax. She'd been hobbling around without complaint for several hours and until we sat her down on the bed, I hadn't realized just how beat up she really was. Her left cheek was black and blue with a dark purple center and her skin abraded in multiple locations. The dress she wore was in tatters.

I set to work removing Lace's shoes and socks. A line of grime outlined her ankles where the socks had provided some protection. I set the shoes aside, thinking they probably were a complete loss; covered with things I didn't want to think about. I caught Gabriella's eye and drew her attention to Lace's damaged ankle. She'd been struck by something long and narrow that left a dark welt and considerable swelling.

"Those animals." Gabriella sighed, taking the same inventory. "We'll need to get you into a bath." She gently moved Lace's bangs from her face, stroked her cheek, and turned to me. "We can't risk infection. Felix, I'm going to need bandages, hydrogen peroxide, antibiotic cream and a wrap for her ankle. She should see a doctor."

"No doctor," Lace said, opening her eyes painfully. "We are still in danger."

"Leave my bag on the bed," Gabriella said.

I didn't have what she wanted in the truck, but knew a twenty-four-hour chain store was nearby.

When I got back to the room thirty minutes later, I knocked softly. "It's me, Felix."

Gabriella unchained the door and let me in. "I'm worried, Felix. She's in bad shape."

"She's in the bath?" I asked.

"I was just about to get her out." Gabriella had laid out some of her own clothing on the bed. "Felix, go in the other room and clean up. I'll be in shortly."

Once I was in the next room, I pulled off my shirt and tossed it into the trash. No amount of cleaning would save it. Unlacing my boots, I was gratified to see they'd fared considerably better than Lace's shoes. Between the preservation enchantment I'd placed on them and their waterproof design, not much needed to be done except knock off a little debris and clean the outside with a wash cloth. My jeans, however, were another matter. I wasn't happy to toss them, but they were torn and the blue material nearly unrecognizable. I removed the belt and dropped the pants on top of my shirt in the trash.

For a few minutes, I simply sat in the comfortable chair, appreciating the quiet. I woke with a start to Gabriella's fingers brushing my cheek.

"Farha is getting antsy," she said. "I told him we needed more time."

I looked at the clock, it was five-fifteen in the morning.

"Help me get cleaned up?" Gabriella asked, unbuttoning her ruined, form-fitting cotton blouse.

I stood, placed one hand behind her neck, the other low on her waist and pulled her in for a kiss. She let go of her buttons and accepted my embrace. As I moved my hands through her hair, my fingers caught on a small piece of debris.

"What is that?" Gabriella pulled back, her hands searching.

I chuckled as she pulled a pinkie-sized bit of something from her hair, relieved upon inspection that it was merely a stick.

I reached for her buttons and finished the job she'd started, helping her pull the shirt tails from her tight jeans. I fumbled while unbuttoning her pants and was pleased when the metal snap cap popped loose and the zipper spread open easily. A reassuring smile from her was all I needed as she wriggled out of the pants, allowing them to pool at her feet. I lifted her to me, her legs wrapping around my waist as I brought an arm around under her bottom to provide support. If I could have frozen time at that moment, I would have.

"Shower, love," she whispered, releasing her legs and sliding from me. She turned, holding one of my hands and pulled me toward the bathroom. With her free hand she reached for the clasp of her once pristine, lacy bra, not quite reaching it.

"Allow me," I said. I used my ability to manipulate small objects and unhooked her bra with a flick of my fingers.

"An interesting skill," she said. "Tell me where you learned to do that."

"Would you think less of me if I said high school?"

She laughed freely, dropping her bra into the trash can. "Let me guess, you used it on the unsuspecting?"

For a moment, I had a difficult time saying anything. As dirty as we both were, I found it difficult to form anything close to a full sentence with her standing in front of me, naked, except for a thin pair of low-hipped panties. My gaze traveled up from her shapely waist, across her stomach and rested for a moment on her petite breasts.

"Not much there," Gabriella said apologetically. Her words were so incongruous with my thoughts that I looked into her eyes in confusion. A smile tugged at the sides of her lips. "No treble, as Thea said."

"For such a brilliant witch, you seem incapable of reading me at the most unusual times," I said, resting my hand on her hip and turning her so she faced the mirror with me behind her. "Read me as I tell you that you are the most beautiful woman I have ever seen." I allowed my left hand to slide beneath the waist band of her panties and my right to cup her breast. My excitement grew as I pulled her back into me and caressed her neck. She moaned in expectation, tipping her head over to rest against my own. We stood for a few minutes simply enjoying the closeness. I finally separated, allowing the moment to pass. I would not have our first time together be rushed. For once, I had hope we could truly be together.

I turned and started the shower. As I did, Gabriella grabbed the bottom of my shorts and yanked them to the ground, pantsing me. "Your body's making promises you better be ready to make good on, Mister." I turned back as she dropped her own panties. I bit my lip, drawing blood.

"Not like this," I whispered huskily. "I don't want to be rushed."

She nodded and slipped past me, brushing her shapely tush across my front side. I bit down even harder and followed her into the shower.

800-ASS CLOWN

"She's really quite beautiful," Gabriella said. We were ready to meet with Jardeep, having texted him that we were heading to the diner. He let us know he was annoyed it was nine thirty in the morning and the night had slipped away.

Gabriella and I stood at the door adjoining our two rooms. Lace lay on the bed, sleeping soundly. Gabriella had lent her a dark dress. It appeared to fit well, a mystery I never could quite put together. Just how could two women, so differently shaped, be able to wear the same clothing?

"She is," I agreed. "I can't imagine what they had planned for her."

"Yes you can, which is why you feel responsible for her," Gabriella said, crossing the room. "Lace." She gently shook the sleeping girl's shoulder. "Lace. It's time to go."

Lace's eyes opened. She looked from Gabriella to me and sat up. "I should leave, I'm endangering you."

"We are sisters," Gabriella said.

"Yeh barely know me," Lace said, her Scottish accent more pronounced. "I deserve what I've got coming; I've done things."

"No more than what was required to survive. I saw as much when we joined," Gabriella said. "Stay with us for now. We'll talk about the future when it finds us."

Lace slid from the bed and stepped gingerly onto her swollen ankle, grimacing. Even cleaned up, she looked like a victim of abuse, bearing a multitude of scars from her ordeal. Gabriella dutifully slipped beneath Lace's arm and braced her, helping her to the elevator and out to the truck. Thick clouds had rolled in and a light drizzle had started. We were in for significant rain.

"We're not sure how much Jardeep knows of our world," I cautioned, pulling up in front of the diner. "He may be on a fishing trip. We have to be careful about sharing too much."

The diner was busy, the morning rush just getting underway, and we found Jardeep seated alone at a deep booth that overlooked the two-lane highway.

"Coffee?" A waitress asked cheerfully as I slid in next to Jardeep. I flipped my cup over as did Gabriella.

"Orange juice?" I asked.

"Fresh," she winked. Her double entendre obviously part of a well-rehearsed shtick. "Do you know what you want, hun?"

I couldn't recall the last time we'd eaten and the smells of baked and fried foods had my full attention. I looked at Lace who was staring out the window. "It's going to rain," she said.

"Lace. Food?"

"I'm okay."

"We'll have two short stacks and whatever fresh fruit you have," Gabriella said.

"What'd I miss?" Maggie surprised us all by appearing behind the waitress and sliding in next to Gabriella.

"Just ordering breakfast. You hungry?" I asked, looking skeptically at her. Last we'd talked, she was concerned about another shift, due to low body fat. The skin on her face was again stretched tight, making her look like someone on a hunger strike.

"You better believe it," she said and proceeded to order more than enough food for the entire table.

"Who is this?" Jardeep asked, once the waitress left.

"A friend of ours. Maggie," Gabriella offered quickly. "Don't worry, she can either hear what we have to say here or we'll tell her later."

Jardeep didn't look as though he approved, but didn't push the issue.

"Walk me through last night," he said. "How'd you figure out that location? Don't tell me it was one of your old hangouts with Althea Sanders. I'm not buying it."

"Pretty mundane, actually," I said. "Gabriella showed me how to track her phone, which Willum's thugs had stolen. I recalled that Thea had a similar phone and guessed her password. That's all it took to track her. I'm surprised the FBI didn't do it."

"We didn't have a warrant for Ms. Sander's phone. We also didn't know she had such a big part in all this," he defended.

"Here we go." The waitress returned with a full tray of food and passed it out, stacking four of the plates around Maggie.

For a moment, the table was quiet as we took a moment to refuel. It was after Maggie had finished her second plateful of eggs and placed a short-stack of pancakes in front of her when she noticed Jardeep's eyes on her.

"I'm starving," Maggie said, drenching the pancakes with strawberry syrup.

"You're a shifter," he said, looking from Maggie back to me.

"Careful," I warned.

"Not much of a guess," Maggie said. "Even Jar-Jar would have put it together eventually."

"Jar-Jar?" I asked. Gabriella covered her mouth, stifling a smile.

"Live under a rock much, bro?" she asked and then moved on. "No, Jar-derp here is part of the group that hunted mom and forced her to go underground."

"Atronia was a danger to everyone," Jardeep said. "She had to be reined in."

"How'd that go for you?" Maggie asked.

"I was reassigned," he said. "I'm sure I don't know."

"What do you mean hunted?" I asked.

"Imagine the knights of the round table hunting the dragon, only in this story the knights always get eaten," she said. "Back in the eighties, Reagan - you know, the actor turned president? Well, his buddy Bush uncovered the presence of witches. Between the two of them, they decided witches needed to be tracked - up until they discovered Mom in the early nineties. Rather than just tracking her, she needed to be brought in - for the safety of the country and all."

"Wasn't Bush a president?"

"Right," Maggie rolled her eyes. "His Dad … never mind, the presidents aren't important. What's important is that Jar-derp here was an up and coming agent. Wait." She looked at him. "You want to tell it?"

"No, I think you've got it about right," Jardeep replied. "Aside from the name calling that is."

Maggie gave him her shoulder and turned back to me. "Well, *Jar-derp* here, sucked Mom into a problem they were having with a demon, not unlike what's going on today. Only when they finished, after Mom saved the day, they came after her. Apparently, *Jar-derp* couldn't wrap his puny little mind around the idea that Mom was a good little sorcerer and everyone would be better off making friends."

"That's when Mom split?" I asked.

"More or less." Maggie stuffed an impossibly large piece of pancake into her mouth.

"What your sister has failed to tell you is we approached Atronia with peaceful intent," Jardeep said. "She simply needed to submit to a few tests and help us when situations arose."

"Why haven't you gone after the rest of our family?"

"Mom was special, Felix," Maggie said. "She wasn't a witch or even a wizard. She was a full blown, fire from her finger tips, call down lightning from the heavens, knock down buildings with a glare, sorcerer. The rest of us just aren't that special, barely reaching a five or six on Epps Thaumaturgic scale."

"Scale?"

"We rank your kind," Jardeep said. "Witches are generally in the one to three range, although I'm guessing Ms. Faa is on the high side of that, given Willum's host's interest in her."

"You know?" Lace asked.

"About the demon?" Jardeep watched Lace carefully for a reaction. She winced at his pronouncement. "Tell me Lace. What is its name?" A prickling along my arm alerted me to the gathering of power next to me. It was coming from Jardeep.

"Uh, well, I'm not really sure," Lace said, fidgeting in her chair.

"It's important. A demon's name is its calling card. It would help us a great deal if we knew this," he said. A wave of power surged across the table.

"Sounds kind of dangerous to give a bunch of bureaucrats the true name of a demon," Maggie said, oblivious to the power struggle taking place at the end of the table. "What? Would you punch it into your computer and anyone with a W10 clearance could read it? It's not like you guys can keep anything secret; pretty soon all wannabe evokers are dialing this guy up. Wait. We could create an 800 number. One eight hundred – a-s-s-c-l-o-w-n." As she talked she counted the letters off on her fingers. "Shit. Too many digits."

"Would you shut up?" Jardeep looked at Maggie in frustration. The second he turned her way, the power dissipated as quickly as my estimation of her increased.

"Do you know where she is now?" I asked.

"Who?" Jardeep looked at me, flustered.

"We were talking about my mother," I said. "Where is she?"

"I have no idea."

"You said you had information about her," I said. "Like what?"

"Yeah, Derp. What information do you have for Felix about his mother?" Maggie asked, stuffing a sausage link into her mouth.

"Maggie," Gabriella elbowed her in the ribs.

"What? I'm on a roll," Maggie complained.

"We're here because I need to understand how you ended up in that cave. Let's start with how you know each other," he said.

"Well. I guess it started when we were young," Maggie jumped in.

"Not you," Jardeep seethed. "Them. How is it that you three know each other?" He indicated Lace, Gabriella and me.

"Not that mysterious," I said. "Lace happens to work at Judy's business."

"Why are you all being so difficult?" he asked, finally reaching his boiling point. "You know what I'm asking."

"No, Jardeep, we really don't. Aside from asking Lace the name of a supposed demon inhabiting Willum Gordon, you haven't asked any questions," I said.

"I want to know how you knew this was about to blow up in Crabtree Valley of all places," he said. "How did you become involved with Lace Faa, the mysterious and missing princess of an

Eppy gypsy clan. And how you happened to be involved with Willum Gordon's second in command, Althea Sanders."

"Let's get something clear," I said. "Thea Sanders was a mistake I made a couple of years ago. I could have gone the rest of my life not seeing her again. As for how we showed up here? I'd say that's like every other part of my life. Shit happens and my friends and I end up cleaning it up."

"And Lace?"

"How many shops in North Carolina profess to sell goods and services for the magically gifted or seekers of the same?" I asked.

"No idea, why don't you tell me."

"This doesn't work if you don't play along," I said. "I'll bet you have a pretty good idea."

"Under a hundred and fifty," he said.

"Of those one hundred fifty, how many of them are run by actual, practicing witches who score better than a one on your witch-o-meter scale?" I asked.

"Less than six," he said.

"Do you really find it that hard to believe that Lace was drawn to Judy's shop?" I asked.

"I get your point," he said. "I also believe you're holding out on me."

"What have I missed?"

We'd been so focused on our argument that we hadn't seen Dana Anderson approach. Her disheveled appearance dispelled any notion that she'd done anything other than come straight from the cathedral.

"Agent Anderson," Jardeep answered. "What are you doing here?"

"We have Willum Gordon trapped," she said. "He and Althea Sanders are barricaded in the big top out at Eppy Faire. They have hostages."

"I see," he answered.

Anderson looked directly at me. "He said he's going to kill the hostages if we don't let him talk to Mr. Slade."

"Felix. You can't go." Gabriella reached across the table and grabbed my arm.

"He's already killed one," Anderson said. "And there are children. We tried to breach, but he had some sort of explosives and several agents were hurt."

"I'll go," I said.

"He's too powerful, Felix," Gabriella argued. "Remember what he did to me."

"I can't let him kill more people," I said. "I'd never be able to live with myself."

"I'll go with you," she said.

"Not this time," I said. "It's too dangerous."

"It's too dangerous for me, but not for you?" she asked, fire in her eyes. "Would you let me go alone?"

"No," I said. "I need to know you're safe."

"No one will be safe if he's allowed to escape," Jardeep said grimly.

"Please," I whispered, knowing I had no right to ask.

"No," Gabriella said simply. "I'll stay back, but that's the best I can do."

"We need to go," Anderson said.

Gabriella pushed Maggie out as I slid from the booth.

"Hey. You're not leaving me behind," Maggie caught up with us.

"No way," Anderson said.

"Like you could stop me," Maggie said.

"Let her," Jardeep said. "That's Sevena Baltazoss."

Anderson lifted an eyebrow, but didn't say anything. She turned back to the car she'd double-parked and left running. "Get in."

"We'll follow you," I said, looking back as Lace hobbled out, a determined look on her face.

"Farha, bring the car," Anderson ordered. "I'll ride with Slade."

The morning's drizzle was turning to a heavier rain as the five of us piled into the Suburban, Gabriella surrendering shotgun position to Anderson. The sound of a wailing siren echoed down the otherwise quiet street as I started to pull away from the curb.

A moment later Sheriff Merritt's white SUV came toward us, slowed and then pulled across the road, effectively pinning us in against the curb, his cruiser pointed in the opposite direction as my truck.

"This can't be good," I said. I rolled my window down as he rolled up even with me.

"Sheriff, you need to move," Anderson said, talking across me. "There's a hostage situation at Eppy Fair."

"That's my jurisdiction," he said. "I just got a call and saw you here. I'll give you an escort."

"FBI has this, Sheriff, and we're already coordinating with the State Patrol," she said.

"I get it, but I have to live here when you're done making a mess," he said.

"Fine," Anderson said, frustrated. "We'll follow. Just move it."

Merritt backed up, fired up his siren and pulled out, temporarily blocking the light traffic in both directions. Vintage 1970s Suburbans aren't well known for their turning radius and I had to swing wide onto the opposite shoulder, u-turning to follow Merritt's SUV. A spray of mud and rock flew up behind us as I accelerated to catch up with Merritt's much newer and more powerful vehicle.

The trip up the mountain in the rain was a combination of harrowing experience and thrill ride. Vehicles on both sides of the highway pulled aside for the sheriff's approach and I struggled to keep up with him.

"What are children doing at Eppy this early in the morning?" I asked. "Shit, I remember. There's a book swap."

"We're fortunate we got there before too many visitors showed up," Anderson said.

"He's using the children," I said.

"I understand," Anderson said. "He's threatened to start killing them."

"No," I said. "The books are cursed. He's recruiting."

"How do you know that?" Anderson asked.

"I saw the curse in Eppy's book store," I said.

"He's trying to draw energy so he can escape Willum's body," Lace said from the back seat.

"Careful, Lace," Maggie warned. "The FBI locks up people they're scared of. Trust me, I know."

"We made a mistake with you, Sevena," Anderson said. "Those agents lost their badges."

"But not their paychecks."

"Jardeep wasn't involved with your incarceration," Anderson said. "We don't have time for this. Ms. Faa, what do you mean? How can whatever is in Willum escape?"

"Can't you guys see it? That's why he wants Felix," Maggie said. "Fuck! Stop the car. We can't go. If that thing gets out, we'll never stop it."

I turned onto the secondary road leading up the back side of the mountain to Eppy Faire, not slowing down. "If we don't go, he'll kill those kids."

"She's right," Lace said. "Ma told me when I was younger, but I didn't believe her until that night Willum was taken. The demons want to walk the earth."

"So it is a demon?" Anderson asked.

"Ghrelin," I said, making a decision. Anderson and the FBI might turn on me, but I'd make sure we had the best chance to win this round.

"Damn," Anderson said.

"Might have thought about that before you tried to lock Mom up," Maggie said.

"That wasn't me," Anderson said.

"Always an excuse handy. And the agents were just following orders when they grabbed me," Maggie answered sarcastically.

"We've made mistakes," Anderson argued. "That changes nothing."

"Other than now you're looking to throw my brother to the wolves," she answered.

"That's enough, Maggie," I said.

Anderson pulled out her phone as we crested the final hill and looked into the valley where Eppy Faire sat nestled in the foothills. While the Faire was no stranger to chaos, today it was accentuated by a myriad of flashing lights atop state patrol cruisers, all surrounding the big-top. Just outside the front entrance, a heavily armored truck boasting an FBI logo sat pointed into the colorful tent's grand entrance.

"Keep going." Anderson placed her hand over the microphone of her phone as we followed Sheriff Merritt's vehicle through the entrance and past a barricade where armed troopers held assault rifles at the ready.

"Felix, you need to think about this," Maggie pled. "If there's really a demon in there, you'll never make it out."

I pulled to a stop next to Merritt's truck and jumped out, looking back at Gabriella. "Promise me, if this goes south, you'll get my sister and Lace out of here."

"I will."

BIG TOP

I walked through the ruined grand entrance of the big-top tent. Red and white canvas fabric hung in tatters, fluttering in the light wind as I allowed my eyes to adjust to the dark interior. Even with Dana's urging, the commander of the FBI team had been completely against my presence. In the end, however, it came down to simple logic. Willum was threatening to kill hostages and the FBI had already failed one breach attempt, which had them baffled given it was just a tent.

"Felix Slade, I find that I'm both disappointed and pleased to see you," Willum announced. The man stood on a stage that had been erected in the center of the hard-packed dirt arena. In front of him sat a score of children along with their parents.

"Disappointed? You asked for me." I approached warily, walking down an aisle between bleacher style seats.

"Surely you know how this will end," he said, spreading his hands wide in front of him.

"Let the kids go," I said. "Or I'm walking out."

"Said the fly to the spider." In the wan light his eyes glowed a sickly green; the same color of the spell he'd spread across the children's books.

"You can't possibly escape," I said. "You might be powerful, but the FBI will never allow it."

"Join us, Felix." Thea stood from where she sat in the darkened bleachers. "With you, we will be unstoppable."

"Two years ago. Was any of it real? Or was it all just an attempt to take my magic?" I still burned with feelings of betrayal.

"A lover's quarrel. How precious," Willum clapped his hands together. "Tell him the truth, darling. He deserves to know."

"You're a nice boy, Felix." Thea stepped over the long benches, working her way down to the arena floor where long tables filled with books had been thrown over. "But really, we're not in the same class. You had to know that."

My heart pounded and my face flushed. I'd seen Thea's cruel side before, but hadn't had it directed at me quite so pointedly. She enjoyed finding a person's weakness and poking at it.

"If I join with you, you'll let all these people go?" I turned back to Willum.

"You wear the lie on your face, Slade," he answered. "You believe that once they are gone, you'll make your move against me. What you don't understand is that I love them all, each and every one."

"Who's lying now?" I asked, impatient with his blathering.

"Not everyone expresses their love in the same way and frankly, some love requires sacrifice. A lesson Althea learned from you," he said.

"From me?" I asked.

"She thought you would give yourself to her fully and yet you nearly killed her," he said.

"I had no idea what was happening," I said.

"True as that may be, your spirit was unwilling to give everything. Let me demonstrate." He stepped down from his platform and stood next to a cowering woman who covered her child protectively. "See what this woman is willing to give?" He grabbed a handful of her hair and pulled her upward as she screamed.

"Stop! Willum!" I cried out.

Even as I did, the woman stopped screaming and attempted to comfort her son, asking him to move away from her.

"I believe I could pull her still beating heart from her chest with her permission, as long as I promised to spare her child."

He cruelly twisted the woman's head around so she was looking at him.

"Yes, yes. Please," she begged.

It was more than I could bear to watch. "*Adoleret*." I incanted, stabbing my arm at him. A gout of flame bridged the gap between us and splashed off his shoulder, burning a hole in his shirt and scorching the skin.

He roared in pain, tossing the woman aside like a rag doll. She flew several feet before landing heavily against the first row of bleachers.

"Felix, no!" Thea screamed, pulling a wand from her pocket.

"*Scutum.*" I raised my shield just in time to deflect a nasty stream of thorned vines. The ghostly buckler shimmered between us as she continued her assault, pulling vines from the ground all around her. The ferocity of her attack took me off guard. I'd never seen her use an offensive spell before.

"Dear me," Willum cackled, having recovered from my attack. "Always the gentleman with the ladies. Why do you not simply kill this one? Surely it is within your power. By my count, this is the third time she's tried to do you in, yet you refuse to respond."

Thea screamed in frustration and changed the direction of her attack, pulling vines from behind me and then from the side. Each time, I repositioned the shield and cut off her attack.

I reached out for the flying brambles and allowed thorns to scrape across my unprotected hand. As the blood dripped, I dropped my shield and incanted, "*Rhamno.*" It was a guess on my part that Thea's magically summoned vines would work with my rooting spell. It was even more unexpected that I ended up turning her spell against her. The vines, instead of attacking me, turned in midflight and wrapped themselves around her. She screamed, first in surprise and then in pain as the thorns bit into her flesh and toppled her to the ground.

"Look at you; shaping her spells. If anything, I've underestimated you," Willum taunted and then reached forward with his hand forming into a claw.

Hastily, I attempted to reconstruct my shield, but I was too late. Pain exploded inside my chest. I could feel his clawed fingers puncture my skin and I frantically swatted the air in front of me, hoping to make it stop. My hands simply passed through the space between us, while Willum laughed but nothing stopped the intense pain.

"I see now that I'll never be successful in turning you," he taunted, twisting his hand. My mind flitted between agony and an attempt at finding a solution. I'd never been in so much pain and it crippled my ability to think.

"Stop," I managed to say through clenched teeth.

"Stop? But we've barely just started." He lifted his arm and it felt as if his fingers were tearing through the wall of my chest.

A blurred shape burst past me and lunged at Willum. It was Maggie in panther form. Distracted, he was too late to do much as Maggie sank her teeth into his shoulder, clawing at his torso with her powerful back legs. Relief flooded through me as he released me and I fell to the ground. With his hands free, he tore Maggie off and flung her from the stage, the cracking of bones loud as she slumped and slid to the ground.

I turned to the sound of automatic gunfire. A foursome of agents hustled down the aisle, weapons leveled at Willum, peppering his body with rounds. Whatever spell had been holding the police back no longer restricted their movements.

"Enough!" Willum cried out, sweeping his arm in an arc at the advancing agents. The gunfire stopped almost immediately as they, too, were thrown back.

"Maggie!" I ran forward to help my sister, who still hadn't moved.

"Felix, stay back." Gabriella cried from a distance. The crack of a much heavier gunshot rang out and Willum was tossed back, pin-wheeling like he'd been struck with something very powerful.

Unexpectedly, Willum jerked to a stop, caught himself before he fell off the stage, and turned back toward the entrance. In a quick move, he pulled Gabriella from the entrance almost as if she was on a string. Her body flew through the air and she hung suspended in front of him. The flaps of the tent sealed closed behind her.

"Humans never learn," he said. "Your FBI has nothing that can stop me. And neither do you. I had so hoped you would be like your mother, but alas, you are just a child."

Gabriella screamed as Willum extended his hand, grabbed her by the neck, and pulled her close. I must have screamed as well when he reached back for me. The pain was so great I blacked out and came to a few moments later when he backed off his grip.

"Don't give in." Gabriella looked at me in anguish.

"Such a pure heart," Willum said. "I can't resist any longer; she is too beautiful."

Distractedly, he clawed at me as he leered into Gabriella's face. The human façade had slipped, the demon fully surfacing. I knew the ghrelin couldn't actually reside on our plane of existence by itself, but it clearly had the capacity to get very close. It licked at Gabriella's face with a long greasy tongue and winked at me.

The motion of Maggie transforming back into her human form caught my attention. She'd told me that when close to death, she would return to her natural state and I hoped this wasn't what was occurring. She only appeared to be semi-conscious as she looked up at me. "Stop him," she whispered.

"I can't," I said, shaking my head.

A fresh scream from Gabriella tore my attention back to Willum. The look of rapture on his face was so hideous that I rocked forward, finding I had some capacity to move. Pain coursed through my body as I fought against the demon's iron grip and moved slowly forward onto the stage. Willum felt my movement and increased the damage his invisible hand was doing, but I pushed against it nonetheless. After closing to nearly an arm's length, his eyebrows darted downward in doubt and he swiveled his head to look at me. His bliss turned to surprise as he dropped Gabriella to the ground, her screams evaporating into whimpers.

"Main course before dessert, you say?" If I'd caught him off guard, it was short-lived. He physically grabbed my chest this time and my hands flew up instinctively to wrap around his wrist. His arm was thick and green, just like when he'd appeared in my vision.

Anger welled within me as his claws sought to penetrate my skin. So many had been killed by this creature and it had, or would shortly, kill Gabriella and Maggie. What right did it have to wreak such destruction? "You have no place here!"

"The earth-wizard lecturing me about survival of the fittest. How deliciously twisted," he mocked.

"You are not of nature," I spat and realized at once what I had to do.

I released Willum and allowed his claw to grab my chest, the pain nearly more than I could bear. I dropped my arms and reached out to the earth beneath us, connecting to the sleepy mountain.

"NO!" Willum bellowed and fresh pain coursed through me as his claws tore into my skin, only momentarily stopped by my ribcage.

The mountain offered a quiet alternative, beckoning me to join it in its slumber. The pain would cease if I gave in. I demurred. The life I was meant to live with my friends was on the other side of that pain.

"Now you die, Felix Slade," Willum said, his claws burning as they pushed into my chest.

Anxiety threatened to overwhelm me and the darkness I'd always lived in fear of welled up. I knew it was part of me and it wasn't without trepidation that I stoked its fire. A fresh surge of energy coursed through my body as I pulled from the mountain. Angrily, I redirected it all into Willum's chest. A look of surprise crossed his face as a bright explosion threw us away from each other.

My head struck something hard and I fought to remain conscious. A scream of terror from Willum as he jumped up from where he'd been thrown was abruptly cut short as bullets riddled his body. Whatever barriers he'd constructed around the tent had fallen a second time and the tactical teams were taking no chances at being locked out again.

The restraint shown by the tactical teams as they rushed in and secured the scene amazed me. In all, I suspected Willum had only been hit maybe twenty or thirty times. If it had been me, I would not have stopped firing until I'd run out of bullets, even with all of the friendlies nearby.

Gabriella made it over to me before I was able to move. I

reached up to wipe away the makeup that streaked down her face. The thought of the agony she'd endured was almost too much for me to bear. "Are you okay?"

"I will be," she answered, gingerly pulling my blood-soaked and tattered shirt aside. "Oh, Felix, you need help."

"Maggie." I pushed her hand aside and struggled to my feet. My eyes fell on Maggie, lying on the ground beneath the stage. Gabriella followed my eyes and gasped.

About half-way there, a firm hand grabbed my arm from behind. "Hold on, help is coming." I turned to find Dana Anderson looking intently at me. "You need medical attention." She spun and called out. "Can I get help over here?"

"What about Willum?" I asked.

"He's dead," she answered. "When you went on the offensive, he dropped his defenses and we were able to breach."

"Help me over to Maggie," I said.

Dana did as I requested. "What's her prognosis?" Anderson asked.

"Severely dehydrated, malnourished," the first paramedic said over his shoulder. "She's also taken quite a blow to her head. Is she bulimic?"

"Something like that," I said, not interested in explaining. "Is she going to be okay?"

"Stop talking about me like I'm not here," Maggie grunted. "I'm not bulimic."

A gurney arrived and the paramedics lifted Maggie, all eighty-five pounds of her, onto it. I ran my hand across her forehead. "I told you not to come in."

"Like I'm going to start listening to you *now*," she said. "I almost had him."

My head started to swim and I reached out for Gabriella. "We'll find you," I said.

"Bring food," she called back as they wheeled her off.

"You need to sit," Anderson said.

"No. Take me to Willum. I need to be sure," I said.

She nodded and helped me over to where a body bag had been

laid out next to Willum Gordon.

I cast my planar view and inspected the body. Part of me hoped the demon was still present so I could burn the body. I wasn't sure what good that would do, but I was willing to experiment. Residual traces of the ghrelin's magic clung to the body, but it was equally clear both the person and the demon had been destroyed.

"Can demons be vanquished by force?" I asked.

"Shh," Anderson stopped me. "We're not to talk about that here."

"Don't be ridiculous. No one is listening to your conversation." Jardeep's voice caught me off guard. "To answer your question, you vanquished the demon with your spell. Even the least sensitive among us felt that surge of energy. It is the simplest explanation, backed up by facts."

I nodded.

"We had cameras all over the place," he answered. "Believe me, if that demon was still here, we'd be dancing to a different tune."

A paramedic approached, looked at the four of us, and took charge. "You need to sit down." He gently guided me to the edge of the stage. "Let's give him some space."

"What about Thea?" I asked, over the man's shoulder as he pealed back my ruined shirt.

"They're cutting her out of the brambles now," Anderson said.

"What will happen to her? And what are you going to do about all of the Dark Folk who helped them?"

"She'll be tried for her crimes," Anderson said. "By a jury of her peers."

"That should be interesting," Gabriella said. "Not sure she has many peers."

"It's something we know how to deal with," Anderson said. "As for the rest of the Dark Folk, the cave contains a trove of evidence and once we lock in on one person, we'll leverage them to roll over on the others. Believe me, we'll undo the entire wicked mess."

"Up here," the paramedic ordered as a gurney arrived. He'd

successfully laid gauze on my chest and handed me an ice pack for my head where I'd struck the bleachers. "You're going to need stitches and staples, but I think you'll be okay."

"What about Petaluma?" I asked Anderson.

"I'll leave her out of it for now," Anderson said. "I'll have to follow the evidence, though."

I shook my head in understanding. I guess I couldn't ask for more.

"Where's Lace?" I asked as we started rolling out. I was glad to be lying down.

"On her way to the hospital," Gabriella said. "She wanted to come help you, but I might have sic'd a paramedic on her."

"Up," the paramedic directed, pushing my gurney into the back of the waiting ambulance.

Gabriella put her hand on my gurney, essentially stopping its movement. "I'm coming along."

"Fine." I heard the paramedic say with a sigh.

I wasn't sure if it was exhaustion or something in the IV, but the next thing I remembered was waking up in a room at the hospital. Gabriella had reclined a guest chair in the semi-private room and was fast asleep, holding my hand. When I rolled my head over, I found that Lace was in a similar bed a few feet away.

"Hey stranger," I said.

"Felix, you are awake. How are you feeling?"

"I think the better question is, how are you?" Her leg was in a cast up to just under the knee.

"Anything is better than that cage," she said. "This will heal. Is he truly dead?"

"I saw it for myself," I said.

"I'm so relieved," she said, although I caught a touch of sorrow in her voice "I just ... I just don't know ..."

"Willum was family," I said. "I'm sorry for my part in this."

"It's not that," she said. "I've just been running for so long. I don't know what to do now."

"You're welcome to stay on at the shop," Judy said from the doorway.

"Lace, you'll not be getting rid of us easily," Gabriella added groggily. "As it turns out, I happen to know of a beautiful little apartment that's coming available in Leotown."

"Yeh barely know me," she said.

"Wait. What apartment?" I asked. "Does this mean you and Clarita are going to finally move in with me?"

Gabriella smiled.

GREAT ESCAPE

"I need to get out of here," Lace whispered. "The people who saw me in that cage know I exist now. They will come for me."

"Willum is dead," I answered, reassuringly.

"That is the problem. Willum had control of the council and with his death, they are back in charge of the Dark Folk," she said. "My ma lived apart from the Dark Folk because she was a threat to them and they wanted to kill her. Once the clan discovers I made it out of that cave alive, they'll come for me, too."

"I thought your mother was the queen."

"With her gone, that title falls to me. The elder council will look to remove me as they did her."

"Do you really think after all the trouble the Dark Folk just stirred up, they'll come for you?" I asked.

"Trouble follows the gypsy clans, Felix. This is nothing new to them," she said. It didn't escape me that she didn't consider herself a part of the Eppy clan.

"You feel good enough to move?" I asked.

"You, my good man, have an appointment with a plastic surgeon this afternoon, so I don't think you're going anywhere." Jason, the duty nurse sauntered into the room, speaking to me and then to Lace. "And you, my friend, could well have an infection from your injuries. So I'll need you both to sit tight until the doc visits. Now, let me get a look at this." He crossed the room and pulled at the bandage on my chest.

"I'll take my chances," I said grumpily. Because of a possible concussion, the nurses hadn't let me sleep until midnight and I was tired of being woken up every two hours.

"Just hang tight. The whole hospital has been crazy - some sort of problem out at Eppy Faire. News is saying a madman had a gun and took hostages," he said, then paused, looking guilty. "Oh crap, you were probably out there. Was it bad?"

"No idea," I answered.

"Your chest looks better, although that's not saying much." He moved on. "You're going to have a nasty scar and these are wicked looking scratches. Your skin was torn in several places. If I didn't know better, I'd say you were mauled by an animal."

"My sister, Maggie. Do you know where she is?" I asked.

"No Maggie is on this floor," he said. "Same last name?"

"Yes."

He typed on the tablet he'd set on my tray. "There's a Slade admitted on fourth floor."

"Is she okay?"

"I can't share information about another patient."

"What's on the fourth floor?" Gabriella asked, standing up from the chair where she'd been dozing.

"A little more security," he said, cautiously.

"I'll go," Gabriella said.

I pulled the IV from my hand. "No. This is crap."

"Hold on there, Mr. Slade. You've had a nasty bang to the head, we can't have you falling on us." Jason gently placed his hands on my shoulders.

"I'm okay." I pushed a small compulsion at him to back up my words.

"You're probably right," he replied. "But orders are you need to stay in bed until the doc has a chance to check you out."

"When will that be?" I asked.

"Shortly." The lie was easy to read. From the corner of my eye I saw Lace waggle her eyebrows and slowly slide from her bed. The movement caught Jason's eye and just as he turned toward her, she vanished.

"Shit, where'd she go?" He spun, searching the room frantically with his eyes. The only telltale was her IV line which made an unnatural bend upward and disappeared from sight. If Jason had been expecting some sort of magic, he might have had a chance at locating her.

"Maybe she went on a snack run?" I asked innocently. When he turned, I tapped the bandage on the back of my hand where my IV had once been. Lace must have seen me because her own line slowly lowered and then hung free.

"She shouldn't be up," he said, worriedly, applying a new dressing to my chest.

"Said something about cafeteria," I said. "She can't be too far ahead."

"Dammit."

I chuckled as he left the room in a rush. From a plastic bag sitting at the end of the bed, I pulled my jeans and belt out and slid them on. Each movement felt like I was reopening the wounds on my chest, but I was not interested in waiting any longer. "Shirt?" I asked.

Gabriella handed me a black t-shirt with a large brown bunny on the front. The caption read 'Some Bunny Loves Me.' I looked at her in shock. Was she kidding?

"Sorry, it was all they had in the gift-shop," Gabriella said with a huge smile. "And Judy said Merritt would see to getting your truck back - maybe tonight."

I pulled out my phone and brought up the car-service app. From the corner of my eye, light shimmered around Lace's figure as she slowly moved and extracted clothing from her own hospital supplied personal-effects bag. It was a remarkable spell; it wasn't that she became visible when she moved, as much as it appeared the camouflage spell took a moment to catch up with her movements.

My gaze must have lingered a bit too long as Gabriella slapped my shoulder. "Stop staring," she reprimanded.

"That's serious magic," I said. It was a shading of truth and I was certain Gabriella caught it. Lace was too young for me, barely twenty-one, but her outlined figure was … well, I suppose you see the problem now.

Lace chose that moment to drop her spell and considered me, smiling. "We should get going."

"A car will be here in fifteen minutes," I said, twiddling my fingers to cause my plastic admittance band to fall off. Lace struggled with her own before I did the same for her. "Let's find Maggie."

I stuck my head out of the room and was pleased to see a stairway door down the hallway only a few feet away, with no nurses in sight.

"Get a chair for Lace," Gabriella whispered, apparently reading my plan and recognizing that I hadn't considered that Lace's leg was in a cast.

"Won't work," I said, knowing the elevators would take us past the nurse's station. Pain coursed through my chest as I attempted to place my arm around Lace and help her walk. My plan was quickly falling apart. There was no way I would be able to help her down stairs. "Shit. Stay here."

I snuck out into the hallway and walked past several open patient rooms. Each room was occupied, but none had a wheelchair. I grimaced as a nurse I wasn't familiar with walked busily past. When she didn't pay me any attention, I continued down the hallway, finally finding a wheelchair just past the nurse's station.

I was just about back to the room with the chair when Jason's voice caught me from behind. "Hey, you there." The sound of jingling change warned me of his hurried approach. "You need to get back in bed."

With a sigh, I looked into the room I was just about to pass. An elderly man slept on the first bed, connected to an array of machines. I twisted my fingers and pulled at the leads with my telekinesis. I must have hit the jackpot as all of a sudden alarms and buzzers went off, making a tremendous racket.

"I think he's choking." I pushed Jason again with suggestion. A pang of guilt tugged at my conscience. I didn't like using suggestion on innocents.

Jason sprang into immediate action. "We're coding!" he shouted down the hall and sprinted into the room, a wave of concern radiating from him. My guilt deepened – he was obviously very dedicated to his work.

Wasting no more time, I spun the chair into the doorway of our room. With Gabriella's help, Lace sat heavily and I pulled back out of the room, pointed us down the hallway and adopting an unconcerned look, pushed Lace past the flurry of activity I'd caused.

Once on the elevator, I hit the button for the fourth floor, but it refused to illuminate.

"Must be locked out," Gabriella observed.

I punched the lobby button as Jason rounded the corner in a hurry and looked into the elevator car. He'd figured out my ruse and I wondered just how far he was willing to go to get me back in my room. He rumpled his eyebrows in confusion and turned away, sprinting down the hallway.

"My people call it shadow walk," Lace said once the door closed.

"I can't even feel an energy drain when you do it," I said.

"Ma always said it was my one real gift," she said.

I pushed her into the hospital's bright lobby and out the sliding glass doors. A black sedan pulled up just as we did.

I waved at the vehicle and the driver returned my wave. "I think our ride is early."

"Do you know where there's a medical supply?" I asked as he stepped out of his car. "We need to get crutches."

"Don't they rent those here?" he asked, hustling around the rear of his vehicle to open the back passenger side door.

"It's complicated," I answered, helping Lace into the back seat.

"Sure, no problem."

"Meet back at Judy's shop?" I looked back to Gabriella. "I'm going to find Maggie."

Gabriella looked from Lace to me and then nodded. "Don't get into trouble."

"No promises." I tried to hand her my credit card but she just shook her head. It was a conversation we'd had a number of times. She made good money and until I gained access to the trust left behind by my mother, she was better funded than me.

After closing the door on the vehicle, I walked back into the hospital and up to a pudgy, middle-aged man seated at the information desk. His demeanor was friendly as he set down the newspaper he'd been reading.

"How may I be of assistance?" he asked.

"Maggie Slade?"

He punched the information into his computer. "You are?"

"Her brother," I said.

"Would you mind if I saw some ID?" he asked. I'd been in enough hospitals to know this was an unusual request. I didn't, however, feel like pushing it with him, so I handed him my driver's license.

"Why the ID check?" I asked.

"Standard procedure," he replied, stiffening slightly. It was a good tell, honest people generally didn't appreciate lying. "I'll have to call Dr. Hornbeck."

"Is something wrong with Maggie?" I asked.

"Sorry, I don't have access to that type of information," he said.

"What's on the fourth-floor?" I asked.

He sat back, surprised by my question. "Uh, well …" he stammered. "Mental health services. But it's restricted access. If you'll have a seat, I'll call her."

"Sounds good." I walked toward the chairs he indicated. As soon as he looked away, however, I diverted to the stairwell and climbed up to the fourth floor. As expected, the door was locked and further announced that an alarm would sound if it were opened. So much for a quiet escape.

I made my way back down to the first floor and took a seat. The receptionist caught my eye and gave me a quizzical look, but turned back to his newspaper. Twenty minutes later a haggard looking woman wearing a white lab coat approached.

"Mr. Slade?" she asked. The smile on her face didn't reach her eyes as she shook my hand in greeting. Without waiting for me to reply she pressed on. "We're very worried about Maggie. If you'd follow me."

"Worried? I know she got bumped around pretty good," I said.

"It's not that," she waved a card across an electronic sensor as she held the fourth-floor button down. For her, it illuminated and the elevator started to rise. "How long has Maggie been anorexic?"

"I don't think she is," I said.

"Your sister is five-foot two-inches and weighs eighty-five pounds," she replied. "There are few other explanations."

"I see," I said. "Is she awake?"

Hornbeck closed her eyes and shook her head affirmatively. "She's asking for you. Mr. Slade. You need to understand; her body is eating itself trying to keep her alive. If we hadn't intervened when we did, she would most likely be dead. As it is, I'm surprised to discover her organs are in as good a shape as they are. She needs help, Mr. Slade. Anorexia is a serious disorder and one that most don't easily recover from. Your denial is not helpful."

"Is she eating?" I asked.

Hornbeck sighed, leading me from the elevator through a short lobby and past an unmanned, glassed-in reception counter that would have looked at home in a police station. "She's currently being fed intravenously."

"And asking for food," I finished her sentence. "Doctor, she needs more calories than you're supplying. She also needs protein."

"In her shape, her stomach would not be able to process food in any volume."

"That's true if she was anorexic," I said. "Maggie suffers from a rare, as yet, unnamed condition. Her body burns through calories at a rate beyond anything you've ever seen."

Hornbeck stopped me in the hallway, placing her hand on my elbow to turn me. "You can't be sucked into this, Mr. Slade. According to Maggie, you're her only family. She needs your help and without it she will die. You cannot be drawn in to her fantasies."

"I'll do everything I can for my sister, but you're not listening," I said. "What is the next level of food once you get past intravenous?"

"Depends on the patient," she said. "But in her case, I'd consider a nutritionally balanced, liquid shake."

"Try her," I said. "If she can't hold it down, I'll do whatever you ask."

"She can't."

"Only if you're right," I said.

Behind Hornbeck, someone pounded on a locked door. The sound muffling in this place was pretty good, but I heard Maggie's voice and she wasn't happy.

"I'll allow eight ounces," she said.

"Sixteen," I negotiated, refusing to use my compulsion.

"She can't possibly … fine, sixteen. But then you'll work with me." Hornbeck turned and unlocked the door.

Maggie sat on a bed, dressed in scrubs instead of a gown. I had to agree with Hornbeck on one thing, Maggie looked terrible, her face sunken and gaunt, shoulder bones poking up into the fabric. She glowered at Hornbeck, but smiled when she saw me.

"Get me out of here, Felix," Maggie implored, opening her arms for a hug.

"You nearly killed yourself," I said. "You weren't supposed to come."

"Gabriella followed the team in," she said. "I couldn't let her go by herself."

"How are you feeling, Maggie?" Hornbeck asked louder than necessary and ignoring our conversation.

"Hungry. I asked for real food hours ago and you still have me on this," she said, pointing to a translucent bag.

"Felix suggested we try you on something a little more substantial. Do you feel up to trying a shake?" Hornbeck asked.

"I'm up for steak and pizza!" Maggie retorted.

"We talked about this, Maggie," Hornbeck replied. "Your stomach can't possibly process complex food yet. We need to train it slowly."

"Tell her, Felix," Maggie said. "She won't believe me."

"Vanilla or chocolate?" I asked. Hornbeck was already being pushed further than she was comfortable.

"I'll take three of both," she said petulantly.

"Chocolate," I answered for her. "Bring two, just in case."

"If she can keep one down for thirty minutes, we can try a

second," Hornbeck answered, walking out the door, locking it behind her.

"You look pretty good," Maggie said. "What's with the bunny shirt?"

"Gift shop."

She growled. "You have to get me out of here. I'm starving."

"Let's play this out a little," I said. "I already broke me and Lace out. This floor has better security; might be best if we have Hornbeck's cooperation."

"She's a fucking zealot," Maggie lamented just as Hornbeck re-entered the room, carrying two plastic bottles.

"I take the lives of my patients very seriously," Hornbeck answered Maggie's jab. "Maggie, I'm the only thing between you and death right now. I know you don't believe me, but I've seen far too many young women die of this horrible disease. I don't care if you hate me if it means you get better."

"She doesn't hate you, doc," I said. "She just doesn't like being locked up."

Hornbeck nodded and uncapped one of the bottles, handing it to Maggie. She opened a cabinet on the wall and pulled out an empty plastic container. "When she gets sick, use this."

Hornbeck left the room as Maggie greedily drained the first bottle. "Oh, hey, this stuff is pretty good." She wiped her lips, holding the bottle up so she could read the label. She shook her head, annoyed, and handed the bottle to me. "Figure out if we can order this stuff."

"How long have you known Jardeep?" I asked.

"I don't know him," Maggie said.

"You sure seemed to at breakfast," I said.

"Okay, I know his name," she answered. "But that's about it. I just know he had something to do with trying to capture Mom."

"Why would the FBI do that?"

"Take her? Because she was too powerful. They're scared of her," she said.

"Are? Present tense? Level with me, Maggie. Is Mom still alive?"

"You know Hornbeck is listening to us." She pointed to a camera in the corner of the room. "I'll tell you what I know, but not here - and I'm having that other shake."

I knew better than to stop her and watched as she gulped down the second bottle, throwing it into the trash thirty seconds later. "I'm serious. Get me a case of that stuff. I'm in love."

Maggie stretched out on the bed, inclining the head and exaggeratingly patting her rounded belly. I hoped she wouldn't throw up, as it would set us back with Hornbeck.

"I'll ask her if she can arrange that," I said.

We waited for better than forty minutes, making small talk until Hornbeck finally returned.

"I gotta pee," Maggie said, grabbing the IV bottle's stand and walking to the door-less bathroom. Maggie had never been one for clothing and before I could look away, she'd dropped her pants to the floor. "What, you still think I'm gonna throw it all up?"

"No," Hornbeck agreed. "Clearly, you're keeping it down."

"Bring me two more and I'll do the same," Maggie said.

"If you do that again for dinner tonight, I'll have you moved to solid food in the morning," Hornbeck said.

"You don't get it," Maggie complained. "I'm ready to eat *now*. I have a condition and I'm telling you, I've already burned through those first two."

"Those bottles are three hundred calories each. You couldn't possibly take any more today. The shape you're in, you haven't ingested more than five hundred calories in a day for months."

"Has Maggie presented any other symptoms of anorexia?" I asked.

"Her interview was inconclusive," Hornbeck said.

"Under whose authority was she admitted to this floor?" I asked.

"Emergency room," Hornbeck answered. "We were called in for consultation."

"Where based on Maggie's body shape, you made the right call to get her help," I said. "Maggie is an adult and has the right to decline services."

"Not if she's incompetent."

"Is it your judgement that she's incompetent?"

"This isn't something you want to get wrong," she said.

"If you can't hold me, I'm leaving," Maggie said. "Although, could you write me a prescription for those shakes?"

"Would you really use them?" Hornbeck asked hopefully.

"They're amazing," Maggie said, overselling.

Hornbeck pulled a business card from her pocket along with her script pad. "Call me anytime, day or night, Maggie Slade."

"That's it?" Maggie asked.

"I'd like to run tests for food allergies," she said. "Make an appointment with my office. Your interest in the liquid formula makes me think your rejection of normal food might be due to external factors."

"You're saying I'm not nuts?" Maggie asked.

"That's not fair to say," Hornbeck chided gently. "This is real, Maggie. You can't ignore it."

The expression in Maggie's face softened, something I hadn't seen very often, and she hugged a surprised Hornbeck. "I'll be okay. I promise."

KITCHEN WITCH

"I need food," Maggie said as we pulled away from the hospital.

As promised, Sheriff Merritt had arranged to have my truck returned and Gabriella had driven back to the hospital to pick us up in it.

"I need real food." This time it was a full-on whine from the back seat. "Chicken fingers and waffles, or tacos. Crap, I don't care, just greasy and lots of it."

"Aren't you concerned for your health?" Gabriella asked, merging with the busy afternoon traffic. "I have fruit in the cooler right next to you."

Maggie lifted the lid and pulled out a plump peach and immediately gnawed on it. "Not enough calories in fruit," she said between bites. "But thanks, this is delicious. Better in pie, but I like it."

Gabriella rolled her eyes and I pointed at a fast food burger restaurant I wouldn't generally consider. Ten minutes later, a very happy Maggie had a bag full of burgers.

"We might have a problem at the shop," Gabriella said as we drove into downtown. The parking spaces, which weren't normally difficult to find, were all full and people milled about in front of Judy's shop.

"What's going on?" I asked.

"Started this morning," Gabriella said. "They're looking for help."

"For?"

"Word's gotten around that the books from Eppy were cursed," she said.

"Did she try salt water?" I asked.

"Yes, but the kids are distraught," she said. "I don't think the salt water is helping everyone."

"Not if they've had them for very long," I said. "The curse will have transferred by now, especially if the kids were actively working with those books."

Gabriella finally found parking several blocks away. We got out and I stood at the back of the truck, looking for clothing.

"I'm going to need to shop for clothes soon. Between Maggie and Lace, I'm scraping bottom." Gabriella helped me pull the bunny t-shirt from the hospital off and replace it with one of my own.

"Word is Asheville has great shopping," I said. "We could run over tomorrow."

"Tempting," Gabriella answered. "But I'd rather stick closer to home."

"I got this," I said, pulling out my phone. "It's going to cost you. There are two dress shops on the square and Luana is friends with both of the owners. I'd be surprised if they didn't have your exact size, but I know they both custom fit their clothing."

"No ..." Gabriella started to object, but I'd already dialed Luana.

"Hello, dear," Luana answered. She couldn't have recognized the number and I doubted she knew exactly who was calling, but she was a savvy witch and would feel a close connection before picking up.

"How busy are you today?" I asked.

"Felix. I was just planning to run over to the hospital and visit. Are you out?"

"You know me, not a big fan of institutions," I said.

"Understandable. The girls and I are working in the garden. The Creeping Jenny is bad this year," she said. In the background, I heard Estelle's voice.

"Is that Felix? Tell him we're bringing him flowers and too bad if he thinks it's girlie," she said.

"You get that?" Luana asked, chuckling.

"I did," I answered. "Tell Bug that no self-respecting man ever turns down flowers from a pretty girl."

"I will, but why do I feel you have an adventure in mind that is more intriguing than weeding and picking flowers?" she asked.

"Gabriella is running short on clothing, but she doesn't want to go all the way over to Asheville," I said. "Neither Maggie nor Lace have anything at all. I thought you'd know how to solve this."

"Let me make some calls," she said. "Get back to you on this number?"

"I'll text you Gabriella's. I'll warn you though, she's a little hesitant and might need a nudge." We'd been walking as I talked and I steered Gabriella and Maggie into the alley behind Judy's shop.

"Leave that to me," Luana said. "Where are you now?"

"Judy's shop," I said.

"Perfect. We'll be there in twenty minutes," she said and hung up.

"Aren't you just the little busy-body," Maggie said. "I'm not going. I'd rather stick needles in my eyes than go shopping."

Two men stepped from the shadows where they'd been leaning against the bricks in the alley behind Judy's shop.

"Can I help you with something?" I asked, recognizing the clothing style of the Eppy residents.

"We're looking for a girl," the taller of the two said.

I chuckled ruefully and couldn't help my reply. "Awfully far from the coast for shore leave, don't you think?"

"I dun know what you're talking about, but if you're being cute, I'm not amused," the man replied, his slight Scottish accent bleeding through.

"What would yeh have me think, laddie?" I asked, attempting a brogue of my own. I didn't think I totally sucked at it.

"Felix," Gabriella chastised in a harsh whisper.

"You need to move on," I said in a more serious tone.

"Lace Faa." The big one stepped toward us threateningly. "We won't take kindly to anyone harboring her."

"Lace is a friend of mine," I said. "And I don't think she's interested in either of you. She's always struck me as more interested in folks from the bathes-regularly club. From the looks of things, you lost your membership cards a few years back."

Whoop, whoop. The short sound of a siren caused me to jump, despite my attempt at maintaining a level of machismo.

"Got a real smart mouth on you, *friend*," the taller speaker said. "Not for nothing, we'll take this conversation up later. Let's go, Phil." The two walked around us and as casually as is possible when being stared at by police, walked to the other end of the alley.

"Everything okay here?" I turned, expecting to see Sheriff Merritt, but instead saw one of his deputies in an ordinary cruiser.

"I think so, officer," I said. "Not sure why those men were loitering behind Judy's shop."

"How do you know Judy?" he asked, pulling on his wide brimmed hat.

"Stepmother," I said. "We're in town visiting."

"Right. Aaron said something about that. You were out at Eppy?" he asked.

"That's us," I said.

He tipped his hat and then removed it. "I'll let you be on about your business." He slid into his cruiser and gave us a friendly wave as he rolled down the alley.

"Lace was right," Gabriella said. "I can't believe they're on to her already."

"Right about what? They didn't seem like admirers," Maggie said.

"Lace mentioned there might be trouble from Eppy," I said. "People who think she'll try to make a leadership claim."

"They really take that royalty thing seriously," Gabriella said.

"I guess so." I pulled at the shop's back door and was surprised to find it locked. A twist of my finger rolled the simple deadbolt back and I pulled it open. The normally bright work area sat in gloom and it took a moment for my eyes to adjust.

Seated in Gia's overstuffed recliner was Lace, her casted leg raised. The spicy scent of a healing poultice cut thickly through the room and stirred memories from times not so long ago.

"There you are," Gia said, stirring the contents of a tall pot over a gas flame. "I had a feeling we'd be seeing you shortly."

"I didn't think you locked the back door during business hours," I said. "What's up with the shades on the windows? Your plants are going to have trouble growing."

"Got a visit from some of those Dark Folk looking for Lace," she said. "Never seen anything like it. One minute she was sitting on the stool making change, the next she was gone. Never seen anyone move that fast before. I didn't even see her go. Good thing she did, too, they were a scruffy bunch. Judy had to push on them to get them to leave. I thought I was going to have to call the sheriff."

"I need to leave. I'll let them know I don't want anything to do with their stupid town," Lace said. "If I don't, someone will get hurt."

"What's to stop them from hurting you?" I asked.

"It's not your fight," she said.

Gia pulled a strip of fabric from her pot. "It is now. Evil men have been hurting our kind for centuries. Witches will stand with our sisters."

"Wizards, too," I said quietly.

"Yes, and wizards," Gia answered, chuckling as she carried the steaming fabric she'd pulled from the pot. "Now lie back and stop your yammering. This will sting from the heat, but trust in old Gia. We'll fix you up, right as rain."

Lace flinched as Gia lay the fabric on her cheek, but to her credit, didn't respond further.

"Do you have anything to eat around here?" Maggie asked. She'd been standing quietly, observing our conversation so far.

"Judy said Felix had a sister in town, but I couldn't hardly believe it," Gia said. "You smell of magic, child."

"I'd like to smell of pizza," Maggie replied.

Gabriella chuckled. "Perhaps I'll go help Judy. It sounds busy out there."

"Order a pizza, Maggie," I said, pulling out my credit card. There would be a financial reckoning when we got back home, but for now, we were in survival mode. "I'm going to help Gabriella."

"We'll be dealing with your chest first, my boy," Gia said.

"What about the books?" I asked.

Gia pursed her lips and shook her head. "Nothing to be done about it. They've waited this long, another fifteen minutes won't hurt them. Now take off your shirt and lie on the couch."

I knew better than to argue. Gabriella slipped through the curtains into the front of the shop as I gingerly removed my shirt. The next fifteen minutes would suck, but I knew it wouldn't be without gain.

I hissed through clenched teeth as Gia removed the dressing from my chest, crusty with dried blood.

"Cutworms and aphid droppings. A demon did this?" Gia asked, her ebony face flushing.

"A ghrelin possessed one of the Dark Folk," I said.

"Its name is Phezore," Lace said.

"Hush child, never speak the name of a demon," Gia reprimanded.

"It is one of its three names," she answered.

"You know its real name?" I asked.

"I do, but I don't believe it knows that," she said.

"I thought you vanquished it, Felix," Gia said.

"That's what they say."

"Best not speak of it." Gia carried a steaming plateful of poultice laden cloth strips. I felt like screaming as she laid the cloths across my wounded chest. For the next minute or two, I focused on ignoring the pain as the boiling rags were laid out. "There, now. That wasn't so bad, was it?" she asked, brushing my hair from my forehead. Her hand was cool to the touch and a small amount of energy was transferred. Tears had run from my eyes and I blinked to clear my vision. Gia had long ago learned that I could take extremes of cold and heat. She preferred to give me the dressings without cooling them first.

"I have missed you, Gia, but dang, was that entirely necessary?" I asked.

"Magic doesn't work if the flesh is cool," she said. "Just the way it has to be." She laid wide gauze across the strips and followed up with a few pieces of tape.

"There were a couple of men at the back door when we arrived," I said. "We'll need to be careful about using it."

"We'll keep it locked," she said. "I'd best get back out front, though."

I didn't know if it was Gia's healing or the fact that I was grateful not to have boiling rags being dropped on my chest, but I found it easier to pull my t-shirt on. After which, I pushed my way through the curtains and into the public portion of the store.

"Felix. Good," Judy said, looking harried. The store was full of people, mostly parents with their children. "I need you to meet Wanda and Max. My apologies … just a minute." She held her finger up to the person she'd been talking to. "I think they're on the front porch."

"Wanda and Max," I said. "Got it."

Weaving my way through a knot of people, I caught Gabriella's eye and was rewarded with a smile.

"Books in the tub." Gabriella pointed at the floor as a worried father entered holding his eight or nine-year-old son by the hand. The boy clutched a colorful book in the other hand. On the ground, next to the front door, a wash tub, no doubt filled with saltwater, sat atop towels.

"Here?" The father asked, looking skeptical.

"Eppy Faire book?" I picked up the conversation Gabriella had started so she could continue to ring up the quickly moving merchandise.

"Is that what everyone is here for?" he asked.

"Mind if I look?" I asked, pointing at the book the boy held.

"Won't that ruin it?" the boy asked.

"Saltwater, yes," I said. "Looking, no."

"But … " The boy started to argue, but the father was having nothing to do with it and pulled the book away, handing it to me.

'Toads and Tree Frogs: Amphibious Creatures in Your Back Yard' was the title. The colorful book had cartoon pictures on the front cover. I felt a small jolt of energy as I touched it. Opening the book, I discovered the content was just as the title suggested.

"It's just a kid's book, but he won't let it out of his sight. My friend said ... well ... you heard what happened out at Eppy Faire, right?" The dad asked.

"One minute," I said pulling out my sunglasses. I'd never tried planar view with sunglasses, but I wasn't about to show the entirety of Crabtree Valley my glowing eyes. "*Altum Visu*" I incanted and held the book in front of me. It had been infected with the ghrelin's curse, but it was very weak. I looked back to the boy who had small splotches of the curse all over his hands, mouth, eyes and legs. "Nothing to be done about it." Before the boy could argue, I dunked the book into the saltwater bath. A small hiss was the only evidence of the dissipation of the spell and I was suddenly grateful that I wasn't wearing rings again, as I'd have ruined them.

"That's it?" the man asked. "What a joke. I'm not paying for this. All you did was dunk his book in water."

"*Finis*." I released my wizard's sight. "Salt water," I corrected. "I don't need to be paid. I would, however, recommend giving your son a saltwater bath tonight. If he feels a compulsion toward death or book fairs, I'd come back and talk to Judy."

"I knew this was going to be a bunch of crap," he said.

I fished his book from the water and held it out to him. The book's curse had dissipated in the water. My best guess was that Willum had cursed some of the books simply so they'd keep kids interested until he could hook them with a real spell book.

"No!" He jerked his hand away from the proffered book. "You crazy bastard, do you think I'm stupid?"

"I have you pegged as an asshole and a cheapskate," I said. "Stupid would have been to ignore the problem. All in, though, I'm thinking not father-of-the-year finalist."

"I'm an asshole?" he started to talk louder. "You're the asshole."

"No argument from me," I said and pushed past him to the open door. Once outside, my eyes fell on who I immediately knew to be Wanda and Max. The plain looking woman wore a black peasant skirt and simple cotton shirt. The boy sat on the boardwalk and rocked back and forth, clutching a leather-bound book in his hands.

"Wanda? Max?" I asked as I approached.

"You were in the tent," she said. "I recognize you."

I furrowed my brows, not expecting to being called out in public.

"You were there? Are you a practitioner?" I asked.

"I am no one of special importance," she answered, holding her hand out cautiously for me to shake. I noticed she wore a wide, ornately carved, leather bracelet, effectively denying me access to her wrist - which I wouldn't have tried either way.

"Judy asked me to visit with you," I said. "How is it you think we might help?"

"I am wiccan," she said. "I don't mean to stir up trouble with Judy. I have respect for her, even though we have chosen different paths." I considered her words for a moment. Some of the covens around Leotown were wiccan, which meant they intermingled a religious component into their craft. Judy seemed to get along with them and I wasn't sure why Wanda was being careful.

"Your respect is appreciated. Is this Max?" I asked, not interested in pursuing the conversation.

"I should have known better," she said. "He found it at Eppy several weeks ago in their bargain books. It's my fault. I was greedy and believed we'd found an overlooked text. He loved it so much and I was thrilled to finally be sharing a part of myself with him." Guilty tears poured from the woman's eyes.

"Max, would you mind talking to me about your book?" I asked gently, sitting on the boardwalk in front of him, careful not to appear threatening.

"It's mine," he said. "You can't have it."

"Want to see something cool?" I asked. "It's real magic."

He looked at me skeptically. "Like what?"

"Well, I'm a lot like you," I said. "I came into my magic when I was about your age, but I didn't have very good control. Now I'm a lot better with it. Want to see a magic lantern?"

His eyes grew wide. "Here?"

"I'd prefer it if you and your mom came into the shop. We have a private area in the back. I bet she's already told you that we

214

don't show people our magic," I said.

"Because they get scared," he said.

"Or angry," I agreed. "They might try to put you in jail. Do you mind coming in, Wanda?" I looked at the woman.

"If it is approved by Mistress Judy," she said.

"I think you've misread her," I said. "If you don't approach her with hostility, I can't fathom she cares a bit if you're in the shop."

"But we're different," she said.

"Then why did you come?" I asked.

"Because I'm nothing more than a kitchen witch," she said, as fresh tears popped out onto her cheeks. "I can't help him."

I took a deep breath. I wasn't about to fix this woman and her prejudices. "I already have permission to bring you back. Mistress Judy recognizes these are special times and that we must band together for the greater good. We even sought help from a Christian pastor."

She gasped. "You didn't. Christians have always persecuted us. How could you?"

"I met the pastor. He is a gentle, kind man as well as a true believer. Without magic, that man walks in more power than I've seen before. What better man to protect a child from a demon?"

"Demons are a Christian construct," she spat.

"I'm tired, Wanda," I said. "I would very much like to help you and Max, but I have no interest in a religious debate."

Max broke the stalemate as the two of us stared at each other. "Mother, I'd like to see the magic. Please?"

She sighed. "Yes. Of course. I'm sorry."

"It is a stressful time for everyone," I said and led them into the shop which had started to empty. Apparently, Luana had walked right past me, because she was leaning against the counter talking with Gabriella. Her eldest, Estelle, stood next to Gabriella, perfectly mimicking her every move.

"Heya, Bug," I said, tussling her hair on my way past.

"Hi, Max," Estelle said, ignoring me and blushing. For his part, Max ignored her.

"What's that smell?" Max asked as we entered the private

portion of the shop.

"You've a good nose, Max," I said. "That's a special concoction my dear Gia uses to torture me with."

"Really?" he asked, immediately concerned.

"Sorry, bad choice of words," I said. "It's for healing poultices and I'm not a big fan."

"Are you really going to show me magic?"

"First one is free," I said, bringing my magical lantern to life.

"That's amazing!" Max's response was so heartfelt that I couldn't help but show off further.

"*Adoloret*." I shaped a hollow sphere of flame and tossed it toward the refrigerator, where it broke apart, leaving behind a small scorch mark.

"Wicked!" he approved.

"Did you learn cool spells from your book too?" I asked.

"You're trying to trick me," he said.

"I showed you what I can do," I said. "It's only fair."

"I can find dead things," he said. "Like bugs or mice."

He opened his book and I pulled my sunglasses off for a better view.

"Your eyes are glowing," he said.

I winked at him. "Best not to mess with a wizard," I said. "Now go ahead."

The ghrelin's curse was all over the book as well as Max. It wasn't anywhere near as bad as Petaluma, but was considerably worse than the kid with the frog book. When he started to read, it became clear why he struggled with the magic - his ability to form the words was poor. My guess was he was a struggling reader, perhaps the best genetic gift he could have received, given the circumstances. A small trail of energy reached out from him to the cabinet beneath the sink and he got up and followed it, pulling out a dead cockroach.

"You have some of your mother's talent," I said. "But you're struggling. This book fights your mother's magic." I was implying a connection between the two ideas, even though there wasn't one. A wiccan would have no room for necromancy and the boy clearly had no real talent for it.

"What are you saying?" Wanda asked.

"You need to train him," I said. Max picked up on it and looked at his mother sharply.

"But he's a boy," she said.

"He has talent, but *this* is the wrong book for him. Would it be so hard to show him the spells you weave in the kitchen?" I asked.

"It's not done."

"I know several male witches," I said. "Some very powerful. I'm here to tell you it is a small sacrifice for ridding your house of this book of necromancy."

"Necromancy?" She all but started crying again. "Yes. I'll show him." She pulled the boy to her chest and clung to him.

"Max. Do you want to chase bugs all your life or would you rather like to learn the secrets your mother has? I bet she has much to teach you," I said.

"I can't give up my ... book." He looked to his mother wistfully.

"This won't be easy for him," I said. "Hell, it won't be easy for me, but I'm willing to help you break this if you'll swear to train him."

"I swear," she said.

I stuck my hand out to her and she accepted it, even when I reached past her and grabbed her wrist. The leather bracelet provided a weak shield which I easily pushed through. She was telling the truth and I released before either of us could get in any real trouble.

"What about her?" Wanda asked, noticing the sleeping form of Lace in Gia's chair.

"Let's stay focused, shall we?" I asked, grabbing a bottle of salt from the cupboard and poured it in a circle big enough for me to kneel in. "Wanda, I want you to hold Max right there. Max, I need you to hand me your book."

"Will you give it back?"

"If you want it when we're done, it's yours. Deal?" I asked. This was the moment where everything could fall apart. Max might be a slow reader, but that didn't mean he didn't have his mother's propensity to witchcraft. It wouldn't take a very strong witch to see through my deception. Certainly, Petaluma would never have fallen for it.

I nodded solemnly as he handed the book to me. "Promise?" he asked, holding on.

"Promise. All yours if you still want it," I said.

He shrugged and let go. The energy trail between Max and the book wasn't particularly strong, but it was evident. After placing the book on the floor in front of me, I closed my eyes and reached out for energy, pushing down into the earth as I'd been doing more and more recently. As I mingled with Gia and Judy's energy, I smiled, their signatures as familiar as their favorite perfumes. The energy was nowhere near as strong as what I'd found in the sleepy mountain, but was there nonetheless.

"*Sphaera*." I invoked the spell circle and a translucent sphere formed around me. Max writhed in his mother's arms as the weak stream of magic between him and the book was cut off. He threw his head back and thrashed as the stream poured from his body and battered against the sphere. His addicted little soul fought for its magical fix and he bucked free from his mother, jumping toward me on the floor, contacting the edge of the sphere and rebounding.

"*Adoloret*." I channeled the energy I'd gathered from below through the wand and into the book. The curse first fought against me, then reached out and spread itself over the surface of the translucent sphere, searching for a way back to its host. I pushed more energy into the book, attempting to burn out the curse. A thumping sound caught my attention as Max wailed on the sphere with his small fists, trying to break through. The sickly green energy stream looked like an alien erupting from his chest, trying to rejoin the book through the impenetrable spell circle wall.

Finally, the edge of the book smoldered and I redoubled my efforts. The curse gave up its quest to link back with the boy and reached around, grabbing me unexpectedly. My throat burned and I struggled for breath as tendrils encircled my neck. Panic welled up in me as I started to wonder if I would have enough reserve to burn it out before I ran out of oxygen.

The edges of my vision darkened and I knew my method was too slow. I wouldn't make it if I didn't change my tactics immediately. I dropped the fire spell and pulled at the oak leaf around my neck as I toppled to the ground. With my remaining strength, I pushed the leaf beneath the tendrils of the curse. Immediately, they retracted and beautiful air once again filled my lungs.

"Shit," I said and looked outside of the circle. Lace had awakened. She, Judy, and Gia all stared at me with concern. Max sobbed, although I considered it good that he was conscious.

With the oak leaf in hand, I cast the shield spell, "*Scutum!*" With my free hand, I shaped the shield, causing it to envelop the smoldering book. I pushed harder, crumpling my fingers as if crushing a tin can. The book began to deform beneath my shield and I pushed even harder, willing more and more energy from my body. I was running out and would not have enough to finish it off. A desperate thought spurred me to action and I pushed my foot across the salt ring, breaking the spell circle.

All at once the noise of the shop found me. Everyone in the room seemed to be talking to me all at once, but I ignored them and reached down into the earth, pulling at the energy I'd found only a few minutes before. It was so sparse that for a moment, I thought all was lost. Finally, I found a small eddy and with a final flourish, I closed my fist, crushing the book into a fine powder.

PINCH OF SALT

"What were you thinking?" Judy asked, annoyed. "You locked yourself into a spell circle with a cursed artifact?"

Judy and Gia helped me onto the couch next to Max's shell-shocked mother. Gia handed me a steaming cup of tea and I got a light whiff of the pungent scent of valerian root - a sedative. I noticed Wanda also had a cup in her hands which she hadn't touched.

"You lied." Max looked up at me from the floor, where he was picking through the remains of his book. His cheeks were tear-stained and I vaguely remembered that he'd been pulled off me while I battled with the book's curse.

"It was a miscalculation," I said, ignoring Max. "Lane's oak leaf saved me. Good news is I have some idea how to attack it now."

"You said I could have the book back," Max pushed. "I hate you and I hate her!" He pointed to his mother who was sitting still on the couch.

"Hard lesson, kid," I said.

"Your shirt," Lace said, hobbling back to her chair.

I looked down and rolled my eyes, I was leaking either poultice or the stuff behind it and Gia would no doubt be prompted to reapply the dressing.

"I don't know how to thank you," Wanda said weakly from the couch.

I gave her a wan smile, my energy level allowing for nothing more. "Removing this demon's blight from Crabtree Valley is the objective. I'm just glad you came."

Wanda sucked in air when I said the word 'demon,' but to her credit, she kept her objections to herself and smiled. I considered it progress.

"I'll see you out," Gia said. "Felix needs his rest."

"Of course," Wanda said, standing. "Max. We're going, get up. You need to apologize to Mr. Slade."

"Never," Max hissed.

"The curse was a compulsion. It's not reasonable to expect his gratitude," I said. "Someday he'll understand. But I think today is probably not that day."

Wanda gave me a hard look. She didn't appreciate my advice on child rearing and struggled to bite back a reprimand.

Gia, always quick to understand, gently guided the woman from the room, with Max right behind her. Just before he cleared the curtains, Max looked back at me and saluted me quietly with his middle finger.

"Making friends, as always," Judy said. "I have two more like Max. I'll ask them to come back tomorrow."

"Not necessary," I said. "Give me an hour and I'll be ready to go. I wasted a lot of energy, but I think I have it figured out as long as they're not as bad as Petaluma."

"I don't think so. Max was the worst we've seen today," she said.

The smell of garlic caught my attention just before Maggie sauntered back through the curtains, carrying three large boxes of pizza and laying them on a folding project table. I hadn't had much to eat and gratefully snagged a slice.

"Smells good for convenience store pizza," Maggie observed, biting into a steaming hot piece.

"How many calories do you think you've eaten today?" I asked.

"Five thousand, give or take," she said. "You'd think I'd gain weight faster; best I can do is a pound or so a week. I'd like to be closer to eight thousand, but it's hard to eat that much."

"This should do it," I said, biting through the thick layer of toppings.

"So good," Maggie agreed, eating a piece that was bigger than her hand. I pulled my phone out and snapped a picture of her and shot it off to Dr. Hornbeck.

"I thought we were going to lose you in that spell circle," Lace said, falling heavily into a metal chair at the table. "You sure take a lot of risks. Aren't you worried that's going to catch up to you?"

"Sometimes, but what was I supposed to do? That kid was enthralled," I said. "You know as well as I do that longer exposure is more damaging."

Lace picked up a piece of pizza and gave me a withering glare. "You won't be able to help anyone if you're dead."

"At least Gabriella wasn't here to witness it," I said.

"I wanted to talk to you about her," Lace said.

I grabbed a second piece. "Shoot."

"Was she serious about helping me find a place to live in Leotown?"

"We both are," I said.

"Why would you do that? I've been nothing but trouble for you," she said. "Besides, I have no real skills."

"I lost my family when I was young," I said. "If it hadn't been for Judy and Gia, I'd be in jail, or worse. I want to honor that legacy of helping without expecting something in return."

"I bring baggage," she said.

"Do you think your clan will hunt you all the way out to Leotown? It's fifteen hundred miles from here."

"Not right away. They want to end my bloodline, especially with Willum and Ma gone now. When I was younger, they left us alone because Ma was a drunk and Willum was nothing more than an incompetent ranch hand. But Willum scared 'em."

"I don't see how they blame you for that," Maggie said. "That's dumb."

Lace turned her glare on Maggie. "Says the woman who all but killed herself to save her brother. Family means something and the Dark Folk understand that. They can't leave me alive."

"Doesn't change anything for us," I said. "Gabriella survived a culling of her own coven. She knows what she's getting into. So does Judy. You'd be safe with either of them."

"I'm not staying this close to Eppy Faire," Lace said with finality. "If I didn't have this broken leg, I'd have disappeared and left you all in peace."

"I'm glad you didn't," I said. "Come to Leotown with us and

help Gabriella rebuild her coven. Be part of something important, Lace."

"You make it sound too good to be true," she said. "Like a fairy tale."

"If, by fairy tale, you mean the kind where monsters keep trying to eat you and Felix makes it sound like we're doing something noble," Maggie said. "Our last go-round had us fighting werewolves and wicked witches. Don't buy his line that you'll be safer in Leotown."

"Help me clean up, would you, Maggie?" I wasn't about to argue with her and Lace needed time to think.

After sweeping up the remnants of my encounter with Max's book, I formed another circle with salt and struck a meditative pose in the center. I'd much rather have been in the forest or on the side of the mountain, but I had two more books to work on and I needed to regenerate.

Some time later, I opened my eyes. From a slit in the curtains I observed the sun, low in the sky. Given the season, I calculated it must be past seven in the evening.

Judy sat on the couch reading and smiled as I acknowledged her and broke my circle.

"I've sent everyone back to the cabin," she said. "Gabriella didn't want to leave you, but I convinced her to look after Lace."

"What of the other two kids?" I asked.

"They're waiting in the shop. You don't have to do this tonight," she said. "We tried the salt bath, but it didn't work - even after a few hours. Cleansing the book looked like it was hard on the girls."

"The curse probably fed on them to protect itself," I said.

"I don't like that it's so strong," she said.

"It really isn't that strong. It's the kid's own power that nurtures it. The curse simply directs them," I said. "There's no way Max is a necromancer. The book perverted whatever purpose he really has."

"Do you think that's the same with Petaluma?" Judy asked, hopefully.

I couldn't lie to Judy. "No. She rode a corpse that was a thousand miles away. I didn't even know that was possible. She's taken to necromancy so readily because it's her gift."

"What if the ghrelin was helping her, adding to her power?"

"Could have been, but Luma sent the first corpse from her bedroom. She was warning me to stay away," I said. "Doesn't seem like the sort of thing the ghrelin would have been interested in doing."

"It's going to be hard on Dolly," Judy said. "She's not prepared for a necromancer. Do you think we'll be able to break the book away from her?"

"I do, but Dolly isn't going to like it," I said.

"How so?"

"We can't approach this as breaking her from her gift. She's a smart girl; she'll understand the idea of the curse even though she'll fight against it. She has to know she'll be accepted," I said.

"How?"

"I'll give her one of my books," I said.

Judy's eyes dilated at my suggestion. "But what if ..."

"What if she becomes a powerful necromancer? What if she learns things she wouldn't have otherwise known?" I asked. "She wants that knowledge and she's not about to give up her book. Judy, I don't think any of us can successfully take that book without doing serious harm to her. She has to agree, if only subconsciously."

"She'll never agree, that's the compulsion of the curse," Judy argued.

"Luma should be here for this," I said. "Let her see firsthand what these curses are doing. I've talked to her; she understands the danger at some level. We need to show her what it's really doing."

"I'll call Dolly," she said. "Change your shirt. Gabriella left you another one."

I looked down. The poultice had soaked through the shirt and looked disgusting. It was a painful few moments as I pulled the shirt off over my head. I knew better than to expect immediate results and I wondered if what I was seeing was better or worse. From my vantage point, all I could see was bright-red skin beneath stitching thread as I washed my chest with a soapy cloth.

Movement caught my attention through the small window over the sink. The two men who'd confronted us in the alley were climbing into a beat-up pickup truck that had just pulled into a parking spot on the opposite side of the street from the shop.

I pulled the shirt on that Gabriella had purchased for me. A sand colored, button-up, the fabric had a rough texture, although not unpleasant. Not having to pull something over my head was definitely a bonus. The shirt felt quite a bit more expensive than any t-shirt I owned. I hastily applied a larger than usual patch of gauze over each wound and taped them well before buttoning up. I'd love to be able to save the shirt, for once.

A second glance through the window proved that the Eppy Faire boys were intent on keeping watch. They were still sitting across from the shop and I was afraid it was going to be up to me to deal with them.

"I'll be back in a second," I said to Judy as I unlocked the front door. "Lock this behind me."

"What's going on, Felix?" Judy asked.

"Men across the street have been hassling Lace. I'm just going to talk," I said.

"Let me call Aaron."

"Just going to talk." I closed the door behind me.

"You got a problem, Slim?" the tall, red-haired, mouthy man asked, stepping out of the passenger's side of the truck.

I stood a few feet from the truck. "I don't know. Do I?"

He extracted a steel pipe from beneath his seat. "Beat it. This don't concern you."

"That supposed to scare me?" I asked.

"Merl. That's the guy from the tent this morning," the driver said.

"So what?"

"They say he killed Willum."

"That right, boy? You take down Gordon?"

"You guys need to beat it," I said. "We've had enough trouble. Don't need the likes of you sniffing around."

"Hear that, Merl? Slim here thinks we need to beat it," the driver said, egging Merl on.

"She ain't even here. I told you that. Let's get going," Merl said.

"You should listen to Merl. I'd hate to have to do something I'd regret," I said.

The red-haired stranger gave me an assessing look. "Mouth of yours is going to get you in trouble. Lucky you, I've got other matters to attend to."

"Like fixing flats?" I asked.

"What flats?"

"*Adoloret*," I said as quietly as I could manage and fired a narrow jet of flame into the nearest tire. The driver – not as dumb as he looked – scrabbled over the middle passenger and jumped out through Merl's door. I loosed another bolt of fire into the rear tire, lancing a finger sized hole through it.

"Those," I said. "Let me know if you'd like to play for keeps."

"You don't scare me." The red-haired man stalked around the truck, pulling up his shirt in the front to expose a revolver. He placed his hand on the butt.

I twisted my fingers and cocked the pistol's hammer back. "Don't fuck with my family," I said, holding my hand out as if it were a gun.

"Please don't," he begged, pulling his hand away from the butt of the pistol.

"Can't shoot what I can't see," I said. "Spread the word that Lace Faa is my family now. You come for her, it'll be through me."

"We won't be the last," he said. "Your threats won't mean nothing to the others."

"Fair enough. Now, if you'd like to keep your coin purse intact, I'd suggest you get to walking," I said. "If I see anything more than a tow-truck over here, I won't be quite so pleasant. Understood?"

"Let's go," the driver said, turning his friend back to the sidewalk.

"Deliver the message, Merl," I said.

"Yes, sir," he said sarcastically as the three of them hustled away.

"What was that?" Judy asked sternly as I re-entered the shop. "This isn't some western. That guy had a gun."

"They're looking for Lace," I said. "I had to push 'em."

"But a gun? You need to be careful. Aaron could have run them off," she said.

"When is Dolly getting here?" I asked. She wouldn't appreciate me telling her that those boys had brought a gun to a wizard's fight.

"Already here. They came in the back while you were playing cowboy."

"Good. Let's get this done." I nodded at the two mothers. "I'm sorry this is taking so long."

"I don't know," the taller of the two said. "I'm not sure what we're even doing here."

"Yes, you do. You can feel it, sure as you're standing there. And - I'm sorry - what's your name?" I asked, smiling at who I assumed was the woman's pre-teenaged daughter.

"Carla and she's Mia," she answered, indicating the girl a few feet away. "You're not taking my book. I've already told Mom that."

"Well, Carla, I don't plan to take anything. Do you know Petaluma Applebaum?" I asked as Luma slipped through the curtain leading to the back room.

Her eyes were downcast and she refused to make eye contact with the girls who appeared to be of the same age.

Carla shot a glance at her friend. Something I couldn't easily understand was communicated between the two. "You mean freaky Luna-Bomb?" she snickered.

I upped my estimation of her age, definitely a teenager. "Petaluma is my niece," I said. "Calling names isn't very nice."

"You guys are all freaks," Carla continued. "We finally get something cool in this stupid town and everybody's freaking out. I can't believe you dragged us down to spooky Judy's."

"Stop it!" her mother reprimanded.

"*Altum Visu.*" I was satisfied to hear both girls gasp as my eyes illuminated.

"What's wrong with your eyes?" Mia asked. It wasn't fear that prompted her question as much as intense curiosity.

"I'm a wizard," I said as I took in the auras of the girls and their mothers. Mia and her mother both had a small showing of light blue energy. If they wanted to, I suspected they'd have some limited success with magic along the lines of Wanda and her kitchen witchcraft. Making potions, ointments and that sort of thing would be within their grasp. That is, if they had sufficient training, interest and access.

Carla and her mother were as mundane as people could be. Their auras read like their personalities - nothing bad, but in the magical realm, not particularly interesting. A thin thread of energy flowed from Mia to Carla, however, and I immediately understood the problem. They were linked as friends and sustained each other.

"We'll work with you all at once," I said. "Follow me, but if you pick on my niece again, it'll go badly for you."

"Felix," Judy hissed.

"Sorry. I'm not a witch," I said. "I'm not always nice."

Judy stood her ground. "We don't threaten children."

"Fine," I said. "Be nice or I'll make you fall in love with the school janitor."

"Felix!"

I laughed as the girls both gasped.

"Just kidding," I said. "I'll let your moms deal with discipline. Apparently, I lack the subtlety for it and they're clearly doing a bang-up job."

"Beth, are you sure this is safe?" the smaller of the two mothers asked.

"The books aren't safe, ladies," I said, leading them through the curtain. "I'm mostly harmless. Dolly!" I crossed the room and gently hugged her. "I can't believe you're up and moving."

"What happened to her face?" Carla asked. Dolly's face still bore the scars from a few nights ago.

"Petaluma's book exploded," I said. "You girls really have no idea what you're dealing with."

"What do we have to do?" Beth, the taller mother asked.

"Your girls are linked," I said. "Their magic is reinforcing each another, which is why the salt bath was ineffective. I'm going to separate them spiritually."

"You're not getting our books," Carla argued.

"Trust me," I said. "I'll give them back."

"No you won't." Mia replied. I raised an eyebrow. I might have underestimated that one.

"I will. You're right, not like they are now, I won't. Petaluma, would you draw a couple of spell circles for me?" I asked.

"How big?" she asked.

"Big enough to stand in," I answered, handing her a cardboard container of salt. She shrugged and did as I asked, careful not to make eye contact with the two girls. "A circle like this is often used for protection. As circles go, this is very simple, which makes it particularly powerful."

"That doesn't make sense," Carla argued.

"If you understand the purpose of a spell circle, it does," I explained, patiently. "It takes more skill and time to construct complex circles and so they fail more often. The only reason I'm explaining this is so you will understand that what I'm doing is about as safe as things get. Now girls, without stepping on the salt, I'd like each of you to stand in one of those circles, please be careful not to scuff Petaluma's line."

"What are you doing?" Beth asked.

"Nothing scary," I said. "Circles are protection. Remember that."

"That's stupid" Carla said. "This doesn't do anything."

"Right," I said. "Petaluma would you get the lights and a couple of candles, if you please."

As Petaluma turned off the lights, Judy moved a heavy pedestal sporting a six-inch diameter candle between the two girls.

"*Adoloret*." I sent a small globe of flame over to light the wick and was pleased by the look of astonishment both girls threw my way as I revealed more of my magic.

The room took on a much different feeling as the evening's last rays disappeared from the sky. The candle's flickering light illuminated only the two girls, leaving the rest of us in darkness.

"Girls, I would ask that you place your books outside the protective circles."

"No way," Carla immediately objected. "This is stupid."

"It's okay. We will all stay over here. Your books will be safe."

"I don't like it," the smaller girl spoke up. "It feels like a trick."

"Up to you," I said. "I'd just as soon go home and get a beer."

"Girls! Just do it," Beth growled. "I tell you Judy, I've had just about enough of this."

Judy didn't answer and nodded in agreement.

"Fine," Carla grumped and leaned over, placing her book just outside the circle, as far away from the adults as she could get it. Mia looked at me cautiously and when I made no move toward the book, she followed suit.

"Thank you, girls. I apologize in advance for this next bit," I said.

Mia caught my meaning first and started to lean over to pick up her book.

Fortunately for her, she was too late. I snapped my fingers and incanted "*Sphaera!*" Twin translucent bubbles popped to life and just as before, the energy of the curse was cut off from its power.

"What is that?" Beth was suddenly concerned and stood up. "My little girl is trapped."

"The girls are safe. They are not the concern," I said. "The book is. Look at it. It's an evil parasite, trying to get back to its host." I had no idea if the fireworks I was seeing were even slightly visible to the mundane.

"I see it," Mia's mother said. "It's like sludge, trying to crawl up the dome - whatever that is - and get to the girls."

"That's why we needed the protection circle." It was an oversimplification, but I liked a good show as much as the next person.

"How do you stop it?" she asked.

"Turns out your little one, Mia, has the big battery and has been fueling all this. Carla is, well, let's say she doesn't have much going on - magically at least. With the girls protected, the books have nothing to feed on, especially when I do this.

"*Scutum.*" I wrapped Carla's book in my shield and crushed down on it with my fist. It fought and sent streaks of putrid tendrils out searching in all directions, but they withered quickly under my assault. I'd like to say it was a heck of a show, but now that I had my sequence down correctly, it turned out to be anti-climactic as I turned both books to dust.

"Just so you know," I said. "They're going to be pissed when they come out of there." Carla was screaming and angrily pounding on the side of her translucent prison.

"Let them go," Beth argued. "You can't hold my baby."

"It's just salt, Beth," I said. "All you need do is run your foot through it and it'll be gone."

A DARK PLACE

"You won't trick me like you did Carla and Mia," Petaluma said.

We planned a ritual tonight to separate Petaluma from her own book and I'd asked her to ride up to Judy's with me.

"You saw what the books were doing to them," I said.

"Mom wants me to give up my magic. She says there aren't any good witches who practice necromancy."

"I don't think that's true," I said. "Did you know the FBI employs necros?"

"They do not," Petaluma said, staring out the window. Her voice begged me to disprove her statement.

"They do," I said. "They help find bodies and figure out what happened to them. Lots of things."

"The FBI doesn't know about witches."

"It's a special group," I said. "I'd bet they don't have anyone as strong as you."

"For serious? You think I'm strong?"

"With almost no training, you were more powerful than any of the Dark Folk," I said.

Petaluma smiled. In the reflection on the window, I saw a glimpse of the child I knew before life had become complicated.

"I was looking through the books my mom left behind. You'll never guess what I found," I said.

"What?" She turned away from the window and looked intently at me.

"Take a look," I said. "It's on the back seat."

Petaluma turned, releasing the seatbelt and climbed toward the back. For a moment, she balanced precariously over the bench seat, reaching for the book. It was too much temptation and I accelerated suddenly, causing her to topple back.

"Hey! No fair!" she complained, laughing.

What a beautiful sound. I hadn't heard her laugh since I'd arrived.

"Do you see it?" I asked.

"This?" She held up the narrow, leather bound book I'd brought from home.

"Yup," I said.

She sank to the floor between the two rows of seats. When I glanced back, she was straining in the dark to read the text, carefully flipping through the old pages.

"This was your mother's," she stated. "It's amazing."

"As you know, wizards don't share their texts with anyone," I said. "That text was written over a thousand years ago. It's in Latin."

"There are so many spells in here. I had no idea."

"How do you know they're spells?" I asked.

"Thea was teaching me Latin," she replied. "I don't know much, but I can read a little."

"Would you like to keep it," I said.

"No way. No. I'm not trading my book for this. I don't care how old it is," she said, closing the book.

"How many times have you read your book all the way through?" I asked.

"Too many to count."

"Then you know it's a good trade." I held my arm over to her, baring my wrist. "Do you know how to read blood?"

"Of course I do," she said. "My sisters and I do it all the time."

"Don't be stupid and go poking around where you don't belong. I don't want to wreck while driving," I said, while her small fingers closed around my wrist. "Read me. I don't want to give you my book, but I believe you will be hurt by the one Thea gave you. You and I both know my mother's book is worth ten times the one you have. Yours contains a curse that has enthralled you and is clouding your judgement. You saw what those other books did."

"My book isn't cursed," she said. The funny thing about reading the blood is it goes both ways. I could feel her insecurity as she recalled the events of the evening. "I don't think I can," she said, letting go.

"Judy and I will both talk to your mom. We'll figure out a way for you to practice," I said. "Do you remember the story of how I came to live with Judy?"

"You burned down a school?"

"Just the gymnasium," I said. "Even though I wasn't a witch, she helped me learn to control my magic, even when it scared her."

"Mistress Judy was scared?"

"Just like she is now, for you," I said.

Petaluma climbed back into the front seat, still holding my mother's book on necromancy. "Why is she scared?"

"I think you know why," I said. "Tell me, did you see what was happening to Carla? How her book made her act?"

"Carla's always been a b-word," Petaluma said, smiling slightly.

"Don't be coy, you know what I'm saying. Do you want to end up like Carla?" I asked. "What do you think was going to happen to her?"

"That book was hurting her," she answered. "Mine would never do that."

"That's the curse speaking, Petaluma," I said. "I know you're stronger than the curse. Carla wasn't, but you have to be."

Petaluma blew out a shuddering breath and I decided to let the conversation sink in while we drove up the quiet mountain road.

When we finally arrived, I had to park at the end of a long line of other cars and trucks.

"What's going on?" Petaluma asked.

"Looks like a Gathering," I said.

"For what? It's not the equinox."

Just then, Petaluma's sister Rosemary and Luana's daughter Estelle came running out through the front garden. Judy's entire home was lit up and the lanterns hanging along the path blazed cheerfully. The girls both wore white dresses and had flowers neatly tucked into their hair.

"Lumaaaa," Estelle hollered as she ran toward us.

"You better go," I said. She opened the door and turned back, holding my book out to me. I smiled at her. "You hold onto it. After you talk with Judy, you can give it back if that's your choice."

When I finally made it through the front door, I'd picked out more than a few women I didn't recognize through the windows. They were all dressed as the girls had been, although most chose more muted colors than white for their dresses.

"Heya, sexy," Gabriella purred, surprising me from behind just as I entered through the front door. I turned and must have had the right reaction as I took her in. She wore a lacey black dress that closely followed her lithe form all the way down to her waist, where it flared out elegantly. Her brown skin showed through the loosely knit fabric and I was surprised to see that she wasn't wearing the body stocking she reserved for celebrations. The white lilies in her hair completed the look and a pang of inadequacy pulled at me.

"Oh man," I said, not able to find words to express the mix of emotions in my head.

Wearing only slippers, she was considerably shorter than me and had to stretch up on her tiptoes to give me a kiss.

"You're silly," she said. "You better not have the same reaction when you see Lace."

"Lace?" I asked, finally gaining enough wherewithal to lean down to embrace her. I winced as I pulled her to me. "Who are all these people?"

"Judy invited two other covens to join us. With Lace and me, that brings the total covens to four," she said.

"So its official? Lace is joining Whyte Wood?" I asked.

"We'll welcome her when we get back to Leotown. I was hoping we could use Tenebrius Manerium."

"Of course. Where is she, anyway?" I asked.

"Some of the girls are already at the glade setting up. She and Maggie went with them." A moment of paranoia captured me and Gabriella must have sensed it. "Why? What's going on?"

"Those Eppy Faire thugs showed up at the shop again," I said.

"I had to run them off."

"They can't be that bad, can they?"

"One of them had a gun," I said.

"Let's go."

On the back porch sat a stack of supplies that needed to be hauled to the coven's ceremonial ground, generally called The Glade. We grabbed a couple of already full hemp bags and I briefly scanned for Judy or Gia, neither of whom were to be found.

Glass canning jars with votive candles adorned the path leading out of Judy's carefully tended gardens and into the dense cover of the darkened forest. A small knot of unfamiliar teenaged girls raced past, giggling and holding hands, their energy causing me to smile while the tension in my stomach pushed me forward.

"You think they'd come out here?" Gabriella asked.

"On an ATV, we're not that far from Eppy," I said. "There are paths all over."

"It's a big forest," Gabriella said.

A flood of relief settled over me as we arrived at the natural opening in the forest. Forty yards northeast, through dense undergrowth, was the artesian spring where the oaks grew together and we'd found Petaluma hiding. It was the same spring that supplied a small flow of water to the brook that ran along the southern edge. Judy, Gia and I had constructed a wood-planked bridge across that brook, allowing easier footing for the older witches. It was there we found Maggie and Lace chatting amiably, sitting next to a jarred candle. Barefooted Maggie had sunk her feet into the cool mud.

"Heya, Bro," Maggie greeted.

"What's going on?" Lace asked, reading my face.

I now understood Gabriella's warning about Lace's appearance. The abused waif we'd pulled from the cave had been replaced by a gorgeous young woman dressed in a white blouse and colorfully adorned black cotton skirt that gave a nod to her gypsy heritage.

"Don't stare." Gabriella poked me unfairly with her elbow,

causing me to wince again as pain shot through my chest wound. "Ohh, sorry."

"I think I confuse him when I wear clothing," Maggie offered.

"I ran into more trouble from those Eppy Faire boys. At least one of them was packing," I said, ignoring the jabs both physical and otherwise. "I wouldn't put it past those idiots to crash the party."

Lace nodded. "I'll leave."

"You'll do no such thing," Gabriella said.

"Are you going to fight men with guns? At a minimum, I'm causing a distraction from the real purpose of the gathering," she said.

"I'll change. I can be more helpful that way," Maggie said.

"You will not. You're weak and that can't always be the answer," I said. "I don't think they want to hurt you, Lace. At least not in front of thirty witches."

"Are you willing to risk these girls?" Lace asked.

"These *women* know the risk tonight," Gabriela said, firmly. "We train our daughters to stand together. Tonight we will be safe. You will join with us and take your place as our sister. Tonight is as much about you as it is about Petaluma."

"I don't like it," Lace said, shaking her head.

Gabriella smiled reassuringly. "You will learn to trust your sisters."

"We could at least check the perimeter," Maggie said. "It's not like wizard-boy and I are needed here."

"That's a good idea," I said, ignoring her jab.

I sat and unlaced my shoes, pulling them and my socks off and setting them aside, next to the bridge. I pulled my pocket knife out and drew it across the palm of my hand. I wasn't a big fan of blood-letting but most of my enchantments wouldn't work without it.

"Felix?" Gabriella asked.

"I'll be back in a while," I said. "Don't worry. If I find trouble, you'll be the first to hear about it." I sank my hands into the brook's soft mud and lifted a generous clump, allowing it to mix freely with my blood. I felt the welcoming presence of the forest around me as I wiped the mud down my face, starting with my forehead, chanting *'lutum ubertatis.'*

"That's disgusting." I barely heard Maggie's complaint as the magic around us washed over me and all the nearby living matter illuminated with a phosphorescent glow. I found I had to turn away from the brilliance of the congregation of witches.

"We'll be back." I waded across the shallow brook, mostly interested in gaining separation from the spectacular display. "Let's go, Maggie."

"When?" Gabriella asked.

"We won't be far. I'll find you and Petaluma when it's time," I said.

"You know, I've seen a lot of disgusting things before," Maggie said. "But a mud mask?"

"You've seen me do this before."

"My raven doesn't care what you do. You're easier to ignore when I'm with her."

My first objective was to swing up through the north, around the quad of oaks and the brook's source. I knew the nearby paths well enough to know that anyone approaching from Eppy would likely come from that direction.

The first thing that struck me once we were far enough from the excited noise of The Glade was that we certainly weren't alone. The forest's animals were hunkered down, their evening plans interrupted.

The second thing that struck me was just how stealthily Maggie made her way through the underbrush in the pitch black. She didn't have the advantage of my spell, which I generally used for collecting spell components.

"You feel that?" Maggie asked.

"I don't see anything," I said. "The animals feel it, though."

"Predator," she whispered.

We'd gone another forty yards when the hackles on my neck rose. A sound, somewhere between a woman screaming and a barn owl screech, froze me in position. I slowly swiveled my head, trying to find the source of the sound. I finally located the sleek shape of a panther resting on a branch, not fifteen feet from where we stood.

"Cat," I said.

"Where?" Maggie asked.

"Just ahead of us, hanging over the path."

"She's warning us to stay clear," Maggie said. "She's hunting."

"Message received," I said.

Gracefully, the panther descended from her perch, dropping fifteen feet effortlessly and bounding off down the path. A moment later, we heard the shout of men and a single rifle-shot rang out.

"Shit, she's going after people," I said and stupidly ran after the cat.

"Not a good idea, brother," Maggie warned but followed anyway.

The scene we arrived upon was something from a hunting show gone bad. A man lay on the ground, holding his bleeding hand and trying to look as small as possible. The panther stalked nearby, warily eying two others who had been separated from their guns. They were yelling at the cat, both with knives drawn.

"Get the gun," one of the two men yelled as we came into view. I recognized him as Merl from earlier in the day.

"Looks like a fair fight to me," I said, keeping clear of the fallen man.

"It's going to kill him," Merl said, panicking.

"What are you doing out here?" I asked.

The panther swiped its paw menacingly at the two, ignoring Maggie and me for the moment.

"What? It's a free country."

"I guess we're free to get out of here then," I said.

"No!" This time it was the man who'd driven the truck, yelling from a fetal position on the ground. "We were told you were having some big shindig out here. Buncha witches. We were just going to break it up. Nobody was supposed to get too hurt, unless we saw that Faa whore."

"Stupid much?" Maggie asked.

"Where are your guns?"

"My pistol got lost when that crazy cat attacked. That rifle's the only gun we got. You gotta help us," he said.

"Doesn't seem like you boys are very bright," I said, nervously eyeing the panther who was chuffing angrily. "Nobody told you about the cats in these parts?"

"Lived here my whole life; never seen a cat," Merl argued.

"And yet, here we are," I said. The cat growled angrily in my direction and I slowly backed off, not remembering if I was supposed to lower my eyes or push eye contact. I decided to just let it know I wasn't a threat by moving slowly. "How many more of you idiots are out here?"

"Are you gonna help us?" Merl asked.

"How many?"

"Just us three. We're trying to keep a low profile," he said.

Just like that, the panther decided she'd had enough and lunged at Merl. He had time to swing his blade but didn't make contact. The cat buried its mouth into Merl's shoulder and raked at his belly with its powerful hind legs.

"Dammit! *Adoloret*." I sent a gout of fire just past the two of them and within a couple inches of the thrashing cat's muzzle. I was firmly in the cat's camp. It had more right to be here than the idiot Merl, but I also couldn't allow even someone as despicable as Merl to be killed while I stood by.

The cat released Merl and roared at me. I ignited another gout of fire and sent it past the beast's flank, close enough that it should feel the heat. Sufficiently annoyed, the proud animal bounded off into the forest.

"Get the gun!" Merl yelled as he writhed on the ground, blood gushing from his wounds.

Maggie lunged forward and picked up the rifle. She held it like someone might if they'd never fired a weapon before, so I pulled it from her. "You want your gun; you can ask Sherriff Merritt for it tomorrow. I'm sure he'll be interested in why you boys were traipsing around in the woods chasing a panther."

"We'll come for you and your family, Slade," Merl growled through gritted teeth.

"Not if you have any brains," Maggie retorted.

I lunged forward and pushed Merl on the shoulder, sending him back to the ground. I fell on top of him, knee in his chest and held my hand in front of his eye. "*Adoloret.*" I allowed a small ball of flame to grow in my hand. "You're bleeding, Merl, and you might die out here tonight," I said, anger building in my chest, causing the blood in my ears to rush loudly. I pushed the flame closer to his cheek. His eyes swiveled between the flames and my face.

"I didn't mean it," he whimpered.

"I am a wizard, Merl," I said. "Tonight, you've picked a fight with a panther and a wizard. Do you know what your problem is?"

"No?" he said, as if asking a question.

"You like to pick fights out of your weight class." I moved the ball of flame next to his bleeding shoulder, allowing it to singe away his shirt. He cried out as the flame kissed his skin. Anger filled me as the edges of my vision darkened.

"Felix," Maggie gasped. "Pull back. This isn't you. Fight it!"

I looked at her quizzically, not really understanding.

"Stop it!" She kicked at my hand and that small contact cleared my mind. The smell of burned fabric and flesh reached my nose and I quenched the fireball.

"Shit," I said, standing up quickly. The sight of Merl's blistered flesh startled me. I'd ruined a tennis ball sized portion of the skin on his shoulder and only had a vague recollection of doing so.

"I'm sorry!" Merl cried and crawled toward his companions who watched us with horrified expressions.

"Get out of my forest," I said darkly. "Tonight is my last warning."

To their credit, they didn't push the issue further and we watched as they raced away.

"Damn, dude," Maggie said. "I thought you were going all Freddy Kruger on me there."

"Who?"

Maggie closed her eyes and shook her head in disgust. "Seriously, would it hurt you to see a movie once?"

I shrugged and continued down the path, not really knowing what I should do otherwise. We came within a hundred yards of the celebration several times, but each time we got close, I veered away. A cloud of darkness still hung around me as I mulled over the encounter. There was definitely something wrong with me. I couldn't hide from it and had no intention of bringing down the joyful energy of the witches of the mountain.

"We better head in," Maggie finally prompted me around eleven-thirty. "I think they'll want to work on Petaluma's deal right at midnight."

I nodded. The cool walk through the forest had settled my anger, but my conscience weighed heavily. If Maggie hadn't stopped me ... the possibilities were endless and none of them were good.

As we approached, we heard the excited sounds of a celebration in full swing. A trio of women sang, their voices carrying preternaturally over the din of laughter and the revelers who joined in with the song. The rifle weighed heavily in my hands and I refused to bring it anywhere near the peaceful group. At the brook's edge, I emptied the rifle's magazine, stepping on the bullets and causing them to sink into the mud. I pulled the bolt from the barrel, flung it upstream and then carefully laid the rifle in the middle of the running water, finally standing atop it.

"I thought you were giving that to Merritt," Maggie said.

I shrugged. "I still can, but it has no place around these women."

"Are you talking about you or the rifle?" Maggie asked.

"What?" I pretended I didn't know what she was asking.

"Uncle Felix!" Estelle had caught sight of us and I hustled up from the bank of the stream. "Dance with me." She towed behind her a girl I didn't recognize and they giggled as they approached.

"What's funny?" I asked.

"Your face, silly," she said. "It's all muddy." Before I could stop her, she rushed over to the river and cupped her hands, pulling a small amount of water out, completely missing the deadly rifle only feet from her position. "Come here," she chastised like her mother might. I bent down and she wiped at my face ineffectually.

Innocently, she kissed my nose. "There. It's the only clean spot on your face." All at once, the darkness lifted from my shoulders and my breath returned, no longer burning in my chest.

"Let me catch up," I said. "I'll cleanup my face first, though."

"Be quick," she agreed. "Judy's looking for you." Estelle and her friend scampered off, having no idea how powerful her simple blessing had been.

"Wait," Maggie said, running after them. "Any food up there?"

"Of course, silly," Estelle called over her shoulder.

With my face washed off, I walked into the camp. For some reason, I didn't find the myriad of semi-naked women of various ages dancing freely in the moonlight to be anything but refreshing. Ordinarily, I'd have been distracted and careful not to allow my glance to linger. I was a man after all, and I'd been taught from an early age to appreciate the human form in whatever shape it was found. To be fair, this wasn't a stretch for me. Tonight, however, was different. Having walked in my own darkness, the beauty surrounding me was much more a balm than anything else.

"There you are," Gabriella found me. "I was worried you'd run into trouble."

I turned and found that she was indeed dancing in the buff. Her long silver hair, still with lilies woven in, was her only cover.

"Uh, gosh," I managed with a weak smile. Ordinarily, Gabriella was an expert at knowing when I had a problem. This time she didn't inquire, most likely because the visage of her in the moonlight had all but blanked my mind.

"This place." She smiled. "Tonight."

My eyebrows shot up. I worked to bring them back into position and swallowed hard.

Judy approached us. "Felix. There you are." I felt a little bad seeing her wearing a semi-sheer gown. It had been a compromise we'd made several years before. I would deal with all the other women as long as she covered somewhat. It was one thing to have confusing thoughts about her friends, but I couldn't reconcile any confusion where she might be concerned.

"Petaluma is ready," she said.

"Dolly is okay with the trade?" I asked.

"Dolly is okay not losing her daughter."

As things often are, the actual ceremony was somewhat anticlimactic. The hard part had been getting Petaluma to accept the change and it turned out she was considerably stronger than the curse. With thirty witches joined together, supporting her, Petaluma released the book to me and it withered beneath my crushing shield. The effort required on my part to destroy the book was nothing more than it would take to crack an egg.

"That was a beautiful thing," Gabriella said, wrapping her arms around me, drawing me back to the blankets she'd set aside for us.

"It was," I agreed. "I didn't have to do anything. Petaluma rejected it and it just disappeared."

Gabriella smiled. "Take a little credit. You might not have done much at the ceremony, but your talk with her set the stage."

"I'll take that, but in the end, it was all Petaluma and the witches of the mountain," I said.

"Of which she's now one."

Gabriella fell back into the blankets and lay supine, gesturing for me to join her. I smiled. Nothing would I enjoy more and I allowed my excitement to grow.

A low thwup, thwup, thwup sound echoed over the forest and I turned, when all of a sudden, a bright light shone from above as a helicopter flew over the peaceful glade. Downwash from the rotors sent material flying through the once serene setting as women and children screamed. The sound of ATVs and off-road vehicles joined the chaos as headlights illuminated the forest around us.

"This is the FBI." I gritted my teeth as I recognized the voice on the other end of the loudspeaker. "For your safety, do not move. I repeat. This is the FBI ..."

The helicopter slowly descended.

LEOTOWN

"Where are your clothes?" I shouted over the noise, just as the bright beams of an ATV illuminated my chest. We'd chosen a remote location at the edge of the glade to spend the rest of the night.

Gabriella's mouth moved and her arm pointed, but the only thing I heard was the high-pitched whine of small engines. I stood and crossed to where I believed her clothing was.

"Freeze and put your hands up," a man's voice ordered.

I stopped and raised my hands slowly to about shoulder height and turned.

"You there," another voice commanded. "Get up."

I watched helplessly as Gabriella rolled from our impromptu nest and rose to her feet more gracefully than I could have managed. She took some care in covering her form with a blanket.

"What's going on?" I asked, shouting over the ruckus.

"Hands behind your back!"

I saw the struggle in Gabriella's eyes. To comply would cause her only cover to fall away.

"She can't," I yelled. "No clothing."

"She doesn't fit either description," the second officer, who'd advanced to a few feet from Gabriella, offered.

"Put some clothes on," the first demanded. "And you. Hands over your head. Turn around."

Gabriella nodded at me, willing me to comply. I'd had a tough enough night and the thought of resistance flitted through my mind. In the short time since they'd arrived, I'd seen at least a dozen agents, so confrontation probably wasn't my best course of action. I turned slowly and complied with the officer's commands as he roughly snapped cuffs on my wrists.

When we arrived at the center of the glade, those who'd

decided to stay the night had been corralled - mostly witches and their daughters. The scene was so different from even an hour before, where the same people had been joyfully celebrating life and welcoming Petaluma into their sisterhood.

"What the fuck's your problem, Farha?" I asked, once I came within earshot.

He turned from one of the coven leaders and grimaced.

"Shut up." The man behind me pushed the butt of his rifle into the small of my back, trying to send me away from Jardeep.

"Uncuff him." Jardeep turned to a female FBI agent who wore a dark windbreaker. "This isn't her." He gestured to the woman whom he'd just been talking to.

"Uncuff Gabriella first," I said, turning toward the state policeman who'd freed me.

"Back off, buddy," he said. "I'm just following orders."

"The girl is fine too," Jardeep said. He sounded tired, which I didn't see as a stretch, given how exhausted I felt. I'd been so looking forward to crawling beneath the warm covers with Gabriella and sleeping.

"Where's Anderson?" I asked, turning on Jardeep.

"Have you seen Althea Sanders?" he asked, ignoring my question.

"Yeah. When you guys carted her off to wherever you take witches who've gone astray," I said.

He let out a loud breath. "She escaped."

"Bullshit, you're fishing for something."

"She overpowered two guards and put an agent in the hospital," he said. "I assure you, we're quite serious about this."

"So you attacked a group of peaceful women and their daughters?" Gabriella slipped her hand around my arm.

"We got a tip that she was out this way," he said.

Gabriella's face grew angry. "That must have been quite some tip."

"Sir?" A younger agent interrupted. "You need to see something."

"Can it wait?"

"I don't think so."

"Come with me," Jardeep said, gesturing to Gabriella and myself. I was ready to throttle the man and he was acting like we were simply part of the team. For whatever reason though, I found myself following him.

We were led back, close to where Gabriella and I were to have slept and then another forty yards into the forest. In the wash of an ATV's headlights was a tarp, lying over several suspicious lumps.

"What's going on?" I asked.

Jardeep crouched down and pulled the tarp back, exposing the dead forms of two of the men who'd been attacked by the panther in the forest. If the slashes on their torsos were any indication, the panther had found them again and this time, finished the job.

"Looks like a wild animal kill," the agent explained. "Big cat by the looks of it."

"You know these men?" Jardeep asked.

I considered lying, but decided against it.

"They're from Eppy," I said. "Maggie and I found them snooping around our camp about four hours ago."

"And?"

"And nothing," I said. "Last time we saw them; they were headed back to Eppy on the path."

"Your sister didn't happen to have a part in their demise, did she?"

"Can't see why," I said. "She went back to the house after midnight," I said.

Jardeep turned to the officer. "Send someone to Judy Babcock's house and have them check her story."

"Copy that," the man answered. "What about these DBs?"

"Wrong place, wrong time," Jardeep answered. "Forest can be a dangerous place."

"What's this really about?" I asked, once Gabriella and I were alone with Jardeep.

"Like I said, Althea Sanders escaped."

"Since when do you need two dozen agents and the state police to arrest one simple witch?" I asked.

"We don't think she was alone," Jardeep answered.

"Someone helped her?" Gabriella asked.

"No. It was the demon," I said, closing my eyes as I heard the truth leave my mouth. It bothered me that the ghrelin had gone down so easily. I looked back at the two of them "It jumped into a willing host. That's why Willum was scared at the end. He was no longer possessed and had to pay the price for the demon's actions."

"I think that was its plan the entire time," Jardeep said. "Althea Sanders has no criminal record and we can't tie her either directly or indirectly to any of the murders. All she needs to do is lie low for a couple of months and the FBI will drop it as a priority. If Willum Gordon had escaped, we'd have chased him to the ends of the earth."

"What now?"

"This was our only lead," he said. "We're back to square one. Tell me something, Slade. You been in touch with your mother, Atronia?" He peered intently at me as he asked the question.

"No." I shook my head. "Why would you ask that?"

"Sort of thing we used to get her help with," he said.

"According to Maggie, you arrested her and tried to lock her up," I said.

He didn't respond other than to dig in the pocket of his windbreaker. He extracted a sparkly chain and held his fingers out to me as if to drop something in my hand. I accepted his offering, which turned out to be the necklace holding the crystal Judy had given me. "Figured you were missing that."

"What will you do now?"

"Question is, what will *you* do," he said. "I'd stay clear of that Faa girl. That demon wanted her for some reason. Whatever it is, I wouldn't put long odds on her making it through the next round."

"You're a cold-hearted sonnavabitch," Gabriella said, surprising me with her cussing.

Jardeep shrugged and started to walk off.

"We done?" I asked.

"Like you said, she isn't here." He pulled out his walkie-talkie. "Wrap it up. There's no sign of the fugitive."

"Do you think Maggie had anything to do with those dead Eppy boys?" Gabriella asked, once Jardeep was out of earshot.

"She wasn't in good enough shape to change again," I said.

"She's been eating hard all day."

"There was a panther in the woods," I said. "Maggie and I both saw it. It looked a lot like her cat form, but it definitely wasn't her."

"What are the odds of that? These men get attacked by a panther who looks like Maggie and are later found dead."

"What are you driving at?" I asked. "I know for a fact it wasn't Maggie."

"You're probably right," she said. "Jardeep was lying when he said he was looking for your mother for help with the demon. "

"How?"

"Not sure, but when he said they used to get help from her, he was leaving something important out," she said. "We should go back and help clean up. I doubt anyone is going to want to stick around after all this."

***

The sky grew lighter in the pre-dawn hours as we finally saw the last of the weary revelers off. Exhausted, we threw blankets on Judy's family room floor and fell asleep. It was well after noon when the smell of breakfast cooking in the kitchen woke me.

"Where are you going?" Gabriella lazily pulled at me as I extracted myself from the mess of blankets.

"Gotta do the needful," I said.

I finished up my business and padded my way into the kitchen where Gia was humming to herself and busily working at what looked like food for an army.

"Coffee?" she asked cheerfully as I slid onto a stool.

"Please," I said accepting the cup.

"Quite a night last night," Gia mused, tipping a large pot and pouring gravy into a serving bowl. "Imagine you'll be taking off shortly?" She phrased it as a question, but I knew better than to hold anything from her. She was more than intuitive on matters like this.

"We're endangering you by sticking around," I said.

"Seems to me the FBI would have shown up last night no matter what."

"Thea is loose," I said. "She escaped FBI custody. She'll be coming for me or Lace."

"Why Lace?" Judy asked, entering from the hallway.

"Farha believes the demon jumped to Thea," I said.

"That what you think?" Gia asked.

"Only thing that makes sense," I said. "We'll stay the night, but I want to head home in the morning. Maybe she won't find us there. Either way, things will settle down here once we're gone, especially all of the FBI attention." I pointed out the window to where a nondescript sedan was parked on the gravel road.

"Witches don't find it hard to locate people they know well," Gia replied. "She'll find you wherever you go."

"That's what Felix is counting on," Judy said. "He's looking to draw Thea away."

Gia slid a plateful of sausage, eggs and home-style hash browns, all covered with gravy, across the small island. It afforded me the opportunity not to respond.

"What smells so good?" Maggie asked, blearily blinking back sleep and sliding into the seat next to me, blanket still wrapped around her shoulders. I pushed my plate in front of her and she shoveled the food in with abandon.

"Child. Where have you been all my life," Gia asked, smiling at Maggie. "I'd have loved cooking for you."

"You always made the best bread," Maggie said, waggling her eyebrows. "Your mistake was cooling it next to the window."

"That was you?" Gia asked as she doled out plates to the late arriving Gabriella and Lace.

"I've probably said too much." Maggie smiled like a Cheshire cat as she slid her empty plate back toward Gia.

"I'll tell you a secret," Gia said.

"What?" Maggie asked.

"I have two loaves for you to take back with you tonight," she answered. "That is, if a curious magpie doesn't pull them from the window."

"Perhaps we should close the window," Maggie accepted a plate, once again filled with breakfast food covered in a thick tan gravy.

"All of God's creatures need to eat," Gia answered.

***

"Home sweet home," Gabriella sighed as we crossed onto the old steel bridge. The Missouri River flowed beneath us and the wheels of the Suburban sang as only the ancient bridge could make them. The river marked the city limits on the northeast side of Leotown. I had to admit, I was tired of traveling and looked forward to sleeping in my own bed and showering in the recently renovated bathroom of my family home.

"I can't wait to see Clarita," Maggie said, bouncing in her seat, causing a pile of chip bags and soda cans to topple to the floor behind me. I winced at the stains I knew she'd leave behind.

"Might have to be tomorrow," I said. It was one-thirty in the morning and tomorrow would be a workday for both Kelli and her husband, Andy.

"Kelli said to stop by, no matter how late," Gabriella said. "We're an hour earlier than I told her we'd be, so I don't see a problem."

"Works for me." I rolled down the window as we pulled off the main highway and onto a street that would lead us to the Brandlemeir home. It had been hot today and I smelled freshly mown grass as we wound our way through the older neighborhood where they lived. The streets were quiet and I appreciated the peace of the night and the sense of homecoming.

When we pulled up, Kelli, Clarita and Kelli's son, Nelson were all dozing on a wooden porch swing that had lost its momentum.

Bugs jumped around the single porch light that illuminated the quiet trio who were protected by nothing more than a light blanket. I smiled, appreciating the serenity I so often associate with late night.

"Who-who-who." The staccato call of an owl caught my attention from just overhead. We'd apparently disturbed its evening hunting and it was expressing displeasure.

"Sorry, buddy," I whispered, stretching to restore circulation to my extremities.

"Felix?" Gabriella's voice carried concern, so I quickened my pace around the front of the truck. "Who's in the house?" She pointed through the window at Thea's unmistakable figure, sitting at Andy and Kelli's dining room table, talking animatedly with Andy.

"Get Clarita and Kelli in the truck," I whispered harshly and slid out of the light that shone from the living room window.

A large form sailed from the tree above and swooped down, startling me as it landed on the house. The owl was reacting to our activity and wasn't pleased. At the same moment, the tinkle of aluminum soda cans falling to the pavement made me wince and duck, the overload of too many simultaneous events.

"Hey. You're back," Kelli announced sleepily as we stepped onto the porch. The groan of old lumber sagging beneath our feet caught her attention. Gabriella pressed her finger to her lips, trying to quiet her coven sister. "Oh, have they fallen asleep?" she asked, misinterpreting the requested silence.

"Kelli – there is danger," I whispered. "Take Nelson to the truck. Gabriella will take you to my house where it's safe."

"I don't understand," she replied, confused. "What danger? And what about Andy and your friend?"

"You have to keep Nelson safe." I intentionally tapped into her protective instincts as a mother. Until the kids were clear, Andy would have to fend for himself. As a witch, Kelli immediately saw through both my deception as well as recognized the truth behind my statements.

I picked Clarita from the swing just as I caught the lithe shape of Maggie in panther form disappear around the side yard followed by Lace, hobbling behind.

"Shit." I said, waking Clarita, whose eyes widened first with joy, then in recognition of my tense mood.

"She's bad," Clarita whispered in my ear as I hustled her out to the truck and dropped her into the rear seat.

"She's very bad and you need to go with Gabriella." I turned and plucked Nelson from Kelli and helped the waking boy into the seat beside Clarita.

"What's going on?" Kelli asked.

"The woman in your home is evil," I said. "Go to my house and have Clarita let you into the basement." I desperately wanted to see Gabriella driving away in the truck, but I knew better than to suggest it, which was why I was confused when she offered.

"I'll drive," Gabriella said, climbing over the passenger seat and into the driver's. "I'll come back for you."

"Don't," I said. "Hunker down in the lab. There's no way Thea will be able to break in. Call Anderson."

I'd like to have said more, but the sound of breaking glass in the back yard caught my attention.

"Help Andy," Kelli begged.

I nodded to her as I closed the passenger-side door and sprinted toward the house.

GONE TO GROUND

Telekinetically, I turned the doorknob on the front door as I ran, kicking the door open violently the second I got there. I wasn't sure what Maggie and Lace were doing, but I knew they were in trouble as neither of them could stand against the ghrelin within Thea. Andy was sprawled on the kitchen floor, blood running from his mouth, but still very much alive.

"Can you walk?" I asked, crouching next to him.

"Dang. What's her problem?" Andy asked, still confused by whatever had transpired.

"She's not who she said. Kelli and Nelson are in danger and you have to go to them."

Andy shook his head and struggled to his knees. "What? Where?"

"They've gone to my house," I said.

"Why would they do that?" he asked.

I'd been around Andy enough to know that while he had difficulty with conversation, he was plenty smart. He used questions as a smoke screen while he worked out complex situations. The problem was I didn't have time.

I pushed him. "Get in your truck and rescue them!"

Between the minor compulsion and the turn of events with Thea, his brain locked on to the simple plan I provided. I helped him to his feet and he was off, unfortunately in the wrong direction.

"Front door!" I said, grabbing his arm. "Thea went out the back. You can't get stopped." It was an unusual ballet we performed as he allowed me to anchor him but used his momentum to swing around. I released him and like a missile, he rocketed toward the front door.

"Godspeed," I whispered to his back.

The sliding glass door stood open and I plunged through into the darkness.

"Felix!" Thea exclaimed in a saccharine sweet greeting. "I'm so delighted you made it."

My eyes adjusted to the dark and I found her standing in the back yard, eyes glowing orange.

"Why did you follow us here?" I asked.

"Can you not smell her?" Thea asked. "The Faa child is so delicious. It's a pesky talent - that ability to hide in shadow. Can you hear me, dear?" Thea raised her voice. "I will release your magics upon the world and you will be the queen you've always been destined to be. And you, Felix Slade, or should I say Baltazoss? You will be her loyal guard and advisor."

"Let me guess, the only thing we need to do is let you possess her?" I asked.

"Only way it works," she replied. "A small price to rule the world."

"You're nuttier than a fruitcake," I said.

The sound of footsteps to my right caught my attention as Andy ran to his truck's cab. We exchanged a quick look. I just wanted to face-palm; coming into the back yard for his truck had been his best idea.

"Never a big thinker, were you, Baltazoss?"

"Name is Slade," I said. "My mother left me when I was six. I took my dad's name."

"Did she now?" Thea asked as Andy's truck engine struggled to start, catching her attention. "How very noble of you. Distract the big hairy monster so the innocent might flee."

Thea reached behind her, grabbing at nothing. When her hand came forward, it contained a fiery ball, which she hurled at the truck. As it flew through the air, the ball grew in size until it was larger than the truck itself.

"*Scutum!*" I strained to form a shield large enough to deflect it. I concentrated on just the cab and was horrified to hear a yelp of pain as Lace and Maggie became visible in the truck's bed. Lace looked at me in panic as her left arm was engulfed in fire. I struggled to redirect the shield and formed it around her arm, smothering the flames. As I did, she collapsed.

"How delightful!" Thea exclaimed. "I had yet to look in the truck."

Just then, Andy's truck roared to life.

"I don't think so," Thea answered, pulling another ball of flame from the air.

I raced toward the truck as Andy's tires dug into the gravel drive. With timing only possible under duress, I twisted in midair as I flung myself into the bed of the truck and punched at the ball of fire streaking toward us with my weakening shield. It was just sufficient to redirect the fireball upward, but not enough to keep it from impacting the cab of the truck.

Andy howled in pain as a piece of the ball peeled off and brushed past him, hurtling out the open window on the other side. To his credit, he stayed focused on his task and the truck bounced off the curb and onto the asphalt as he turned onto the street, plowing over his mailbox as he did.

I caught a fleeting glance of a giant-sized soda cup splashing in Andy's face as I struggled to gain balance. With nothing to hold, I was thrown into Lace and pinned her against the truck bed's sidewall. The momentum in the truck shifted as Andy accelerated down the sleepy suburban street and we all slid backward. I grabbed hold of the tailgate in time to see smaller, twin fireballs streaking toward us. Flattening myself onto the truck's bed, I watched one sizzle overhead and strike the steel cab, exploding on contact with the window. The truck jerked to the side as Andy howled again in pain, no doubt from flying glass, but the tough little bastard didn't give up and roared around the next corner, cutting through a neighbor's lawn.

"Are you all okay?" Andy yelled through the back window as he straightened out on the road.

I looked around for Maggie and when I didn't find her, recalled an image of her jumping from the truck's bed, still in panther form. I looked back to Lace's crumpled and unconscious form, her head still in contact with the hard steel of the truck's sidewall. Her arm was a bleeding mess. I didn't know much about fire injuries, but it didn't take a genius to realize she'd been badly hurt. I pulled her onto my lap as I rotated to a seated position facing the back.

"Find a hospital. Lace is hurt," I yelled back.

"What in the hell was that?" Andy yelled back through the window. As he turned, a streetlight illuminated bits of glass, still embedded in the side of his bloodied face.

"You wouldn't believe me if I told you," I answered, too quietly for him to hear as I searched for and found Lace's pulse. I pulled Lace and myself closer to the back of the truck's cab, where I knew the wind would buffet us less.

"My arm," Lace complained as she regained consciousness.

"I know. Don't look at it," I said, trying to sooth her. "It was burned by demon fire. We're headed to the hospital."

"No hospital. Not safe," she said.

"But your arm," I protested. "It's burned."

Agonizingly, she twisted her head and looked down at her arm, flexing her hand. I cringed when I saw the side of her head where a softball-sized spot of hair had been burned away. "I'm alive, don't let it be for naught."

It was a horrible choice. The burns on her hand and arm were disfiguring and I didn't believe her neck or the side of her face would escape scarring as the skin had already started to blister.

"We can't, you're hurt," I said.

"You must!" she said. "Don't let the demon have me, Felix. You're my only hope."

"Dammit! Andy. My house. Go!" I said.

He shouted over the roar of the truck. "We're almost at the hospital."

"No. It's not safe."

At the next street Andy turned and I pulled the phone from my pocket to dial Gabriella.

"Felix? What's going on? Are you safe?" Gabriella asked in rapid fire.

"Lace is hurt," I said. "Burned. Thea attacked us with fire."

"Where are you?"

"Ten minutes from the house. Where are you?" I asked.

"Just pulling in the drive."

"Call Willow," I said. "We need her to help Lace."

For a moment, we argued about the relative safety of the hospital, but in the end, Lace took the phone and painfully explained that it was her decision.

"I'll call Willow," Gabriella agreed.

I sat back against the truck and did my best to comfort Lace as I inspected the damage the fire wrought. I found it ironic that the bandages on her cheek from where Willum had slapped her had, in the end, shielded much of her face.

"It's better this way," Lace said through tears. "No one else need die because of me."

"You're very brave, Lace," I said. "I'm sorry I was unable to protect you."

"I've already lived longer than I'd thought to."

"Why did you go in the back yard?"

"Your friend's family didn't need to lose their father because of me and my family," she said. "If Willum hadn't summoned this demon – if the Dark Folk would simply leave demons alone …. I don't see what's to be gained and yet it is my family's legacy. We brought this destruction."

"Rest, Lace," I said, smoothing her hair. "We'll figure it out."

Finally, we arrived at Tenebrius Manerium. Even with all the work, the stone façade still bore the scars of the witch's assault the previous fall. Old houses might look cool, but they sure demand a lot of attention, especially when people hurl rocks at them. I shuddered to think what a demon-fueled ex-girlfriend might do.

"How is she?" Gabriella met us as Andy parked his truck next to my blue Suburban.

"Lace? Can you get up?" I asked, helping her to a seated position.

Headlights illuminated the end of the long drive that joined to Happy Hollow Blvd.

"Who's that?" Gabriella asked.

"Get her inside." I leapt from the bed of the truck and walked forward, hands at my side, fingers stretched out, reaching for the power stored within the bounds of my family's property. I breathed deeply as the energy greeted and filled me.

A convertible, still a hundred yards away, paused and revved its engine.

"Give it up, Slade," Thea shouted, standing up on her seat. "I've got you boxed in this time."

"Turn around Thea," I yelled back, still approaching. "This is *my* home and I'll defend it. Leave before you're hurt." I knew I was tilting at the influx of power and no doubt overstating my position. The fact was, however, if I couldn't take the ghrelin here, I stood no chance anywhere.

"You are no match for me," Thea said, hurling three watermelon-sized fireballs.

With power to burn, I pulled my shield up and stood firm as they splashed away harmlessly. Thea sat back in the car and floored it, hurtling toward me.

"*Adoloret,*" I shot flames down the lane, impacting the car dead center but it continued to roll forward, undeterred, even as the engine gave up. The darkness within me rose and I laughed as I pulled more and more energy from the stores beneath and intensified the stream of fire. I cackled with glee as the car burst into flame and small explosions rocked the engine compartment, bits and pieces flying apart. I would burn it to the ground before it reached me.

Unfortunately, I was not in my right mind as flaming wreckage barreled toward me. At the last moment, a hard shoulder caught me beneath my ribcage and I was thrown to the side, rolling down the embankment next to the drive. Entangled with a panther, I came to rest on the edge of the rocky stream bed that cut through the property.

"Rawr!" Maggie cuffed my face with her large paw. Even with claws retracted the smack hurt, but her message was well deserved. I'd lost control again and nearly died.

"How cute," Thea taunted, walking up from behind the vehicle. "Saved again by the broken sister who'd rather live as an animal than face a life without any real power. Felix, though, I'll say it now, you've really got something there. That was quite a display; it left me all tingly. Now I can't figure out if you're a snack or the main course."

Thea reached out and pain lanced through my body as my limbs stretched and I was lifted from the ground. I screamed in agony, all the while, still able to clearly hear her speaking.

"So much faster this way," she said. "I'd heard rumors that Atronia had a place in the suburbs. It's so much more inviting than her others. If only she was here to defend it."

I attempted to activate my shield, but the pain in my body simply increased.

"Tsk, tsk. None of that now." Thea's voice had changed to that of a man's and I knew it was the ghrelin's own. "You do bend so wonderfully." Fresh pain and the cracking sound of my finger being bent back at an impossible angle caused me to snap back into reality, from which I had started to fade.

"Why?" I asked.

"Why the pain?" the ghrelin asked. "It feeds my soul. Anguish, despair and loneliness are tools of the trade for my compatriots, but not me. I'm all about pain, suffering and death. I won't lie to you, Felix. I feel I owe you that much. You were a strong adversary and you weakened me back there in the Carolinas. I had a good thing going, but you exposed me and I had to give up much. Don't worry, though, I'm not angry with you. Really, life was becoming repetitive. Capture, torture, kill. You'd think the mountain air would be nice, but I got tired of it. It was time for a change and this will be even better."

It spun me in the air and a fresh wave of pain caused me to cry out.

"You know; I've been arguing with myself about something. Maybe you could help me. I smelled that child. Your daughter? No? Niece then? That Faa princess is one thing, but maybe I'll just take the child instead. Humans are so quick to forgive children. And wearing the skin of a Baltazoss, now that's got cachet. I'm just giddy with opportunity."

I opened my eyes and realized it was not just me suspended in the air, but Maggie also, still in panther form. Anger welled up within me and I pushed against the ghrelin. The more I struggled against the demon's hold the more pain I felt.

"Good. Fight, Baltazoss, fight," it replied to my struggle. "Bring forth the Fury within. It will rip you apart as I reduce you to dust." The intensity increased as two more of my fingers snapped backwards. "Only seven more to go." Maggie roared in anguish, her panther form thrashing, suspended above the ground.

We continued like this for what seemed like hours, although I had a suspicion that it wasn't anywhere near that long. I knew that pain had the effect of extending perception of time and it stood to reason that great pain would be no different. At some point, however, the mind becomes used to the idea of pain and while you feel it all the same, it becomes more manageable. It was at times like this that the ghrelin allowed us to rest.

"You're becoming desensitized," the ghrelin explained. "It's not as good for me when you do."

"I'll hunt you," I said through gritted teeth.

"Let's say you live," it said, contemplatively. "Do you really think you could kill your niece? I assure you, Althea Sanders is still quite alive in here. When I take the child, it'll be just the same. She'll ride along for every evil thing I do. Eventually, she'll grow to enjoy it. They all do."

"Never!" I dug deep and pulled at the energy from beneath without regard for my own self-preservation, allowing the darkness that I feared to flow through me. I had no idea what I could do to this demon, but we were going to find out. If it killed me – so be it.

The energy burned as it blazed through my being, tearing through me like strong alcohol. At first, I found it difficult to focus; the energy and darkness pushed at the edges of my consciousness. I fought to maintain a grip on the dim reality around me, but still I pulled at the earth, ignoring the pain.

"So valiant. The brave little wizard finally finds his true calling and is yet tragically too late," the ghrelin taunted, smiling through my onslaught. "Your last moments on this world will be spent with the knowledge of the wonderfully vile things I'll do to your witchy girlfriend and to your brother's daughter. Ooh, the things I have in store for them."

I closed my eyes and pulled harder, feeling the damage the wild energy caused as it coursed through me. I could feel the demon's defenses as it resisted and deflected my attack. Slowly, its grip lessened, but my efforts would not be enough.

"You're losing it," I grunted.

"Too little, too late," it replied, sending a fresh wave of pain through my body.

"Then we'll go together … " I paused. For a third time since we'd started this journey, a large barn owl crossed my vision. For me it was a magic number and I followed its progress as it swooped low over our heads, landing behind Thea. I watched as the owl transformed into a shapely, middle-aged woman with waist length black hair. "Mother?"

"I've heard you cuss before," the ghrelin chuckled. "That's all you have for me?"

The woman smiled, the love in her eyes bringing tears from my own. I understood I was dying and knew I'd lost contact with the pain. I appreciated whatever power it was that could give me this vision before I finally passed. I'd so longed for one last moment with her.

The ghrelin in Thea's body jerked as the woman raised her hands and lightning arced from the sky above, striking it in the back. The howl of pain sounded more like a wounded werewolf than anything human. For a moment, Maggie and I remained suspended and then we fell to the ground. Fresh pain savaged me as I attempted to break my fall with broken fingers.

"You're real?" I asked, holding my arm up to her.

"I am, but do not let up," she answered quietly although her voice was easily heard.

"Baltazoss?" the ghrelin roared as a fresh bolt of lightning grounded itself through Thea's body.

"You were told to leave my family alone."

I breathed deeply and pushed my right hand out to Thea and the ghrelin, willing as much destructive force as I could into the powerful being. For once, the darkness I'd so often felt within myself didn't take over as I became a conduit of energy. For several minutes the three of us stood, locked in a deadly embrace. Finally, Thea's form began to shake, as if two bodies were trying to share the same space.

Shimmering, as if caught between two states, the much larger ghrelin demon pulled away from Thea only to be snapped back into place. Each time it did, Thea cried out.

"You may have won today, but you lose, Baltazoss." The ghrelin grasped for Thea's body. "The Synod will reward me for outing you. I hope this was worth it."

"A woman will risk everything for her family," she replied, smiling. "And where you're going, I doubt even your Synod will find you."

The ghrelin looked confused for a moment and then slipped away from Thea – its form translucent, sailing toward the house.

"Felix. Sevena." Mom ran across the drive and fell between us, pulling us to her, tears falling down her cheeks as she kissed my forehead.

I breathed in, recognizing the familiar and pungent smell of wild lavender as her hair brushed my skin.

Headlights fell across us once again and old brakes squealed as a heavy vehicle rolled to a stop. I felt the tension rise in my mother's arms and I painfully laid my arm across hers.

"No. Friends," I managed, as consciousness ebbed from my body.

FINALE

Warm, dappled sunlight streamed through tall windows and I rolled lazily away, not wanting to awaken. By lucky coincidence, my hand came to rest on Gabriella's hip. Instinctively, I pulled closer and allowed my hand to follow the curve of her body until it rested on her abdomen. She murmured sleepily and pushed back into me with her legs, her bottom coming to rest against my growing affection.

She must have become too warm while we slept as the white coverlet had been thrown back, giving me a perfect view of her as she slowly awoke. Over the years, I'd had my share of girlfriends, each beautiful in their own way. Gabriella however, was beyond anything I could have imagined. Certainly, she was gorgeous by any definition, but for me it was much more than that. Gabriella had given herself to me emotionally as I had to her. The bond we shared was much deeper than anything physical we might share in the future. For now, however, I simply reveled in our closeness, breathing her in as I kissed her back, just below her neck.

"I'm glad you're finally awake." She turned beneath my arm and brushed her hand down my face. The length of my beard surprised me. Deftly, she popped a small mint leaf into my mouth and followed it by bringing her face close to my own, her lips meeting mine.

"Careful," I said, when we separated for a moment. "You're starting things you won't be able to stop."

With her knee, she rolled me onto my back and slid on top, still kissing me. Her silky nightgown lifted as she straddled me and I eagerly encouraged the gown's progress with my hands. There's something about a smile from my partner whilst kissing that I find particularly engaging. It's not actually conducive to kissing, but I enjoy the communication of happiness and mirth.

"You are mine," Gabriella said, sitting up and teasing the gown over her head. "And I am yours." She reached back for me and helped us intimately join. I reached for her and pulled her nakedness to me, running my rough hands down to her hips.

For what seemed both like eternity and precious few moments, we gave ourselves to each other. Finally, lying back on the bed, exhausted, I lay my leg across her waist and stared into her eyes, stroking her silvery hair.

"Thank you for waiting for me," I said.

Gabriella smiled. "I love you, Felix Slade."

We both jumped as the bedroom door was abruptly opened, slamming noisily into the wall, dislodging plaster dust. In the doorframe stood Maggie. "It's about time! Now maybe we can move on with our lives without you two always mooning after each other. It's like I live in a damned, teenage vamp movie. 'Oooh, Felix, will you ever love me?'" Maggie mimicked Gabriella, dramatically spinning around.

Gabriella quickly pulled the twisted coverlet up to her body, attempting and failing to cover herself.

"Maggie, get out of here." I threw a pillow at her, which she easily dodged.

"Look, Rumpelstiltskin, I heard you were awake and thought maybe you needed help," Maggie said. "You've been in bed for almost a week."

I turned quickly to Gabriella, who'd finally found enough material to cover her critical bits, alluringly leaving broad patches of brown skin that weren't ordinarily viewable. The events of the last weeks flooded my mind. One of the last things I remembered was the sight of the ghrelin being dragged, ethereally toward Tenebrius Manerium where we now sat.

"The demon," I said. "My hands." I pulled my hands into view. I'd felt aches while loving Gabriella, but I'd pushed it out of my head.

"Mom and Willow got you all fixed up," Maggie said. "Amak's been calling every day. I told her you were up and she said she's on her way over."

"What about Mom?" I asked.

"Are you kidding?" Maggie asked. "She took off right after Lace ..." She gave a sideways glance. "Maybe we should save that for a moment."

I looked dumbfounded at Maggie. I'd never known her to hold back anything.

"What?" I asked, emphatically.

"There's something you need to see," Gabriella said, stroking my arm.

"What's going on, Gabriella?" I asked.

"Trust me, Felix. Let's get a shower and we'll work through all of this," she said.

"Mom just left me again?" Over the years I'd dealt with a lot of abandonment issues. I felt like the long covered wound had been painfully reopened.

"She didn't want to, Felix," Gabriella said. "She said that every minute she stayed endangered us all, especially you and Clarita."

My throat felt tight and I fought back angry tears. I couldn't believe she'd abandoned me again. "I guess that's her thing."

"That's not fair, Felix," Maggie said. "She was with you every time you needed her."

"She's the owl?" I asked.

"Of course she is," Maggie said. "And the panther in the woods."

"She killed those men," I said.

"What can I say? She's protective," Maggie answered.

Gabriella ran her hand across my chest and allowed her cover to drop as she positioned herself directly on top of me. "She was heartbroken, Felix. She only had a few moments with Clarita, who she didn't even know existed. It nearly broke her to leave her family again."

Gabriella slid her wrist into my hand and I caught a glimpse of an emotional exchange between her and my mother. I pulled away, not able to process the rush of feelings.

"I thought I'd dealt with that." I said as I looked into Gabriella's concerned face.

"Felix. It's okay to love your mother," she said. "She clearly loves you very much. Trust me when I say she didn't believe she had another choice."

"She left a letter for you," Maggie said, pulling an envelope from a dresser near the door, holding it up and walking it over to me.

"Why don't you come downstairs after you've cleaned up," Gabriella said, climbing off and slipping into her satiny night gown.

"No," I said, accepting the letter from Maggie. "Stay. This concerns you too."

"Twenty minutes," Maggie said. "Amak is on her way and you're not going to act like a nutter at breakfast, so pull yourself together. Got it?"

I nodded and ran a finger beneath the envelope's seal. A release of magic tingled through my hand as I pulled the letter out and held it so Gabriella could also see it.

Dearest Felix –

Today, I've placed you and your new family in grave danger by once again showing myself at Tenebrius Manerium. I would not have done so if I hadn't believed that by my actions, you might live and that without, all would be lost.

The demon, who prefers to be called Lord Gester, cannot be allowed to return to its plane of existence. The knowledge he gained, specifically that I yet live and that my progeny also live, must not make it back to a consortium of evil that call themselves The Synod. Please heed this warning as The Synod will take any and all measures to eliminate the Baltazoss bloodline.

My heart weeps with both joy and sorrow in meeting my precious granddaughter, Clarita. I mourn the loss of my son and her father, Geoff. His death weighs heavily upon me as it was my trap that he willingly fell into. I had instructed him not to attempt to claim Tenebrius, but I suspect he found this unacceptable.

I wish we had been able to spend more time together. I will treasure always the moments we had, where I was able to hold both you and your sister, if only for a short time. You cannot know the depth of pain it causes a mother to give up her children. This pain is only offset by the joy I feel when I realize the man you've become.

Don't pull away from your friends. They are the strength you'll need for what is to come.

With Enduring Love —
Your Mother, Atronia

"That's beautiful," Gabriella said, kissing my shoulder as I struggled to compose myself.

I sighed and slid from the bed, placing the letter on my nightstand. As I released it, it crumpled into dust.

"Shower?" I asked.

Twenty minutes later, I heard the sounds of excited voices as I walked down the stairway from the second floor.

"Look who the cat dragged in," Amak said, grinning as I pushed through the swinging doors into the kitchen with Gabriella right behind.

Clarita threw her head back, slid from Amak's grasp and ran over to me, climbing up and wrapping her arms around my neck, kissing my cheek affectionately. "Love you, monkey," I whispered in her ear.

"Love you," she whispered back. I raised my eyebrows at her response. She wasn't much for talking and rarely expressed emotion when she did.

"Rawr!" Maggie, who'd just moments before had been in human form had transformed to a panther. It was too much for Clarita who slid from me and chased after her.

"Amak." I crossed the room and embraced my tall friend.

"Ooh, you smell good. Like sex," she said, grabbing my butt with both hands. "It's about time the two of you worked that out."

"Hey now," Gabriella complained, laughing. "Hands off the merchandise."

"I'm a twenty-first century type of gal," Amak said, releasing me. "I'm willing to be flexible."

"Your flexibility was never in question. Thanks for bringing

breakfast," I said, turning to the already open box of gooey cinnamon rolls.

"Want to tell me what happened to your truck?" Amak asked. "It looks like you drove through a fence."

"Maggie did," I said, pulling a roll onto a plate and handing one to Gabriella. "Not really her fault though."

"Maggie drives?" Amak asked.

"We're still debating the subject," I said. "So what's this big surprise you didn't want to tell me about until after breakfast, Gabriella? And where's Lace?"

"She's in the lab. Standing watch," Gabriella said. "With you out of it, we couldn't let the door shut or we couldn't have gotten back in."

"Why would you care?"

"Let's go," Gabriella said. "Amak, you might as well see it too. We're all going to have to deal with it eventually."

"Ooh, a mystery," Amak said.

"Not a fun one," Gabriella said. "Trust me."

I grabbed a second plate, loaded a roll onto it for Lace and followed Gabriella to the basement door which had been propped open with a shoe. I wasn't comfortable leaving access to the lab open and as we descended the stone stairs an uneasy feeling settled on me.

"What in the hell!" I exclaimed, reaching for the oak leaf that hung around my neck. Amak roared angrily and jumped across one of the lab tables, picking up a steel stool menacingly.

Lace, who'd been sitting in the leather desk chair, jumped up, spurred by our sudden activity.

"Felix. No," Gabriella warned. "It's contained."

The object of my angst sat within a translucent bubble confined by the runed, silver spell circle that occupied the marble floor in front of the fireplace. Within the bubble sat the ghrelin demon, grinning evilly at me.

"Are you nuts? We can't have this here," I said.

"Damn, Slade," Lace said. "You nearly gave me a heart attack. By the way, this was your mother's idea."

"She summoned the demon into the lab?"

"No. I did that. I know its name," Lace replied. "She said this circle would keep it contained indefinitely as long as we don't break the continuity of the circle."

"Can it hear us?" I asked.

"Not according to your mother," Lace said. "But I believe it reads lips quite well. We shouldn't talk here."

"Is it safe to leave it alone?"

"This is the first time in days it's been quiet," she said. "Up until now, it's been throwing itself against the circle, trying to find a weak spot. Apparently, we're lucky the ghrelin is so small. According to your mother, your circle wouldn't hold most of the greater demons. They're just too big."

"Didn't seem small to me when it was breaking my fingers," I said.

"It's not even a full demon," Lace said. "It's just a sub-demon. But according to your Ma the big boys wouldn't be satisfied in setting up a death cult and milking it for several years."

"What happened to Thea?"

"Anderson picked her up a few days ago," Gabriella said. "It was sad; she's just a shell of the woman she'd been."

I sighed, my feelings for Thea still a jumble.

"Your mom left these books," Lace interrupted my thoughts, waving her hands across several leather-bound books. "She wants us to transcribe them so they can be returned."

"What are they?" I asked.

"The ghrelin is watching you talk," Gabriella warned.

"Can you leave the room?" I asked.

"Certainly," Lace said. "I'm doing nothing that keeps it in there, the runed spell-circle does all of the work. Your mother said you should make sure to keep the stores of energy high within the well. I wasn't sure what she meant."

For a moment, I felt jealousy at her conversation with my mother, but I let it pass. "I understand. It's something I can see to."

"This is insane, Slade," Amak warned as we exited. "You can't keep a demon bound for long."

"According to his mother's books, demons only escape this type of trap when released," Lace answered.

"You smell of witch," Amak said, invading Lace's personal space.

"You're not human," Lace replied, tilting her head back to look up into Amak's face, not giving ground.

"Hold on, ladies. We're all friends here. Lace Faa, meet Amak of the Senwe," I said, stepping between them. "Amak, meet Lace of Clan Eppy."

"What happened to your arm?" Amak asked, looking at the bandages along her right arm. "It's a fresh wound."

Lace had shaved the side of her head where the fireball had melted her hair. While the exposed skin on her scalp was still reddened, there were no obvious scars. Bandages, which started just below her ear, extended down her neck and followed her entire arm to her hand, were more of a concern.

"The demon attacked," Lace said simply.

Amak raised her eyebrows. "You are otherwise unscathed?"

Lace pushed her leg forward, exposing the cast on her left ankle. "Nothing that won't heal."

"Then you are more than meets the eye, Lace of Clan Eppy," Amak said. "But it changes naught. To keep a demon under your roof is the worst idea I've heard yet. Are you serious, Slade?"

"I'm just getting caught up," I said, shutting the basement door behind me.

"She's right," Lace agreed. "I've yet to read of an instance where a captured demon doesn't escape and kill its captors. The stories in your mother's books are all cautionary tales."

"Then I guess we'll just have to figure it out," I said. "Any ideas?"

"I have a couple," Amak said.

But of course, that's another story entirely.

ABOUT THE AUTHOR

Jamie McFarlane is happily married, the father of three and lives in Lincoln, Nebraska. He spends his days engaged in a hi-tech career and his nights and weekends writing works of fiction. He's also the author of:

Privateer Tales Series
1. Rookie Privateer
2. Fool Me Once
3. Parley
4. Big Pete
5. Smuggler's Dilemma
6. Cutpurse
7. Out of the Tank
8. Buccaneers
9. A Matter of Honor
10. Give No Quarter

Guardians of Gaeland
1. Lesser Prince

Witchy World
1. Wizard in a Witchy World
2. Wicked Folk

Word-of-mouth is crucial for any author to succeed. If you enjoyed this book, please consider leaving a review at Amazon, even if it's only a line or two; it would make all the difference and would be very much appreciated.

If you want to get an automatic email when Jamie's next book is available, sign up here. Your email address will never be shared and you can unsubscribe at any time.

CONTACT JAMIE

Blog and Website: fickledragon.com
Facebook: facebook.com/jamiemcfarlaneauthor
Twitter: twitter.com/mcfarlaneauthor

www.ingramcontent.com/pod-product-compliance
Lightning Source LLC
Chambersburg PA
CBHW070324260626
47160CB00003B/946